"Dr. Davis is a gifted writer. She uses literary techniques to hold the reader in the story and basically takes you inside the mind of twins as they deal with tragedy and life unfolds.

The creativity of the story line coupled with the content makes the book easy to read and hard to put down. I found myself visualizing the moments as the author laid out the opening action and developed the plot in a clever and masterful way.

The book is outstanding. It is well written, holds the readers attention, and will have you experiencing most every emotion under the sun.
Thumbs up from me. Five stars and then some."

Dr. Bo Brock, author of Crowded in the Middle of Nowhere: Tales of Humor and Healing from Rural America

"Relevant issues of the day are skillfully woven together in this murder mystery. It will captivate you from the beginning, through many twists and turns, to its gripping end.

An excellent choice for any high school library."

Claudia Park, Librarian

Inside Voices

Sarah Davis

www.darkstroke.com

Discover us online:
www.darkstroke.com

Find us on instagram:
www.instagram.com/darkstrokebooks

Include **#darkstroke** in a photo of yourself
holding this book on Instagram and
something nice will happen.

I dedicate this novel to superman,
tiger bait,
little mouse,
chewie monkey,
and the overly jealous hound.

About the Author

SARAH DAVIS is a veterinarian who one day decided to write down an idea for a story. A book dragon to the core, she enjoys stories that transport her to imaginary realms and honestly has read more books than she will ever admit. She and her wonderful husband share their remote prairie home with three extraordinary children and a Weimaraner who has a licker problem. INSIDE VOICES is her first novel.

Facebook: www.facebook.com/sarahdavisdvm
Twitter: www.twitter.com/SarahDavisAuth1
Instagram: www.instagram.com/sarahdavisauthor

Acknowledgements

I am tremendously blessed to have so many people who patiently gave me their time and expertise.

Firstly, a huge shout out to Laurence and Stephanie at darkstroke for their faith and encouragement. Their extremely warm welcome and support, as well as the wonderful team, is beyond imagination.

To the early (alpha) readers: Dr. Oleg, Dr. Elizabeth, Nicole, Michele, Dr. Carolyn, Morgan, and Sharon. You are the brave souls who looked over my early work...the whole entire story. Yes, it could be a trilogy. But it won't (probably).

Thank you to the brilliant and kind developmental editor, Maria, who offered insight when the story was in its infancy! And to Tessa, who reminded me to cross my Is and Ts and dot my Ts and Is.

To Shelby for giving me critical insight for which I will be ever grateful; Dr. Vern, Russ, Lanell, Vivian, Kaylee as well as the local book club members...Cathy, Joanne, Michelle,

Lori, Mary, Marydean, Jo, Georgianna, Deedra, Lisa, Sonali...your encouragement means the world; to Harvey, who graciously and unblushingly provided criticism for my blurb; and to Sylvie for your suggestions, encouragement, and smiles - RIP my friend.

Hugs to my sweet grandma Eunice.

To my mom...for reading and rereading and rereading (etc). I'm glad you continue to put up with me as an adult.

To my understanding family for your constant loving support and their constant loving interruption. I love you guys. Meow!

To all the grey ghosts who I hold close to my heart...there are no greater companions then the noble humans masquerading in Weimaraner bodies.

Last but never least, to you the reader who will give my story a chance...I do hope you enjoy it. And if you do, please consider to take a moment to review the book on Amazon. Every review for authors helps increase the chances of reaching more readers.

Inside Voices

BEFORE

Our Father

The buzzing beneath eighteen-year-old Penny Osborn's skin started while she spoke to the officer. It worsened during the car ride from her high school in Pasadena to her mother's veterinary clinic north in Eaton Canyon. As she rested her palms in her lap, atop the wrinkled and blood-crusted jeans, she wondered why her hands were still while everything beneath her skin vibrated.

A whine from the back of the Jeep pulled her from the depths of her daze; the school's security dog, Zeus. They were taking him to her mother's clinic for a complete exam, possibly surgery to remove the bullet. Or bullets. Penny had forgotten he was in the vehicle. She had forgotten getting into the Jeep.

Her gaze returned to her hands, the hands with the intense buzzing beneath her skin. The hands she earlier tried to clean with hand sanitizer. Many rust-colored crusts still flecked the backs and stained her fingernails. Penny considered the mess she would leave behind.

"Don't worry about the seat, sweetheart. It will clean easy enough," her mother had said when Penny climbed into the passenger seat.

She scrunched her eyebrows together and tried to recall leaving the school grounds. Her mother, Dr. Eelyn Osborn, and Penny, loaded Zeus in the back. No, that wasn't right. Billy, the school Security Officer, helped her mother with the dog. Left unattended, Penny sought to focus on something, anything, instead of the pandemonium surrounding her. Her attention drifted to the clear, sharp outline of the mountains. The overnight rainfall had washed away the smog allowing an uncommon view of the mountain tops so sharp against the blue, clear sky - a jagged tear in the ether.

Upon reaching the clinic, her mother parked in the unloading zone. Penny climbed out with care and walked to the back of the vehicle to help lift the German Shepherd. Several technicians swooped in like white geese coming in for a landing, their white frock coats billowing behind them in their haste. They had with them an electric wheeled cart: one able to lift and lower a hefty animal with ease leaving Penny jobless, standing at the curb, distracted by the buzzing beneath her skin.

Her mother led her through the back door of the clinic where the antiseptic nasal blast both embraced and comforted her. The fragrance she had known since childhood. While in the employee locker room her mother spoke quietly. How are you doing? Fine. Do you need something to drink? No. Do you mind waiting while I check on Zeus? Sure. Please clean yourself up. Okay.

The glimpse Penny caught of herself in the locker room mirror revealed the extent of her disheveled appearance. Her hair, mostly freed from its ponytail, fell around her face like limp noodles; the excess blood on her face, arms, and clothes suggested she played the target at the shooting range. But, no external injuries, so said the EMT who examined her. No *external* injuries. Of course not. She had not been in the field with her senior class but had witnessed it from the picture window in the science room just as in her nightmare the previous night.

Not a nightmare. A vision.

Drenched in sweat she had awoken at 11:07 p.m. and unable to sleep the rest of the night. Weary and on edge the following morning, she found it impossible to concentrate during class. Checking out of her second period self-study group under the pretense of searching for props for the upcoming drama club production, she sought to consider what the vision meant. Past visions Penny had experienced foretold future events. Ones that she was thus far unable to prevent or alter.

Willy, the white rat from the science room, appeared in the

drama storage room in a space between two shelved boxes, startling her and distracting from her worries. He was a white apparition of whiskers and tail. He had been missing for weeks, and as the fire alarm signaled the routine fire drill, Penny returned the rat to his habitat in the science room. It was a drill, after all. Her life was not in danger for being late to joining her senior class that would gather on the athletic field. Perhaps, if she were caught, she might receive a warning or even detention. Perhaps. It was only a drill. She could be late.

Because of a white rat, she watched the massacre unfold from behind bullet-proof glass in the science room. As she sprinted out of the school and across the road to the chaotic athletic field to help, the white van carrying the shooter sped away, disappearing.

She moved through students on the field with the efficiency of one who spent years working as an aid at the emergency room with her father, or as an assistant at a veterinary emergency room with her mother. She instructed the injured to apply pressure to their wounds or asked uninjured students to apply pressure if they were able. She placed tourniquets. She closed eyelids on Mark, Sofia, Taylor, Lorenz and whispered apologies to their unhearing ears. Their dreams snuffed out beneath their lids as she watched.

She was handing out blankets when emergency personnel pulled her from the field for questioning and examination, so she left the blankets for another to hand out. She was cleared with no injuries by a medic. The stressed policewoman thanked Penny for her quick action and then dismissed her, releasing her to her mother's custody. Penny did not mention the scene she witnessed from the science room was the same she saw last night in a dream.

Now, in the veterinary clinic employee locker room, clothing on, she stepped into the hot shower and regarded the blood spots expanding across her shirt like her internal injuries broke open with grief for the lost. The scarlet-tinged water pooled and swirled on the white tile floor before

7

disappearing down the drain. When the heat became too much, Penny peeled the clothing off. She scrubbed herself with a vigor out of place on the zombie-like girl. The blood slowly dissolved and washed away leaving behind tan skin. But the memories remained. So she continued to scrub until the tan skin became pink. Then standing naked in front of the sink mirror, she scrubbed at her face, salty tears adding their aid.

Penny wiped up the pink water that pooled on the changing room floor with her towel and disposed of it in the laundry hamper. She disposed of her clothes in the trash and dressed in an overly large pair of crisp, green scrubs. Her long hair, the color of espresso, hung heavy upon her back, rivulets of water creating patterns on her scrub top. She stood for a few moments in the quiet locker room before the ever-increasing buzz of the overhead lights became more unbearable than the buzz beneath her skin.

She didn't want to help with the surgery, so she made her way to the waiting room. The buzzing beneath her skin distracted her. Would she have rather gone home instead? Of course. But Zeus required care, and her mother was one of the best veterinarians to care for him. The room around her hummed with motion from its occupants, and soft overhead music played in the background.

With a vacant stare, Penny faced the muted television which hung on the eggshell-colored wall opposite her. The few people and their pets, many whom Penny knew from years of working at the clinic, refrained from speaking with her, offering instead sympathetic smiles that Penny didn't notice.

"Penny, can I get you anything?" came a soft voice, temporarily breaking through Penny's oblivion. She blinked slowly, the young woman's face coming into focus.

"Blair." Penny's voice sounded rough in her ears. Clearing her throat, she began to answer until the "Breaking News" flashing across the bottom of the screen drew Penny's attention from Blair's earnest face. The surrounding music ceased, and the television volume rose, amplifying the voice of the Pasadena Chief of Police speaking at a news conference.

Blair stood next to Penny, her hand over her mouth. Two chairs over sat Mrs. Bailey with her miniature schnauzer, Betty, who hopped to the floor and trotted over to Penny. The salt-and-pepper dog with his massive beard sat down on Penny's foot and leaned against her leg.

"Please hold your questions until I finish. Understand I do not have all the answers currently. More information is coming in, and we will do our best to keep the public updated as best we can. There may be some questions I cannot answer due to the ongoing investigation into these events." He paused in the heat of the afternoon sun to mop the sweat from his brow. His miserable look stemmed from more than the heat.

"So, to start...at 9:25 a.m. today, two suspects arrived in a white utility van on Cooley Place during the performance of a fire drill at Pasadena High School. Using military grade, high-round automatic weapons, they fired into the five hundred to six hundred and fifty gathered students. One-hundred-fifty-three students and faculty were wounded; their conditions range from minor to critical. Ninety-seven students and faculty were fatally shot. The shooting event lasted approximately one minute, with the suspects firing continuously from the moving van. Before the van fled the scene, a third person exited the school and entered the vehicle. The suspect wore a bright orange vest. Witness reports indicate this third suspect was a Pasadena High School student."

Ahrin. It had been the new student and her recent lab partner for the past two weeks. A hot flush spread through her body. He ignored her attempts at discussion during lab and kept to himself, hardly ever speaking a word to Penny or anyone else.

Wrapping her arms around herself, Penny found herself wishing her sister were here with her. No, she didn't wish that. Of course not. If Lucy had been there, then she would also have been at school. She surely would have been out on the field. And perhaps Penny, too. A shudder wracked her body. The mental link she shared with her identical twin was inaccessible; their connection impossible at such a great distance. She needed to hear her sister's thoughts.

Swallowing back bitterness, she closed her eyes and concentrated on the relief that had come crashing through her veins when her mother finally picked her up from the school. The relief was swiftly overpowered by grief and guilt. Penny was alive when many of her classmates were not. Survivor? No. A powerless witness.

A client, whom Penny didn't know by name walked in. The man sat on Penny's right; his golden retriever whined softly, and its head found a resting place on Penny's other knee, opposite the schnauzer which had started pawing with gentleness at Penny's calf. Both dogs recognized her discomfort. She sensed them distantly in her mind, though, as the thousand bees buzzing underneath her skin obstructed their connection to her thoughts.

The broadcast continued as her gaze slid out of focus and a mental fog obscured the turn of her thoughts. She allowed herself to disappear inside the fog as the news played on.

"Abandoning the van near the intersection of East Del Mar Boulevard and South Roosevelt Avenue, it is believed the suspects transferred weapons, including explosive vests, to a previously stolen vehicle and drove to South Arroyo Boulevard. At that location, they again switched vehicles, this time to a stolen Glendale Hospital ambulance. Video surveillance confirms these movements and that all three suspects made these vehicle changes.

"The suspects then drove the short distance to Huntington Memorial Hospital, arriving on the scene at the same time other ambulances arrived from the scene of the shooting. The suspect in the orange vest was presented as a wounded student and taken into the hospital for emergency care. The two remaining suspects were detained due to improper emergency vehicle protocol."

The mention of the hospital where her father, Ben, worked in the ER drew Penny's attention back into the now and unease rolled down her spine. Of course, her father would be back to work after his night shift, helping however he could. The message she received from him said as much. Also, he was thankful she was safe, and he loved her very much, always in this lifetime and beyond. She crossed her arms and hunched her shoulders.

"Unknown to the authorities and hospital staff, the suspect taken into the hospital wore a vest containing explosive devices. The vest detonated shortly after the suspect went inside the hospital's ER killing the suspect, five hospital personnel, and two students who were treated for gunshot wounds. An additional twelve hospital employees were injured in the blast." His voice broke with emotion.

Penny swallowed back rising bile while darkness gathered around her and her breathing grew shallow. The schnauzer nosed her leg. The retriever barked; the sharp, earnest sound pulled Penny back from the tunnel she fell towards.

"At the moment of detonation, the two suspects being detained began firing at hospital security officers and at anyone else in the area. Both suspects also wore explosive devices; however, only one suspect detonated his. The third and final suspect was shot and killed by officers. An additional four people were injured in these incidents."

The Police Chief continued as Penny stood, her thoughts in turmoil. Retrieving her phone, she messaged her father. Then she called, but it went immediately to voicemail. She tried the nurses' station, but a busy line greeted her. Her heart beat thunderously in her ears. The nurses' number responded. Always. She tried the number again. Busy, again.

She heard Blair as if from far away calling her name, but she ignored it and walked behind the receptionist desk and through the closed door beyond to seek out her mother.

The overhead speaker crackled as Penny walked down the hallway leading to the surgery suite where she knew her mother would be working on Zeus. A female voice announced an urgent phone call for Dr. Osborn.

Penny picked up her pace to the treatment area. She did not notice the staff paused in their motions, fear, and pain etched onto their faces as they focused on her mother who stood leaning against a doorframe, her face as white as the wall behind her.

No…

A heavy weight draped itself over her shoulders, an oppressive cloak, that made it difficult to breathe. Something else happened. Something more than she'd dreamt.

"An explosion?" her mother choked out.

*Oh my God …*Penny clutched at her head, sucking in a rugged breath. *No, not daddy.*

Not her father.

Dr. Eelyn Osborn let the phone drop from her hand and a technician close by picked up the dangling receiver and placed it back on the wall. Mother reached out to daughter.

"Penny," she cried. "Oh, Penny. There was an attack at the hospital. Ben—" her mother choked on a sob— "he didn't make it. He died. Your father's dead." Eelyn pulled Penny tight against her while sobs shook the woman's lean frame.

No, no. He can't be dead. He just hasn't had time to call us.

At least Lucy stayed home today. Aunt Bianca, their mother's sister, had arrived for a week-long visit to pick out dresses for her upcoming wedding to the guitarist and would be home with Lucy. She escaped the carnage…but no, of course, she had seen…through Penny, through their bond, their link.

Their mother slid down the wall, pulling Penny with her.

Penny, can you hear me? came the whisper of Penny's identical twin in her mind.

Lucy, oh Lucy. Penny's sluggish thoughts seemed like wading through molasses. *You are alright!* Penny's weeping intensified.

Penny, I'm here now. Tell me what happened. Lucy urged, the fear in her voice crushing Penny's spirit.

Our father. Daddy. He's gone, Lu. He's gone!

TWO YEARS LATER

Edge of the World

"Penny, hand me the sponge forceps," Dr. Osborn requested, her face mask muffling her voice.

Penny reached across the pale blue surgical drapes that covered the anesthetized dog and found the clamp that was needed on the neatly arranged tray. She palmed the cool steel shank and handed it to her mother, handle first.

The longer Penny stood at the table in the stifling blue surgery gown, the more sweat beaded and ran down her neck. The muscles in her right calf cramped and she wished in vain she had taken a few extra moments to stretch after her early morning run before answering her mother's call for surgical assistance. Luckily, the slow, rhythmic whoosh of the ventilator covered any whimper that might have escaped Penny's lips. Her mother, understanding as she was, wouldn't appreciate an interruption of her concentration. Penny stretched out her leg as best she could while standing and retracting the abdominal wall of Fred the dog.

Her mother spoke, mostly to herself, providing something like a running commentary. "Okay...would you look at that...oh, boy...you would think...at least they paid closer attention this time..."

The mixed-breed dog on the table had eaten two socks and a pair of little girl underwear. Doc Vincent Utqiaġvik (Barrow), Alaska's sole veterinarian, removed underwear from the dog three months earlier, just a month before Penny and her family arrived in May. Her mother worried there would be adhesions and scarring to complicate the operation.

Not saying much for the dog's tastes, Lucy commented in Penny's thoughts. "His intestines look much better than what Vincent documented in the file. Less inflammation. The old incisions healed well," her mother said.

Penny envisioned Fred's folder and the handwritten notes

15

in Doc Vincent's surgical report. She had snuck a look at it before the surgery. An "old schooler," he refused to use modern technology, like a computer, when a pen would suffice. Penny's exposure to years of her mother's atrocious scribble at home, and while working as her assistant, made it easy to decipher the aged doctor's notes. Indeed, the reddened intestines presented with a better prognosis than those the color of grape juice with spots of yellow peritonitis. Amazingly the dog had pulled through with a complete recovery from the first surgery.

The iron tang of blood overpowered the disinfectant scent of the small surgery room. It surrounded Penny, and she imagined it collecting on her exposed skin, absorbing and working through the many cracks in the mental barrier she built and fortified over the years. She swallowed hard and closed her eyes for a moment, forcing back unwelcome memories.

Clearing her throat, she returned her attention to her mother preparing to suture the abdominal incision. Penny piled the sponges into a neat pyramid. Once she counted twice and was certain all were accounted, she began cleaning up, following a protocol she learned when she was twelve. Turning all garbage into her used gloves, she aimed and tossed her make-believe ball into the garbage can, with her blue surgical gown and cap following. She heaved a sigh of relief as her dark hair fell free from its constraints and hung in her typical ponytail.

Finally, air flow.

After a quick wash, she returned to the room's sole surgical table to check Fred's level of anesthesia. Per her mother's instructions, Penny altered fluid rates and administered medications to help ease recovery and prevent pain. She began tidying up the room, hopeful it would speed things up.

Her mother's presence was essential on today's flight. The removal of a polar bear's tracking collar required a veterinarian to oversee the tranquilization, health monitoring, and reversal of sedation.

The sooner they were airborne, the sooner Penny could focus on her own. The only thing preventing Penny from performing the same job as her mother on this trip was her lack of credentials. The countless hours spent assisting her mother over the years lent her a glimpse behind the curtain, as it were, but led to Penny's understanding that her path did not follow the same as her mother's.

Penny mentally listed her week's duties.

Begin the prelim report for research paper, check on the status of females with COYs (cubs of the year), guitar lessons with Noah's students, catch up on Army's blog, get Blue started on pulling heavier loads, hopefully weather cooperates for more flyovers...

Aren't you forgetting flying to the moon, tea with the prince, and rescuing the last viable dragon egg from the alternate universe? Lucy asked.

Penny smiled. She and her sister communicated telepathically. In fact, she couldn't recall a time when her sister wasn't in her head. She was rarely distracted by the faint tingle in her skull signaling her sister's presence. Their mute conversations filled any emptiness in Penny's wakeful hours.

Early on, and into their childhood, her sister Lucy struggled with verbal speech. Practice, practice, practice was the best way for her to improve. The rule stuck until those times when the twins were too loud. Then their mother or father would tell them to use their inside voices. Of course, this meant something quite different than the common understanding of not yelling inside.

One hour later, Penny went in search of Sam Little, the clinic's everything man. He cleaned kennels, cleaned the facility, took dogs out for walks, checked on animals during evening hours, and even answered phones. He did not assist in surgeries unless absolutely necessary, and only during his normal work hours. Today was an exception as he covered for Linda, the clinic's only technician. He was taking care of Linda's weekend animal caretaker duties so she could visit her sister in Juneau. He had an engaging smile, one he showed often and, although he was their mother's age, Penny and her sister found him charming and very easy on the eyes.

"It really is crazy what some animals will eat," she murmured.

Yeah, remember that corgi back in Pasadena, the one that ate nine used tampons?

That poor puppy was so sick, even after the surgery. Mother didn't expect her to make it, Penny responded.

Mother expects everything to die, especially right after she works on it. Easier to take the loss, if expected.

Penny rolled her eyes as she thought of her mother. Lucy was right. That woman never sugarcoated anything when it came to patient prognosis. There had been many times a tender lie would have sufficed over the blunt, probable truth.

Taking a steadying breath, Penny smoothed the wrinkles that resided between her eyebrows with her fingertips. Inhale peace, exhale pessimism.

"You okay?" Sam appeared in front of her in the hallway to the kennels, one eyebrow raised over his icy blue eyes. She noted the buzz cut of his hair and wondered if it would be curly or straight hair should he ever grow it past a half inch length.

"Yeah. Ah, thanks." She presented her best smile.

"So," he leaned against the wall and placed his hands in his pockets, "I guess you're studying up to be a vet like your mom, are you?"

"No," she said.

"No? Don't like fixin' up animals?" A tiny bit of southern drawl snuck into his otherwise local accent.

"Oh, I like helping her. Great mother-daughter bonding," she replied wryly, considering plenty of their bonding was over a surgical table. She suddenly found it difficult to meet his gaze. She didn't care for the unexpected twists and turns with which her mother dealt. The emergencies, the different types of owners. Realizing her thoughts were running away with her, she mentally shook herself and made eye contact with Sam. "I'm leaning more toward a career in arctic marine biology."

"Polar bears aren't as cuddly as on the holiday commercials, though, are they?" his grin shrewd.

"No, they are rather amazing predators, though." Her heartbeat quickened thinking about the thrill of seeing a polar bear, much less standing beside one. She knew not everyone landed their dream job. She never really imagined she'd have such a prospect when she started at the University of Alaska-Anchorage three years earlier. Opportunities were very rare due to tough competition for limited funding.

"Well, you be careful out there," he said as he stepped away from the wall.

"Yes, sir. Here." She held up the bag and shook it. "Can you hang this by Fred's kennel? Mother wanted to show the owners later."

"Little girl's underpants. And a couple of socks," he clucked his tongue. "Wonder if ol' Fred will be back a third time? I remember the first time he came in." Sam shook his head. "Ah, well. Nothin' doing. I'll take care of these and the patient. Army's here. Been waiting outside for you," he said giving her a smile and a slight wave as he walked away.

Penny jogged to the end of the hall and opened the side door of the clinic. The bright sun greeted her while the 40°F chill took her breath away. It was 7:30 a.m. yet the constant presence of the mid-June sun gave the impression of mid-day. She waved, then held up five fingers to her boss, research leader, Native Alaskan, professor, and neighbor, Dr. "Army" Armstrong Volkov.

Army nodded from inside the black, jacked-up, twin-cab truck. Grey exhaust puffed out of the straight pipes. The bone-rattling grumble guaranteed it was not a vehicle made for sneaking around in, unless you lived near an erupting volcano. Penny loved it and hated it at the same time. There was irony in studying an (almost) endangered species, due to the warming arctic, while driving a loud, exhaust-spewing monstrosity. Army insisted the truck was not as bad as it sounded or looked. His nephew, Noah, modified it to be better for the environment. Better didn't equal beneficial. But then again, when living at the top of the world, you made do with what you had.

Back inside, Penny attempted to stretch out her still-cramping leg, tendrils of dark hair hat escaped her ponytail tickled her face whenever she bent forward.

I really, really, really hope this dog figures out little girls' clothing is not good to eat. Don't care to do this again. This girl has her own job to attend to!

Her proclaimed five minutes ticked by. Penny stretched her soreness to almost the point of relief. She searched for her absent mother and found her in the small clinic office. Eelyn was changed and getting her coat on.

"Hurry up, pokey," Penny said. "Flight is being delayed for your slow self."

Eelyn groaned as she stood up, nearly every joint popping in the process. "Just let me grab this," she said while reaching for an open yogurt container.

"Utensils aren't that expensive here, mother, especially if you wash them afterwards." Penny lifted an eyebrow and shook her head at Eelyn's use of a tongue depressor for a spoon.

Eelyn snorted. "Oh, but hurry, hurry, hurry" she said, her arms pumping in a fake run. Spikes of her short pixie-like hair bounced before Eelyn pulled a knit hat onto her head. They were a contrast. Although the same height, Penny was lean with long espresso colored hair where her mother was softer with mousy-brown hair. The softness was deceiving, though, as Penny had seen her mother pull calves, wrangle tiger cubs, and carry large dogs without breaking a sweat.

She and Penny locked eyes as slow smiles spread across both their faces. Eelyn reached up and placed a warm hand against Penny's check, her thumb caressing one of the two dimples that Penny and her sister inherited from their father.

"I just need to speak with Sam. Will be quick," Eelyn said, breaking the moment. Penny stifled a sigh.

As they approached him in the hallway, Sam waved his hands.

"Go on, git going. Everything will be fine. I got it," Sam muttered, shooing them out into the cold.

20

Penny took a deep breath of the beautiful Sunday morning. Releasing it slowly, for a moment she imagined herself the dragon she pretended to be as a child.

At least her nose wasn't freezing up like when she first arrived mid-May. They were in the middle of a significant heatwave right now in mid-June, with temperatures expected to stay above freezing and even reach the sixties by the end of the month.

"Come on, dragon breath," her mother said as she tugged on Penny's grey down jacket.

Penny broke out another eye-squinting grin, put on her sunglasses, and jogged to the truck. She was not yet used to the constant light that infused the area, even though most days were overcast, or a hindering fog encased the oppressed landscape. Today was a welcome oddity: clear skies and little wind.

It would be a good day to tag polar bears.

"Pablan, Penelope. Ready to hunt Nanuq?" Army asked as she hauled herself into the back seat.

She responded with a broad smile and a nod. "Please, call me Penny, Dr. Armstrong."

"Only if you call me Army."

Army drove the three of them from Doc Vincent's clinic near the center of town, south to the airport where Army's helicopter and two other passengers awaited them. The unusually clear, endless blue sky fused at the horizon with the slate blue of the sea as Army drove out of town along the coast. While Eelyn and Army chatted away amiably in the front, Penny directed her attention to her intended research on arctic species' acclimation to the warming north and what impact the exhaust-spewing vehicle had on said environment.

Funny how you can't research something without making an impact on it in some way, thought Lucy.

Yeah, funny ... not funny.

The scenery drew her attention from her thoughts. Houses stood above the ground on pilings to keep the heat away from the tender tundra, as if pulling up their pants against the wet ground. While shades of grey and whitewashed out the scenery, here and there, muted colors caught her eye…a faded teal home, a bright red truck, a yellow four-wheeler, a sign with bright green lettering. Many yards held varying degrees of junk. A refrigerator scrapped out for parts. Three sorry-looking snow machines in obvious stages of disrepair or dismantle. The newer parts of town to the north didn't have as many such lawn decorations, but no matter the money coming in from oil drilling, the town was a bit too far off the beaten path for the majority to ship parts overnight. Residents sensibly used what was available for parts.

Her fingers found the pocket-sized figurine of a polar bear she carried in her jean pocket. Their parents had given them a set of arctic animal figurines for their fifth birthday. Disgusted, Penny gave the penguin back to her parents, much to their delight. Lucy confiscated the polar bear and marked the cheek with a black marker, much to Penny's displeasure. On presenting it to Penny as if bestowing a precious gift, Lucy announced that the bear was Penny's guardian, and she must always keep it close. And Penny had.

Although her sister did not dream of future events like Penny, she only recently inclined to ask why her sister had made those marks. Three small marks. Scars across the left cheek. Lucy avoided answering, instead referring to the guardian nonsense.

Since moving to Alaska for college, glimpses of the scarred polar bear snuck into Penny's dreams. And the more recent move to Utqiaġvik had resulted in an increase in dream sightings. Be that as it may, Lucy presented no further answers on why she had marked the bear figurine all those years ago nor had any idea why Penny was now seeing the bear in her dreams.

The sight of the partially open ocean, when visible between the buildings, drew Penny's focus back to the day's work. It stretched out away from town, a vast grey mass, unfriendly, uninviting. Especially for the bears that relied on the ice for hunting.

The black truck pulled up to the airport where the other three team members lounged in the hangar office.

Noah Volkov, Army's nephew, was seven years Penny's senior. An army veteran too, he worked security in Prudhoe Bay on a three-week-on/three-week-off rotation. During his off time, he flew helicopter for hire, assisted his uncle and the team, or tinkered on some machine or another. Penny had spent less time working with Noah and more time playing guitar with him. He didn't pry, didn't find the need to fill silence with words, and she found his aloofness comforting. His unique eyes still gave her the chills, slate blue with an inner vibrant ring of green.

Winter, Noah's constant canine companion when he was not in Prudhoe, had amber-colored eyes set within his wedged-shaped face. His ears were black, as was the band that draped across and down his back, ending at a black tail tip. The colors blended smoothly to varied shades of grey and white throughout the rest of his body. Lanky and thin, there was a lot of body to fill out. From nose to rump he was longer than any dog Army had, close to five feet long. And he was a wolf-hybrid.

Winter sired a litter, and one puppy now resided with Penny. Almost an exact copy, only in miniature at present, Blue was only a few months old but with the striking blue eyes of his mother.

Dr. Bill Barosevik, Army's second-in-charge, held a PhD in arctic geophysics. He also worked with the USGS on a separate project, studying the effects of increasing populations of migratory birds in the area.

As Penny approached, Bill grumbled under his breath. Although he was harmless, his normal grouchy demeanor only accentuated his resemblance to a black bear. Dark, curly hair sprouted fur-like from almost every inch of exposed copper skin with matching dark eyes. He was completely different from his assistant and partner, Rita Wickerson, with her tall, lanky frame, pale skin, short spiky blond hair and blue eyes. Bill and Rita had been working with Army for years and years and years, as Rita liked to say, and Rita liked to say a lot. The ride would be quiet without her along for the day.

While Noah and Army stood next to each other, Penny took in their similarities. Or tried to. There were more differences between them. Noah was tall and sinewy, whereas Army was thicker around his midline and closer to Penny's five-foot-eight height. Army kept his black hair slicked back into a long braid while Noah held his shoulder-length black curls tucked beneath a black beanie. A beard graced his face and most of his neck. Penny wondered what he looked like without the beard. Then again, did it matter with his amazing eyes? The fact she found him attractive disconcerted Penny; she hadn't ever truly been attracted to anyone. Plus, he seemed out of her league. Although if she were honest with herself, she never fathomed a league she did fit in. It had been hard relating to her peers before her sister's illness, and not since the shooting and her father's death had she cared to try.

"Penny, help me load up this equipment." Bill's rough voice broke her from her musings.

She jogged over and began handing up the cases for Bill to pack inside the helicopter. The bird, as Army referred to it, was an older Bell helicopter updated with a rotor system that used smart technology to reduce the noise output during flight. Quieter meant less interference with natural animal behaviors. And it yielded a lower carbon footprint.

Her mother added her cases to the mix. Winter jumped in, settling his canine frame into the seat next to the window behind Noah's pilot seat. Penny climbed in and sat next to the dog, receiving a friendly sniff and lick on the cheek. A mixture of joy and contentment oozed from the dog. Bill and her mother sat across the aisle.

"Don't worry." Bill tapped her knee. She bent her head toward him, their headsets not yet on, as Noah and Army continued to run through their pre-flight checklist. "Your man is a brilliant pilot." His dark bearish appearance contrasted with his Irish lilt.

"Ah, he's not my man, Bill," Penny said, her voice quiet. Her skin burned, and she hoped no one else heard the bearish man's comment.

He shook his head, a disgusted look on his face. "No, I mean him, Noah. That chap. Guy. You Americans take our slang literally, but we are supposed to not take your slang literally." He continued to grumble under his breath as he placed his headset on his blocky head.

Penny shared a rueful smile with her mother. "I know he flies. He does at Prudhoe, right? I."

Bill lifted his chin quickly in response.

"Easy peasy, Billie," said Noah through the headset. "The weather couldn't be more perfect, so we should have a great flight today." Noah gave Penny a grin over his shoulder. Curling edges of black-inked tribal tattoos peeked from underneath the sleeves of Noah's blue plaid shirt, the long sleeves rolled up to his elbows as if challenging the cold outside to interfere with his flight. "Buckle up kids. Time to be airborne."

Penny's excitement teetered at the reference to kids. To change the direction of her thoughts, she pulled out her tablet and brought up a map of the area with an array of colored dots.

The team's research was funded under the USGS, in which Army held a position, so the team coordinated efforts to remove or repair collars during their biochip research. The chips offered a way to monitor both sexes of bears as male polar bears' necks grew so think a collar would fall off.

On their electronic mapping system, red dots marked the uncollared bears the team had tagged thus far. Purple dots indicated collared and chipped bears. Blue dots indicated the collared bears the team tracked to remove the collars and replace them with the biochip. The green dots showed the location of collared bears that would stay collared.

Army gazed at the same map on his handheld in the front, guiding Noah in the direction of the day's target, the collared bears.

As the helicopter took to the skies, Penny's stomach plummeted to her feet where it would undoubtedly stay until they landed, or until she fell asleep. She maintained a firm, one-handed grip on the seat while her other hand manipulated the computerized map.

"Off to your left, folks, you will see the edge of the world on the horizon," came Noah's voice in Penny's headset. She smiled at the never-ending joke the team shared—not the end, just the edge.

The arctic waters off to the left reminded her how small and insignificant she was, and the question rose within her, "How exactly will you make one bit of difference?"

A pod of eight Beluga whales appeared below, their sleek, white torpedo bodies sliding through the frigid waters. The suddenness with which the sorrow hit her stole her breath. Her father would have loved this. He would have finagled Army into giving him a role on the team. Penny lived her family's dream without her father. Her eyes burned, and she stared off toward the sun, willing the tears away. No one needed to see her emotional meltdown. She bit her lips together as Winter nosed her shoulder. It would be alright. Her father was still with her in spirit. She cleared her throat and wiped at her eyes as inconspicuously as possible while she rubbed Winter's head. She didn't think anyone noticed.

If she looked closely out the side window, the two houses to the east of town where Army and Penny lived would be visible. Houses and buildings blended into the bland landscape, standing out with their symmetrical shadows. The research station sat further south of the airport and was not visible with their current course.

The ice long ago retreated significantly from the coastline and most bears were landlocked earlier than normal. The warming arctic continued its push on the bears to alter their routines.

The whale bone pile, located at the point of Utqiaġvik, held the hulking remains of the carcasses that were dumped following harvest by the indigenous hunters. That and the local garbage dump happened to be a popular hangout for many polar bears.

On her tablet, Penny counted three biochipped bears at the bone pile at the point of Utqiaġvik. On a whim, she asked Noah to do a flyby.

Bill and Army searched out the windows, counting the bears rummaging through the decaying carcasses.

"Six bears," Bill grumbled through his mic.

"Alright, Bill. Doc. Set up to tag the other three," Army responded.

Eelyn pulled out biochips encased within a syringe apparatus and passed them to Penny to be scanned. Once Penny logged the tracking number and returned them to Eelyn, she loaded up the dart gun that would inject the biochips into the thick back fat of the bear. The bear's own body would provide energy to activate the chip. Embedded, the chip would begin sending its data to the team's database where it would be broken down into useful information. Should the bear perish, the chip would only function for a brief period, and the team would receive notification.

While Noah held the helicopter steady, Bill shot each bear out of the window. The appearance of a red dot coinciding with a beep. That notified Penny of the activation of each chip on her monitor, and Eelyn confirmed the purple dye through binoculars. The retraction mechanism created a flash of non-toxic purple dye that would be visible on the back of the bear and demonstrated a successful retraction of the needle and release of the syringe case. They would be able to retrieve the waterproof and buoyant case after the bears had left the area later that day.

Due to the size differences, the three unchipped bears most likely were a mother and her two cubs so Penny keyed in that information. Noah did a wide sweep to ensure the bears didn't react poorly to the tagging before heading out along the coast.

Penny rubbed the tiny figurine in her pocket and wondered how the rest of the day would present.

Bear(ly) There

It was another hour before the next bear came into view. With the thump-thumping of the helicopter blades, the lack of conversation, and the bright sun, Penny dozed. Bill nudged her, startling her awake. As she attempted to slow her heart rate, she brushed her mouth, removing any drool that may have snuck out before Winter might assist. The fuzzy image of a scarred polar bear fading into nothingness.

Army called out one of the collared bears they sought. She traveled upon the tundra along the coastline far from the town of Utqiaġvik. Noah hovered over the tundra so Bill could hit his target that had come into sight - an adult female, eight years old. Bill called out the young cub he spied that trailed the female. Penny itched to perform the darting, but she had yet been given an opportunity to prove her skill.

After a smooth landing, the crew disembarked with their equipment. Army placed a loose-fitting rope around the neck of the cub to establish some control over it although the cub, small for its age, clung to its mother. Penny longed to cuddle the furry cub, but its anxious mental outbursts were too much even from ten feet away. Besides, her outerwear worked best without tear marks, and the little cub was still formidable at over ninety pounds. Her mother eyeballed the cub and provided a tranquilizer dose for it as well so that the team could accomplish a complete exam on both.

With the cub sedated, Penny approached the female. Overwhelming awe cuffed Penny for the umpteenth time as she stood near the six-hundred-pound bear. Her throat tightened as she took her gloves off and buried her fingers into the bear's thick coat. The sunlight glinted off the long, luminescent hair shafts. Bits of twigs and short grasses adhered to the dingy coat turning her into more of a muddy tan bear than a white one.

Squatting down at the female's feet, Penny inspected the paws. The forepaw dwarfed her hand by a good four inches. The black pads were thick and highly sensitive. The scent glands on the toes left behind a unique marking wherever they walked, allowing a male to track a female for great distances. Penny ran a fingertip over the length and curve of the smooth claw, perfect for grasping seals from small holes in the ice.

Eelyn called out parameters to Penny for recording, so Penny stood and began entering the data into her handheld computer. The doctor collected samples: blood, hair, and fecal for later analysis as it was imperative to get a read on the animal's condition.

The adult appeared to be in fair condition. Her cub did not. It was small, borderline emaciated. Normally, females give birth between October and December, so at this stage the cub would be seven to nine months old and about the size of a giant breed dog. Noah relayed the cub's weight from the hanging scale to Penny - ninety-two pounds.

The team hoped to discover a way to help the creatures in the warming climate, to improve understanding of the animal's biology, and to lead to recovery in their status in the years ahead. Greater periods of time on land meant fewer fat reserves from the consumption of seals by the threatened bears and harder maternity periods for the females who spent roughly five months in a den nursing cub(s) without taking in any sustenance. Other bears hibernated during winter months. Polar bears hunted. They required significant fat to sustain them in their frigid environment and during denning. Unique to the marine bear, their metabolism slowed when faced with limited food sources.

Penny stood and surveyed the scene; she was stricken with the plight of not just this, but all the creatures faced with a changing world. Her mother needed a bit longer with her sample collection, so Penny took a short walk away from the bear. The wind was brisk, but the pungent musk of the bear had started to become intense. Plus, she could only fawn over the slumbering creatures so long before the others started to think her odd.

The cold breeze carried the tang of the briny sea from the nearby shore. Impressive pinkish-purple blossoms of dwarf fireweed opened for the sun. The fragrant flowers were much too small for their scent to overpower that of the sea. She glanced up to watch the geese flying low overhead, honking noisily. The extreme numbers of geese around the area caused destruction of the tundra, which in turn released more carbon dioxide into the air and escalated warming of the area. The geese might very well provide a supplemental food source for the bears. The teams' studies thus far indicated it was occurring, but would it be enough overall?

Noah stood off closer to the ocean, his beanie hanging out of his back pocket while he play-wrestled with Winter. His shiny black curls bounced and glistened in the sunlight. She heard his laugh and the frisky growling of Winter.

The tundra behind them ridged and then dropped off to an unseen beach. Army, Bill and her mother were still gathered near the mother bear and cub with the helicopter waiting silently behind them. Penny began to pull her phone out to take a few pictures.

As her gaze returned to Noah and the jumping wolf-dog, black spots swarmed her vision. She attempted to blink them away without success. Heat surged up her back, and the horizon swayed. She bent over, hands on her thighs, and closed her eyes. A vision rose up of Noah and Winter, almost like a memory. Only this wasn't a memory. She had not before witnessed a great white bear appearing behind Noah on this same crest. A rearing bear with three long, black scars across its left cheek.

The strange visions Penny perceived lately were foggy and difficult to understand, like the overcast landscape. This vision, however, was distinct. The vision that was not a memory continued: Noah turned and fell on his knee as the bear advanced. Winter launched himself at the bear's throat.

She blinked rapidly. Noah and Winter were still playing.

Glancing at her watch, she calculated the time they had been on the ground. The team had not spotted any other bears in the area before landing. Another bear could have approached given the time they had been working on the female.

Her heart thumped in her chest as she scanned the area. She began to walk toward Noah, the clear vision replaying in her memory. Noah, with his beanie removed, looked just like the Noah from the brief vision. The bear would be coming from behind Noah, most likely from the unseen beach.

She jogged over to Noah, her heart thrumming loudly in her ears, and tapped him on the shoulder.

"Hey Penny." Noah flashed her a toothy grin. "Everyone ready to go?"

"Noah..." The odd sensation of déjà vu hit her with urgency. "Bear!" she yelled back over her shoulder to the other team members. "Big bear!"

Two fistfuls of Noah's coat in hand, Penny pulled him away from the slope, tripping on a stone in the process. She discerned Winter's confusion in her mind and pushed aside her fear, hoping to soothe the dog. She tripped and pulled Noah down to the spongy ground.

Bill ran past them with the dart gun extended. As he peered over the ridge, he fired the gun.

"I need another dose. Hurry," he shouted.

As Eelyn ran past, Penny dropped her head against Noah's chest where she rested atop him. So...the vision had not materialized. Could she have really just prevented a situation? That would be a first. She slowly rolled off a silent Noah. The relief that momentarily greeted her soon became drowned by a guilt that constantly lurked in the depths of her mind.

Penny, you cannot stop every bad thing from happening.

I would like to prevent just one. Save one. Although, would it make up for anything? The lives snuffed out? Her father's death? These questions she replayed over and over but without resolution. If only the vision had provided a glimpse of the person from her class who aided in such violence. If only she had known her father would die. If only she had known. If only. But the vision had not granted her the information she wished to have had, and wishing for something was as futile as the worrying. What was done was done. She should focus her energy on figuring out how to use the visions instead of worrying about what she couldn't do. So, then, why couldn't she stop the brooding?

Noah gave her a questioning look as he rolled up. Standing, he offered her a hand up before hurrying to Bill's side and gazing at the scene below on the beach.

"What happened?" asked Eelyn on her approach.

Penny remained silent as Army rushed past with a second tranquilizer gun.

"I'll be damned," he said as they all looked down from the ridge.

Below the steep drop off on the pebbled grey beach lay a massive polar bear. A dead walrus bobbed in the sluggish surf nearby.

"He's a monster," said Eelyn. "I bet he weighs a ton."

Army handed Noah the gun and retreated to get more supplies.

Eelyn informed them that the female and her cub still slept; she had not administered the reversal injection, so they had plenty of time to work on the bear below. The team made their way to the beach via a precarious route down the eroded tundra, between blocks of frozen ground tangled with soggy, slippery mud and slick gravel.

"It was a good thing I loaded up a backup tranquilizer," Bill groused as Eelyn made a quick exam of the massive male bear. With the extra rope Army procured from the helicopter, the team struggled to roll him far enough from the water.

Standing at his head, the three jagged, black scars that marred its left cheek captivated her. "It's him," Penny breathed, her hand hovering over her pocket.

Noah, standing beside her, glanced at her. "Him?"

Before her laid the bear that crept into her nightmares and appeared in her daydreams since her arrival in Alaska. Him... the bear in her pocket.

Penny didn't respond but crouched and ran her hand along the scars marring the massive, beautiful face. An old wound from another bear paw by her guess. The overwhelming stench of clams and bad farts stung her nose. She swallowed hard against the bile rising in her belly.

Army injected the male with the chip and locked in his information into the electronic tablet. The bear that appeared in her visions, as well as rested in her jean pocket, would now be trackable.

She pulled her hand back into her lap and stared at the vacant, small black eye. The eyelid closed in a slow blink. When it reopened, the vacant stare had departed, and the eye fixed on Penny. The bear inhaled a deep, slow breath. Noah pulled her up and away from the bear.

He shouted. "Coming to."

Eelyn reacted with speed and administered another dose of tranquilizer as the male had started to paw and lift his head. Army nearly drug her away, although the bear's movements were slothful and uncoordinated, he could still do a great deal of damage.

"Sorry, I should have been paying closer attention," said Eelyn as they stood a safe distance away waiting for the dose to take effect, and the bear relaxed into sleep once more.

Can you imagine him turning into a man? That would be a big dude, thought Lucy.

Penny snorted while snickering at the comment, recalling a favored childhood tale of the White Bear Prince.

Noah nudged her arm with his. "What's so funny?"

"Just thinking about *East of the Sun West of the Moon.*" She glanced sideways at him and noticed his contemplative stare at the slumbering bear.

"So, did the wind tell you there was a bear down here?" he asked quietly, his thick beard hiding a half-grin or a grimace. It was too difficult for Penny to tell, so she moved away pretending not to hear.

It was surprising the wind hadn't brought the pungent odor towards them. The dead walrus saturated the air with its strong marine perfume. Penny wrinkled her nose and held her breath as much as she could while helping to take measurements of the bear.

As they finished up their physical exam of the male, Eelyn returned to the original scene with Bill to inject the female and cub with a reversal drug that would revive them. Waking them before the male would allow enough time for the female and the cub to leave the area without being harassed by the male. The four humans hovered quietly in the bird over the area to ensure no bear confrontation occurred following the bears' recoveries.

Over the next few hours, Bill darted six more bears, and they removed three more collars from females before the team headed back to Utqiaġvik. Noah flew the bird through miles of air over the course of the long day. To the north of the route, vast expanses of open water brought a somber tone to the bird. On Army's request, Noah scouted the retreating ice. Army swore at the incredible distance they traveled over open ocean. During springtime, the ice should still mostly cover the ocean's surface. Below them, one whaling boat traversed the open sea.

Spring whaling in Utqiaġvik customarily occurred out on the ice with snow machines, dog sleds, and umiaks, the Native sealskin boats. The current year was proving one of the more challenging of the whaling seasons thanks to the past three years of record arctic highs and temperatures above freezing during long stretches in the winter months.

By early evening a heavy fog rolled in, so thick that Noah flew them back relying on his instruments. A heavy silence shrouded the group on the return trip and during the ride back to the research station, at least in the vehicle in which Penny rode.

Penny hadn't been impressed the first time she observed the station, little more than three buildings enclosed by a chain link fence. Like most other buildings in Utqiaġvik, the colors were faded, blending into the environment. The primary building was a wood frame covered by corrugated steel the color of muted ochre. The most interesting part of the exterior was the truck tailgate that sat out front, propped as a bench. A grey shipping container made up the second building, and a small, dilapidated woodshed the third. Rita once informed Penny that the woodshed held an entrance to an underground bunker. Bill claimed it was an underground ice cellar. Either way, Penny had not taken liberties at exploring it as it was locked.

The team arranged their equipment inside the single room that held storage closets, shelves and ample space. During Penny's last trip out to make sure the equipment had all been taken inside, Noah stopped her by the truck.

"Seriously, Penny, how did you know the bear was down there?" His deep voice chased the cold from her veins.

Penny looked around, unsure of what to say. "I caught a glimpse of him." Not a lie. Conscious of his hand on hers, her heart beat faster.

"But you were behind me," he said. "I was closer to the beach, but I couldn't see it over the cliff."

Penny shook her head. "I saw the bear, Noah."

He released her hand. "Yeah. I just don't see how when I didn't."

She let out a shaky laugh and ran her hand over her hair, brushing back loose strands. "Well, you were playing with Winter, right? You were a bit distracted." She couldn't share how she knew; she liked that Noah looked at her like she was normal.

"Hmm, perhaps I was distracted," he said faintly, his gaze contemplative. "Why did you tackle me?"

Oh, that. "Well, I worried he would come after us, and, um, I didn't tackle you. I tripped when I tried to pull you away..." she broke off as the slow smile creased the corners of his eyes. He was teasing.

She shook her head and walked back inside without a backwards glance at the young man.

Unusual Death

Penny returned home that evening, weary down to her bones. After dropping her mother off at the veterinary clinic, a persistent throbbing began in her right temple. Replays of the vision and what occurred plagued her. On top of that, other older nightmares weaseled their way from her memories so that one blended seamlessly into the next.

She repeated her mantra. *I'm not broken; I'm only damaged. Healing takes time. I'm not broken, only damaged.*

Parked in front of her temporary home, Penny rested her forehead on the steering wheel.

What is wrong with me?

Nothing is wrong with you, her sister replied.

Obviously, something is. The headaches are back. She had nightmares of explosions filled with rapid fire of gunshot for months before the school shooting. The gunfire troubled her so much that she had stopped going to the shooting range to target shoot with her father on their free weekends together. Headaches had plagued her then, occasional brief twinges that coincided with the strange visions.

Healing takes time. You are stressed, hence the headache. And you have a gift, dear sister, reminded Lucy.

Curse was more like it. The dark visions terrified Penny.

She removed her boots and dropped them in the small porch. As she walked in, her pup, Blue, jumped and yowled, ready to go outside for some playtime. He shared his thoughts of injustice at being stuck inside with Lucy.

Army provided the home for Penny and her family to use as part of her research stipend. The porch led into a slightly larger kitchen. Dividing the open floorplan was a kitchen table and four chairs. The quaint living room had a flowery couch, a threadbare brown recliner, and a television. A blue-black bird sat on a perch nestled against the wall between the kitchen and sitting area. The house contained two bedrooms and a miniscule bathroom, so small Penny found difficulty changing her mind, much less her clothes in the closet-sized space. But she did her best.

Penny hefted Blue into her arms letting loose only a few grunts. *Dude, you are getting too big.* His unfaltering excitement to see her might have helped to eliminate some of her fatigue if her head hadn't felt like it ticked closer to an explosion. The young dog's thoughts were but ketchup compared to the spicy mental assault she would receive at Army's dog barracks. Penny placed the wiggling dog back on the ground, and he nosed and sniffed every reachable part of her legs. Sighing, she searched out a pain reliever. Mercifully, Blue picked up on her pain and patiently waited by the door.

Lucy rested on the top bunk in the tiny room they shared. Beside the bunk bed there was only enough room for a dresser, a chair, and a thick throw rug on the narrow floor space. Huddled beneath a green blanket, the outline of Lucy's body was barely visible. The thick curtains blocked most of the light, but as an extra measure, newspaper had been taped across the frame to prevent sunlight seepage.

"Hey, how's it going?" Penny asked, fearing using her inside voice would inflame her headache.

There was no movement from beneath the green blanket—green because that was the color of spring and summer and, therefore, was Lucy's favorite color.

"Did you get much writing done today?" she probed. Lucy, in her disabled state, still found joy in writing and reading. A lot. Her intended majors had been in creative writing and journalism. Since they arrived in Alaska, she had been dabbling in short stories when not working on her lengthy sci-fi/fantasy novel.

Lucy remained silent.

"You alright?" Penny asked, although she already knew. There was very little that could be hidden from each other. Lucy's ongoing illness left her tired most days. The few times she left the comfort of the house, Lucy usually went with their mother to the veterinary clinic; although truth be told, she kept to the office rather than helping.

Okay. I'm tired. Her sister's mental voice soothed the chaos in Penny's cranium.

"Too tired to come with me?"

Yeah. Don't worry about me. Go have fun.

"It would be more fun if you came."

I'm always with you, Pen. You know that.

"Yeah, I know."

There were times when Penny would have liked alone time in her mind and certainly vice versa. But it would be callous to think such a thought now. Although they shared many discussions about privacy over the years, their connection wasn't something easily shut off, although intense emotions weakened it. Sometimes it was unsettling, Lucy being privy to all her experiences and thoughts. And so, Penny tried not to think about it. Their bond differed from the mental connection Penny developed with animals; her animal link diminished with space, which was fortunate otherwise she would have a permanent migraine from Army's sled dogs.

The older sister walked out of the bedroom, leaving her younger sister alone once more. Truth be told, Penny craved some alone time herself, but she still had work to do before supper at Army's house. The sled dogs couldn't feed themselves. A smile tugged at her mouth at the thought. Before leaving, she greeted the solemn-looking crow sitting quiet on its perch.

"Hello, Edgar. How are you today?"

The bird ruffled his feathers and gave her a steady look with one beady eye. Penny sensed the melancholy that rolled off the bird in waves now that Blue's excitement waned.

As she reached out to pet him, Edgar stretched his head toward her and leaned into her touch. Penny stroked his glossy blue-black feathers, something he would not have allowed weeks before.

"Oh buddy, I know. It sucks losing someone you love."

Edgar's pupils dilated and contracted in response. "I need to head back out. You want to come with, do some reconnaissance flying for the dogs?" Penny projected images of Edgar soaring through the sky. He fluffed up his feathers and shuffled down into his roost. Not today, then.

I'll see you both soon, she thought as she and Blue left the house. Her head no longer twinged and as thoughts of the bird filled her mind, she shielded them from Edgar until her connection to him fell away.

The crow had been rescued as a fledgling and lived with one owner, Kate Kingston, up until several weeks ago. He had not spoken to anyone since he was rescued from his owner's home. Kate had gone missing in early spring; her body was found days after Penny's family's arrival in May. The remains pointed to a bear attack at her hunting cabin outside of town. No one had come to claim the bird, so after a short stay at the veterinary clinic, Eelyn brought Edgar into the Osborn household.

Penny and Blue walked over to the dog runs behind Army's neighboring home where Noah waited with the dogs.

As she approached the tall chain link fence that surrounded the dog enclosure, the yard lights blazed ineffectively in the white fog that hovered just overhead. Within the fence next to the front gate sat a lone shed that served as storage and dog food prep. It was nothing more than a wood frame covered by planks of tundra turf with patches of moss stuffed haphazardly in the collection of cracks.

Army's horde, as he referred to the twenty-two dogs, overwhelmed Penny at first. The lack of boundaries between the dogs and her mind was like a dam breach of flooding senses. After feeding the dogs the first few weeks, she would leave with headaches that often grew into migraines. As the dogs grew accustomed to her though, they eventually settled down, responding to her mental requests for calm. The fact that with Penny's arrival the dogs got out every day for exercise correspondingly played into their more mollified natures.

Noah slipped out of the shed as Penny walked into the yard, his heavy boots clunking on the wood steps. He joined in untethering the dogs for their daily walk.

The odor of wet dog surrounded Penny and triggered memories of early morning jogs with one very different canine. Her throat closed, and her eyes burned causing her to blink rapidly against the rising moisture. He, too, had been named Blue—an exceptionally large, gun metal grey Weimaraner, all lean and no mean. Her childhood companion and running partner for over twelve years. His life had been snuffed out by cancer only weeks after her father had died. Life was full of loss, and she had suffered several in a short period of time.

She was still musing about Blue when Noah handed her a . 243 rifle to carry. They set off on a different path than yesterday, south toward a creek, silent partners to the dogs' vocal jaunt.

The dogs worked so well together that taking them out for exercise was quite simple. They leashed a few dogs while the others ran free, including Blue who responded quite well to her unspoken requests. Because of Army's diligent training, the dogs responded extremely well to verbal and even physical commands, but Penny unconsciously directed them with her thoughts.

Penny's knack of working with animals extended beyond physical cues, and its usefulness was undeniable. Her mother enjoyed having Penny work with her during veterinary calls. Eelyn was aware of the twin's ability to communicate mentally, so it was not out of line to acknowledge Penny's similar ability with animals.

Although not interested in career as a veterinarian, Penny thoroughly enjoyed the summers spent working at her mother's clinic during high school. She enjoyed helping her mother, even though she grudgingly accepted her mother's use of her abilities. It was time she was able to spend alone with her mother who was often absent from home due to one emergency or another.

"You bringing the new Laguna over tonight?" Noah's

voice pulled her back to the present.

Their footsteps were soft in the moist tundra as they ventured east with the dogs, away from the houses. The howls were overpowered by the mental noise and excitement that spilled over into Penny's mind since she had arrived. Fortunately, the ache had receded before the short walk over and stayed tucked away. The dogs jumped, sniffed and nosed, and ran circles around each other and the two human companions. Winter, Noah's near constant partner, padded silently alongside, unwilling to partake in the puppy-like behavior but nonetheless tolerant of Blue who bounded about and licked his sire's face.

Penny brushed at the mosquitoes dive-bombing her, then gratefully accepted the insect repellent lotion Noah offered.

Annoying bugs ...

Yeah, hence the name bugs. *They bug*, chirped her sister. Penny mentally groaned.

"Thanks..." She handed the lotion back to Noah. "I suppose I could bring it. Not sure I want to let you touch her, though." Her dimpled smile was mischievous.

"What? Come on, I let you play my Gibson last week," his voice bordered on a whine. Noah's Gibson Les Paul guitar was his new baby or as Rita had coined it, his girlfriend. She claimed he hadn't spent money on dates in ages, just his guitars.

"And I didn't even put a scratch on her, did I?" Penny ribbed the young man who so willingly met her to help with dog chores.

"I suspect you play all my guitars when I'm gone."

"You do? Huh, the thought crossed my mind," she admitted with a chuckle.

"I still can't get over how your mom hustled us," Noah said.

His comment took her back to her family's second night in Utqiaġvik back in May. She and her family had been invited next door to Army's home for a welcome meal with the entire team. Eelyn had found a pair of drumsticks on the kitchen counter and twirled them between her fingers. Poorly. She smacked herself hard enough in the head to cause a small bruise. When Bill asked, Eelyn admitted she liked banging on a set of drums every now and then. Not to be left alone in the spotlight, she outed Penny's talent with the guitar.

"So can you bloody play guitar?" he solicited in his gruff voice.

Penny grinned at her mom and the question and then admitted that, yes, she played guitar. Not very well, though.

They then descended a narrow staircase into the cool air of an underground bunker buried beneath Army's home where Eelyn's bumbling with the drumsticks was revealed as a gaff when she and Penny played. They, of course, had been playing together for years.

The team had a comfortable, family-like quality. Relaxed, Penny dropped her guard a fraction. Noah sang that night; his voice was deep and smooth like liquid dark chocolate. It stirred emotions within her she didn't fully understand but very much liked. She sang only once that night. Noah's comment on wanting to listen to her sing on repeat thrilled and embarrassed her for she was sure that he was being overly kind. Her voice was raspier and lower than her mother's soprano, and she rarely shared it with others.

Pulling back from the memory, Penny countered with a shrug, "My mom was just playing around. She does that, you know?" She stroked Winter's back as he walked beside her.

"Yeah, I thought we were in for a good laugh," he chuckled.

"She had that black-and-blue mark on her forehead for quite a while."

"And you, though... 'I don't play very well.'" He pretended to twirl his hair, bumping his shoulder into hers as they walked.

"Well, I would like to play better." She pushed him away. "And I don't twirl my hair."

"We can't all play like Steve Vai," he said. As far as Penny was concerned, Mr. Vai was one of the best guitarists of all time. "But if anyone could match him, it would be you."

"Aww, stop. I don't have that kind of talent." Penny failed

to hold back her blush.

"I'm just kidding. You're alright." Noah snapped his fingers.

"Yeah, right? I can keep up with you, mister. That's all that matters."

The fog gradually descended as the dogs played and worked off energy. Visibility fell to a quarter of a mile. The world held them close beneath a cloak of eerie half-twilight.

Penny had quickly checked the data logger before heading out, just to make sure no bears were in the vicinity. Of course, untracked bears and other predatory beasts lurked in the tundra, but with over twenty dogs encircling the two humans, their risks were slight, so she hadn't even considered bringing the handheld on the outing. After their lengthy and uneventful walk through the fog, they returned the horde to their respective areas in the backyard to begin feeding.

Inside the shed, the dust motes rose and swirled around Penny in the washed-out light streaming through the two small windows. Abundant shelves and cabinets lined three and a half walls with sleds hung in between. Kennels, wheels, and other crates of supplies filled the cramped room. She collected two buckets from the countertop along the far wall facing the dog yard.

When Noah returned from tethering the dogs to their houses, Penny handed him a bucket of canine entrée - a gourmet dish of whale blubber (or muktuk), white fish, and dog kibble. As they distributed the delightfully smelly meal, Penny worked to quieten the enthusiastic dogs with her mind, a feat that would leave her with a headache.

The yard held rows of square wood dog houses. Each dog was tethered by a six-foot chain to a rough wood box house, arranged in groups of four. Several of the dogs stood on top of the houses barking and howling their anticipation.

Once they were all fed, Penny ran back to her house to grab her guitar and a box of French Toast cupcakes she had made the night before, a special treat for her boss and his nephew. Noah waited with the dogs so that Winter and Blue could finish eating. When they arrived at Army's house, where Noah also lived, Army greeted them at the door with a grave expression. He waited until they were all settled around the kitchen table before speaking. Blue and Winter curled up on the rug by the door.

"Autopsy results came back," he said. "About Kate."

Kate. Edgar's owner.

"Anything abnormal?" Noah asked him.

"Yes..." Army ran a hand through his long, wet hair, unbound from the usual long black braid. "Kate died before the bear got to her."

Penny asked, "How?" A sense of dread settled on her shoulders. She leaned forward, pinning her arms between the table and covered her mouth with her hands.

The authorities reasoned a polar bear, or bears, caused Kate Kingston's death. She was the second victim of an attack that spring. Both were young women in their twenties, and were found in their hunting cabin. Only now one's death could not be blamed on the white beasts.

"There were marks around her neck indicating strangulation, but her spinal cord had also been cut, most likely with a scalpel. The mauling was postmortem but not very long after her death." Army stood and began pacing. Noah leaned back heavily in his chair, his face ashen.

"Wasn't there another polar bear attack? Before I arrived? Ah, Rena, I think," she asked. Army nodded in response. "Do you think that's what happened to the other girl?" Penny asked.

"Based on this discovery, the sheriff's department is requesting an exhumation. Rena's family declined an autopsy when Rena died, but they are willing to allow one now. I guess we'll see, but I suspect...well." He exhaled and rubbed a hand down his neck, resting his other hand on the back of the chair. "I knew both girls. So did Noah. Rena lived here her whole life and Kate most of hers. Those two girls would have known better."

Trepidation settled along Penny's spine. A person murdered. Possibly two people. Did that mean a killer lived in their midst? Her nightmares of an ominous, shadowy figure lurking in a shadowed background - were they warning premonitions instead of shadows of past nightmares as she had once thought? Was she sensing a great evil skulking about the town?

Perhaps your gift is evolving, her sister considered. The vague dreams Penny had in Anchorage had intensified once they arrived in the North Slope community.

Penny would not describe past nightmarish premonitions as a gift. Her life was shattered in Pasadena with the shooting that upset nearly the entire country. The one that took her father's life.

She had brushed off the recent nightmarish dreams that hindered her sleep as nothing more than bouts of fear and self-doubt brought on by living in a barren landscape. But they persisted.

Yes. Look at today. Although it didn't happen, I believe what you envisioned with Noah and the bear might have happened if you had not interfered. I don't know why the visions have changed, but maybe it's a good thing. Leave it to Lucy to see the good in the bad.

The ever-present guilt over not having been able to stop the violent event in Pasadena gnawed at her. Her premonition had been of the aftermath, not the chain of events.

Penny wondered then whether she should share her visions of the shadowed figure with Army and Noah or her mother. She didn't understand the visions, nor could she make out details, just like before. No, surely they would find her strange. Or stranger. And her mother had her own worries; Penny had no desire to add to them. Besides that, the visions couldn't be anything more than a response to anxiety or stress induced by the constant daylight. She stayed silent as Army and Noah discussed the possibility of a serial murderer. No other unresolved disappearances occurred in the past year, and no other polar bear attacks happened due to vigilance of the community and swift action of the Polar Bear Outreach and Patrol. Nothing that could be out of the ordinary like the two girls.

Noah leaned closer to Penny.

45

"You know, it might be best to stay on the safe side and take extra precautions. Safety in numbers and all that," he said.

Penny allowed a small, crooked smirk, exposing a dimple. "I can take care of myself." Seeing the concerned looks working onto the two men's faces, she added, "but I'll keep that in mind."

"I haven't noticed any strangers in the community. No one and nothing that stands out," Army spoke, his gaze unfocused at the ceiling. "But that doesn't mean much."

"A killer usually blends in well with the environment. Camouflage. Not unlike a polar bear, right?" said Penny, reminded of saying something similar to Sam that morning.

"Perhaps the police will find some other clue, knowing what they know now. We aren't going to figure anything out tonight." Noah sniffed. "Come on. Let's go play."

"Wait a sec. Brought you all snack."

Inside the box sat six delectable looking cupcakes, decorated with a swirl of cream cheese frosting. The warm aroma of cinnamon and maple infused the men's home. Eagerly, they grabbed a cupcake.

"I think my life is complete," Noah remarked, finishing off his second helping. Crumbs clung to his beard.

Army said, "These are unbelievable. Where did you get them?"

"I made them and can bring more by later."

"In that case..." Noah ate his third and Army grabbed for the remaining cupcake.

"I'll save this one for later. You kids have fun. Leave the door open so I can listen." Army grinned and plopped down on the well-worn recliner in front of the television.

Penny followed Noah down the stairwell into the underground bunker. Basements were unheard of in the tundra; the heat given off would cause a melting of the ground around the foundation and a whole mess of problems. The bunker gave off a feel of intense protection for both the bunker as well as the surrounding earth. Heavy rugs were strewn over the floor and hung on the walls like odd tapestries to help with sound during their playing. The one time she kicked aside one edge of a rug, she exposed metal plating. She had not yet asked to explore outside the room where they played their music.

She took her newest guitar, a very expensive, very late birthday gift from her Aunt Bianca, from its case and tuned it.

Penny suspected the guitar was part of her aunt's divorce settlement (a Vegas rock guitarist), but who was Penny to look a gift horse in the mouth? The Laguna guitar was painted, giving the impression of smooth water ripples, transitioning from sapphire blue to turquoise and then to teal. Embedded along the fretboard were opalescent birds, wings out in various stages of flight. The icing on the cake was its name: Dragon Breath, her childhood nickname. And now, lucky girl that she was, many more opportunities for Dragon Breath existed.

For a short time as Penny and Noah exercised their fingers along the tight strings of their guitars, strumming out their emotions in the melodies and harmonies, Penny was freed from her fears and dark thoughts.

Colossal Attack

"Oh, come on," Penny said. "I didn't go to the Wisteria Festival, the Avocado Festival..." She listed multiple other celebrations that her friend Liam attempted to get her to attend when she had lived in the L.A. area. Now, roughly three-thousand miles away, he was insisting she attend the spring whaling festival, or Nalukataq. Where she stumbled over the Native pronunciation, but he avoided pronouncing it altogether.

"Penny." Liam sounded exasperated on the phone. "You'll be missing a cultural event. The chance to experience Inupiaq Eskimo traditions." Penny pictured his shaggy blond hair shaking in frustration over her non-desire to venture out for a cultural event. Science, though? Now that would pull her any day.

He has a point. Lucy joined the razzing.

"You guys don't understand. Being around lots of people...crowds make me claustrophobic. Plus, I'm an outsider. I don't fit in. I'm not from here. I'm like a tourist."

"Didn't you say two native Barrownians invited you?" Liam asked, his tone jealous.

They had, in fact. However, Noah was currently in Prudhoe and unable to make the late-June festival. She felt the need to correct Liam's use of Barrow instead of Utqiaġvik, but withheld. It would not make a difference, only irritate him.

"My puppy is getting big, Lee. Blue is already pulling a snow machine track around. Won't be long before he can start to train with a team," Penny said. At four months of age, he was gangly and rowdy, and was presently curled comfortably on her lap in her lower bunk instead of being tethered with the rest of the dogs outside. Her hand stroked his soft fur, light enough so as not to awaken him, although his ears flickered when she spoke his name.

"That's great, Pen. I picked up a puppy myself. Golden Retriever. Got it from a friend," Liam said cutting her off when she began telling him of training her puppy to pull. "I know. Me and pets, yeah right?" He hadn't been able to keep a fish alive longer than a week for years. "But mom is excited about having a dog."

Penny rolled her eyes at her friend. Years earlier, when the Osborns moved to sunny southern California, the twins had met Liam, who was a year older and a close neighbor. He asserted himself as the Osborn's third child. The three grew to be exceptionally close, but Liam and Lucy took it a step further and began dating during high school. When Lucy became ill during the twin's junior year of high school, she broke up with Liam. He never quite got over it. Over time, and with Lucy's continued self-induced isolation, Liam clung tighter to Penny, but she refused anything more than friendship.

When she could, she snuck in tidbits about her life in the cold north. Darting bears from the air, trying her hand at blogging about the team's activities, running on the treadmills at the small workout facility in town (it was soul-sucking but unavoidable), reading research material, the horrendous onslaught of mosquitoes now that temperatures stayed slightly above freezing, walking and sledding with the dogs, and the latest fantasy novel she was reading.

"How much work do you actually do?" he asked.

Penny laughed, the light sound filling her artificially darkened bedroom.

"Not much. Seriously though," she confessed. "I have plenty of time to do other things and still find myself getting bored. I started writing like Lucy to fill in the gaps, but I might still need to find some other job to take up time when the tagging season finishes."

"Still playing guitar?"

"Yeah. Turns out my boss - well, my team – has a band of

their own. They are pretty stoked mother and I can play."

He snorted. "You still call her 'mother?'"

"You still call her 'Mrs. Osborn."

"Touché. So, this Army, he plays guitar?"

"No, he plays keyboard. And sings. Nice voice."

"Any other guitarists?" Liam probed.

"Noah, Army's nephew. He also gives guitar lessons, and because he spends three weeks here and then three weeks at the oil field in Prudhoe Bay, I keep everybody going while he is gone."

"Oh. So, you don't get to hang out much then?"

Oh my gosh, he is jealous! Lucy sniggered from the chair across the bedroom.

He isn't, Penny disagreed, her eyebrows drawn together in a scowl.

So, tell him you two hang out all the time.

We do not! Penny retorted.

Oh, okay.

"Yeah Lee, we hang out. He is a bit older than us, but we have similar interests, I guess. He lives next door with his uncle, my boss. And we do work together. You'd like him."

There was a long pause on Liam's end, and Lucy chimed in that Liam would in fact not like Noah. Penny ignored her twin and checked a notification on an incoming message on her phone from her mother.

Mother: Hey girl, head to the beach. Bowhead hauled in!

"Sorry, Liam, gotta run. My mother is calling me," she said, a bit ashamed of her relief to end the call.

After their goodbyes, Penny grabbed a warm jacket and headed out. Lucy declined going, opposed to the harvesting of the magnificent creatures no matter that the harvest was for sustenance of the Native population. She insisted that currently, most shipping companies delivered better tasting and smelling food within days. Penny declined to argue that particular point; the aroma was something she didn't care for either but dealt with every time she fed the dogs. The ritual harvesting of whale and seal provided sustenance for those who had made the arctic climate their home for tens of thousands of years.

Discussions during college classes in Anchorage focused on the status of the arctic ice or rather the extreme loss of it and the effects on the local populations. Many of the lectures touched on research that predicted ice-free summers at the North Pole within the next twenty to thirty years. Penny attended a summer field trip to Kaktovik to observe wildlife on Barter Island. It had been an exhilarating and eye-opening trip to experience firsthand the devastating effects of the warming arctic.

It was during this excursion that she met Army, with his PhDs in everything. A resident of Utqiaġvik, he gave lectures on climatic transformation at the UAA. Penny took the opportunity to talk with him about arctic work during the trip. His research focused on climate changes, trends in melt and freeze of arctic ice, and the current population decline and adaptation of arctic species. He appeared especially animated about assisting polar bears in attaining the endangered status.

Bill and Rita met Penny at her vehicle, and together they walked to the beach. Rita was wearing a fluorescent pink, short-sleeved t-shirt that complimented her ever-changing blue eyes. Today, her eyes were the color of new ice. Bill wore his trademark black sweatshirt. Penny wondered at how they ever became a couple.

"Opposites attract, don't you know, Penny? Bill and I are like magnets," Rita said without prompting when Penny first met her.

Rita did not play a musical instrument, or at least hadn't since high school, but she made an enthusiastic audience of one, claiming she could listen to Bill beat on the drums for hours.

As they walked to the beach, Bill's characteristic deep voice rose as he shared that the whale was the last for the spring season. Wings of nervousness fluttered in Penny's belly. Although she often glimpsed pods of whales from overhead when she was flying, this was her first up close and personal with a fresh bowhead whale carcass.

A large crowd gathered around the even larger whale carcass. Penny knew it to be 38°F, but many people worked in short-sleeved shirts. The hazy air warmed as they drew closer. Steam rose about the workers as they made their cuts on the beast. The equipment used to haul it ashore stood off to the side, behemoths in their own right. It was close to 9:45 p.m., but as usual in late June, the sun made it appear closer to early afternoon.

The leviathan's carcass lay on the beach where workers cut and pulled long rectangular slabs of white blubber away from it. Penny eyed the slabs critically, wondering at the cleanliness as it laid on the ground while people milled about.

Bill and Rita distracted her by pointing out the Game and Fish technician, deep in discussion with Eelyn and Army. Rita broke from their little group to chat with the G&F official, while Eelyn excused herself to join Penny and Bill.

Penny's attention focused on the small children that ran about, screaming and laughing. One child with black pigtails squatted down beside the dark blueish-black skin of the carcass, digging her hands into a red puddle. She suddenly slapped both palms against the whale's skin, leaving behind two perfect bloody handprints.

Drawn to where the child had played, Penny stood beside the carcass. She laid her palms against the warm skin while the opaque steam swirled in eddies around her head. The heady fish aroma permeated the heavy air and clung to her, making her feel heavy and slow. Breathing through her mouth didn't help.

She turned and surveyed the many people standing, walking, talking, the younger folk running and screaming around her. The sounds became muffled, as if far away. Penny peeked back to the carcass from beneath her eyelashes, splashes of red appeared everywhere. Streaked handprints, dripping crimson. A coppery tang snuck through the whale odor and caught in her throat, immobilizing her.

Her vision tunneled and memories spilled forth of another time, another place where sounds of death and chaos and the coppery tang of blood filled her head. She stumbled backwards away from the whale, tripping over two kids running behind her, their faces painted crimson. Their mouths opened in laughter, but Penny only perceived screams.

"Penny!" called Rita.

Penny held her palms up to her face, blood dripping from her fingers. Her gaze shifted downward, her breathing shallow and her heartbeat thrumming in her ears as she caught sights of the streaks of red on her white jacket. Something inside her had broken long ago, and the edges were still raw and quivering.

A sob tore free, and her chest hurt as her broken pieces fragmented yet again.

"Noooooo," wept Penny. *Not this again.*

Strong arms embraced her.

"Come on, Penny, I gotcha. Let's get out of here," said Rita.

Penny, I'm here. Penny, focus on me, sissy. Stay with me, called Lucy's faint voice.

Penny's legs gave out, and she slid down the length of the person holding her, her knees hitting the cold, wet ground.

Divine Confession

"Penny, honey, can you hear me?"

Penny's surroundings slowly came into focus. She was back in her house, laid out on the couch. A dull pain pulsed at her temples, and her thoughts were sluggish. Overall, though, a state of calmness blanketed her. Medication coursed through her veins. Blue lay atop her legs. She absently stroked his head while he licked her hand.

"Mom," she croaked. Clearing her throat, she tried again. "Lucy..."

I'm here, Penny, her sister said faintly. And there she was, peering over the back of the couch. Their connection was odd, distorted. What medication had she been given?

"I'm right here, sweetheart. How are you feeling?" said her mother as she knelt next to her.

"Tired. Slow."

"Do you remember what happened?" Eelyn brushed Penny's forehead.

"I would rather not," said Penny, concerned over her foolish reaction to the whale. She inhaled deeply, catching the scent of cinnamon and vanilla in the air.

Army and Rita appeared within Penny's vision. She imagined the look on Rita's face was pity, whether it was or not.

"Penny, don't be sorry, sweetheart." Her mother continued to stroke her hair.

Try as she might, Penny couldn't hold back the solitary tear that escaped.

"We were all worried about you..." her mother broke off, her hand rubbing Penny's shoulder. Penny met her mother's eyes that were filled with worry and grief. Neither escaped unscathed from the day that caused Penny's anxiety.

"I'm sorry," Penny began.

"Oh, sweetheart, don't be sorry. It's not your fault. I should have thought about it more before I asked you to come down." Her mother sighed.

Army cleared his throat. "It may not be my place, but I don't think either of you are at fault for anything that happened earlier."

When the silence stretched out longer than manageable, she replied, "It was the screaming, I think."

Army and Rita glanced at each other before returning their attention to Penny.

"The kids were running around, laughing and screaming in the blood. All that blood." Penny stopped to take a shaky breath. "Then I just heard screaming. And the red handprints were everywhere. It was just like that day, mother. I couldn't stop thinking about it. I'm so sorry. I wasn't able to stop it." She fought back a sob.

Not a day passed when Penny didn't think about that day. It was always in the back of her mind along with the guilt and sorrow and shame.

"You don't have anything to be sorry over," Army spoke up. "We all have demons. Some more than others."

Penny covered her face with a pillow. "There are too many…nightmares…memories," she said, her voice muffled. "This was a nightmare, the same nightmare," her voice all but disappeared with the final word.

A stronger person could handle this, she thought.

You are not weak, came her sister's sharp retort.

"Penny, you are one of the strongest people I know. You are talented, smart, hard-working. And you are fortunate to be surrounded by so many people who care about you," said Rita. "Army wouldn't have picked someone who couldn't handle the job."

"Thanks, Rita," came Penny's muffled response as she teetered on the pit of grief.

Army placed a cup of tea next to Penny. The mint aroma reminded her of her father. She tilted into the pit. It would be so easy to fall into the overwhelming sadness. Her father's birthday was two days ago. Or at least would have been. Penny failed to notice how her mother was coping.

Penny exhaled and let the tears fall.

"I miss him so much, mother. I wish I'd been able to stop it. Done something to prevent it. I was there, but I couldn't do anything to stop it." She couldn't stop the words from flowing.

But you did prevent the one with Noah and the bear, her sister reminded her faintly.

Unsure what to think about that, Penny let the comment slide.

"It's not your fault. I don't blame you. No one does. You need to stop blaming yourself. You did not pull the trigger. There was nothing to be done." Eelyn sighed and pulled Penny close. "What you saw the night before...what would you have done? Told someone? No one would have believed you. You didn't understand it. Hell, even afterwards I didn't understand it, sweetheart."

Penny had shared her recollection of the vision, albeit in a brief, censored version, the morning before the incident. As much as she blamed herself, Penny hoped her mother did not hold any resentment towards her. Penny was only 99% certain her mother didn't but the "why" of her visions ate at Penny constantly. What good were the visions when she didn't have the ability to stop or change them?

"You are so lucky to have such support, Penny. Family is so very important," said Army.

Penny recalled meeting Army that first year in college. She had written a research proposal for the use of a modified biochip to track marine mammals, and it had caught his attention. The chips, fitted with GPS and biotechnology, would not only track tagged animals via satellite, like the standard collars, but also would provide details about health and body functions as well as alert the scientists to any deaths. Marine carcasses tended to be lost to the sea and so determining causes of death proved challenging. Perhaps the chips weren't as cool as the solar-powered video collars in use, but they could provide useful information without much interference with the animals. The chips could be used on any age and sex and would add to the research obtained with the collars. The collars would continue to be used unless they malfunctioned or were no longer needed.

Over the next couple of years, the professor stayed in contact. Once he secured funding, he requested Penny work with his research team on the project over the next two years. The opportunity piqued Penny's interest in focusing her future career on the marine bears, and she gladly agreed. Completion of the two-year project would secure her standing in the graduate program.

When Army learned that Penny's mother was a veterinarian, he mentioned the need for one, as his usual vet in Utqiaġvik was close to retirement and a bad hip prevented him from much field work. Eelyn agreed and was hired on part-time at the veterinary clinic to help out ol' Doc.

Not to be left behind, Lucy also agreed to move to the small community of Utqiaġvik but not to work with the arctic research team. Lucy preferred writing and staying indoors, ever the recluse. The debilitating illness that Lucy suffered through resulted in restrictions with her physical activities, but she stayed mentally fit and more than comfortable to settle into the role of a writer, insisting that she lived vivaciously enough through Penny's eyes.

They knew eventually they would live apart, a point their mother had made more than once. They wouldn't be able to rely on each other forever. But throwing into the equation that their mother, too, had made both moves with them placed a significant flaw in her case. Their prognosis of staying together was excellent.

"Me, too," Penny responded. She sat up, pulled herself together. Life was easier wearing a smile. Obviously hers was forced, but her friends and family accepted her effort.

When Noah returned the following week, the spring whaling festival had come and gone. The panic attack Penny suffered the few days prior prevented her from attending, and she stayed busy with work instead.

Outwardly Penny hoped people saw a happy, recovered Penny. Behind the mask, her dark thoughts tormented her. She refused additional medication, as it interfered with hearing her sister. Medicated, she displayed the abnormal happiness, knowing it was false but not caring. It bothered her. Medication free, her true feelings, the good and the bad, rang loudly in her ears. She pursued a lifestyle of fitness, preferring running and martial arts to blow off steam and help focus her mind. No one offered martial arts in Utqiaġvik, so she ran through her perfected patterns and techniques alone to maintain her skill.

Alone one morning, Penny donned a pair of sweatpants and a tank top and began running through every taekwondo belt pattern she knew starting at white and ending with black. The small home was a simple, open floor plan. She had only to move the kitchen table and chairs off to the side next to Edgar's perch, and the kitchen floor opened before her.

She repeated each pattern three times before advancing to the next colored belt. Music helped her concentrate, and she wore ear-engulfing headphones to pull her into her zone. They canceled out all sound, and she soon became lost in the motions, ignoring the puppy until he lost interest and disappeared. She finished the last move of the first-degree black belt pattern and held it, her back to the front door. A song ended followed by a brief period of silence in which Blue barked. Penny glanced around, looking for the dog, when a figure loomed from behind her.

Startled, she jumped away and landed in a defensive stance, ready to fight off the intruder. The intruder, however, held his hands aloft with a sheepish grin beneath a thick, black beard.

Self-conscious she cursed and stood, removing her earphones.

"Have you been standing there long? Don't you knock?" she asked.

He glanced down with the sense to look apologetic. Perhaps his cheeks were ruddy, but with the beard it was hard to tell. "I did knock, but Blue was the only one to come to the door. I thought I would let him out for you since I riled him up. Sorry, I…" he trailed off and scratched the back of his head. As he did, his black, long-sleeved crewneck pulled up revealing the large hunting knife he wore on his belt and less than an inch of smooth, white skin. "So, you know, ah, taekwondo?"

Penny tucked a loose strand of hair behind her ear and then crossed her arms, tucking her fists behind her upper arms. "Yeah, a bit."

He leaned sideways against the kitchen counter and folded his arms in front of him. One of Lucy's notebooks, the one with ink doodles of a flying horse with lightning trailing his aerial hoofbeats across the sky, rested nearby and caught his wandering gaze. He reached for it and studied the drawing.

"This is cool. You do this?"

Stepping forward, Penny took the notebook from Noah. "It's my sister's. One of her writing notebooks. She filled a ton of these."

"Any good stories in this one in particular?"

"There's one about humans colonizing an alien planet." Penny pointed to the sketch in the center of the notebook. "This illustration here was her inspiration for a race of creatures that lived there."

"Nice artwork. Not your typical Pegasus with rainbow hair," he said in a tentative tone, as if not wanting to reveal a manly specimen such as he knew the proper term for a flying horse.

"They had horns, so not a Pegasus. She called them A'Sarien." She tucked the notebook under her armpit for safe keeping and glanced away.

"Is the story any good?" he asked.

Penny shrugged. "What she told me about it, or at least what I needled out of her, sounded amazing. But maybe I'm a bit biased, right?" When he smiled, his eyes crinkled at the corners. She tried not to lose her wits when their eyes met. "Anyway, it isn't finished."

She flashed a quick smile before looking away. Perhaps if she had the ability to disappear, it would have been an opportune moment. The notebook crinkled, and the metal spiral binding pinched the sensitive skin in her armpit as she twisted her arms in front of her, weaving her fingers together.

"My sister painted those," Noah said as he nodded to the underwater scenes painted on the wall behind Edgar.

Since moving in, Penny wondered who the artist was behind the diving seals and breaching whales, but she never remembered to ask once outside the house. Edgar appeared so out of place perched in front of the murals, a black splotch in a sea of blues and greens. He seemed to stand up straighter with the thought. She tried to convey that he was in the perfect place, and she was happy where he was. His feathers ruffled, and he settled lower on the perch.

"They are very good," she replied. "Is she into art or was this a hobby?"

"She's a lawyer in Juneau. This was a hobby...*is* a hobby still, I think."

"Um, do you have any other siblings?" She tried to recall if she ever heard. She was getting a bit chilled standing still having turned the heat down to practice.

"Yeah. A younger brother, Harry. He started at the U in Anchorage last fall. He's working at one of the canneries this summer."

That last statement elicited a hundred questions in Penny's mind, but Noah suddenly looked like he had other things on his mind than discussing family. Besides, Lucy probably wouldn't want him reading her stories.

"I was wondering if you wanted to hit the beach on the bikes?" he asked. "I think I finally have the 250 running decent. You up for it? We could pick up a few rouge containers."

When she first discovered Noah owned motorcycles, she was ecstatic. The dry riverbeds and sand hills near the greater LA area provided ample room for her to ride motorcycle growing up. Penny had even considered buying her own bike, but the few for sale in Utqiaġvik were pricey. On top of that, Army insisted she not ride alone. Safety in numbers and all that meant even more with the possibility of a murderer in the area, two-legged or four. Noah often took out a bike on his own (but he was from this area) to retrieve dart casings. This would be the first time he asked her to join him.

They followed a trail on the tundra to the beach several miles away. The wide tracks that replaced the bike's tires provided traction on almost any terrain. They raced the wide stretches when side-by-side riding was possible. Penny whooped into the wind when she pulled ahead.

The round rocks of the beach gave the modified bikes good traction. They passed an enormous piece of tundra that had eroded and broke from the mainland, forcing them to ride out into the water. The ocean splashed up against her jeans, but the bikes continued without so much as a splutter.

As they approached a small strip of beach where a creek emptied into the ocean, Noah slowed, and Penny followed suit. They slowed to cross the eroded beach and then throttled it once again. Penny's bike skidded slightly and as she corrected, she peered back and caught sight of a huge polar bear standing atop the bluff overhead. From the distance and the angle, she didn't see any black marks on his face and then wondered at the thought. No visions of a scarred bear bothered her that day.

Ten minutes later, Noah slowed, coming to a stop on a wide swath of beach. Penny stopped and removed her helmet, happy for the breeze that cooled her scalp.

"So, what did you think? The bike give you any trouble?"

"No, it rode great! Did you see the bear?"

He peered over his shoulder back down the beach.

"On top of the bluff where we crossed the stream?" she continued.

"No, I didn't see one, but I didn't look up either."

"I doubt it was my dream bear. The one that we tagged that day." The day she knocked Noah over. The words had escaped her mouth before she thought them through.

Noah got off his bike, rested it on the kickstand, and approached her. "What do you mean, your 'dream bear?'"

Penny leaned back, a nervous laugh escaping her. She waved a hand at him. "Oh. You know. Nightmares about

61

being attacked by a polar bear. Paranoia at seeing a polar bear during the day. It's just the job and the constant daylight wearing me down."

He crossed his arms, waiting. "You said 'dream bear' not 'nightmare bear.'"

"Please, don't laugh." She picked at a frayed string on her glove. "Okay, so I may have been having dreams about that same polar bear that I tackled you over." *Every day and night.* There was something raw about sharing such a secret with a stranger. Not a stranger, but not familial either. "I mean, before I tackled you."

He shoved his hands into his jean pockets and stared out across the Beaufort Sea. After a few minutes of tense silence for Penny, he spoke.

"So, the day you knocked me over, you dreamt about that?"

Penny rubbed her furrowed forehead as if she could suppress the memories. "Well, not exactly. There was this indescribable sensation, right before I pulled you - pulled you down, sorry again. I got dizzy and saw a scene play out of a bear attacking you."

"You got dizzy right before?"

"Yep. Usually. And a headache follows later."

Noah drug the toe of his boot through the rocky beach. "Have you ever experienced this before?" He stared out over the frigid waters, the hushed waves lapping at the pebbles.

"No. Well, yes and no, I guess. I mean, not of you being attacked before that day. I have had other dreams or nightmares the night before things have happened."

The visions that visited her before moving to Alaska almost always occurred while she slept. Those would play out the following day. Only since arriving in Utqiaġvik in May had the daytime visions started, but none so far had been as vibrant as the vision of Noah and the bear.

Noah continued to gaze over the sea. Penny studied his handsome profile. He appeared serious, perhaps in contemplation. When he at last returned his attention to her, there was a definite solemnness to his expression.

Does he think I'm crazy?

"So, you have visions?" Noah asked.

Now it was Penny's turn to shift her gaze from Noah's searching eyes. Only her mother and her sister knew the horrible truth Penny hid from the world.

"Yes. I don't get the full picture, just a part. I saw a bear attack you. The bear with three scars."

"During your visions, at any time has the bear harmed you?" he asked, his raised eyebrow echoing the question.

Penny considered it and shook her head. It was true, the bear scared her, but not because she had seen it come for her. Except in her vision it attacked Noah.

"And in your vision, did the bear harm me?"

Again she brought up the memory. There was the bear rearing up behind Noah, blood staining its front. Blood from the walrus it dined upon. It roared. But it had not attacked.

Her eye shot up, meeting his gaze. "No, he reared up behind you. You weren't harmed. And the blood on him, I guess that was from the walrus."

Lowering his eyes to the beach, Noah shuffled his feet, kicking at the small rocks. "Maybe he was saying hello?" he offered.

"Crazy, right—" She broke off with a strangled laugh, brushing at aberrant hairs that escaped her stocking cap to tickle her nose.

"Penny." He said her name with an intensity that made her insides simultaneously soften and clench. "Have you considered the possibility of a spirit animal? In my people, there are shaman, or angakkuq. People who are psychic." He leaned toward her, grasping the handlebars of her bike. "My grandmother was well known for being able to perceive future events. When she said something was going to happen, people took notice or suffered for it. Don't ever think I would laugh at such a thing. I can see that you are serious about it."

She closed her eyes, blocking his gaze. Was this possible? She communicated with her sister telepathically. She could do so with animals as well, albeit in a different manner. How would this be any more impossible?

A calming breath settled her, and she opened her eyes. She was hesitant to share more, but the look he gave her was reassuring. "I also have visions of a Shadowed Man. This figure. This man—he terrifies me. And there are echoes of screaming even though I don't see anyone else." The memories of the visions threatened to conquer her.

"Did you experience the visions of the Shadowed Man before you came here?"

She nodded. "I couldn't say for certain when they started, but it was not long after I agreed to move here."

"And we found two missing girls, one just before you arrived," he said, his voice so quiet, barely audible over the wind.

Noah rubbed a finger along the clutch handle and then slapped his other hand against his thigh as he straightened.

"Look," he said. "I don't think it is just anxiety or paranoia. I think it is better to let someone else in on it. Be a sounding board. I will not judge you; I promise."

"Oh, okay," she said, thinking that sharing her dreams with this beautiful man may not be the best idea, especially if she was losing her mind. But, what could it hurt?

"Maybe this scarred bear isn't there to hurt you. I mean, we can track him through the chip."

Penny nodded.

"So, let's check out where he is when we get back."

Penny reached into her inside jacket pocket and pulled out her phone. Why wait that long when she carried the means to check immediately? She brought up the app and quickly located the red dot and corresponding number that signified the scarred male bear. Noah moved to look over her shoulder. His breath warmed her cheek.

"Look at that. It was him," Noah confirmed. "We aren't far from where we tagged him, though, so we shouldn't jump to any conclusions just yet."

The statement did little to dispel the fear that blossomed. Noah stood up and put a hand on her shoulder.

"Guess I will need to start checking the app, too."

"So you plan to stalk this bear?" Penny received a nod in

reply.

"Wouldn't that make you a stalker in your own right? Of me, I mean? You would need to know where I was whenever you check on the bear..." She detected the slow half-smile appearing on his face. He raised an eyebrow and winked. Noah was utterly striking when he smiled. When he winked, well, he was gorgeous, beard and all.

"In a completely sincere way, yes, I will become your stalker. That's what friends do. Look out for one another, right?"

"Stalker. You are offering to be my stalker or the bear's?" She crossed her arms, holding tight to the fluttering of her insides even though he used the friend word.

"Yours, I guess." He scratched at the beard on his chin and neck.

"That is a bit creepy, you know that, yeah?" she teased.

"Best job I will ever have, stalking a beautiful creature." His eyes twinkled as his grin broadened.

She shifted her bike into neutral and stood, ready to start her bike, hoping she hid the flush that rose in response to his words.

"I'm curious. Do you have any other abilities?" he asked.

Please don't tell him about our connection, Lucy requested.

"Besides seeing awful visions?" Penny chewed on the inside of her cheek. "I guess I might have one or two." She strummed an imaginary guitar before kick starting the motorcycle.

Harried

True to his word, throughout July, Noah maintained an eye on the red dot that was the scarred polar bear. Having downloaded the app, he would send Penny messages checking on her and letting her know about the bear's whereabouts when he was working at Prudhoe. He didn't really need to, since Penny was also monitoring the bear, but she didn't dissuade him. Any nearness of the bear would be nothing more than coincidence as he was land bound until the sea began to freeze. Although the great white bears are not territorial, the mapped wanderings of the scarred bear showed him staying relatively close to the town.

Each message sent a jolt of excitement through her. She mentally chided herself over the elation. He was older than her. He held no interest in her beyond friendship. She had almost zero real-life experience with romance, but she was pretty sure no part of their relationship thus far resembled any trace of romance. She was feeling things her mind told her were improbable.

Well, if you won't hope, I will, her sister declared. *We both know you need some enjoyable daydreams.*

Upon his return in late July, Noah invited himself over to Penny's house late one afternoon to play guitar. He didn't want to hole up in the bunker any longer, it seemed, and wished for a bright, sunny living room in which to play. Having warmed up to the handsome young man, Edgar glided across the room to perch on Noah's shoulder while Noah began tuning his guitar.

They played a new song together; one Penny had been eager to try with a second guitar. After railing though multiple riffs, Noah called for a break. As he walked into the kitchen to grab a drink, Blue stretched out against Penny's feet, and she stroked him absently. She listened to Noah stop to allow Edgar to climb onto his perch before returning.

Noah handed her a glass of water, their fingers brushing in the exchange. It meant nothing, the electrical zings in her arm.

"That guy has some sharp claws," he said, rubbing his shoulder.

"Yeah, I know. I need to file them. They are like daggers." Penny drank half the glass before placing it back on the coffee table. She ran her fingers along the strings of her guitar, fingerpicking a song. As usual, their talk was minimal. Neither felt a need to fill the silence with words.

With fall's approach came preparations for Army's return to teach at the college in Anchorage. He made the decision to discontinue tagging at the end of July and planned to resume the following spring. The team had tagged more than the planned number of bears, and there was already several months of data on less than half of them. So, although the physical work was stalled until spring, Penny's computer work was about to hit full swing.

Bill and Rita would stay another few weeks before heading back to London for a short vacation with family. They then planned to travel to Australia as they had the past three years before proceeding further south still to Antarctica for penguin studies.

Eelyn took the offered opportunity to work full-time at the small animal clinic. Penny really didn't see it as much of a difference. She was there almost full-time anyway. That left Penny to tend to incoming data and maintain the research station over winter, which required daily visits at best. And help tend the dogs. And give guitar lessons, although two of the kids she was giving lessons to were moving out of town. Overall, Penny figured she would stay busy enough.

Noah told her during their last guitar session that his younger brother, Harry (short for Harrison), was coming up next week during the first part of August to visit before he started college later in the month. He was a year younger than Penny.

On the morning Harry was to arrive, Army and Eelyn had taken the Twin Otter out for a flight to survey a piece of land off to the southeast. After much urging on Penny's part, Lucy tagged along. Penny faced a solitary afternoon in which she promptly fell asleep while trying to read a research paper on DNA mapping.

The phone buzzed and woke her.

"Hey, busy today?" came Noah's voice.

She cleared her throat before speaking. But her voice still sounded like it was full of sleep. "Umm, no. Why?"

"Did I wake you?"

"No, no, it's fine." She sat up straighter, hoping that would help.

"My little brother is flying in, and I was wondering if you wanted to come with me to pick him up. If you aren't busy."

She wasn't. She should have been, but time with Noah would be better than trudging through DNA mapping sequences.

"Are you sure you want me to tag along? I'm sure you two have loads to catch up on," she said.

"We will have plenty of time to catch up. You should bring Blue. He can keep Winter company."

Penny smiled, that weird electricity shooting the length of her arms again. "In that case, we accept."

The foursome arrived early in the black truck and quietly waited to watch the plane land in the afternoon sunlight. Noah explained that his younger brother was studying to be a brewmaster, not a profession openly paraded in the dry town. While he spoke, his leg bounced out a wild tempo.

"Anxious to see your brother?" Penny asked.

His leg stilled.

"I am. We haven't spent much time together since I entered the army. He was a little boy the last time I saw him," he explained quietly.

Penny recalled a recent discussion. During a lull in playing, Vale had asked Penny about Noah, what she thought of him. Of course, Penny wasn't about to tell Noah's little cousin that she found him caring and funny and attractive. Definitely not the latter. So, she said little. Vale, on the other hand, said a lot, relaying most of Noah's upbringing. He and his older sister, Sanna, didn't share the same father with the youngest sibling, Harry. Sanna and Noah's father ran out on their mom, Raina, when Noah was two. His mother moved to Washington, the state not the capital, where she met David, Harry's father. They married, and Harry arrived when Noah was seven. Then Raina and David were killed in a car accident. A truck driver fell asleep and swerved into them on the highway. Sanna was in college in Anchorage at the time. Noah moved to Utqiaġvik to live with Army and finish high school. Harry stayed with David's parents, his blood grandparents, to finish school. Penny listened, sad for Noah and his family and happy for Vale's willingness to share.

"Harry. Short for Harrison?" she asked, hoping to cover the well of grief that opened within her as thoughts surfaced of the three siblings losing their parents. She couldn't imagine how it would feel to have lost both at once or grow up knowing her father didn't care enough to stay.

He chuckled oblivious to her discomfort. "Yeah. But after my ataataga, uh, grandfather. Not after the actor, although Harry seems to forget that I think."

"And your sister?"

"She is named after Sedna, the Inuit goddess of the sea."

"And you are named after the dude who built an ark?" She sniffed and gave a tentative half smile.

"Yup. Good old Genesis."

"Vale told me about your parents, Noah. I'm very sorry."

"Not your fault."

"No, but it still sucks. Have you, ah, ever met your biological father?" Penny asked tentatively unsure if he would want to talk about it.

"No," his answer was what she expected. What love could one feel for someone else who failed to put any effort into your well-being? "David was my father in all ways that mattered. Most people think we all look more like him, anyway."

He pulled a worn photo out of his wallet to show her. As he moved closer, she inhaled his scent, a tantalizing combination of shampoo and fresh mint gum. The familiar combination caused a skirmish in her belly, like a mess of butterflies were trying to break free. She hadn't realized how much she craved his scent, his warmth, his ease. She tried to focus on the photo he was showing her. The three siblings and their parents all smiled broadly at the photographer, dressed in matching sweaters. Noah smiled, but it didn't reach his eyes.

"So, what, he's twenty?" she asked.

"Twenty-one."

"Oh, so he's my age," she said, contemplating Noah's age. Twenty-eight. He wasn't that much older...

Older men are much dreamier, her sister thought.

You dated Liam, and he is our age, Penny responded through their bond.

That was when I was young and stupid.

Oh stop.

The dogs nosed their way into the front seat then, distracting them from any real conversation until the plane they waited for landed. Penny and Noah exited the truck, the dogs tumbling out behind them, and walked to the airport entrance to wait next to the concrete barriers outside the Wiley Post-Will Rogers Memorial Airport.

As they waited in the nippy afternoon, a cloak of darkness descended over Penny's vision, and she glimpsed the back-lit silhouette of a menacing figure. The menacing figure. She sucked in a sharp breath and stumbled backward against a concrete barrier. Her fingers found the skin at her temples, and she pushed hard to force the image from her mind.

A hand gripped her shoulder, giving her a little shake and returning her to the present.

"You look pale. Are you sick?" asked Noah, his brow furrowed and eyes tight.

Sick of the visions.

"Did you see something?" he asked so close to her ear that his breath warmed.

She licked her dry lips and whispered, "Yes."

Before more words were exchanged, a dark-haired young man wearing sunglasses and a fur-trimmed down jacket exited the terminal. The roller suitcase bouncing and clamoring on the uneven ground as he approached them. Noah stepped back from Penny with a worried face. The young man who resembled Noah stopped in front of them, crossing his arms. His face was as blank as a beach stone. Noah stiffened beside Penny. The young man in turn stared hard at Noah but was the first to break as a smile spread out across his face. They gripped each other in a welcoming embrace complete with back patting and growling. Penny backed up a step, unsure of how close she wanted to be. Harry broke free and turned to Penny.

"And you brought your new girlfriend! You dog, bro."

"This is Penelope Osborn." Noah slapped his brother on the shoulder.

Penny's heart stuttered when Noah said Penelope, the recent image briefly forgotten. Or perhaps it was because he didn't deny the girlfriend part. Shaking off those thoughts, Penny shook Harry's outstretched hand and smiled. He did look like Noah. Same dark hair, same nose, same chin. But he had brown eyes, and was shorter and thicker.

He held her hand longer than necessary, bringing it up to his lips.

With a slight kiss he said, "This is Penny? *The* Penny?" His firm grip prevented her from gracefully retrieving her hand, so she left it in his grasp.

Penny looked hesitantly at Noah and then back at Harry.

"I'm sorry. What do you mean?" she queried.

"What I mean is *the* Penny that everyone is talking about. Noah, Uncle, Auntie, Vale. Noah. Tiki, even. After all they said, words still could not convey what stands before me." He placed his free hand over his heart during his speech. As he gazed intently at her, she shifted uncomfortably. Fear, humiliation, uncertainty tried to crush her.

What does he mean? she thought to Lucy.

He bowed. "My family is besotted with you. And I can see

why. You are a beauty. Angels would gather to be in your presence."

She glanced at Noah who stood with a wide grin on his face. *Oh, joking. I get it. Well, whatever.*

"I'm sorry, Penny. I forgot to warn you that my brother can be a bit...much."

"You did mention you two are very different." She finally extricated her hand from Harry's, worried he'd try to kiss it again, and said, "Look, how about we head out. We are blocking traffic."

Blue barked as if in agreement.

Harry looked up with amusement plain on his face. The brothers sat together in the front so they could catch up, while she hid with the two furred creatures that she understood. More than once, Penny caught Noah casting her cautious glances in the rearview mirror.

Vale greeted them upon their arrival at the Volkov homestead. Penny stood awkwardly while the three chatted, wondering if it was polite to just melt away. The dogs stuck close by her side.

Once she decided it safe to wander off to her own house, Vale yelled to her.

"Oh, Penny! Wait a minute! Are you coming to my party tomorrow?" Vale asked.

Deciding honesty was the best policy, Penny divulged her fear of water to the young girl.

"You don't have to swim, Penny. Just hang in the shallow end and help Noah with the kids! Come on Penny, please? I only turn sixteen once!"

You only turn any number once. "I don't own a bathing suit."

Vale snorted. "We *do* have a store in town. If you can't find anything there, one of my taller friends could lend you something."

"Um, I'll see what I can find." She secretly vowed not to go if she suffered a nightmare, though Lucy thought she should just chill out and go no matter what.

"I'll see you guys. Nice meeting you, Harry," she said with

a wave to the boys.

Her phone dinged with an incoming message from Noah later that night.

Noah: You coming tomorrow? Please don't leave me to hang alone with the children, my brother included.

Penny: Don't worry. I will be there. Probably.

As it turned out, Eelyn possessed a bikini that fit Penny nicely. Eelyn had held onto it, hoping to someday fit back into it. There was so little fabric that it exposed the large wing tattoo on her back. Where they had once comforted her, she now felt threatened they would fly off without her.

Eelyn sighed. "You should be proud of that body, Pen. You look fit. Strong. Like a young panther. All sleek and defined."

"That is just so not appropriate for a mother to say. And what are you doing with your hands?"

Eelyn laughed and discontinued gesturing to Penny's body. "You can cover with a towel when out of the water and when in the water, well, you will be covered again, won't you. Please, don't be so self-conscious."

"No boobs." Penny stared dejectedly downward, contemplating her nearly flat chest.

"You have the right amount. Nothing is threatening to throw itself from your bikini top." Eelyn paused before asking Penny if any nightmares plagued her.

Penny sighed. "I will admit no, sadly. Just normal anxiety, I guess."

Eelyn grasped her daughter by the arms. "You'll be fine. I am proud of your courage to go to the pool, dear sweet girl. I'm proud you are not giving in to your fears."

"If I have a nightmare tonight, I won't go."

"But isn't it worth seeing your friend happy for her shining moment?"

"Mother, she is turning sixteen. Not getting married. And I'm not sure we are friends, not really. I give her part-time guitar lessons."

"Sixteen is a magic time. Big changes."

"I think she had her big change already, but I get your drift. And I will wear my rash guard and board shorts. The shirt will cover my wings."

"Baby, you need to spread your wings more often."

"You want me to expose myself? Is that what you are saying?" Penny held her hand over her heart feigning astonishment.

Eelyn playfully swatted Penny on the arm as she turned to leave.

Don't see why you won't come, she thought to Lucy.

Then you are apparently blind, sis. I am of failing health.

Oh, bull. You float as well as me.

But mom gave you her only suit, the *only suit in the house.*

Healthwise, Penny knew her sister could manage a visit to the pool, but she sensed Lucy was ashamed of her physical condition. Instead of pushing the issue, Penny let it drop.

I think you are beautiful, and it might be fun... her thoughts dissolved as she felt Lucy pushing her away.

She walked into their room to find Lucy curled up facing the wall on the top bunk blatantly ignoring her.

Penny crawled into her bottom bunk and thought, *Good night, Lu. I love you.*

Pooling

The night passed without terrifying dreams, and Penny awoke earlier than normal. As she readied herself for and the day, she found a near illegible note left by her mother that said she left early for an emergency.

That woman is one step away from being a cryptographer.

You know what mother says, her sister chimed with an imitation of their mother. *My brain pumps out thoughts faster than my hand can record them, hence my messy penmanship.*

Penny choked on her orange juice.

No vision of drowning. Looks like you're going to the party, sweet sister.

Sure you don't want to come, Penny chanced to ask one more time.

Absolutely.

Four of the dogs jumped on her during feeding time and another peed on her leg. Blue tripped her three times on their run, luckily resulting in her falling only once. Edgar spoke, finally, but told her off in a few rude words for turning off the TV. While she showered, Blue jumped onto her bed and sat on her outfit. Her hasty cleaning of his muddy feet resulted in several long streaks of brown across the front of her rash guard, which she had planned to wear over her swimsuit. By the time she found something different and changed for the early afternoon pool party, she was running late and not in the best mood. She remotely started the truck as she quickly checked her backpack, ensuring she had everything she needed for the birthday party.

In the meantime, Blue crumpled up the blue scatter rug on her floor. As she turned to walk out of the room, she tripped and fell, face-planting on the wood floor. Groaning, she rubbed at her stinging nose, tears welling up with the pain. She blinked back the sudden moisture and stared hard at the smooth crease that was wider than the adjacent ones between each plank in the floorboards. As her mind worked through the dulling pain, she realized that the ends of several boards lined up. She pushed herself up and back onto her heels, turning her head this way and that. She prodded at a square piece, no larger than two inches and one side yielded, its opposite end lifting above the surface.

She pulled the tip up and exposed a metal hook at which she pulled. The boards lifted at the seam, a hidden door revealing a narrow, dusty wood-framed chamber with a short ladder leading to a circular hatch below. The bedroom light only reached part of the cavity, so after grabbing a flashlight, curiosity lured Penny down with Lucy on her heels.

She wondered at how she had overlooked the hidden access in the floorboards, but then again, the rug covered most of her floor. She shook the rug out several times, but... well, housekeeping wasn't her strong suit.

The hatch opened by rotating a wheel. The dust was heavy and clung to her fingers. She brushed her hands together and descended the metal rung ladder into a silent, dark tunnel. Dust motes danced in the beam of her flashlight, and she moved it to examine her surroundings.

The passageway was cramped with a low-slung ceiling and narrow walkway. Next to the ladder was a switch and conduit that ran along the outside of the wall. She pushed the switch, and light flooded the passageway. Situated on either side of the hall were hobbit-like door hatches with metal wheels for door handles. As Penny walked forward, she realized with excitement that this underground area most likely connected with the underground beneath Army's house. She trotted down the passageway until she came upon the open area where they played guitar. She headed back to the entrance from her room, checking the doors. Those that opened either held unmarked containers or sleeping areas. One small room held a hammock, a bookcase filled with worn books, with Christmas lights strung across the ceiling.

Many were locked and retained their secrets.

As they returned to their room, Penny's sore nose and morning troubles forgotten, she contemplated her discovery and whether she should mention it to Army or Noah. It was obvious Army knew about it, being he owned the property on which both houses stood. But did Noah? Probably. The hammock room could be his. The thought left her excited and perplexed. Upon Penny's arrival, Army had informed her that the underground was hers to use any time. Was this why he made that comment? Did it truly matter, this find of hers?

Since he had to stay home with Lucy, who would not play with him, at least not while she was sleeping, Penny gave Blue an extra treat before she left for the party.

Army left a different truck for her to use since Eelyn used the black one. It was rather fortunate Army owned as many means of transport as he did; while a local vehicle was within their means, the Osborns saved money by not purchasing an insanely priced vehicle.

It started to flurry as she headed off to the party. With the wind whipping flakes about, it was hard to determine how much actually fell from the sky. Her face tingled from the vicious battering of frozen flecks.

Oh, no, she thought as she spied the flat tire on her departure from the house.

With her mother at work, and Army and Noah already at the party with their family, it was on her to change the flat.

She began gathering up the tools from under the back seat to jack up the truck and remove the tire. As she did, her thoughts churned over the raven. She pitied the coal black raven who remained quite stoic, his feathers ruffled.

Her father used to say that it was only through his own sheer willpower that their family hadn't been overrun by animals that people tried to beg off on Eelyn. On the occasions her mother couldn't say no, she had worked hard to find homes for every unwanted pet she brought home. Usually the Osborn's only had more than one pet at a time for a week or two. The longest they had ever fostered an animal was three weeks, and that was for a wallaby joey. The young joey needed to be carried around in a pouch, which Eelyn fashioned from a towel and hung around her neck. Penny once took it to school for part of the day without anyone the wiser.

Penny wondered briefly every now and again where the joey had ended up. Probably not in a wildlife refuge in Australia but hopefully somewhere similar.

Her thoughts drifted back to the raven's unfortunate owner, Ms. Kingston, as well as the first missing woman, Rena. Army had recently informed Penny that the autopsy for Rena came back with evidence that she had been drugged with a similar spinal injury to Kate. Both women were once assumed to have been victims of a polar bear attack. Although polar bear attacks on humans were rare, that they had been victims wasn't a far-fetched conclusion. With the exoneration of a polar bear attack as the cause of both deaths, murmurs abounded of a serial killer around the community. The dark, terrifying visions that Penny experienced convinced her of a stalker in their midst.

She struggled with the lug nut wrench on the flat tire with fingers that were quickly losing feeling. Cursing the weather, she had to run into the house to warm up before replacing the tire.

What's up? I thought you left for the party, her sister said while Penny held her hands in front of the heater.

Flat tire.

Did you call Mom or Army?

Penny rolled her eyes. *Uh, no. I'm a big girl now.*

She checked the temp as she headed back out. It was just above freezing. In August. Awesome.

She checked for the spare beneath the back of the truck bed. The cradle was empty. As was the bed of the truck.

Are you kidding me? she thought.

Gonna call Mom now, big girl? teased Lucy.

She spoke to Army instead. It was his truck. He probably stored a spare at his house.

"Just leave it be, Penny. I'll take care of it later. You removed the tire already, you said?" Army asked, his surprise obvious.

"Yes. So, I guess I won't make the party. Please tell Vale I'm sorry."

"Nonsense. Noah will pick you up."

A few seconds later Penny received a message from Noah.

Noah: Be there in a few. Dress warm, riding bike.

She grabbed her backpack, a scarf, and a pair of mittens, excitement building overriding the bike or seeing Noah, she wasn't entirely sure.

Wow. I never thought I'd see the day where my sister would freak out about a guy.

I'm not freaking out.

You are very much looking forward to seeing him.

Oh, shut it.

You look like a sexy snowwoman in your snowsuit, Lucy joshed. Penny wished she'd picked blue bibs instead of white. The ride would be short. She could forego the extra layer, so she left the bibs at home.

Noah was waiting next to his motorcycle. Penny raised a hand in greeting. The wind whipped at her as he handed her a neck wrap and a helmet. She caught bits of what he said over the noise of the engine and the wind. Something about a speaker in the helmet.

She removed her warm cap, pulling on the gear. The outside noise was replaced with rock music as she pulled on the helmet. *Cool,* she thought.

Penny stuffed her hat in her jacket pocket and waited for Noah to mount the bike. She got on behind him and wrapped her arms loosely around his waist. Her grip tightened as he rocketed out of the yard, the whine of the motor breaking through the song. She started humming to the chorus to calm the racing of her heart. It was an older rock song, one her dad loved to play on guitar. She sang the second verse.

"I didn't realize I would get serenaded on this ride," Noah's voice cut in after the song finished.

Even though she sang before while playing guitar with Noah, embarrassment warmed her face. "Oh, I didn't realize you could—I'm sorry. I didn't hear you say we could talk to each other with our helmets on. Why didn't you say anything right away?"

She felt him shrug, his shoulder moving against her helmet.

"I like the song. And your singing."

Her embarrassment morphed into delight.

"Thanks for the ride."

"Not a problem. Not every day I get to ride with a pretty face."

"Technically you do every time. Yours." *May I fall off right now and add to global warming. What am I saying?* She thought her sister giggled.

"Yeah, but mine gets boring. Any more visions?"

She shook her head before remembering he couldn't see her. "Not really." Unease ran down her back. "Not sure that makes me feel better."

Noah remained quiet during the remainder of the bumpy ride into town.

The warm, chlorine-rich air clung to her when she and Noah entered the indoor pool area at the high school. All thoughts of the hidden door dissolved in the loud and humid space.

Rose and Tiki, Vale's young mother and toddler sister, walked up to greet Penny as Noah moved off, most likely to change. Vale easily resembled her mother with their long, straight black hair, smooth, pale skin, and frequent, friendly smiles. Sam approached as they greeted each other, and Rose introduced him as her boyfriend.

"Oh, we know each other, sweetheart. Penny's often with her mother at the vet clinic where I work." Sam rested his arm across Rose's shoulders, and he winked at Penny.

"That's right. Army said your mom was called in early this morning. I sure hope my pager stays silent. I'm covering for someone else who has the flu." Rose looked a bit flustered as the toddler wiggled in her mother's arms but shot Penny a kind smile. Tiki was already wearing a swimsuit. "I better get this one something to do. Hope you have fun, Penny," Rose said as she excused herself and walked off with Sam.

Winking again, Sam said, "Later, Penny."

Working as an EMT seemed to be every bit as demanding as being a veterinarian. Every time Penny ran into her, Rose was usually on her way out for an emergency.

Sam, huh? Well, why not? Penny thought.

He seems a bit old for her, replied her sister critically.

Well, the 'younger guy' who was Vale's and Tiki's father didn't work out well, replied Penny. He split right after Tiki's birth. The Volkov family heard rumors that Rose's ex-boyfriend moved to Texas and overdosed on meth. No one had heard from him since Vale's birth. *So, in that case, younger was not better. Besides, Sam seems nice enough.*

Army's sister, Dolores, waved as she and Rita walked up. "Penny, I just wanted to thank you again for sharing that recipe! Those French toast cupcakes are a hit at the restaurant." Dolores ran The FrostBite restaurant downtown. "I just warm up the bottoms and drizzle on a bit of warm maple syrup. Anytime you stop by, whatever you want is on the house!"

A rush of warmth flooded through Penny. She dipped her head and grinned. "No worries, Dolores. Glad they are liked."

"Liked? Loved is more like it. Who could pass up a tiny cup of cake that tastes like breakfast heaven?" Rita said, going on and on about the blend of cream cheese, maple, and cinnamon with a hint of nutmeg, making Penny's smile broaden. If one listened to Rita, Penny's recipe included the first rays of morning sunshine and the comfort of a grandmother's kitchen.

Penny caught a glimpse of Noah from the corner of her eye. He wore teal-and-white-striped swim shorts. His broad, muscular chest on display distracted her. She offered a wave in greeting before turning her attention back to Rita. "I'm sorry. What did you say, Rita?"

"I was just mentioning how I finally convinced Bill to give his beard a trim. He was starting to look a bit wizardly instead of grizzly. I mean, how much food do you need to hide within the hair grown on your face. He looks so handsome, doesn't he?"

"Ah, yeah, Rita. Bill looks good," Penny said.

"So, do you like hairy faced men, or do you prefer faces smooth and hair-free?" Rita posed the question with a wry smile. Dolores even grinned at Penny, looking a bit like the Cheshire cat.

Looking up at the ceiling did nothing for Penny's response. She felt a twinge of pain as an image of her father shaving before a shift at the ER zinged into focus. He never grew more than a medium stubble. "Oh, I don't know. Guess I don't have a preference, really." Her face reddened as Noah and Army approached, sure that her thoughts played out for their viewing.

"Oh, I love a good growth of stubble on a man. Rugged handsomeness and all that," Rita said, wiggling her eyebrows at Army.

"What's this?" he asked as he rubbed his whiskers.

"Just chatting about facial hair, whether we girls fancy such things or not," Rita replied.

Sporting a pair of wild floral swim trunks and work boots, Army's appearance offered an opportunity to take the conversation in a different direction.

"Army, those boots look like they might take on water," said Penny.

"No worries, Penny. The trunks are more for show." He smiled warmly at her. "Great to see you here, by the way. Vale will be thrilled to see her rocking guitar teacher here."

"Hey, what am I then?" interrupted Noah, trying to look offended since he was her first guitar teacher.

"You're her cousin. Totally not very hip, you know. Or something," offered Rita.

Penny smiled.

"Penny, Penny, Penny! Looking awesome!" Harry said as he slid up next to her. He threw his arm around her shoulders as he continued. "I would have come to get you, if I had a vehicle. My brother has all the fun." Penny's eyes flicked toward Noah who winked at her. "You know, this is a pool party. You will need a swimsuit to get in. They don't allow shirts and shorts."

"Uh, yeah, I'm wearing a suit underneath." Penny clenched the bottom of her shirt.

"Great, can't wait to see it," he whispered in her ear.

She shrugged out of his embrace as politely as possible and stepped away.

Over by the tables, Tiki started throwing a tantrum. Her mother, Rose, looked harassed. As Penny watched, Tiki threw her bottle on the ground. When Sam picked it up and handed it to her, she screamed loudly and batted her hands at him. Rose lifted her up and walked her away from the group sitting at the table.

Army struck up a conversation with Harry, allowing Penny to make an escape. She walked the length of the pool to a chair on the far side where she could leave her towel and bag. Here, she was on the opposite side of everyone else in the shallow end. She sat down and drew her long hair up back into a fishtail braid. Then, wrapping her arms around herself, she regarded the water filled with splashing children feeling more than a little out of place. The family talked and joked with each other, and she very much wanted to go home.

A few moments later, Noah sat down next to her on the lounge chair and bumped her with his elbow.

"Penny for your thoughts?" His friendly smile had a warming effect on her mood. He sat close enough the heat rolling off his body radiated between them. Black tribal tattoos covered his usually covered arms. They traveled up his right arm all the way to his shoulder and ended at the elbow on his left.

"My thoughts are certainly worth more than mere pennies. And you would be disappointed to find that they focus on water, drowning, and such."

"Such dark thoughts on a bright fun-planned day. No premonitions?"

She shook her head.

"Not a swimmer?"

She shook her head again with a dry smile.

"Is that why you look so uncomfortable?" Noah possessed

the gentleness of a concerned friend.

She sighed with the next shake of her head. "I had to borrow a suit from my mother."

Noah laughed a bit. "I will never borrow any of Army's trunks. Ever. Flowers are not my thing." His swim trunks accentuated his lean, ribbed abdomen. "Due to my considerable charm and ability to lift heavy objects, I am charged with staying in the shallow area to care for the little kids. Would you care to assist me in this daring endeavor? Never fear, I would never let you drown."

"I would be more than happy to help, as best I can. But you shouldn't use the absolute word 'never.' You won't always be close enough to rescue me."

"Ah, but didn't you just use the absolute 'always,' therefore nullifying your request to discontinue my use of 'never'?"

Penny smiled as she shook her head with downcast eyes. "Whatever. I just am not looking forward to being in the water."

Harry approached them, saying, "Come on guys. It's a pool party. Time to get wet!"

Penny muttered to Noah under her breath, "He has no idea how stupid he sounds, does he?"

"No. That's what makes him so much fun. He has an incredibly high IQ, but he adamantly refuses to let people know. Goes very far out of his way, I think." Noah grinned as he stood and walked off. Unsuccessful in her attempt to not watch him go, she glanced at his bare back multiple times.

He reached Aunt Dolores and took a quieted Tiki from her grasp. As the two approached the side of the pool, Tiki fretted. Penny took the moment of distraction to remove her rash guard and board shorts. As she approached, Noah and Tiki remained sitting on the side. As Tiki held tight to Noah's neck, Penny sat down on Tiki's side, the cold, hard cement biting at her bottom and the tepid water inciting goose bumps. She asked Tiki what the matter was.

Tiki lifted her head from Noah's shoulder and peered at Penny, her eyes rimmed with tears.

"No, Pen. No get in."

Penny held her hands out for Tiki, and the little girl practically leapt from Noah to Penny's embrace. Grabbing on tightly around Penny's neck, Tiki continued to sob. Penny shushed the girl as Noah entered the water. Without loosening her grip with one arm, Tiki started sucking on her thumb.

Penny said in a reasonable voice, "You know, Tiki. Penny is very afraid of the water, too. But you know what? The water is warm, like a bath..." *one you are ready to get out of* "...and there are a lot of other kids who really want you to come in to play with them. I will make a deal with you. If you get in, I will get in, too, okay?"

Tiki minutely let loose her death grip on Penny's neck. Looking into her eyes, she said sadly, "Pen's scared, too?"

"Mm-hmm." Penny brushed the child's hair away from her face, wiping away her tears in the process.

"And if you will try to get in with Uncle Noah, I will too. How does that sound?"

The little girl released her grip around Penny's neck. She placed a little hand on either side of Penny's face and whispered, "Okay, Pen. Okay."

Tiki turned around and held her hands out to Noah, her bottom lip sticking out. Noah lifted the girl up high, swinging her down gently next to him and into the pool. With his encouragement, she started splashing with him as they moved away. Penny took a deep breath and slowly lowered herself in the water.

Crap, this is not warm, she thought.

Take a deep breath. Release it. Continue. You will be fine. Don't even need to get your hair wet, Lucy responded.

Just then, a chubby boy cannonballed into the pool beside them, soaking Penny, Noah and Tiki in the process. Tiki laughed. Penny forced herself to relax.

If she can do it, so can I. For a little bit, anyway.

Penny soon found herself enjoying the time in the pool. Vale bobbed up to her in the water and gave her an enthusiastic hug while Tiki giggled. Vale then swam off to hang out with her friends in the deeper water.

Little kids swarmed, hung off her, and asked her to catch them as they jumped into the pool. Several even asked to touch her back. She acquiesced, and their curious fingers stroked the feathers of the large wing tattoo. One asked her if she was an angel.

Just then, Rose called to everyone that it was time for cake and ice cream. Noah collected Tiki and set her poolside. As soon as her pudgy little feet hit the concrete, she ran to her mother, her pool diaper hanging precariously low. Noah winked at Penny and drew himself up out of the pool, water splashing down around him. Penny tried not to stare outright but was rewarded with another good backside look as he walked over to his brother.

Penny moved through the water and exited closer to her pool chair where she retrieved her towel and wrapped it around herself.

Vertigo hit her as she straightened up, so she quickly sat on the chair and rubbed her temples. Behind her closed eyes, an image of a shadowy figure appeared backlit by a bright light. And there was a polar bear, blood dripping from its open mouth. Three black scars marred its left cheek. She sucked in an unsteady breath.

It took several long moments for the vision to fade and for Penny to find her calm center once again. She pulled on a pair of board shorts and a sweatshirt, even though it was rather stifling. As she turned around to stuff her things into her bag, she caught a glimpse of Harry, Noah and Sam looking in her direction. Noah smiled, while Harry and Sam stared. She looked quickly away and rewrapped her towel protectively around her waist for added coverage and grabbed her bag before she walked over to the cake line.

"Now why did you go and mark yourself up like that," drawled Sam who stood beside her. "Your skin's beauty is smothered beneath such dark ink."

She glanced sideways at him. "I suppose the same reason anyone else does. They mean something to me."

"I don't understand it, I guess. You cause yourself pain.

For a pretty picture that will fade and distort with time."

"Isn't that life, though? All beauty fades and distorts with time. But the beauty remains."

"In life? There is much beauty but also a great deal of ugliness."

"So, more beauty and kindness are important, don't you think?" she asked, curious as to the depth of the conversation.

Since she entered the line and spoke with Sam, several small children gathered around her cooing at the watercolor dragon tattoo gracefully wrapped around the inside of her left ankle.

Well, my tattoos are a hit with the kiddies, she thought. Looking about she saw that plenty of tattoos were on display, so a novelty she was not.

"Just saying, you are a pretty girl, Penny. No need to adorn your body with such garish displays."

"I'm smart, too," she grumbled as he strode off. She reached down for a piece of cake hoping the chocolate cake with vanilla ice cream and caramel sauce would overpower her irritation.

"Hey, you okay?" Noah said quietly.

"Umhmm, yeah." She glanced at him briefly, surprised at the concern on his face.

"It looked like you were dizzy back there," he said.

"It was nothing. Nothing new, anyway. Really."

He nodded and walked with her to two open seats next to Rita. The children, jacked up on sugar, began to chase each other around the eating area. Rita's genuine delight at the commotion was infectious and before long Penny's tension eased. She listened without comment to Rita and Noah's exchange on the environmental impact of drilling for oil in the arctic waters. Noah was adamant that his position in security didn't encourage the drilling but ensured the security of the rigs and personnel.

"Yes, yes. But by working there you are in a sense supporting the drilling."

Noah held his hands up in surrender. "Agree to disagree, Rita. If it wasn't me, it would be someone else."

"Fine. Then when are you going to shave the beard, Noah, and show everyone that handsome face? Might be why you are single." Rita said.

Noah cocked an eyebrow and glanced between Rita and Penny. "I don't know, winter's coming."

"Oh, don't use the weather as an excuse. It's always cold up here," she said, scrunching up her little upturned nose.

Vale and her friends entered the pool, and Penny excused herself, anxious to return home for the day. While Vale's excitement over Penny's presence was genuine, her interest in hanging out with her friends prevented her from visiting with her family. Exhaustion clung to Penny, and when Vale pleaded for her to join them later at Army's to play guitar, Penny declined.

She retreated to the locker rooms to change. Rose was washing a bottle at the sink and barely glanced up, her petite frame hunched and her long, dark hair cascading forward into the sink.

"Hi Rose, how are you?" Penny asked.

Rose leaned on her hands against the sink ledge, her head bowed. When she at last met Penny's gaze in the mirror, Rose's eyes were red, and streaks of mascara ran down her cheeks.

"I don't know what to do. Tiki absolutely will not behave with Sam around. I really like him, Penny. But he can't even spend time with me and the girls without some major tantrum action." She wiped at her cheeks and gave a deep sigh.

This was unknown territory for Penny. She barely knew Rose and had little experience with romantic relationships. Aunt Bianca, with her extensive experience with boyfriends and marriages, would have been the more appropriate counselor. Or maybe not.

"Ah, what's meant to be, will be?" she said, her words hesitant. She was still irritated at Sam's comments, but withheld any judgement. People would have their own opinions, after all.

Rose laughed wryly. "Yeah, I guess."

"Just give it time," Penny suggested.

"Yeah. I've been working a lot of overtime at the hospital. Being on call is no fun. And helping Dolores at the restaurant on my days off. I think I am just tired." She said with a yawn. "Yep, definitely tired."

"I'm sorry. Need any help? I could babysit for you some nights. Give you a break?"

"Ah, thanks, Penny. You are too kind. I didn't mean to coerce you into helping me," Rose said, yawning again.

"No, I mean it. Most likely Noah would help, too."

"You two are fairly inseparable these days."

Before Rose could go further, Penny held up her hands. "We are just friends, Rose. Trust me."

Rose peered at her as if looking for the answer to an unasked question. "Shall I put in a word for you? Mention something to Noah?"

"Absolutely not. Please. In fact, do something like that, and I will rescind my offer to babysit."

The comment brought a warm smile to Rose's face, erasing many of the tired lines and making her seem her youthful self.

"Okay, okay. Settle down. I won't say anything." Rose's smile waned as a piercing beep echoed in the locker room.

Rose sighed. While she checked her cell phone, Penny dressed quickly listening to the short, one-sided conversation. Rose was an emergency medical technician for the local hospital and a primary helivac crewmember. She indicated she would respond immediately.

Penny exited the locker room shortly after Rose and found her deep in discussion with Army, who also received a call. Noah approached with Harry and Sam along with another distant relative of Army's, whose name eluded Penny. The small group gathered in close.

"Hey, what's going on, Army?" asked Noah as he moved in to stand shoulder-to-shoulder with Penny. Army seemed to have aged ten years in the few minutes since Penny entered the locker room.

"The sheriff called. They found another woman's body." Several sharp intakes of breath followed from those gathered nearby listening.

"Is she alive?" asked Sam.

"No," said Army heavily. "They found evidence that there was a bear. Possibly dogs or wolves. Her body is in bad shape."

Sam looked angry while the others stood in shocked silence, digesting the news of a third death within a few months' time.

"Sam, I have to go. I'm sorry, I know, I know. EMTs aren't needed for the deceased, but the sheriff asked me to oversee the transition to the coroner at the hospital. I'll get mom to watch the kids," said Rose before she walked off toward Dolores.

"I'm going to head out with Rose," Army said, then nodded to Noah and added, "Noah, why don't you take Penny home when she is ready. Harry, you take your aunt and cousins back to the house. I don't know how long this will take. We might need to hold off on the evening celebrations until tomorrow."

"You think this girl is linked with the other two?" Noah asked the question that surely everyone in hearing distance was thinking.

Army sighed heavily. "I don't know for sure. I hope not. I hope there isn't a serial killer."

On the quiet ride back home with Noah, Penny thought back to her episode earlier. Had it really been related?

Penny, you okay?

Shocked, I guess. It is alarming to consider, more devastating if there is a link. What can we do?

Do? Be safe, obviously. Stay vigilant. Don't go out alone.

Alone? Lu, Army will be gone soon for teaching, Noah is going back to Prudhoe. It will be us and mother. How can I check the research station without being alone?

Take Winter and Blue, I guess. They will protect you, right?

"Well, aside from that ending bit, did you enjoy today?" Noah broke the silence of their drive back home.

"I guess so." She smiled. "Did you?"

"Yes, I love being the shark in the water. Was my favorite game as a kid."

Penny imagined him as a child. Dark curly hair, pudgy cheeks like his little cousin, Tiki.

"Did you see something earlier? When you said you were dizzy?"

Her nod came slowly. "The shadowed figure," Penny relented. "And the scarred bear. I have no idea if the two are related, or if I'm going crazy." Not wanting to linger on that thought, she added, "Do you know where they found the body?" That knowledge would allow her to cross check the area bears, see if the scarred bear was somehow involved.

"I'll find out. I don't think we should narrow to just him, though. Can we check on all movement around a specific area?"

Penny nodded. She could check on any of the chipped and collared bears' movements. But if the body was discovered by a pure bear, as they called the ones without a tracking device, then the information would be useless.

"Wish we could chip the humans. That would help us more if someone killed her."

"Yeah, that won't ever happen. Not in our lifetimes," Noah said. "Would you want the government tracking your every movement?"

That thought sobered her, and she shook her head.

"Penny, what do you think about meditation or some other way to bring on or focus the visions?"

Getting them was bad enough; she didn't consider forcing more into her mind to be a better situation.

"I mean, it might not work. But if it did, any additional information could help. What do you think?"

She answered slowly, working through the potential benefit. If it worked. "I can try. I wouldn't know where to start, though."

"Army'll guide you through the meditation. He is a guru or something," he said.

If she were honest, she did mind a smidgeon. "Would you mind not sharing my visions with him?" At his inhale, she interjected, "At least for right now." *Don't need him thinking I'm weirder than he already does.*

Noah agreed.

Folk Style

She researched meditation after Noah left and decided she would try some techniques before bed. Her sister allowed her mental space, retreating to the top bunk once again. Penny sat cross legged on her lower bunk, and as she attempted to clear her mind of all thought, her attention was overcome with aberrant thoughts and worries. She eventually fell asleep, but it was not a peaceful sleep. Nightmarish images of a mutilated body startled her awake multiple times.

The following morning, giving up on sleep, Penny attempted her own type of meditation with a run at the school gym. As she was finishing, Harry and Noah walked in, surprising her. Then again, per Noah's request, she had sent him a message alerting him to her whereabouts. Alone. She sighed at the thought of having one more person knowing where she was and what she was always doing.

Oh please, it's for your own safety, her sister grumped.

That I know, that I know...

Penny gave a brief wave as she cleaned up her treadmill and grabbed her water bottle.

"How far did you run?" Noah found her distances interesting.

"Umm, five," she said.

"Just five, are you kidding me? How far do you normally run?" Harry asked.

Penny shrugged.

"Well, you must run a lot to keep so fit." His sticky sweet words irritated her, and she longed to leave them.

As Penny tightened her ponytail, Harry perked up.

"Is that another tattoo?" His eyes focused in on her right inner elbow.

93

"Obviously," Penny bristled.

Sheesh, calm down, sis, her sister's thoughts interjected.

Penny didn't understand the anger but stomped it down. She was tired after all.

"Can I see it?" he asked, breaking her from her sour thoughts.

She groaned inwardly but held out her arm close enough for Harry to see and yet far enough away to pull back if he tried to touch her. He did not. He peered at the outline of a polar bear walking amidst a color washed aurora in the starry night sky.

"How many do you have?" he asked. Her grey sweats and sweaty black tee covered the others.

"Hey man, leave her be," Noah said, coming to her rescue.

With a grateful smile to Noah, she told them. "That's okay. I believe I displayed the others yesterday. There's the dragon on my ankle I got when I was sixteen. The wings—I got those after my father died. This polar bear...right before I moved here. So. Just the three."

She threw her towel over her shoulder and was ready to bid them good morning when Harry asked if she wanted to stay and watch them wrestle. Something in her snapped.

With a Cheshire cat grin and a sugar-rich voice, "Oh, like you really want me to watch you two big guys wrestle. That sounds like...so...much...fun!"

Noah appeared taken aback by her sudden change in attitude. Harry seemed surprised, as well as encouraged.

"And if you find yourself so inclined, maybe you could wrestle me afterwards." Harry's trademark smirk was in full force as he stepped toward Penny.

"Oh, I don't know about that. You might hurt me," she said, her sugary tone lowered as she took a step back.

"Nah, I would never hurt you. We could even make it interesting by adding some stakes. Winner gets granted one request by the loser."

"Well, I am already warmed up, shall we go now?" She smiled as sweetly as she could.

Harry was all but salivating. "I'll go change."

As he ran off to the locker room, Noah asked, "You know, he is a very good wrestler. You sure you want to do this?" His gaze was full of concern.

"Ahh, it will be fun. I doubt he will try to hurt me. And I can handle myself, Noah."

"He's harmless with his words, but with wrestling…that is a different story. He's ruthless. No taekwondo moves."

"I know I can't kick and punch him. What makes you think I am not ruthless as well?" At his raised eyebrows, she said, "Sorry, my runner's high is more of an aggressive grouch."

A small smile appeared on his face. "Be honest, do you know how to wrestle? It's not like taekwondo."

"Yes." She returned a small smile of her own.

"Yes, you have, or yes, you know?" His smile widened.

There was a pause that drug out into a bit longer silence.

"Not really into sharing information about yourself, are you?" Noah ran a hand through his black curls.

"Isn't that like the pot calling the kettle black? Mr. Tightlips." She rested her weight on one leg, hand on her hip.

"Alright, Miss Sassypants. Keep your secrets." He chuckled as he shook his head.

Harry burst out of the locker at a jog, interrupting her doubts on challenging Noah's younger brother.

Noah agreed to referee, reminding them both that it was a friendly match. Penny asked about the rules, to which Noah explained that there would be three two-minute bouts. A win occurs when one wrestler causes a fall or pin, ends with the most points, or scores fifteen points more than the other wrestler.

"Okay, folk-style," Penny said, rolling her shoulders and loosening up her neck. "I'm sure it will be over quick." She batted her eyes at Harry, flashing what she hoped was innocence.

Noah dropped his hand and whistled. Penny briefly wondered where Noah got the whistle before she made her first move. Then, reaching out with her left hand, she grabbed Harry's left wrist and threw a flying headlock. She threw him on his back, pinning him in less than eight seconds.

As he lay under her hold struggling, she whispered, "As winner, my request is that you treat me with respect. As a friend. Not as an object. You may be pretty, but you are not my type." With that she let him go. He lay there on the mat, looking slightly confused.

"Did you see how fast she moved? I think we got hustled."

"No, little brother. *You* got hustled. You should know better than to underestimate your opponent. Especially in her family." He turned to Penny. "Confess."

"I did participate in a wrestling club in middle school. And it was only for a year. For complete disclosure, I hold a second-degree black belt in taekwondo. This past year I advanced to level nine of Krav Maga and just started learning grappling techniques. And I ran cross country in high school. As for this match, I planned to take you off your guard and move faster than expected."

"And Harry here was two-time state champion, so I guess you two both failed to air out your levels prior to the match."

"So, Noah teaches self-defense at the school during the school year, did you know that? And that he also dabbles in Krav Maga?" Harry asked, seeming to want to enter their conversation in a more mature way.

Penny's eyes lit up. "You do? Do you instruct here?"

"Not officially. I teach self-defense and oversee fitness programs here in the afternoons during the school year, like Harry said. I also assist coaching wrestling."

"You coach wrestling?" Now who was withholding information? "Seriously." Penny met his gaze. "How does that work? With your security job at the rigs?"

"I usually take a lengthy vacation to cover for Army when he is gone teaching. To take care of the dogs and such."

"I've been taking care of the dogs, though," she spit out without thinking.

Nice, sis.

Shut it.

"Sorry, already planned. You'll have to put up with me full-time."

"Well, would you consider sparring and working on Krav Maga techniques with me during the classes? I mean, the better I am at defending myself, the less likely I would ever be a target." She looked meaningfully at Harry, who smiled.

"If you are level nine, I would recommend you help me coach wrestling, so you can work on those skills. During self-defense classes, I would be more than happy to work on advanced techniques, so long as you would agree to help me teach the less advanced."

Penny thought on this. "So, you are asking me to fight for my right to fight?" They both smiled. "Sounds like a deal to me."

Harry chimed in. "Great! Now that the deals are made, how about the winner treats the loser and his brother to a nice hearty breakfast?"

"Don't you need to work out? Or work on your headlock deflection?" Noah was laughing as he threw a play headlock on his younger brother, rubbing his hair with his free hand.

"Hey, back off. I didn't see you jump to challenge her." Harry sulked.

"I suspect I will get the opportunity. Loser pays for breakfast."

"I need to run out to the station and pack up some equipment for Army first," Penny said.

"If you hold off, I will come with you to help," Noah offered.

I don't need a babysitter. "That's alright, I'll take Blue."

"Yeah, I'll come, too. We can stop by The FrostBite and grab breakfast from Dolores on the way," Harry said, making every attempt to stay in the conversation.

"Oh, okay." *Guess I don't have a choice.*

The boys dropped her off at home after their trip to the research station, insisting they carry all the boxes of equipment to Army's house. Blue bounded up to her mother, who was relaxing in the living room area. Penny stopped to give Edgar a scratch on her way to the living area. Edgar lifted a leg, indicating he wanted her to hold him. She placed him on her shoulder and sat down on the couch.

"Hey, bud, what have you and Penny been up to?" Eelyn asked as Blue jumped into her lap and licked her face. "Wow, I missed you, too!"

"Went to the stations. Are you off the rest of the day?" Penny asked.

Eelyn pushed the energetic dog off her lap and slowly stood up from the worn brown recliner. She wiped her face and shook her head. "Nothing scheduled for this afternoon, so I thought I would hang out here. But I fell asleep." She yawned and stretched her arms overhead, her back popping as she twisted and bent. Dark circles stood out beneath her mother's brown eyes, and her normal smile was absent.

She looks so tired, Penny thought.

"A nap, huh?" Penny's own body felt weary and not from carrying heavy boxes. "I could use one, too, I guess."

"This whole dead girl...thing..." her mother's voice trailed off.

"Does Army really believe there could be a serial killer?" Penny dropped her bag in her room quietly to not wake her sleeping sister.

"He seems convinced."

The small hunting cabins where the women were found had been decimated. A bear, or bears, made certain that evidence discovery was unsuccessful.

"Well, a birthday party for Noah should help, hey?" Eelyn said attempting to lighten the mood.

Yeah, cause the last birthday party didn't result in everyone scattering after a dead girl was discovered.

So negative, Lu. I thought you were sleeping, too?

Only stating the obvious. And I heard you come in. Rather, I heard the dog.

"He isn't too excited about having a party," Penny said.

Noah had grumbled about being too old not that long ago, which brought on a snarling response from Army. "Too old? Wait until you are my age. Then birthdays will be a celebration that you made it to such an old age." He then smacked Noah on the top of the head. "Be respectful. If your family or friends want to celebrate your birth, then go with

98

it."

Two days later, as Penny got ready to head to the Volkov residence next door for said party, Eelyn wondered aloud about them being invited to family functions.

"I think Army feels like he is our foster host or something. Wants to make sure we feel comfortable here, have things to do. You know, so we don't sit inside our house and shrivel up from no use." Penny said. "Or maybe Army likes you."

Eelyn looked aghast. "He is at least twenty-five years older than me!" She shook her head. "I am still in love with your father. No, if there are any seedlings of love, my dear, it would between you and—"

Penny held up an open palm, cutting her off. Lucy snickered. She decided to tag along for which Penny was grateful.

"No, no, no, nonono. You will not mess up my head with your maniacal mumblings. It's hard enough with my own. I get it, you and Army are friends. Just like Noah and me."

Eelyn snorted. "Yeah, okay."

Am I missing something here? Penny wondered.

You two do seem kinda chummy, more so than you and Liam. And you weren't so defensive about Liam when someone teased you about him, Lucy responded.

"I am just teasing. I realize you and Noah are friends. He wouldn't be a bad catch though. Very polite, helpful, hardworking, empathetic," Eelyn said.

Penny rolled her eyes. "Empathetic."

"Strong relationships are good, and the Volkov family has treated us with nothing but open arms. I just hope they invite us because they genuinely like us, not out of charity," Eelyn said. "You know, one day I was bumming. This job…this climate." Eelyn cleared her throat. "I'm probably bummed more days than not. But this one day, Dolores found out I was alone. I think you were out messing with Noah—oh quit with your eyerolling. I mean, *running* with Noah and the dogs. Dolores asked me to go out to lunch, but I declined. She showed up on our doorstep. Brought me soup and a flowering plant." Eelyn paused and glanced away.

Oh, that's where the violas came from.

"That is something family or very good friends would do. It's just nice is all I'm saying." She smiled and they, including Blue, headed outside across the yard to the neighboring house.

It was a small gathering: Dolores, Harry, Army, Noah, Vale, Penny, Lucy and Eelyn. Plus, Winter and Blue. Vale, Tiki, and their mom dropped by earlier in the day and left gifts, which were already opened and sitting on the table. Rose had not been up to celebrating after attending the call the night before, but Vale was at least able to celebrate her birthday with her family as planned.

Penny placed her card, including a gift card for fuel, on the table. She always offered to fill up the bikes when they took them out, and Noah always refused. So, she thought that a gift card for fuel might be an okay present.

There was cake and ice cream. Rita brought Penny's new favorite, caramel apple pie with a top crust that looked like a dahlia. Penny also brought along French toast cupcakes.

They played board and card games, talked about the Christmas holiday, and made plans to see Harry again. Sanna called to wish Noah a happy birthday and to tell him that she already booked her flight for Christmas vacation.

A small cloud hung over the party. The apprehension over the recent dead woman, Pam Iverson, finally worked its way into the conversation.

"No, there hasn't been any further word from the police. There seems to be a lot of accusations. Pam's brother returned yesterday and wants to blame Pam's boyfriend, Doug, because he had been previously abusive. Doug has a solid alibi, though. He was with his other girlfriend, which doesn't exactly paint the best picture."

"You don't see any connection between the three women, do you?" Eelyn asked Army.

He shrugged and shook his head ruefully. "Aside from how they were found, not yet. But I have suspicions. The forensic specialist in Juneau should complete the autopsy soon. Maybe it will confirm the possibility of a serial killer or maybe not. I'm guessing any findings suggestive of murder will lead to more civil unrest and finger pointing. I would say to keep this information to yourselves. No need to encourage gossip."

Mosquitoes and Dogs and Bears (Oh My!)

The day before Harry left was predicted to be gorgeous and unusually warm with a high of seventy degrees and a light southern wind. Army gave Penny the day off so that he could spend time with his nephews, beginning with an early morning flight to watch the 5:18 a.m. sunrise. By mid-morning temperatures were in the sixties, which felt downright hot to Penny. She realized that it would also mean an increase in the insect population, but a truck went by last night spraying what she hoped was insecticide.

After pulling her hair back into a ponytail, she donned a pair of shorts and a tee and headed outdoors with Blue for a walk. His growing frame, already knee-high to Penny, led the way but not so far as to tighten the leash. The bug population that blossomed overnight whirred around them as they crossed the lawn between the two houses on the property. Army's truck and SUV sat parked in front of his house, and she wondered how the morning flight went. If she were honest with herself, she was a bit put out she hadn't been invited.

Suddenly Blue stopped. His hackles rose, and he growled. Penny walked up beside him, wondering at his behavior. Nothing out of the ordinary appeared between the dog shed and the back of Army's house. Blue faced straight ahead, between the two.

Penny's mouth went dry, and her eyes narrowed as the reason lumbered around Army's house. Before them paced a large, very dirty polar bear. It stopped when it saw them, nose lifting in the air. Hyper-focused and momentarily paralyzed, her grip loosened on Blue's leash. Her heartbeat pounded loudly in her ears. No premonitions had warned her of the beast before them.

She willed herself to action and took her phone out of her pocket. Her ear bud was in place. As she began recording the situation, she simultaneously video dialed Noah. He answered, but if he was surprised to see the bear instead of Penny, she knew not.

"Are you back?" she whispered. Glancing down, she saw his questioning face.

"Yeah, we are at the house. Where are you?" he asked.

"Out between your house and the dog kennels. Please come out and help me," she said.

Blue lunged forward, jerking his leash out of Penny's hand. He rushed up to the bear, and the bear sat down on its haunches. Blue stopped before it and yowled a greeting. The bear's arms rested on its hind legs at first, and then it raised one giant paw up as if in a wave and cocked its head to the side.

As Noah strode through the back door with Winter at his side, the bear leaned forward and came nose to nose with Blue. Blue licked it on the nose and jumped at the bear's muzzle, persistently licking its lower jaw. The bear's front legs encircled Blue as it fell to its back. Penny jumped as Noah appeared at her side.

"They are playing." His quiet voice reached her ears.

As if hearing Noah, Blue extricated himself from the bear and raced back to the three of them. He approached Winter and barked, lowering his front half to the ground. Then he raced back to the bear that had risen on all fours. Blue playfully attacked the bear's throat, and the bear opened his great maw and pushed Blue around with it. Winter suddenly leapt away and tore up the ground between them, launching his body at the very much larger bear...and joined in the frivolities. Penny chanced a glance at Noah, finding the expression on his face to be as amazing as the scene before them. Harry then appeared at the back door.

"No freakin' way!" they heard him say. Then he disappeared back inside the house.

Noah glanced at Penny. "We need to get to the house right

now. Quickly, but walk," he said.

"Yeah, sure," she breathed. A hiccup and a giggle escaped her mouth as she followed.

As they neared the back porch, Harry re-emerged from the door.

"I called the PBP." Polar Bear Patrol was a group of volunteers that responded to bear sightings within and close to the town. The volunteers responded to the calls as quickly as the ambulance in some cases.

Noah and Penny simultaneously called to their canine charges. Mesmerized, they witnessed the dogs slowly extricate themselves from the bear. The bear stood on his hind legs as the dogs jogged back to their people, tongues hanging and tails wagging. The bear made an "aahr" sound and chuffed. He bobbed his head as he dropped down to all fours again and began walking toward them.

"Should I get the gun?" Harry asked in a voice almost too quiet to be considered a whisper.

Noah shook his head. "Wait."

The dogs climbed the steps onto the back deck. Penny stared at them and said, "Down. Stay." They complied. She glanced back to see the bear had stopped and sat down as well. Looking at them. Judging them. Trying to figure out if it wanted to get closer.

"How about that. It is wary of people but wants to play with the dogs," Noah said. He lowered his voice for only Penny to hear. "Did you see this one?"

She knew he meant via a vision. She shook her head, her gaze never leaving the bear. She wondered how many polar bears it would take to see in her lifetime before they didn't completely captivate her.

The PBP arrived in their orange-and-white truck. Rotating lights atop the roof did little to light up the afternoon glow. The man at the wheel leaned out the window as a horn sounded. The bear got up slowly and began to roam away from the homestead. They watched the truck follow the bear several hundred yards before they heard a gun fire. The bear picked up its pace and lumbered heavily away, the truck trailing after it.

Penny stopped her recording. "Did they shoot that bear?" she demanded.

Noah still looked to be in awe, but he shook his head. "No. They only shoot in the air. They don't shoot at a bear unless it is absolutely necessary. Dire circumstances and all that. But the guns shoot rubber projectiles anyway, so even if they did shoot the bear, they wouldn't actually kill them."

"You said once that they could also tranq them," Harry piped in.

"Yes, they will tranquilize repeat offenders. Depending on the time of year, they will then either relocate them or place them in the holding station until they release them. I am sure they can destroy a bear if it endangers human lives. But they wouldn't want to advertise that. Too many bleeding hearts. I hope they can at least protect themselves. I can't imagine that every bear, every time, will oblige to their tactics."

Penny wanted to know more, but she also itched to watch the recorded video. They entered the house as the sun's glare made an outside viewing next to impossible. Penny was surprised to see the video lasted seventeen minutes. It felt like seconds. Both dogs lay down on their sides once inside, tongues lolling as they panted loudly in the small entryway. Blue gazed up at her, his head falling so far back, his ears splayed out like bat wings.

A bit too warm for their playing, I see ...

Wow, Penny. That was amazing! Penny knew Lucy was pacing the floor in their bedroom. She too needed to move, or her muscles would burst out of her skin.

That was awesome, she agreed. *Something you could use in a story?*

The guys chatted while the video played. Penny was surprised to learn that they had never seen such a thing happen.

"Really?" she asked, entering their conversation.

Noah looked up. "Well, there are stories of it happening. And Army claimed he had seen a male bear and two wolves hanging around several different times together near the

105

research station earlier this spring." Penny recalled a passing comment about it but hadn't considered the three hung out together. "He wondered if they could have been to the area Pam was found." They all three sobered at that thought. "Army's been searching your data, Penny, to see if any of the tagged bears were around Pam at the time of her death." Penny had considered searching as well, but Noah refused take her out to the locations. Noah's gaze bounced between the video and the dogs before he left to grab the two fur balls some water.

Harry focused on his cell phone, attempting to get a copy of Penny's video. While the dogs panted at her feet, she leaned against the wood-paneled wall, surveying the house from where she stood. One of the bedroom doors stood open along the hallway leading to the kitchen. Noah's bedroom door. Penny had been shown around the house when she first visited. There were two bedrooms, Army's and Noah's, an office and a bathroom down this hall. Noah's door had been closed at that time and each time since. This was her first glimpse inside his room. The bed was neatly made. A USA flag adorned the one visible wall above a dresser that was, for the most part, bare. It was not the messy room of a bachelor that she expected.

"Who would have guessed a polar bear and a wolf would get along so well." Noah's comment was barely audible from the other room.

"Well, my last name means bear and yours means wolf. Did you ever think of that?" Penny said, tearing her gaze from his room as he returned with a full bowl of water. He closed the door as he passed by and glanced up at her from where he knelt, the dogs descending upon the water. She saw his smile widen, and he looked up again, this time holding her gaze longer. She found it hard to breathe.

She cleared her throat. "Do you mind if I stick around for a bit, leave Blue to cool down?" she asked. "We were going for a walk, but now…"

Noah suggested they all sit out in the back yard and enjoy the warm weather. Harry grabbed a few chairs from the deck

106

at the rear of the house and arranged them on the lawn in full exposure of the sun. After a few minutes, they returned to the deck. Noah sprayed the area with a fog to reduce the bug population that swarmed them. A few more minutes passed, and Penny reluctantly asked to borrow long-sleeved shirt and sweatpants, but she refused to go inside. Harry offered her a beer that he had brewed, and Noah pointed out that it doubled as insect repellent. She politely declined.

"I thought you were going to screen in this deck, bro," Harry said.

"Not much use for one of those when a warm day like this happens once every five years," Noah said.

"I don't know. It has been getting warmer. Remember when we visited as kids? It was never this warm."

Harry asked if Noah worked out the plans for a sauna yet. They laughed about that and joked around over the next half hour. Their discussion turned more serious when Harry brought up the deceased girls.

"Are there any leads on who the killer might be?" Harry asked.

Since Army had his hands in just about everything that happened in the community, this question wasn't farfetched. But no, the perpetrator was still unknown. And at large. If he even lived in the community.

The guys continued their discussion while Penny quietly listened, pretending she was not surrounded by flying demons, dive bombing her and her surroundings. Her thoughts fluttered around the dead women and her nightmares with the shadowed figure. Were there details or clues that could be helpful with the investigation? Noah insisted she notify him first, wary of how others might take information from Penny, an outsider. He also insisted she tell Army, but she balked at sharing. She hadn't even told her mother, not wanting to unsettle the woman.

When at last she could not discern the conversation over the buzzing, she gave up. She thought Noah tried to steer the conversation in a different direction based on his comments about topics unrelated, but Harry was insistent, presumably being out of the loop. She bid the guys good day and entered the house to retrieve her cooled-down dog. Harry followed her, offering her a bottle of water as she woke her slumbering canine. She declined.

"You know your brother seems an awful lot happier and relaxed with you around. I'm almost sad to see you go just because of that," Penny said, her mouth curving into a half smile.

"I was thinking he seemed happier and more relaxed with you around. I think that's part of the reason I acted the way I did when I first met you. I was jealous of you. Both of you. I am sorry, by the way. I think you are cool...and hot," Harry said, winking at her.

The shock at his heartfelt disclosure made the heat rush to Penny's cheeks. He threw an arm around her as they walked back to the back door, and she allowed his arm to rest companionably on her shoulders. She decided that perhaps she would be sad to see him go after all.

Black Eye

September's approach was swift. For three weeks after Harry left, Penny spent much of her time at the computer or running out to the research station collecting and sending data for Army to review. During that time, the visions hadn't visited. Several times when she talked with Noah on the phone, he encouraged her to speak with Army about her visions, but uncertainty prevented her.

"Oh hey, Army. I've had these creepy visions. Possibly of the killer although I never see a face, just a shadowed figure accompanied by these feelings of dread. Something I should worry about? And, these aren't the first premonitions that I've had. Like, I had them of the school shooting. But not of my father being killed. And I've been trying meditation. Have any tips?"

Probably best to keep her mouth shut.

Her fear remained, but it was pliant. She could push it to the back of her mind and focus on other, higher priority tasks as she continued with her life. Succumbing to recent fears would allow her grief and guilt and shame to join the pity party.

It helped that the shadowed visions had abated, although Penny fretted the lack meant the predator was holed up, planning out the next victim.

When Noah returned from his last three-week turn on the oil rigs, he offered to give her a ride to the first self-defense class of the fall. She had been looking forward to this night since Harry had mentioned it.

"What happened to you?" Penny asked. She heard from her mother that Noah had a shiner but was still shocked to see it. Although he worked security at the rigs, she didn't figure there would be much in the line of physical altercations.

He shifted, looking away from her inspection as he stood in the kitchen wearing his heavy black leather jacket, black tee, and black sweatpants. He was going ninja-style tonight, the black eye making him look even more intimidating.

"Ahh, that." He ran a hand through his glossy black locks. "Well, I fell asleep on a boat ride out to the rigs, and I woke up to gun fire. My first thought was we were under attack. Not a great way to wake up. Some of the new crew members, two that I was training in as my replacements, were shooting at a pod of narwhals. I, ah, stopped them."

"You stopped them? How many were there?"

"Four. I was lucky I didn't get shot after I was knocked unconscious."

"Yeah, right?" she marveled.

She stepped closer and reached up as if to touch his face but withheld her hand.

"I'm okay," he said, waving her hand away. "Unfortunately, several narwhals are not. They killed three and hauled two of them onto the deck after they knocked me out. When I woke up...I...well. I took care of the situation and radioed for help."

Penny felt an inward shudder as she considered the strength of the man before her. He was adept at fighting, handy at so many things. And, per Army, had served in active combat for the military. Furthermore, Army requested Penny not ask Noah about it. The topic was off limits, unless Noah brought it up.

"Why would they do such a thing?" she asked.

He shook his head. "Because they thought they could? They were bored?" He shrugged. "I don't understand people's desire to kill things for sport. Anyway, I already gave my notice that I was quitting. Not sure how this will play out. I messed up a couple of the guys. On the brighter side, here is a present. For you."

He handed her a twisted, four-foot long, cream-colored horn. It was a narwhal tooth.

Penny was startled by the gift. "This is for me?"

"Yeah. Thought you might like it. You read all those fantasy books and stuff. Here is your very own unicorn horn," he laughed lightly.

"I don't think I can accept this, Noah," she said and attempted to hand it back.

"My black eye says differently. Take it."

A warmth spread through her that had less to do with the gift and more to do with Noah gifting her a present. So, she reverently placed it inside the sparse bedroom she shared with her sister, leaning it against the wall next to her bedside table. The bed covers were rumpled, and her laundry basket overflowed. Next to Noah's pristine bedroom, hers looked like a slob lived there. She hurried out of the room, closing the door behind her. Picking up would have to wait. Again.

They were the first to arrive at the high school gym. The nostalgia of high school struck her—the perfume of old sweaty socks, floor polish, and the hint of popcorn took her back to a different time, before the event that marked the end of high school. It was almost comforting.

As she sat down on the lower bleacher to change her shoes, her vision narrowed, and the room spun with glittering stars. Another vision. The images blurred together - the polar bear and the man hidden in shadows. A deep, low chuckle emanated from the Shadowed Man. An evil hunger rolled off him, unlike the bear's image, which felt like a fierce challenge. She continued changing her shoes while she focused on breathing and clearing her mind. A third image, one of a woman's face, one she didn't recognize, flashed briefly.

"Hey, you ready to warm up?" Noah sat next to her.

Penny nodded, not confident she could speak.

"You alright?"

"I, ah, yeah. Bit nervous, I guess." She wanted to share her vision, but the arrival of participants prohibited her from sharing it in secret. Several greeted her and Noah before milling in small groups or sitting off by themselves. She didn't relish the thought that others might overhear her.

Standing, he squeezed her upper arm, as if to reassure her, then walked off to greet the newcomers.

On the ride over, Noah had commented on the small group of people of all ages from the town attended. There were a few die-hards who came every meeting. Some only came a few times. On average, a dozen people gathered each time they met Wednesday evenings.

Noah was an excellent instructor, providing individual assistance when needed. Half-way through the class, Noah and Penny sparred to show different techniques that could be used to escape or defend against attacks. They showed basic, but effective, moves, fluidly responding to each other's moves to make for a great demonstration.

During the cooldown they had a bit of fun attempting to free their wrists from duct tape. For those who tried it, a challenge rose to see who could free themselves the quickest. Penny used to practice when she was bored, so she figured she would easily win. Turned out, a young boy in the class practiced on more than a few occasions. They tied multiple times, with Penny only barely winning in the end.

After the hour-long class, Noah worked with Penny alone to gauge her skill level, so he knew where to take her in her training. He couldn't officially train her, but he could show her some things that she would be presented in the more advanced Krav Maga classes.

Over the course of several Wednesday nights, Penny discerned Noah would not spar with anyone aside from Penny. She asked him about it, but he just shrugged and mumbled something about not wanting to hurt anyone.

"But you aren't worried about hurting me?" she challenged, a bit confused at his reasoning.

"Nope. You are as tough as me."

She flushed, and his smile broadened. If he used his charm during a fight, it probably would catch her off guard.

Penny went home with new bruises, which surprisingly did not come from Noah. He was firm with his attacks and defense but not hurtful. The others in the group, however, could get a bit aggressive without realizing it.

Turbulence

"After many months of research, it's time we goofed off," Noah said, mimicking his uncle's voice. He laughed, then in his own voice, added, "More. Goofed off more, he should have said."

The October day had started miserably, as many had since the sunlight began to ebb its way closer to winter and the impending weeks of endless night. The week-long fog made it more the worse. Moreover, Penny awakened in a grouchy mood. Her mother had stayed out late the night before playing cards with Rose, Army, and Sam, then had gone to work early leaving Penny to stew in her petulant silence. Lucy knowingly shied away from her temper, having a matching one of her own. When alerted to Noah's call, Penny had only reluctantly answered in the hope that his voice might cheer her up. It had.

Noah asked if she wanted to go out flying the following day as the fog was predicted to clear by then. Home for a two-week stay from Anchorage, Army planned to fly down to the mountains.

"That sounds like fun. Anyone else tagging along?" she asked. She imagined Noah shrugging and laughed.

"Not yet. Just the three of us. There is room for more," he added. They would be flying in Army's Twin Otter plane. The small plane could seat six and carry quite a bit of equipment.

"I would like to see the Brooks Range. I slept the first time I flew over them. I'll let you know later if I find another passenger," she bid him goodbye, feeling her spirits had lifted.

How about it, Lu? Want to take a trip to the mountains?

No, Lucy quietly reverberated through Penny's mind. *I don't really feel like going.*

Her sister's illness was something they didn't talk about. Everyone was aware of Lucy's poor health, and they shied away from mentioning it, which made it easier for Penny to cope with her sister's disinclination to leave the house most days. The harsh, cold, dreary tundra climate made it difficult for Penny not to stay in bed most days. But she had a job to keep her busy away from the small home, whereas her sister's writing kept her indoors. Where some authors traveled to gain inspiration for writing, Lucy relived Penny's daily activities and used them for her compositions.

Do the best with what we have, right? Penny thought.

And be happy because we have a lot. I know. Wallowing in self-pity does nothing. It gets so very quiet when you, mother and Blue all leave. But the quiet helps me focus, and I do get a lot of writing done. I envy you, Pen. But I also look forward to each and every day I can spend watching the world happen through your eyes. It is more than what could be.

It was in that moment that Penny was so very grateful for their mental connection. A random thought occurred between them, one that both vexed and humored. The giggles transcended into fits of laughter that left both breathless with tears streaming down Penny's face.

It is a bit disturbing, knowing you see everything that I do. Sometimes I don't even realize it. I take it for granted! Penny thought.

Okay, first of all, I can ignore you or tune you out. I don't recall observing you in the bathroom, with limited exceptions I suppose, Lucy thought in a sarcastic tone.

Penny snickered as she realized the truth of this.

Secondly, you block me during times of high stress. Lucy continued more soothingly. *When the incident happened back in Pasadena, I saw more on the television than I did through our eyes, Pen. I do believe you blocked me, intentionally or subconsciously. Doesn't matter. I think that whenever you and Noah finally get together…*

The shift in subjects caught Penny off guard, and her

114

mental shout of *What?!* cut her sister off. *Noah is my* friend!

Lucy continued in a placating tone. *Or when you fall in love and get married to someone, anyone, I think we will be able to ensure your privacy during most times. I would still sense your feelings, though. Just like I can breathe without thinking. You know what I mean.*

Penny understood, although it helped discussing it with her sister. She shook her head.

Friends, Lu. Nothing more.

Penny sighed and left the room to call her mother about taking the trip the following day. Eelyn was always excited for an opportunity to fly.

The fog cleared that afternoon along with Penny's sulk. With the retreat of the white veil, Penny's breath came easier, the claustrophobic feeling having disappeared. In the early hours before twilight the following morning, Blue bounded out of the truck behind Penny at the small airport and ran up to greet Winter. Winter wandered close to Penny and licked her hand before leading the rambunctious puppy away.

They secured the simple provisions for the short trip along with emergency gear. After a quick cup of hot chocolate with the airport manager and the resultant emptying of bladders, they boarded the plane.

Penny and Noah buckled and secured their headsets in the back seats as they waited for Army and Eelyn, co-pilot for the day, to complete prefight. The Otter had the capability for a land or water landing and with its main and reserve fuel tank could travel great distances. It easily accommodated the four people and two dogs.

Blue and Winter curled up at Penny and Noah's feet. The weather called for sun and a light breeze. Their route to the Anaktuvuk Pass in the Brooks Range took them roughly two-hundred-and-twenty miles to the southeast. Excitement rushed through Penny as she pictured the mountains.

"Winds are due to increase later this afternoon. My plan again is to do a run down to Anaktuvuk Pass for a short visit. My buddy Jake plans to meet us. We are fueled to capacity and should have plenty of time to stretch our wings," Army relayed after take-off.

Penny could hear the smile in his voice. He had mentioned Jake in the past and knew him to be a long-time friend. They served in the army together for twenty years. His son and Noah also served together, although for a much shorter period.

The dark blue sea vanished quickly behind them as the expansive grayish-green tundra took over. Here and there winding rivers sectioned off the tundra. Because of the prolonged heat wave of the summer and fall, the green stretched out before them like the sea. Penny patiently longed for the view of the Brooks Mountain range as the two pilots discussed airstrip conditions at the little town that was their destination.

A jostling of her shoulder drew Penny from her dreamless sleep. Noah was leaning into her and looking out her window. Her usual first reaction at being woken from a slumber was to lash out, but the shock of his near proximity doused those feelings. She gazed wonderingly at the shades of black within his thick hair inches from her nose. His eyes met hers as he turned.

"Wakey, wakey, Penny. The mountains are in view," he said with a smile. An exciting warmth spread through her chest and up her face as they stared at each other. She tore her gaze from his and peered out the window.

The carpet of green ran along the edge of the grey mountains, their sharp peaks poised beneath a clear blue sky. The homescape she left was a sharp contrast to this scene before her.

Home, she wondered, *when did I start to think of Utqiaġvik as home?*

Eelyn gracefully landed the plane on the clear gravel runway, and a small crowd greeted them as they exited the craft. The dogs ran about, happy to stretch their legs. There was much exchange of hugs and a joyous reunion for Army and Noah and their comrades. The people were friendly with Penny and Eelyn, exchanging pleasantries with them as well. Multiple packages were gathered near the plane, the caribou that Army had so looked forward to. Penny avoided the light and friendly chatter by arranging the packages in the coolers inside the plane, her mouthwatering at the thought of roasted caribou.

As she backed out of the plane, she bumped into Noah, who surprised her with a small bundle. Curious, she unfolded it, revealing a suede-soft face mask. Noah confirmed that it was tanned caribou hide. She stroked the velvety material and handed it back to Noah. He held up a hand.

"It's yours. You will be thankful for it when it gets colder." Colder. Right. She considered putting it on right then.

Confused, she asked, "Did my mom buy it for me?"

His cocked his head to the side as he watched her. "No," he said slowly. "Jake made them and gave us a box full. I thought you should have one, unless you don't…"

Interrupting, she said, "Oh, in that case, thank you." She smiled, casting her head down. Her sister would say he gave nice presents.

Army strolled up. "Well, kids. Sorry to have to cut this short, but we need to be leaving. Forecast changed. The winds are supposed to pick up, possibly carry in a sudden storm. Lucky us, hey?" If they left now, they should make it back home before it became too bad.

They were lucky. Lucky to have two very good pilots. Turbulence struck halfway back, and the visibility degraded so much that Army and Eelyn navigated only by the instruments. The freak storm hit them with all it could muster. At one point, Penny thought they landed. The plane shook and dropped. Metal groaned, and the windows rattled. Penny held her fists tight in her lap until a touch startled her. Noah had reached over and picked up one of her hands, turning it over to show her the blood beading around her fingernails.

"Let me help you." He pulled a rag from his pocket and wiped her palms, then tore it in half to wrap her hands. Their heads narrowly escaped knocking into each other with a sudden drop. "I would recommend you clean that better when we land. I don't want to chance a concussion to retrieve the emergency kit right now."

Penny looked down at her hands, eyes wide, tears gliding atop her freckled cheeks. Noah scooted as close as his lap belt would allow and took her hand in his.

"I could use a hand to hold right now," he grunted as the plane dropped and rose abruptly. "Not much for roller coaster rides." A shocked giggle escaped Penny.

"Roller coaster? I have been in worse than this. This is nothing, right, Eelyn?" Army yelled to his co-pilot.

Eelyn nodded with a plastic smile, her knuckles white on the controls.

"Almost there, guys. No worries," Eelyn said.

Within minutes, Army turned on the landing lights and hailed the control tower on the radio.

The reply came, "Hold...Tango Zero...visibility zero... other plane to land..."

"Message not clear, repeat. Repeat instructions," Army barked into the microphone on his headgear.

"Do not...ten minutes...southeaster..." Static filled the void between audible words.

Army worried out loud. "Could be another plane attempting to land. But coming in from what direction?"

Static. "Repeat. Good to go."

"Cross your fingers," Army said as he modified the controls dropping the plane's elevation. At least, that was what Penny gathered from the sharp change in pressure in her ears.

Eelyn set the flaps while Army dropped the airspeed to one hundred knots. He activated the intake deflector, because as he mentioned to Eelyn, the amount of blowing snow probably transformed the runway. Penny only vaguely understood what he meant at that point. Army continued decreasing the airspeed until the tires bumped against the runway. Penny felt the reverse thrust at the same time she heard it.

They made it. Alive.

"Everyone okay?" Eelyn asked.

Penny scanned the occupants. A faint buzzing resonated in

118

her head, and her body shook. Noah's face paled with a slight green tint. She wondered if she looked similar. *We are okay. We made it.*

"The dogs are shaken and are ready to disembark," Penny said.

Ha, terrible pun, Lucy replied.

Getting the plane moved into and parked on the carousel inside the private hangar luckily didn't take very long, its south-facing door offered some protection from the windy assault.

They stopped in at the terminal and found out that another plane had indeed been attempting to land at that same time, only it crash-landed several hundred yards off to the north of the runway. Emergency crews were already out. The blinding flashing red and blue lights hidden by the stormy night.

"What would have happened if we went down? Could we have landed somewhere without a strip?" Penny asked after the four of them returned home and sat eating a quiet meal at her house.

"Yes, we could land around here without much difficulty. Might have banged the plane a bit. That old bird has been through a lot and can go through a lot more," said Army.

Army gave the impression they could survive any type of landing, but Penny knew he was only trying to lessen her fears. How could they have survived if the plane plummeted to earth?

"But if something had happened," she fretted. "I mean, I'm good with first aid and all that. But do you think winter survival would be good to know?"

"Hopefully, you will never be far from town if your vehicle breaks down. But knowledge is power." His look became thoughtful, and he suggested that he and Noah take her out on a few trips close to town. "Heck, we could do it in the backyard, but that wouldn't provide the same experience. But the dogs need some sled time away from the yard." He winked. "Want to start tomorrow? This storm shouldn't last too long and should leave a bit of snow to blow around," Army offered, as if he had nothing better to do during his brief vacation from the college.

Penny studied the blinding white, wondering how much was "a bit." She thought snow usually didn't stick around until October. Then again, October was only days away.

In the days following the turbulent trip from the mountains, Penny's anxiety over what happened, or could have happened, gradually waned. She busied herself with the research and other activities, which now included rigorous dog sledding training. In this she was distracted from the possibility that a serial killer was hunting in the small town she considered home.

Revealing

The day Army had planned for an overnight trip with the sleds, Lucy and Eelyn fell ill with rather severe sinus infections. They decided to stay home, leaving Penny to go with Army and Noah.

They set out past the road to the research station for the first part of the trip. Army rode behind the team with the sled. Penny and Noah trailed with a second team, trading off who skied behind the sled. Being pulled by a larger dog team was thrilling.

Wind-burnt and exuberant later that night, they set up camp near a frozen lake. Noah showed Penny how to set the trip wire that would alert them to a wandering polar bear (if the dogs didn't sound the alarm first). Then, after they started several fires for practice, procured and purified water, the three huddled in the small yellow tent discussing scenarios, though the wind howled so loudly it was hard for anyone to hold a conversation below a shout.

Penny was amazed at how much the trip was like being in a class. Army quizzed her over techniques that they practiced throughout the venture.

As anyone desiring survival skills in the northland might, she asked what to do if a bear attacked the tent.

Army patted his front pocket. "Well, I sleep with a knife." The implement he extracted from his pocket...well, she was amazed it fit. It was long and of a dull grey metal, thicker in the center with one end curving toward the tip. He nodded to Noah, who also produced such a knife.

"And we have our guns." Noah then produced an AR from under his bed roll, not the .22 or .243 they normally carried on walks or in the sleds.

Shivers of fear trickled down her back. It was nearing the freeze-up and the bears, anxious to be back out on the ice, had become more active on land. She found herself wondering if it was smart to go out camping with land-locked bears.

As if reading her thoughts, Army said, "When our time comes, there is nothing we can do about it. But until then, it is necessary to enjoy life. We are, of course, safe here. Besides, I have this." He winked at her, and she realized that he carried his small computer and could monitor any chipped bears. Knowing that allowed her to breathe a bit easier.

Army went over the plan for the next day, which started with netting fish from the nearby frozen lake.

A lull dropped into their conversation, stretching out for a million hours.

"Penny, forgive me being a nosey old man, but Noah tells me that you experience frequent dreams about a polar bear. One in particular."

Penny glanced quickly at Army before returning her gaze to her hands. "Hmmm," was all she said.

"In your research role in looking out for polar bears, there would naturally be some anxiety and other emotions associated with that. Our work, while trying to answer questions and do what we can to assist the marine bears, does result in leaving a bit of an imprint on them and is not without risk, both to the bears and to us. It is impossible to study a subject without some level of consequence." Army's voice reverted to his lecture tone.

She furrowed her brow and chewed on the inside of her cheek. Noah may have mentioned Penny's dreams but perhaps not the significance.

"I've actually been meaning to talk to you about them. I don't think it's the stresses of life." She rubbed at her eyes. "The bear I see is the same bear every time. Three black scars on its left cheek. The visions started before I moved here. In fact—" she broke off, shifting to remove the child's toy from her pocket and presented it to Army "—I have carried this around since I was a child."

The wind died down suddenly, as if it too wanted to hear the conversation. Army took the bear figurine in his hands and studied it like it was a polar bear necropsy before passing it to Noah. A look flashed across Noah's face. Disbelief? Irritation? She had not divulged the contents of her pockets to him, even though he already knew of her visions.

"Only now, since I have been up here, I see that bear," she pointed to the figure that Noah turned over in his hands, "in my dreams and during daytime visions. Day or night. And a man usually appears with the bear. There is the sense of fear and warning with the images, which honestly scares the crap out of me. Noah and I think the man may be the killer, but I cannot make out any details. I just see this vague, frightening shadow. And I have no idea what the bear means."

The wind returned, tugging and wrenching at the tent. Noah shifted, handing her the small plastic toy. A trickle of apprehension ran along the back of Penny's neck.

"Well, he hadn't told me that," Army's gravelly voice sounded surprised. "You think what you are having are premonitions"

She began to nod her head, then realized the lantern that hung above their heads from the center of the tent danced with the buffeting wind and cast much of the tent in shadow, so she gave a verbal yes.

"Have you had others? Before your move here?" he asked.

"Yeah. I dreamt of the school shooting the night before it happened, but only a piece of the event. I saw the students fall on the athletic field at school," she said, her voice low. Once again, she watched it play out, unable to do anything to stop it. If only she had visualized what was to happen to her father. Perhaps she could have done something to save him. Or at least said goodbye, given him one more hug. She shook free of the memory and persistent guilt. "The first actual vision I remember was of my own drowning when I was five." She sheepishly looked over at the shadow that was Noah. "That's why I don't like swimming. I normally see images of an event. Clear but without context. The shadowed visions…they are different. They are flashes of emotion and shadows."

Noah cleared his throat, and Army asked, "You have had many more visions?"

"Yes, but nothing much to talk about." Her voice was soft, barely audible above the wind's returned assault on the tent. She wanted to take the hanging lantern down and place it on the ground to stop the light from swinging.

"So, these visions with the man and the bear...how else are they different?" he asked.

"Before I watched a scene play out when I was asleep. Now, though, they come when I am awake or asleep."

"Like the day you tackled me?" Noah interrupted.

"Actually, that day the vision I saw very clear. And not to repeat myself, Noah, but I didn't tackle you. That day, though...the bear we chipped. That was the scarred bear. My scarred bear," Penny said as she rotated the bear figurine in her hands. "For as much as I see him, either my mind just can't get rid of his face, or I am destined to meet up with him again." She made a guttural sound.

"Or it could be this bear has become tied to you. A spirit guide," Army said.

Penny looked up at his words. Spirit guide. She had heard of the concept before but had not connected it to the scarred bear.

"Spirit guides can be animals." Army continued, "Shaman teachings tell of them as a link to the afterlife or otherworld. Since the bear is alive, it may mean something different. What, though, I could only guess. Perhaps he is linked to the killer in some way...perhaps he was the bear that came across the first two women after the killer left them."

She said, "I'm not scared of the bear. Wary, for sure. Awed. But not fearful. At least not the kind of fear that I sense when I see the Shadowed Man. I think it might be best to say there might be meaning to my visions, even if the meaning is elusive. But not many people would think me sane if I began sharing actual details, although to this point there aren't any details to share." Penny felt bile rise as she recalled the image of the woman's face that had flashed in the premonition she had at wrestling practice. If she disclosed details, would it change anything for the woman?

"We believe you," Noah said.

Army agreed. "We understand you have faced a lifetime of traumas in your young life. You are not so far gone a bit of salt won't save you."

A barking laugh burst from Noah. "True words."

"These visions should be viewed as a gift," Army said.

It was Penny's turn to laugh, albeit with a bitterness. "They sure don't feel much like a gift, Army. I don't understand what they are showing me. They are confusing and frightening."

"What I mean to say is that being tuned differently means you can play in a unique key. Do you think I haven't noticed the way you have with the dogs? I think you possess more gifts than foresight."

"I did see a woman's face during a recent image." From the periphery, Penny noticed both Army and Noah leaned closer to her. "Not someone I recognized or anything. She was screaming. I'm worried what that means. Do you think it might help if I tell you what she looked like?" Unease flooded her as she recalled the forgotten vision, certain that the woman had already met her demise. After providing the limited description, Army and Noah confirmed her suspicions: they did not immediately recognize the woman. Few women in the community had flaming red hair that matched the age of the woman Penny described, and no one with black tips, although it was possible the girl was someone new or someone they had not yet met.

"Noah suggested I try meditation," she began.

"And has that helped?" Noah interjected.

Rueful was her expression. "It has helped me sleep better, I guess."

"Tell me what you have been trying," encouraged Army, and she did. He offered several tips to quiet her mind and suggested once she reach that state of calm awareness, she should then recall the images from her premonitions. Perhaps it would trigger details that hid from her.

"If it is alright, I would rather not try it now. With the wind and how tired I am, I doubt I will stay awake much longer."

The conversation turned to other, lighter subjects, for which Penny was thankful. With the need for sleep descending upon them, she exited the warm tent one last time to relieve herself, stretch a bit and check on the dogs.

The sky was clear. As she gazed upwards, she found Orion, the Big Dipper, and Polaris amidst the colorful brushstrokes of the Milky Way. The stars twinkled, unfazed by the evil that prowled the town. The view mesmerized her, and she could have stayed out all night observing the night sky. As it was, the wind lashed at her, finding and hauling away her warmth. Upon her return to the tent, she found her two companions asleep. She crawled to the center of the tent to the open spot Noah and Army left her and within minutes fell into a deep sleep.

The next day, before their return trip, Army and Noah showed Penny how they caught fish in the winter. Flags marked where nets had been set previously, and after chopping out blocks of ice, the trio hauled loads of whitefish. They collected the larger ones, threw the small ones back into the lake and re-set the nets. Penny paid careful attention since the job would be her responsibility every now and again. The fish would be laid out and frozen, then used as dog food for the winter. The fish, in addition to the whale they stored, a bit of dog kibble and a vitamin supplement would be adequate to sustain the dogs over the winter.

Wrestling

Since Penny had agreed to assist with wrestling, she met with Noah and the head coach, Mark Winkler, at the school for a conference in mid-October. The coach had already worked out a practice schedule, so they went through her duties and how best to use her during conditioning.

Although overwhelmed at first (but trying hard not to let it show), by the second practice Penny found her stride and settled into her role. Noah's pointers on form and technique during practice for the wrestlers were not lost on Penny, and she worked to improve herself. Very few of the kids, as Penny referred to them initially, complained and even then only after the end of the conditioning drills. Even so, all worked hard.

Ten days into practice, Penny happened on one of the two female wrestlers who was crying in the locker room after practice. Molly, a junior, was teased earlier that day by several girls in her class about the winter dance. Penny asked if that was what brought about the girl's meltdown during takedown practice. Molly nodded sadly.

"No one asked me to go, and my friends are all going with dates," she sniffed.

"To be honest, I didn't date in high school. I just didn't find any guys in my school...enough...no, I don't know the right words. No one ever caught my eye, no one I wished to date. So, I didn't. And the other students made fun of me for it. But I told myself that if it bothered them, then that was their problem, not mine. I would do things on my own terms or not at all," Penny told her. "If you don't want to go to the winter dance, don't. You can hang out with me and play guitar. If you want to go, then ask someone. Anyone. Or go by yourself. It's not like you won't know anyone there. Just be the brave girl you are when you are on the mat wrestling."

Molly was one of the toughest wrestlers on the team, having been raised with three older brothers who also wrestled.

"Did you go to many dances?" Molly sniffed and wiped at her nose.

"Not one. But that is not the same as never been dancing. My father and I danced a lot when I was younger. Never met a guy in high school that I thought would be a better partner than my father."

"My father can't dance at all. He is in a wheelchair," Molly said.

"Are you sure? Guys in wheelchairs can do some pretty incredible things…"

Molly was quiet for a few moments.

"Look, people can and will say or think what they want about me, but the only one who can make me happy is me. Other people's negativity is a waste of their own energy, not mine. We are in control of our own thoughts and feelings. Sure, it is hard not to let comments and remarks eat away at our confidence. Self-doubt is a tough opponent - but only if you let it be. We are only human. You know what I feel good about now? I am not ashamed of who I am. I didn't do things to please other shallow people. I didn't give in to peer pressure on sex, drugs or alcohol. I did pressure peers into being respectful to elders and veterans, but I also gave respect to those who didn't because I was good enough to be respectful." Penny paused, gathering breath. "Look, I've seen more death and loss than anyone ever should. Life should not be taken for granted. It should be cherished and shared with those you love, not wasted on those who do not love you."

Penny patted Molly on the back. Molly, much like Rita, who apparently preferred the closeness of a hug, grabbed Penny into an embrace and held her tightly. Penny felt the girl's hot tears on her shirt.

"Shh, it's okay. You might not get exactly what you want…like how much I want millions of dollars…" Molly choked back a laugh. "But you should learn to appreciate what you do have. Your family and friends love you very much. These girls, they talk big and pretend that nothing hurts them, but they are just like you and me. They're scared. They're self-conscious. They bleed red."

Molly took a deep, shuddering breath and released Penny. "Thank you for talking with me."

"Anytime." Penny watched Molly gather her things and leave, wondering if she said the right words. She walked out afterwards to discover Noah leaning against the wall around the corner.

"What are you doing in here?" she whispered. "Stalking?" She gasped in mock horror. "Not eavesdropping, are you?"

"No, no. Stay calm, woman," he smiled. "I saw Molly leaving. Is she okay?" He stood upright as Penny neared him.

"I hope so. She was worried about some girls making fun of her for not going to the dance."

"Really? I heard three of the wrestlers argue over who was going to ask her to the dance." He paused. "Are you going to chaperone?" Noah raised an eyebrow her direction.

"Chaperone?" She raised an eyebrow back. "No, I'm sure the thought has not crossed their minds."

"You would be surprised. You are an assistant coach. And female. They need female figure heads to chaperone."

"Are you chaperoning?" she asked.

"No, not this time.

Penny shuddered. Dancing scared her almost as much as swimming, but she had yet to have a dance-related vision.

Penny, could you make time to spend with your sister? asked Lucy as Penny walked out to the truck with Noah to head back home.

What do you mean? I see you every night.

Silence stretched out in her mind for what seemed like eternity until Lucy finally answered. *Look, you are busy. Research, wrestling, self-defense classes, guitar practice with Noah, Blue and the other dogs, and Noah...I know why you like to be busy, but this is borderline ridiculous.*

It's no worse than before, really, if you think about it, responded Penny.

Sure, Penny.

As the hours of sunlight had waned, Penny made increased efforts to be outside as much as possible. The temperatures dipped lower, too, especially at night, and the wind seemed incessant. The winds of darkness, as Lucy dubbed them, gusting down their necks.

Over sixty days of night neared, and Penny was starting to become apprehensive over the thought of the sun's complete disappearance in less than a month. Snow settled and stayed during the beginning of October. The small drifts shifting back and forth like the sands in the desert.

Penny promised to make some time for her sister, just the two of them. After she and Noah returned from their little trip they had been planning for a week. It was the last they would take before wrestling officially started next month and took up Noah's time.

After Noah pulled up to her house, she went inside to grab her bag that was packed for a three-day, two-night excursion. Blue was already out with the other dogs. The plan was to make snow shelters both nights, but they did pack a tent just in case.

Penny smiled as she recalled how Eelyn had fretted over Penny going out alone with Noah for the extended trek.

"Based on the ratio of formality and friendliness that Noah showcases in my presence, I'm pretty sure he is either repulsed or completely unattracted to me. So, your worries are all for naught, mother. Fear not for my safety, for my guide is a master of self-preservation and survival, and I, a worthy assistant, should he become overwhelmed by my wit and beauty."

"I was more worried about your environmental safety and how you two will fair in near-zero temps with twenty-two dogs to care for," her mother said.

The trip was a success in that no one died nor had Noah been overcome by her wit. They built individual snow tunnels for practice, but their true nighttime shelter was big enough for both so they could huddle and share warmth.

The first night, they spread a Mylar blanket on the ground

and used the capsized sled as a windbreak. They hung a tarp above them to provide more cover, like a makeshift tent. Penny dug down beneath the snow to find bare ground on which to establish a fire. They boiled a rabbit Noah shot earlier in the day over the hot flames and shared the meal. Penny wished for utensils and napkins but made do with a clean sock and her fingers. They then shared the liquid in which they boiled the rabbit. Although they were in survival mode training, the dogs were not. Noah claimed they ate better than the two humans. Penny disagreed. The reek of muktuk, dog kibble, and fish were not at all appealing to her nostrils or stomach.

"So, tell me about your sister," Noah prompted as they settled in their sleeping bags.

The tarp sides luffed in the gentle breeze. Penny focused on the thin clouds that glowed pink from the aurora. The air was cold, and her breath fogged as she exhaled deeply.

Penny tried to gather her thoughts. Where to start?

"She used to be more like me. More than me. She was active, involved in taekwondo, wrestling, drama. When she began losing her balance, my parents took her to the doctor." Penny shrugged, thinking back. "It took a lot of tests, but they finally diagnosed her with a brain tumor. Inoperable."

The silence stretched between them.

"She underwent treatments, radiation, chemo. They stalled the growth of the tumor, but by then her balance and coordination were permanently affected. She turned from athletics and started keeping journals, writing stories to distract her from the pain."

Huddled up, Noah switched subjects. "What was it like growing up in Pasadena?"

"Warm," she said.

Although he was supportive about her visions, she kept her and her sister's telepathy a secret. Perhaps in time she could share; it seemed even more private than sharing her visions. Instead, stories from her childhood fell from her lips.

"Once we grew out of the band phase, she decided she wanted to become a veterinarian. That made mother happy…

and irritated."

"Why irritated?"

"Being a vet is hard. I understand it more now. It isn't just about helping animals. The long hours, emergencies calling you away from time with family, the difficult owners…it was worse in Pasadena. Our father was an ER nurse and his shift rotated, so sometimes both our parents happened to be home together at night. Most times, we had one or none. When we moved to Anchorage, mother worked part-time and went back to college part-time. I think it was actually a struggle for her, not having emergencies to tend to at all hours of the day and night."

"Did you ever want to be a vet?"

"Yeah, when I was younger. Then Lucy and I decided she would be the vet and I would be a marine biologist." *Now all she does is write her stories.*

"What about a nurse like your dad?"

"People are gross," she said with a laugh. "Being a nurse didn't appeal to me. I am not made of the tough fiber that one needs to be a nurse."

"Oh, I think you are tough enough. But I agree, the first time I would have to look at someone's foot, I'd be done." Noah asked tentatively, "So, your father has been gone for how long?"

"Two years. It was my senior year in high school," she told him, her voice soft. "I left during my off hour to go search for props for an upcoming play. I was stage manager. While I was in the storage room reaching for a box, I felt this soft, furry thing with my hand. Scared the shit out of me. It was Willy, the science room rat, who disappeared for a couple of weeks. Someone forgot to latch his cage or something. He was skinny. I fed him part of a granola bar I carried in my pocket. Then the fire alarm went off for the fire drill, so I grabbed the white rat to take him back to the science room. I didn't want to chance losing him outside. While I was putting him back into his cage, I heard these sounds. Like at the shooting range. Pop. Pop-pop. Like popcorn, over the sound of the fire alarm. And when I looked out the window…" she paused, thinking, and took a deep breath before continuing, "…there was chaos. Gunmen drove by in a van, shooting at the kids on the lawn. And I just watched."

Noah turned on his side, and she mirrored the move. Their eyes met and she found his gaze steadied her.

"There was this new kid, Ahrin, who wore a puffy orange vest, like in *Back to the Future*. He ran out of the school and entered the back of the van. I first thought he was going to help, but then he turned around and shot the security dog that ran after him. He climbed into the van, and then they left. I called 911 and went out to help as many as I could. When I arrived on the field," she broke off, refusing to remember the sounds and smells that had assaulted her, "the scene was exactly like I had dreamt. A piece of the puzzle fell into place. I replay the events over and over and cannot figure out what I could have done differently to have prevented it."

"I remember seeing the news reports. I'm so sorry, but it's not your fault. You didn't pull the trigger, Penny." He pulled down his sleeping bag and reached a hand across to rub her shoulder.

"The shooters switched vehicles and drove a stolen ambulance to the hospital my father worked at." Still, after all these years, the grief swelled. She didn't even try to hold back her tears.

"Two of the shooters distracted police at the entry, while the new kid was taken into the ER for an evaluation. And my father was the first to…" Penny cleared her throat and stared at the light of the flashlight to thwart the tears. "The kid was wearing a suicide vest. He detonated it and destroyed half the hospital. My father didn't make it."

She rolled back onto her back, her stretching silence broken by the light breeze that lifted the tarp above their heads, as tendrils of smoke reached up to kiss the stars. Blue shifted near her legs.

"He used to take my sister and me hunting for bear when we lived in Wisconsin. Not actual bear, we were little kids then. He would put teddy bears inside colored plastic bags and hide them in snowdrifts. Then he would help us track the bears to their snow caves, and we would dig them out. Lucy always said she 'loved her bear so hard'" Penny broke off to shake her head and chuckle. "My father, he possessed such a love for the outdoors. My parents met in Alaska, and we took a family trip there once, before Lucy got sick. We decided to return one day to live, once my sister and I finished school. I applied for college in Anchorage…and well, we decided to continue our plans after father died." She reached up, her black gloved hand swiping at the wispy clouds that drifted overhead, obstructing her view of the stars. She failed.

Noah said, "We lived in Washington state for many years."

Penny nodded. This she remembered.

He went on. "It was alright. Very green and wet, but I craved the place of my birth." She heard the smile in his face. "I spent many summers with Army. He was more than an uncle, more like a father. When my parents passed away, moving here seemed the only real option for me."

A dog woofed in its sleep. The aurora seemed to respond, jetting radiant bursts of pink and green bands skyward. A second dog howled, sparking a chain reaction. The hairs on the back of Penny's neck rose in response to the melancholy serenade.

Noah's words came more softly, as if trying not to interrupt the music. "I joined the army after school. Spent six years. During the first round of active duty, I was wounded. Took a hit in my shoulder. I spent three months recovering in Australia. It is amazing down there. I would like to go there again."

His admission to being wounded was not lost on her. That explained his habit of gripping and rolling his right arm. She thought it a nervous twitch or something, and perhaps it still was.

He spoke then of his brief adventures in Australia, when he wasn't in the hospital for surgery or rehab. She wasn't sure about the number of poisonous insects and snakes, much less the crocodiles and…

"You are aware we are camping in prime polar bear

territory, right?" he teased after she voiced her fear of deadly creatures less than one inch in length.

Sobering thought, that.

"I will admit that Australia is on my bucket list. Red sand and kangaroos and misty green mountains. My favorite show of all time took place in the Great Dividing Range."

"Which one is that?"

She told him. "It's based on a poem by Banjo Patterson."

Eventually he circled back to talking about being in the military. Stationed out of Fort Wainwright, his active duty took him into the Middle East and South Pacific. He saw a great many wonderous places; Penny felt by omission the many terrible sights he also witnessed. He would serve his country all over again if he was needed. But it took great effort to deal with the experiences, many of which he was not allowed to speak of. "Top secret" and the like.

She bittersweetly talked about gliding with her father. How she and her mother would go rock climbing some weekends with her sister. She talked about her and Lucy's first tattoos when they were sixteen—how her mother took them to the tattoo parlor.

"Really, I think mother just wanted another. That's when I got the dragon on my ankle."

"When did you get the others?" he asked.

"I dreamt about my father the night before his funeral. These enormous, beautiful, white wings embraced him. I couldn't get that image out of my head, so I had them inked before I left California. The little polar bear," she absentmindedly touched her arm, "down in Anchorage, before I moved to Utqiaġvik."

Noah asked to see them all again. Penny laughed. "No way in this cold."

"What? It is warm enough that you can't see your breath. Look." He breathed out slowly, the white fog giving away the lie. She giggled.

"You show me yours, then, tough guy," she said.

"Nope, not tonight." The wind whipped around them deep into the night as Noah shared his own adventure stories about rock climbing during high school. He enjoyed the open air and the sweet agony his muscles experienced. He and a buddy once spent the night in a hanging tent.

"Vertical camping, we called it. We would hang about two-thousand feet up the cliff face. But that wasn't the scariest part of that trip. The next morning, I reached up for a hand hold and grabbed onto a snake sunning itself along the ridge we climbed." Apparently, he really didn't like snakes. Just the memory gave him chills. "Good thing about this cold weather is the extreme lack of snakes."

"Do you still see your friend that you went camping with?" she asked, thinking he sounded like a fun guy. The silence stretched out until she peered over at Noah. "Hey, you okay?"

"Nick committed suicide after he got out of the army. We were planning a trip to discuss him re-enlisting. He was having trouble readjusting at home. But we never did make that camping trip."

"When life becomes the blackest, sometimes we only see the way out of this life. Where it may bring relief for the one in the darkness, it never makes it easier for those left behind. But like the tree that loses its leaves and stands barren and naked against the cold, eventually the warmth returns and with it renewed spirit." she said. "I'm so sorry, Noah. And I'm sorry for all that you have gone through."

The solemn words echoed in the quiet. The dogs' howling had subsided, and the rising, waxing moon quelled the auroral display.

He reached over and squeezed her hand, the bulk of their gloves unable to hold back the tingles that crept up her arm with his action.

"I'm sorry, too. But I would do it again if that path led me to you."

Mother

On Mischief Night, or the night before Halloween, Penny went out in the early afternoon, taking advantage of the mere six hours of daylight to run a small eight-dog team - not to create mischief of any kind but to get the most out of the shrinking daylight hours. During one leg of the venture, she turned into the wind, which forcefully whipped at her face causing her to halt the team to readjust her goggles and face mask. As the dogs pulled on their harnesses, Penny double-checked her ground spike holding the sled in place. The sudden increase in the frenzied chorus made her take notice, and her sweeping gaze caught on the polar bear digging in the snow along a grey rocky outcrop not far from where they had stopped. She was momentarily transfixed by the scene.

Thankfully, the wind was in the bear's favor, and it neither heard nor cared about their proximity. Penny pulled the reluctant dogs away and traveled swiftly in the opposite direction.

The next day, Penny convinced Noah to go for a short run down the coast on the snow bikes, secretly planning to go by the same spot. Noah was more than happy to indulge.

Although anxious to share her finding, she withheld until they stopped on a ridge downwind of the spot. They argued in hushed tones about getting closer before Noah acquiesced and followed Penny up the ridge on foot, pushing the bikes along the way. He checked his pack to make sure the bear spray was easily accessible. After parking the bikes, they crawled up to the top of the ridge. Both pulled out binoculars as Penny gestured in the general direction where she saw the bear yesterday.

Several minutes of quiet passed. The wind blew in their

faces while they scanned the vast shore that reached out for miles. Under the overcast sky and offshore fog, the land was a tumbled mix of shades of white and grey. Through her binoculars, Penny spotted the dig marks and the entrance hole, no more than a darker area on the leeward side of the exposed rock outcropping.

"There," she pointed.

He scanned the area for several minutes, the wind pulling any noise they made away. There was no activity to be observed. Penny scanned the entire area to make sure the big female was not sneaking up behind them for a snack.

They returned the short distance to the bikes and drove off, heading back into town. After cruising the streets, they finally pulled up to his aunt's restaurant, The FrostBite.

Noah followed Penny inside, the warm air enveloping them in a suffocating embrace. The cute waitress took their orders of hot chocolate and sweet rolls, barely taking her eyes off Noah. When she finally retreated, he asked Penny to explain the trip and her secrecy. As she did, she asked him if it could have been a denning mother.

The waitress, Kitty—per her nametag—placed cups in front of them.

"One for you and one for your sister."

Penny was confused. *We don't look alike, do we?*

No, she is trolling her line, hoping for a bite, Lucy thought.

Oh.

"Fortunately she's not my sister," Noah said and winked at Penny.

The waitress retreated.

He leaned back and pulled his hands through his hair, waves crashing back down around his face. He stretched and then asked why they had ridden out to look at a polar bear. Hadn't they tracked enough of them already for the year?

"I think it was a female, Noah. I checked, but she wasn't a chipped or collared bear. Do you think we can keep checking on her? Maybe set up a camera?" The prospect of witnessing the female and cubs emerge in early spring excited her, although how to time it eluded her. Once the snow began to accumulate and blow around, setting up a camera would be a challenge. Perhaps they could secure a camera to a metal post...

No Penny, Lucy thought to her. *Not a good idea to be around a polar bear momma and her babies.*

He puffed out his cheek in slight exasperation. Noah echoed Lucy's thought and continued, saying that because of the short days and stormy weather approaching, it would be unsafe to venture back. A severe storm was anticipated in the next several days, bringing with it the possibility of a record snowfall for this early in the season. He thought it best to make note of the location to avoid in the spring unless in an enclosed vehicle or in the air. Ever the voice of reason.

"Look. I mean it. Be safe." Noah tapped her fingers. "Don't do anything stupid like go looking for a polar bear on your own."

Penny nodded. *Of course, I'll be safe. I'll take you with me.* "Any more word on the women's killer?" she asked.

Noah frowned as he shook his head. "Nothing. Army said they are looking into missing women reports from surrounding communities and have contacted the FBI. No leads yet. What about your visions? Anything new?"

"No."

"Meditation still not helping?"

Penny cringed. She had tried meditation since the night Army gave her pointers. Some. A bit. She sighed. "No, I'm not having great luck with it. Usually find myself waking up an hour or two later without any new visions."

A vicious blizzard it turned out to be. The snow came down in great sheets, encasing the tundra in white. Army ran a rope line from the dog shed to each house to make sure chores could be safely done. Penny never imagined such a loss of sight and hearing that the blinding snow and howling winds brought. She coordinated with Noah to visit the dog shed together and messaged Eelyn prior to their departures. And upon arriving safely in their homes, Penny and Noah notified each other through messages.

On the second morning of the blizzard, Eelyn walked out of her bedroom to find Penny typing away on a report.

"What is this horrid music?" Eelyn asked, her face twisted in a grimace.

"You don't like it?"

Eelyn cocked her head as if trying to determine from whence it came and to where she should run. "Are we preparing for a sacrifice to the ancient gods?"

"No. Not today at least."

"Then I don't think I'll make it a preset music selection." Eelyn shook her head as she poured a cup of coffee. She turned and leaned against the counter, blowing the steam from her cup.

"Are you happy we moved here, mother?" Penny asked. The ritual-like drumbeats and throaty warbling ended, and a haunting folk song took its place.

Eelyn's eyes were focused on some distant memory for a moment before shifting and turning to her daughter. "Happy? Now that I've been hooked by archaic folk music, I'm ecstatic."

"Gah," Penny said and turned her music off. "Seriously."

"Seriously. I think I might like this band. I mean, it matches the desolate, starving environment we live in, yeah right? Although it seems like it would be more fitting in a different cold land with active volcanoes and great sheets of slowly moving ice and Scandinavian longboats." At the look on Penny's face, Eelyn relented. She sat down at the table across from Penny and pulled her fuzzy robe tight. "I am glad we came. Two years isn't that long, really. While winter will be tougher than back in Anchorage, I think we will manage."

Penny nodded. "But are you glad you tagged along?"

"Yes. I'm grateful for the experience and to be with my family. Someday I'll be an empty nester while you go off on some grand adventure." Eelyn had reached across the table and laid her hands upon Penny's.

"Some days I catch myself thinking of father. And it catches me up, how long it might have been since the last time I thought of him."

"He would have enjoyed being here too, right?" Eelyn rubbed Penny's hand before leaning back in her chair. "That you think of him less doesn't mean you think lesser of him. He is always here," she patted her chest, "and here," she tapped her temple. "We have awesome memories to draw from."

Wounds heal with time, but scars - visible or not - remind us of the journey, chimed her sister.

"How about you, dear? Do you like it here?"

"Very much."

Her mother shot her a wry smile, her eyes twinkling. "It's the scenery, isn't it?"

Before Penny could reply, Eelyn continued. "The flat expanses rippling with bogs and streams during the summer. The snow and ice of the winter." Oh, so she hadn't meant Noah. "The brawny men. I mean, Noah is—"

"A little young for you, mother," Penny interjected.

A snort was her reply. "But not for you, dear."

The heat rose in Penny's neck, a blush she was unable to prevent.

"Anyway, as much as I love it here, I need a break. At least, that is what your aunt figures. She booked me a flight down to Vegas. I will be staying with her for a week to help her move her things to Pasadena. She's going to rent our old house."

"Cool. I remember you mentioning that earlier. When are you leaving?"

"Well, depending on the storm, this Friday. Bianca bought a ticket this morning."

The announcement took Penny aback.

"So soon?"

"You know your aunt…" Eelyn said, an eyebrow raised high.

Penny did know her aunt. Aunt Bianca was loyal to a fault and unquestionably credulous when it came to men. She was coming off her fourth marriage. Penny's latest guitar, the Laguna, had been a gift from Aunt B and her recent ex-husband, a guitarist in a Vegas band. A very wealthy guitarist who insisted Aunt B not work and just follow him around like a puppy. When that became too difficult for her to do, he moved on to a new puppy, or rather, woman. Aunt B acquired one heck of a lawyer and half of everything he owned was now hers with an additional monthly alimony. She quickly liquidated the material items, and along with alimony from her third husband, was retiring to Pasadena it seemed for however long it was until the next boyfriend.

"No worries. We will be fine without you for a few days. Besides, you need a break. Go get refreshed before you must help keep us sane for two months without the sun."

"I am a bit nervous about leaving you, with the murdered girls and such."

"I am very capable of taking care of myself. We have Blue and Edgar, who are both excellent guard animals." Edgar puffed up with her mention of him. "Besides, Noah and Army are next door."

"I could ask Sam to stop by, too," Eelyn offered.

"Why? Army and Noah are next door. I'm sure Noah will be here visiting every day when you are gone." Penny attempted a joke, but they both knew he would be over every day. "I would rather Sam not stop over. I don't know him very well."

"Don't look at me like that, neither do I. He and Rose are still dating, I think."

She got up and hugged her mother. "We will miss you. And don't worry. I will be perfectly safe."

Cub

Penny had a vision, late the night before Eelyn was to fly out. As her mind wandered amidst the depths of a deep sleep, her translucent self detached from her sleeping body and floated in the air. She lifted her hands in front of her face, able to see the land through her fingers. In the cold, she failed at warming her hands with her breath. Gleaming in the half-light of twilight, she soared miles over the grey terrain. As she neared the place where she spied the female bear, the area was illuminated by a blazing sun. She floated in the air above, a ghost above the white landscape.

The scene below stirred into motion as she turned her gaze downward. A polar bear pounced down heavily onto an incline in the snow. It pawed and dug at the snow for several long moments. Then, shoving its head into the hole, it began wrenching and walking backwards. It pulled out another bear by the neck. A female. The new bear appeared sluggish and did not react as Penny expected a defending mother bear should. The aggressive bear proceeded to attack the female, ripping at her. He pulled her further away from the den. Claws raked bright red channels across her body. He shook her neck in his maw and set his weight onto her shoulders. With several rough side-to-side pulls, he tore her head from her body.

Penny's scream was silent, and she felt her translucent self flying backwards, away from the scene to settle back into her existent body. She awoke sweating and sat up on her elbows. She looked around, unsure of where she was and her dream. Unease penetrated her consciousness. Blue whined and nuzzled her hand. She absently petted him behind the ear.

Penny, you okay? It was just a nightmare, Lucy thought to

her.

Yeah, a nightmare...or perhaps... Her thoughts trailed off, and she shuddered as she recalled other visions. *I hope it was just a nightmare and nothing more.*

Like Noah said, the Inuit believe in astral projection among their shaman. You could have been drifting over an event taking place-

Penny cut her off. *I am not Inuit and am certainly no shaman, Lu. Ah, it's alright, just a dream, a night fantasy that was scary in its brutality. I saw that female several days ago, and my mind was over-thinking things. Too many papers read, not enough sleep lately. Go back to sleep, Lu. I will be fine.* It was also possible that it was another premonition, which made her more anxious over the female bear.

She guiltily recalled telling Noah she would continue to try meditation. Ask Army for more help. But they had had no further discussions, so perhaps he forgot as well.

Okay, Lucy thought skeptically. *Night, Penny. Love you.*

Love you too, Lu.

It took Penny a long time to fall back asleep. She invited Blue up into her bed but only for a short time. She snuggled up to his large frame that he wedged between her and the wall. His warmth and steady breathing were a soothing balm to her raw soul. He reacted to the increase in heat and stretched out. As he did, his legs pushed against the wall, and his back pushed against her body, thrusting her out of bed. He was subsequently encouraged to return to his dog bed on the floor.

When Penny awoke the next morning, the unsettled notion still stayed heavy within her. It held on through the still, early morning hours as she dropped her mother off at the airport.

Eelyn, however, was very excited, and while normally her happy attitude was infectious, Penny found herself faking her smiles. She hated to see her mother leave, even if only for a few days. The way they behaved today, Penny wondered if she was acting more like the mother and her mother acting more like the parting daughter.

"Goodbye, sweetheart. Be good. Be safe! Have fun!" her

144

mother told her as they hugged.

"Same to you, mother. I love you."

"My love for you expands beyond the farthest universe, to Neverland…"

"Okay, enough, goofball." Penny kissed her mother on the cheek and stepped back.

As they regarded each other, neither wiped at their tears until they turned away from each other. Penny left the airport before her mother's plane took off to fly south to warmth, palm trees, and sandal weather. And millions of other people. Penny shuddered at the thought of all those people surrounding her. She did not miss the claustrophobia of big city life.

As her thoughts turned to life in Utqiaġvik, the vision from last night flashed. The unsteadiness returned and with it, nausea and vertigo. She needed something to ground her. Lucy was silent this morning.

She called Noah.

Hours later, after lunch, Noah and Penny left town, each running their own team. Sympathetic to her bumming about her mother's trip, Noah suggested the outing, one last run before the next storm. There would not be too many more days of daylight dog sledding in their future with the onset of the endless night. He had also consented to venturing near the site where she had seen the digging bear.

As they set out, she found herself guiding her team toward the location of the polar bear den. Noah attempted to call her off her path, but she was deaf to his calls and her faster team pulled away from his. His slower team followed.

They stopped further out and staked the teams. She insisted they crawl up a ridge overlooking the area. Noah shot her a questioning look but followed without comment. The snow drifts had transformed the landscape, hiding the supposed opening to the den. As they looked, a polar bear wandered into their view.

"It's not the same one I saw before. This is a male. No scars," Penny spoke into the mic she earlier attached to the inside of her hood—her direct line to the earpiece Noah wore. "Has to be. Check out the urine staining."

"A young one, too, by my guess.," responded Noah. "Look at the absence of a very shaggy coat around his legs."

"Noah, is that blood on his face?"

"Not just his face. What was he feasting on this far inland?" Noah asked. Penny felt her blood draining from her face as she focused on the bear. *No, please no. It was only a dream.*

The bear pushed its face into the snow and dropped its body, rolling around. After his snow bath was complete, he stood up and shook off the excess. Blood still covered the front of his body. The bear wandered off behind the den and east toward the coastline. Noah followed until the bear could not be visualized in his binoculars.

"He's leaving, Noah. Let's go check it out."

"What?! No way, Penny. It's too dangerous. He could come back."

With a heavy heart, she responded. "Not likely, he ate, he's full, he's going to sleep for a while. Other bears or scavengers may come, though. Both our teams should be enough to keep them away and help us make a quick getaway if needed. Come on. Let's hurry."

"Did you see this happen? Is that why we came out here?" he asked.

She inhaled fear, exhaled resolve. "Yes."

"Will it be safe to go out there?" he asked.

"I think so. I only envisioned the female's death. Which, by the looks of it, already happened."

Noah sighed and climbed back onto his sled. They urged their teams forward.

He wants to see what happened, too.

As the sleds capped the final drift blocking their full view, both were stunned by the violent scene. A bear, the presumed female bear Penny originally had seen, drug a hundred yards from her den. Her head and a front leg ripped from her body, and her belly ripped open.

Penny and Noah anchored their teams and walked shoulder to shoulder toward the carcass.

"What a waste," he said with a disgusted look on his face.

"Why on earth would this happen? He didn't look to be starving. Do you think it was a territorial thing?" Penny asked. *Looks like some of those papers mother read were accurate. Polar bear cannibalism.*

"I don't know. I can't tell for certain by just looking, but it doesn't appear that he ate much, he mostly killed and dismembered."

Noah approached the carcass and inspected it thoughtfully.

"I think I will try to skin her." He regarded Penny gauging her response. "Army could tan the hide, and we could use it for warm clothes or a blanket. The storm coming tonight will most likely cover this up as well as our tracks," Noah said.

Penny agreed.

With his sled positioned closer to the bear, Noah tied a couple of ropes to the handle and attached them to two chains from his packs. He began cutting the hide away, secured it with the chains, tightening the rope to hold the hide tight. He then removed his outer coat and changed gloves. As he continued skinning, he asked Penny to keep a look out.

She took her dog sled in the direction the male ventured, up and behind the den. They would be downwind of anything approaching from this direction and it provided a vantage point to see off in the other directions.

Penny staked the dogs and scrutinized the collapsed den. The snow was pushed up from the attack, but it appeared that only the opening was collapsed. Dark red blood discolored the area around her. She refused to think of what crafty hunters polar bears could be or that he could come up downwind of them at any time. The dogs would never smell him in the wind.

Noah called out that the bear showed signs of nursing. That made Penny even sadder than before. She contemplated the fate of the offspring.

Surely nothing could survive that, she thought, as she considered the collapsed den.

Without a second thought, she double-checked her sled's anchor and scanned the area one last time to make sure there was no sign of any approaching danger. She took a deep breath of fresh, frigid air and slowly exhaled, willing her fear to leave her to face only the wind and what lay before her in the den.

Once at the den, she began digging by hand down into what she assumed was the main chamber. The wind blew loose snow in her face, her goggles protecting her eyes. Within a short time, she reached the floor of the den where a fishy odor assaulted her nostrils. With the wind cut off in the den, she noted there was still a great deal of warmth left inside. The size of the den was quite large and held up relatively well from the assault.

She pulled at the large chunks of snow-ice and pushed them away until she discovered what she thought was a smaller room off the main chamber. The walls to this area were intact, but the entrance was too small for her to enter. She pulled herself out of the den and scanned the area, checking on the surroundings, the sled, and Noah.

She was surprised she missed the absence of the wind down below, although the cold was still creeping into her bones. She pulled her fingers down into fists inside her mittens, attempting to warm them.

Satisfied the coast was clear and her hands had warmed a bit, she dropped back down. Turning her head lamp on, she swept the new-found chamber. Her goggles began fogging up, and she removed them to see better. The walls remained intact, perhaps sheltered by the rocks. She reached in blindly, her fingertips painfully pulsing and preventing her from really feeling anything. She pulled back and removed the mitten from her right hand and reached back in. This time, she could feel a warm, smooth body encased.

Yes, there is movement.

She pulled back out and replaced her mitten. Using a pick from her pocket, she began chipping a larger entrance. Once satisfied, she reached back in with both hands and gently extricated two very small cubs. Her headlamp illuminated the small bodies. Less than a foot in length and weighing about a pound, each was covered by a fine coat of translucent fur

148

over pink skin. She removed her mittens again and handled each cub, as she held her breath, looking for movement that would signal life. The rise and fall of a chest. The thrum of a heartbeat in the thin chest. She slowly let her lungful out as she saw movement from one cub. The second was cold to the touch and beginning to stiffen.

As she reached for the other cub in her lap, it stirred and made pitifully weak noises, responding most likely to the change in comfort. Her fingers touched the little cub's body, nudging it, to which it responded with a weak wriggling. She opened her coat and found a pocket inside her warm coveralls loose enough to hold the cub snug against her. The cub nuzzled its head weakly into the bulk of her coat, which hid the slight bulge well enough against her almost nonexistent chest.

Hold on, buddy.

With one last look at the dead cub, she doused her headlamp and turned back to reality. Pulling her goggles back over her eyes, she worked her way back into the blinding whiteness.

Once her eyes adjusted, she checked her sled team, scanned the area and checked on Noah's progress. The coast was clear, and the dogs relaxed. She was surprised to see Noah was already cleaning up.

"I knew you'd go looking for cubs," he said. "There any live ones?"

"I found a dead one," Penny said. Her heart heavy with her half-truth.

Noah nodded. "Not unexpected, I guess. Not sure what we would do with a live one anyway."

Toast

As they sledded back to town, the cub occasionally wriggled inside her pocket. A crowd of thoughts milled around her brain, bumping into and jostling one another.

When did the cub last feed? Did it feed at all? Did it get chilled? Of course it got chilled. How long had it been chilled? Hold on, buddy.

It was Penny's fear that the cub, fallen still for the last mile of the journey, had plausibly died, but she didn't want to risk checking and alerting Noah that something was up. Really, the bear cub had a poor prognosis for life.

Breaking down the teams, Noah and Penny worked quietly and quickly cleaning ice out of the dogs' feet, filling water bowls, unpacking sleds. Noah stashed the hide into one of the empty bins, locking it to keep out unwanted attention.

Upon exiting the barn, Penny noticed a different truck parked in the driveway. Dolores was visiting.

While Tiki, who Dolores was babysitting, ran amuck around the house, Army asked them how the run went. Noah glanced at Penny first and then to Army. "There is something we need to discuss with you. But later. I smell pie, so that should come first." Noah walked over to the kitchen table.

"It's peach, your favorite, Noah," Dolores said, handing him a slice half the size of the pie pan. "You want some, Penny?"

She declined, citing a headache and rough stomach. She caught Noah's worried glance out of the corner of her eye before bidding them goodbye and heading back to the door. Tiki ran over to her and grabbed her leg, shrieking with excitement. She threw her bottle at the door, held both hands up in the air and cried, "up!"

She wanted to hold the toddler, but that action might very well snuff the life out of the small white thing hidden in her jacket. While she hesitated, Noah walked over and scooped Tiki up in his arms. "Up, up! You want to go up?"

Tiki giggled as Noah swung her up in the air. As the focus turned to Noah and Tiki, Penny squatted down to check the laces on her boot. She scooped up the bottle that laid on the floor beside her boot and slid it her jacket pocket. Throwing a half-hearted wave in their direction, she withdrew.

On the way back to her house, Penny almost tripped over Blue, who tuned into her urgency and bounced around as if encouraging her. The cub remained still. Penny ran into the house, partially unzipping her jacket to get a quick look at the cub. She couldn't sense its mental presence, but the chest rose and fell with slight breath.

Up on his perch, Edgar ruffled his feathers, puffing up like a ball of feathers and began walking the length of his perch, bobbing his head. His curiosity and excitement over the cub streamed into Penny's consciousness, and she collected her thoughts for a moment to calm the rambunctious dog and energizing bird.

When her efforts took effect, Blue lay down on the kitchen floor, and Edgar glided down to rest next to the dog. Blue nuzzled the bird and refocused his attention on Penny. Meanwhile, Edgar climbed up between Blue's front legs and nestled in. Continuing her undertaking, Penny grabbed a couple of towels and threw them on the couch. She collected a heating pad from the storage closet and plugged it in. Rushing into her room, she unceremoniously dumped the contents of a wood storage crate onto her bed and put it with the other supplies. She then laid the heating pad on the bottom of the crate, layered the towels over it, and placed the cub within the folds.

Penny, what are you doing with that?

Trying to see if I can save it. Do me a favor, Lu, and help me look up what I need to feed a polar bear cub. There should be something online.

Penny removed her outer clothing and joined Lucy in the

search for information. Penny was the first to find an instruction manual on the feeding and care of polar bears in captivity.

Newborn polar bear formula:
Esbilac powder
Pediatric vitamins
Heavy cream
Lactase
Cod liver oil
Boiled water

Penny began looking through cupboards as Lucy repeated the ingredients and measurements mentally. There was the carton of cream in the fridge—so much for the planned creamed peas and potatoes for supper. The medicine cabinet held a bottle of cod liver oil pills. Eelyn stored cans of Esbilac, a puppy milk replacer, beneath the kitchen sink.

Well, mother is a vet.

Penny mixed as Lucy recited the recipe and heated up water as she searched for the missing lactase ingredient. Luckily, their mother developed lactose intolerance over the past year. Once their home-concocted formula was complete, she poured thirty milligrams of the solution into the stolen bottle and blew on the top to cool it down.

Do I even ask where you got a baby bottle? Lucy thought.

You can, but I won't tell you I stole it from a toddler, that's for sure.

Won't it run too fast for the newborn?

Don't think so. Rose and Dolores mentioned going back to a newborn nipple. They hoped the slow flow would make Tiki want to take to a cup.

With Lucy monitoring her actions mentally, Penny lifted the cub out of the crate and laid it back in her lap. She gently held its belly to keep it in position. While presenting the nipple, she smeared some of the formula against the cub's mouth. It made weak sucking and whimpering noises and rooted around the towel.

"Come on baby, take the nipple."

If it does, it probably won't like the fake bear milk.

152

"No, it is so hungry that it will gladly eat it. Won't you, baby? There you go, latch on. There's a good baby bear."

Stop with the baby-talk already, Penny! Seriously, not cool.

"Look at it, Lu. Look how tiny it is. It must be about a foot long. No more than a couple of pounds. And soft. And it is eating. Look at it, Lu."

It looks like a giant baby rat.

"Shush." Penny helped her mother feed many an infant dog or cat and the occasional foal. Although she enjoyed these times, something felt different with this baby.

They stayed quiet while the cub finished the bottle. It sneezed and rooted around for more.

"No more for you right now, little one." Penny walked over to the kitchen sink and wet a washcloth to wash the cub's face and body. She finished with a massage of its belly to express its bladder.

Well, that looks like it may be a boy. She noted that the urine streamed out more between the hind legs than back near the tail.

Penny, it says you should use baby oil to rub it down daily.

We will worry about that later, Lu. Let's see if it, he, makes it through tonight, first.

It says here that their diet when older will consist of dog chow. Lucy laughed. *You don't even feed dog chow.*

Blue looked at Penny and yipped, cocking his head in an expression to match his thoughts. Penny did give him dog chow but only as treats. A full bag of dog food for a growing dog his size was a bit cost prohibitive.

Penny held the cub for a few minutes longer before placing him back in the crate. A quick check of the temperature revealed the crate was 87°F.

Darn near perfect if I recall the information correctly. Penny adjusted it a bit lower just to be safe. She quickly showered and changed, readying herself for the long night ahead of her.

You do know having that cub is illegal, right? Like a federal offense. That train of thought broke off with the ring of Penny's phone.

It was Noah calling to see if Penny needed anything before the storm started up. The snow started falling, but it was still light enough. Penny considered her meager supplies that she needed to last through the night, if not several days.

"Uh, Noah. Yes, I guess I could use a few things if you are going to the store. Lactaid...baby vitamins - in liquid...yes, those are for Blue...and baby oil. I'm out of baby oil. And, ah, peanut butter. And bread. For toast."

Bread for toast? Lucy giggled. *Can you make me some toast, Pen?*

An hour later, after Lucy succumbed to sleep, Noah knocked and brought in a few small bags for Penny. She greeted him at the door and took the bags from him all the while attempting to act normal. This, of course, meant that she acted very much abnormally. When he told her what she owed him, she hurriedly retrieved money.

"Are you anxious for me to leave, Penny?" Noah said as she shoved the dollars and coins into his gloved hand, dropping some in the process.

"What? No. Why? Did you want to stay for a minute?" She looked at him, biting her bottom lip and raising her eyebrows.

Doe eyes, Lucy thought. *Too innocent of a look to not be guilty.*

So, you are not asleep, huh? Come out and give me some help.

No, I think I will pass, thanks.

"Sure, if that is okay," Noah said.

"Uh, okay." Penny then turned to unload the sacks of groceries. She noticed a bar of her favorite chocolate candy.

That was nice. Unexpected.

Noah appeared next to her with his coat off. A warmth that had nothing to do with the furnace spread over her.

They talked about the groceries a bit; Noah curious about her lactose intolerance. Penny tried to briefly explain that it was for her mother, that she wanted to be prepared for her return. She was sure that Noah could tell something was up, but he didn't challenge her. Finally, he pulled up a chair at the table and sat down.

"She was fine all her life, and then suddenly agonizing gas and severe diarrhea every time she drank milk or ate ice cream," she said.

Please shut up now...

Noah laughed as Blue sidled up beside him vying for his attention. He leaned down to pet the growing dog.

"I know something about that. Army is dealing with eating too much pie as we speak. He is gluten intolerant, apparently. Or just ate one pie too many. He is confined in his room for the evening. You want to play cards or something?"

"Uh, sure. Maybe a game or two." Penny was unsure why Noah was asking to stick around. Unless they were stuck in a tent together trying not to freeze, he normally spoke little. Which was fine with Penny. She wasn't good with minor chatter. Tonight, though, he was talkative. He chatted away without requiring Penny to respond to most comments. He suggested a card game. Penny quickly became aware of how competitive he was and felt a small amount of shame after he won every hand.

Unbelievable. Completely wrong, Penny. How could you let him win? thought Lucy.

Oh, you are up and capable of helping me out. Come out and join us, pleaded Penny.

No, you are on your own on this one. He suspects you of hiding something.

Penny began shuffling the cards for the next hand, but then stopped and set them on the table. She crossed her arms and leaned back. "Noah, what's up? Why are you here so late?"

"So late? It's only 8 p.m. Is it past your bedtime?" He raised one eyebrow and displayed a lopsided, heart-skipping grin.

"No, of course not. But you're acting weird."

He stood up and ran his hands through his hair, walking around the room.

"I'm acting weird? Me?" He huffed. "You are. After seeing that bear, you hurried back, rushed through checking

155

the team, unpacking. You refused to pick-up Tiki. Wouldn't eat any pie. That is not like *you*, Penny." He sighed, turned around and sat back down. He leaned into the tabletop. "Did the sight of...what happened...did that bother you?"

She gazed back at him finally understanding. "You are wondering if I am alright."

They sat in silence for a brief few minutes, their gazes connected. The resumed onslaught of wind against the house suppressed even the sound of their breathing. A warmth spread through her.

"Well, thank you. I guess I am. I mean, seeing what animals can do...it isn't far from what humans are capable of. It wasn't the scarred bear, either. I checked. But I don't think we can say for sure if it isn't the same one that, ah, interfered with the deceased women's bodies."

Noah leaned back. "I was worried. Thought I could listen, talk, whatever." He shrugged and absently reached down to stroke Blue, who continued to stick close to him.

"Noah, are you taking it okay?" she asked.

"Not really. The brutality of such an attack is abnormal but not unheard of." Penny recalled several papers she read in college on the subject while Noah continued. "The desire to survive, to find nourishment, drives all. Survival of the fittest. In utero cannibalism in sand tiger shark pups. Bearded vultures and northern goshawks eating nest mates. Male fish consuming eggs. Mothers may even eat their young due to scarce resources. Whether it was for competition, nourishment or some other madness does not change the fact that it occurred. Or that we saw it. I just wanted to make sure that you were okay, especially with your mother away. If you wanted to talk about it, I just wanted you to know that I am here for you."

"Thank you." Penny was touched he thought of her. "I guess I was trying to focus on the fact that the bears are animals, and I trust that animals will behave as they do, for whatever reasons they do." She looked down and away. "It seems easier to understand animals' basic needs and drivers than to try to understand man's madness."

The weight of murders in the small community pulled at her. The missing women that turned up mauled by bears but not killed by them. How brutal life could be.

Just then, the cub began whimpering. It made enough rustling and grunting to be audible over the brief lull in the wind.

"Penny, what's that noise?" Noah asked, tilting his head searching for the source of the noise. "Do you have mice?"

"Hmm? I don't hear anything. No, no mice. Probably the wind. You know, I am exhausted. Maybe it is better if you head home. Call me when you get there, so I know you made it safely." She repeated their joking mantra to call when they got home safely. He lived a little over two-hundred yards away. She rose as he did but headed in the direction of his coat, while he and Blue headed toward the rustling sound.

"Are you hiding something from me?" he asked quietly, his brow creased.

You should tell him. The cub will climb out of the bag, eventually, Lucy pointed out.

Penny took a deep breath and let it out slowly. "Look Noah, please don't be upset with me..." She trailed off as she walked past him to the crate. She lifted the blanket covering the crate and withdrew the cub, holding him close to her chest. "I just couldn't leave him to die."

Noah walked over to Penny, focused on the cub in her hands. She brought it up closer to her neck as it pushed his nose into her. She stroked the sparse, soft fur.

"I know he won't likely make it, but I just wanted to give him a chance."

Noah caught her eye. His eyes sparked with excitement, a small smile upon his lips. But then he frowned. "What do you think will happen if he does survive? A polar bear does not make for a good pet, Penny. Cubs stay with their mothers for at least two years before going off on their own. How the hell do you think we can keep a bear that long?" His surprising use of "we" was not lost on Penny.

"I was just thinking about the next few days. When I found him, I couldn't just leave. I wanted to give him a chance."

"But should you? That is the question I want to know. Should you try to raise it? Should you try to raise something that could kill you?"

"Noah, what I do know is that right now this tiny creature needs something that I can provide. And he may or may not survive. And if he does, I will do what I can to help him. That's as far as I am willing to take this discussion right now."

Penny walked over to the kitchen and began preparing the concoction the cub would drink. She heard Noah move up behind her. She stiffened.

"Here, give him to me. It will free your hands up to make his meal."

She turned to him, hesitant. "Thank you, Noah."

He shook his head, but awe and excitement replaced the anger or fear on his face. Noah smiled down at the cub before winking at Penny.

"I guess I see why you stole him."

"Pft," was her response.

Noah held the tiny cub gently against his chest, murmuring to himself or the cub, Penny was not sure. Once finished, she walked over and sat down with the towels in her lap. She nodded to Noah, who passed her the cub. He watched her as she fed the cub, who struggled to latch on. The cub kneaded her knees with his paws. He sneezed several times, losing his grip on the bottle. Hiccups assaulted him, and he refused the last half of his bottle.

She took the bottle over by the sink and set it on the counter. Under Noah's watchful gaze, she wet a rag and began washing the cub, saying, "A clean hair coat makes for the best insulation."

When she finished, she placed the cub back into the crate, and returned to the discarded bottle to begin the clean-up. Noah leaned back against the counter as she stood at the sink.

"Funny. That bottle looks just like the one Tiki and my aunt searched the whole house for before they left tonight."

"Huh, imagine that. I hope that they have more. Although

may I say she doesn't need one?"

A chuckle emanated from Noah as he helped Penny dry the dishes and wiped the counter, their actions shrouded in a comfortable silence.

"It will need to be fed every two to three hours for several months, you know..." Noah laid the towel on the counter.

"Ummm."

"One person cannot keep that up for very long, not a schedule like that." He leaned back against the sink.

Penny nodded. She wrapped her arms tightly around herself and stood gazing off into the distance.

Noah sighed and looked down, thoughts playing in tandem across his face.

He lifted his head to meet her gaze. "Look. I can help, Penny. I obviously have the time. For the record, I don't think this is a good idea. I don't know what good will come of it or how much trouble we can get in. But I don't think taking it out back and killing it is an option." He paused, then added, "Let's begin a new adventure."

Penny's smile blazed, her eyes wet. She could only nod at his words. When she knew her emotions were once again contained, she said, "But he is mine. Nothing happens to him without my say."

Noah nodded. "Fine with me, Momma Bear." The nickname came out smoothly. Penny pretended nothing was out of the ordinary with such a nickname. He smiled.

"I will send you the files on the care of captive bears I found," Penny said

"Why don't you let me look at those now? It looks like the cub is out for a while." Noah lifted a curtain and peered out into the darkness. "And by the disappearance of the yard light, I think it best to stay out of the storm for a bit. We should get a game plan together." He let the curtain fall back into place across the window as he turned back to her.

Noah read through several of the manuals, then they watched videos of hand-raised bear cubs at different zoos. She took more handwritten notes as they did so, realizing too late she might look like an obsessive nerd.

159

"You know, if it survives, it shouldn't be released back into the wild. Not just because the information says it, but because I know we can't teach it to be a polar bear," Noah said, scratching his beard.

"I don't think we should try to predict what opportunities will present by the time he needs to be weaned."

"You keep calling it a he. Are you sure it is?"

She nodded. "Yes. I am pretty sure, anyway."

Noah scratched at his cheek again.

"You need something to treat that?" she joked.

His brow furrowed as his gaze met hers. "What?"

"You keep scratching. Lice?" She feigned horror, placing a hand over her heart. "You shouldn't be handling the wee one until that has cleared up!"

"Funny. My skin is just dry."

"I suppose you can't just put lotion on…that," she made a vague circular gesture at face level.

He sniffed, and a smile peeked out behind the lengthy whiskers. "Not really."

"Essential oils?" she offered. "Or a shave?"

He pretended to be horrorstruck at that. "And let my face be naked?" he said.

"One you could lotion," she said, releasing a chuckle.

Several episodes into a new series of Viking drama later, the cub's whimpering alerted the pair, both having relaxed on their respective sides of the couch.

Once again, a gentle nudge in her mind notified her that the cub woke well before the cub's rooting around became audible. She held off reacting until the cub was well awake. She noted the time and recorded it in her notebook, then picked the cub up and placed him into Noah's extended arms. Since he had asked earlier, Penny rolled the wriggling cub onto his back to show Noah why she thought the cub was a he.

Noah insisted on feeding the cub. She hovered about, critiquing his actions with the guinea pig-sized baby until he finished. Without killing the cub.

He laid the cub back inside the crate and then patted Penny

160

on the back. He asked if he passed and if he could feed the cub again without supervision. She apologized as she wrung her hands.

Half an hour later, they penciled out a tentative schedule for feeding. Noah would take over midnight to 6:00 a.m. while Penny took the rest of the day. She could work easily on the research project in between feedings, playing her guitar, and exercising. She would get a full night off every Friday and he every Saturday. They argued about this until they both conceded - it was too soon to tell how the cub would fare. Penny secretly hoped her mother would help some so Penny could continue assisting with self-defense class and wrestling.

Nightmares from the Past

Penny awoke, unsure where she was. The clock read 4:00 a.m. It had been an hour since the last feeding. She performed a quick mental check on the cub; he slumbered peacefully. Penny crawled out of bed and tiptoed into the other room. Noah tossed on the couch, moaning loudly. Edgar cawed softly, anxious about Noah's behavior.

Penny reached over the back of the couch to gently shake him awake. Noah shot up to his knees growling and grabbed Penny around her throat, squeezing down hard. His eyes were blank, void of any emotion. Penny instinctively placed her left hand over his mouth, using the flat of her pinky to push his nose up. With her right arm, she reached in between his arms and grabbed the inside of his armpit, squeezing on the pressure point. She succeeded in breaking his hold, but, off balance, Noah fell forward over the back of the couch and landed on top of her. Recovering quickly, he pulled himself up on his hands and knees as she struggled beneath him.

Blue snarled and lunged at Noah, but Penny called him off, worried for both their safety.

"You're not getting away," he mumbled, his voice harsh.

Although she couldn't lift her hands, she could slide them across the floor, so she circled her right hand toward his left hip. She bridged her hips to the right to throw him off balance. He fell forward and rolled onto his back. She quickly pushed herself up, straddled his chest and slapped him full in the face.

The blank look slowly lifted from his eyes as he blinked. In her relief, she slid off him and sat to the side, hugging her knees to her chest. He stayed on the floor, rubbing his face with his hands. When he finally peered at her, he saw her

162

rubbing her neck gingerly. Blue barked a warning at him, which made Noah wince.

"Are you okay?" he asked.

Penny, are you alright? came her sister's quiet thought.

She nodded, not meeting his gaze.

"Did I hurt you?"

She flinched as he sat up and reached for her, tears suddenly spilling over her cheeks. He scooted away, his back settling against the wall across from Edgar, and pulled his legs up against his chest, mirroring Penny. His large, blue and green eyes were wide and glistened in the light of the kitchen nightlight.

"Why did you do that? Some sick and twisted idea of practice?" she asked. The attempt at humor failed miserably.

He pressed his thumbs into the bridge of his nose.

"Do you usually have such active dreams?" she asked but suspected she already knew the answer.

"Yes," he whispered. "I attacked a nurse when I was hospitalized for my shoulder. And Army a couple of times."

"And you are asleep when it happens? You don't remember doing anything?"

He shook his head.

"And we go out overnight camping together?" she voiced her now most immediate concern, "knowing this happens?"

"They have been better," he said as he tilted his head back against the wall. "Only a few in the past year and a half. I was worried my reaction to the guys on the boat was one, but I was fully conscious and aware of what I was doing. I don't believe I would have reacted any differently had I been awake and walked up to them shooting narwhals."

The silence hung heavy between them.

"I have Post-Traumatic Stress Disorder from my military service." He rubbed his shoulder. "I was shot during, well. I can't really say. There were skirmishes with hostiles. Anyway. I've tried different sleeping medications, antidepressants, antipsychotics. Everything made me...numb. I became a zombie. I didn't want to relive the pain and grief, but I also didn't want to be trapped by a drug-induced freeze.

I didn't want to resort to alcohol or other drugs. Army offered a place for me here to help him out. My counselor has me trying behavioral therapy, sleeping medicines only when absolutely necessary." He paused with a shuddering breath. "There are many times when I think that I will spend my life with Army. Or alone, because how could I put someone else through that?"

Penny arose and walked over to him. She slid down the wall to sit next to him. The sound of Edgar ruffling his feathers drifted to their ears in the quiet. Blue dropped down next to Penny and laid his head on her leg.

"I started having nightmares and panic attacks months after the death of my father...and the school massacre. I would be sitting in a college lecture and sweat would start to roll off me, soaking my shirt. The doctors and counselors prescribed meds that messed me up. It didn't help to talk. I couldn't find the words. So, a counselor suggested writing. My sister wrote because she liked making up stories, but she also used it to cope. I tried it. It helped me separate reality from fiction. A year went by before the attacks and nightmares became less frequent." She ran her hands through her hair pulling it back from her face. She winced from the pain in her neck. "I guess you never completely get over it," she huffed. "There is too much joy in life to fall into despair. The days I allowed myself to stay away from activities like playing guitar or exercise...even the fighting in Krav Maga...were the worst. The days I made myself get up and live...those were the days that saved my life. But an awesome support system helps." She reached over and grabbed his hand, giving it a slight squeeze.

"My counselor has encouraged me to write down my experiences and nightmares. My feelings." He snorted. "I am not good at talking or writing about my feelings."

"If nothing else is working, what could it hurt, hmmm? They would be just for you, not for anyone else to read or look through. Mine are too raw and too intimate for me to read through, but they are to help me and me alone. You could try to draw pictures of your feelings. You know, doodle. No, don't laugh. Doodling is a form of expression. I could show you some of my doodles, if you wanted."

Noah looked at her out of the corner of his eyes. "Right now?" he asked, voice subdued, as if frightened to ask.

She released his hand and retrieved her journal from her room, then thumbed through the heavily inked pages until she found several drawings. She slid back down the wall to resume her position alongside him on the floor. Hesitantly, she held the book out to him.

"Don't try to figure out what they mean. I am not sure I could even tell you without reading the before and after pages. It's safe to assume there was fear, anger, sadness, resentment, guilt, yadda yadda blah blah."

He peered at the two pages before him.

Anxiety pulsed through Penny over revealing her journal. *Maybe this isn't a good idea, maybe he will judge me...* Doubts started to fill her mind until her rational brain took over. *Maybe this will help him; maybe he will know he isn't alone in how he feels.*

Noah cleared his throat. "I am not sure my doodles would be so vivid or convey such feeling, but I think that I am willing to give it a try." He closed the book with a snap. While still holding it, he grabbed Penny's hand and placed it on the cover, holding it down with his own. "Thank you for showing me this," he said, his voice husky. "I know it wasn't easy. And I'm sorry I hurt you. I hope you can forgive me." He leaned close and gave her a feathery kiss on her cheek. She responded by throwing her arms around his neck, hugging him tightly. They stayed like that for several heartbeats before releasing their hold on one another. Penny smiled shyly and retrieved the book that had fallen between them.

"I have faith in you, Noah. Just don't lose faith in yourself," she said as she walked away, returning her book to its hiding spot in her room. The cub snuffled, and his cries grew across the room from the wooden crate. She picked the crate up and walked back to the living room.

"Here, take Fjord," she said, as she handed the cub and a

blanket to Noah.

"Fjord?"

"Yeah, I just came up with it. It sounds good, right?" she asked nervously. "It would work for a male or female, although I suspect it is a he. Plus, I am a Viking descendant, or so I am told. The dark hair is a dead giveaway."

Noah shook his head. "Whatever you say. Fjord sounds like a good enough name to me, although it may be too soon to name him. He may not make it more than a few days."

"Yes, yes, but right now I needed something more than 'it' or 'the cub.'" Penny started to gather the ingredients to make the formula. When she glanced over her shoulder, Fjord suckled on Noah's hand. A quiet humming emanated from the tiny creature. She swatted Noah on the shoulder, reprimanding him for providing his fingers for a pacifier.

Much later that morning, Eelyn called to check in. Penny asked her mother hypothetically if it would be possible to raise a newborn polar bear cub.

Eelyn paused to consider this question. "Of course, they raise them at zoos where there is enough support staff and medical intervention should it be needed. It would take much more supportive care than a puppy or a foal. For an individual, I think it would be quite hard and most likely illegal."

Penny asked if anyone would really care that much. "The polar bear is a threatened species. Rescue and survival of any of the species should be of great importance."

"Yes, threatened, threatening, respected, and feared. For good reasons all." Eelyn changed the topic, sharing several brief stories of her and her sister's activities. Her mother's enthusiasm over spending time with Aunt B lifted Penny's spirits.

Penny and Noah continued feeding the cub every two hours. During the first twenty-four hours, he failed to finish even half of the intended amount. But his appetite grew, and he finished more each time until he was eating the entire amount after three days.

The mental connection between Penny and the cub was

vague, akin to what she experienced with newborn puppies or foals at the veterinary hospital in Pasadena. Its mental state focused on feelings of sleepiness, feeding and evacuation. His desires stirred within her mind like leaves dancing lightly in a breeze.

She was a bit worried about how much he sneezed when he nursed, but she listened to his lungs with her mother's stethoscope and took his temperature twice a day. Thus far, all appeared within normal limits per her internet reference materials. The day her mother would return approached, but another strong storm system pushed through central and southern Alaska, extending down to the lower forty-eight states and shutting down airline travel for twenty-four hours. She was unable to reschedule her flight back into Utqiaġvik for an additional two days.

Since the discovery of the cub and subsequent seclusion indoors, Penny and Lucy spent a lot of time together unless Noah was visiting; then Lucy shut herself away. Penny missed how her sister used to be: social, energetic. Happy. But she refrained from accusing her sister of being rude for that would have been unhelpful. Lucy did not participate in feeding the cub. Because of her frail condition, Penny didn't push the matter; although, she would gladly have accepted the help and a chance to get a bit more sleep. After only seven days, she was becoming exhausted.

Noah continued sneaking over before midnight, determined to keep their secret from Army a bit longer. Army pestered Noah about Penny's absence from wrestling and self-defense class. Word got around in small towns. "She has a really bad cold," was enough to prevent Army from visiting, although he dropped off soup and cold pills. Bless him.

As the days progressed and Fjord began eating more, his cries began to take on more volume, becoming less kitten-like and more baby-like.

Noah allowed Fjord to suck on his fingers, against Penny's protests. Fjord would massage back and forth with his tiny paws while a loud gravelly vibration emanated from his tiny frame. Because the literature indicated it should not be done, Penny avoided allowing Fjord to suckle on her fingers, but she caved eventually as it pacified the little bear while his food was prepared.

She received a message from her mother indicating the time her flight would land the following day. After an uneasy night due to excitement and anxiety, Penny fell soundly asleep on the recliner and slept through the scheduled time to pick her mother up at the airport. Her phone, void of charge, sat next to her.

Sometime later, she was shaken awake. Angry at the interruption, she puffed up, ready to throw a punch at whoever spoiled her nap. Blinking away her grogginess, she realized her mother stood next to her.

"Oh my gosh. Mother! I am so sorry. I fell asleep. How did you get home?" Penny rubbed her eyes one-handed. The other held a tight bundle. Nervous energy prickled up and down her.

Completely awake, she stood to give her mother an awkward one-armed hug.

"Army came to get me, dear. Are you okay?" Eelyn took a moment to brush hair from Penny's face. "You look exhausted. Army is worried about you. Says you missed practice because you haven't been well." Blue approached and nuzzled Eelyn's hand. Her attention briefly diverted to the canine.

Penny motioned for her mother to sit opposite her on the couch. Not knowing the best way to present her case to her mother, she sat next to her and passed her the now moving bundle. Eelyn folded back a corner of the blanket, revealing the head. In his wakefulness and hunger, his wiggling and rooting caused more of the blanket to fall away.

"Penny, tell me this is not what I think it is," she said quietly.

A nervous chuckle escaped Penny. "Well, that depends on what you think it is. A white wolf it is not. Nor is it a white dragon. No scales, see. Just white fur and pink skin that will change to black skin. With white fur."

168

"So, this is what the talk about polar bears was about. And here Army was concerned about your physical health. About the possibility of you and Noah sneaking around. Where in the world, how did you, when…" Eelyn faltered. Then she just said, "Talk."

Penny started her tale with crossing paths with the female bear digging in the snow. Then the nightmare she had the night before Eelyn left. About Noah and her taking the teams out and finding the scene that disrupted her dreams. How they inspected the area once the male departed. Noah collecting the female's skin. Searching the den and discovering two cubs, one dead and one holding on to life.

"I acted without really thinking, Mother. I couldn't leave it to die. Not if I could do something to help it." Penny knew the longer her mother held the cub, the better her chances were at keeping him, so Penny rose to start making Fjord's formula.

"We can't keep him. I could lose my license. We could get kicked out of Alaska…or have an indefinite stay at some nice penitentiary…" Eelyn's voice trailed off.

"You won't lose your license. No one will turn you in. I'm the one who took Fjord." Bottles rattled, and Esbilac sloshed on the counter in her haste. "I found information on the care of captive polar bears, which, all-in-all, is pretty detailed. It is amazing what you can get from the net. Anyway, Noah has been helping me with Fjord. We made a schedule so that I can get some sleep at night."

Eelyn followed her to the kitchen commenting that, yes, she most certainly could lose her license and that obviously Penny had not been getting enough sleep or she wouldn't have forgotten to pick up her mother at the airport.

"I really am sorry about that. And you are right. But it will get easier. He will grow out of this stage."

"Noah. And Fjord," Eelyn said.

"Yes, Noah has been helping. And I named him Fjord. I am quite certain the cub is male."

Eelyn almost tripped over backwards on top of Blue who followed closely behind her. She said something that rhymed with lamb hog.

Penny extricated Fjord from her mother's grasp and sat down at the kitchen table to feed the hungry bear.

Penny glimpsed Eelyn's dumbstruck gaze before placing her attention on the cub.

"Look, I know there are a lot of 'ifs' and other questions. But bottom line, I won't kill him, nor will I let you do it. Think of it like an unexpected pregnancy. We accept and we adapt. Figure it out."

Penny thought she heard her mother mumble about a preference for an unexpected pregnancy before she more audibly asked if Army knew about the cub.

"No, just this family and Noah. At least for now."

Eelyn then sent an emergency meeting request to Army and Noah.

Tough Decision

"Well, now that you are fully aware of what has been transpiring on your property, what do you think? What do we do?" Eelyn asked after Army was brought up to speed.

He sat, quietly chewing on his bottom lip, looking down at the table in the Osborn's kitchen for several long moments. And then a bit longer.

Finally, Eelyn broke the silence.

"Army?"

Do you need me to join in the discussion?

No, Lu. It's fine. I can handle it.

Penny, get a pencil and paper and make a list. Penny did and began writing down the things Lucy listed off in her head as the rest of them continued to sit in silence as they watched her.

1. Kill it.

2. Find someone else to take it...zoo, wildlife sanctuary, etc.

3. Keep it.

She placed her pencil on the table and cleared her throat.

"Okay, here is a list of things we can do with Fjord. First, we can euthanize him. We could, but we won't...at least not without good reason. Second, we could investigate placing him in a zoo or other sanctuary. And finally, we can keep him and do the best we can. I picked him up out of the cave where he was sure to die and brought him back and cared for him. We," she pointed to Noah, "researched the care and habitat for captive bears, and I think the first six months of life are manageable."

Penny studied Army to judge his reaction. State law prohibited the owning of a wolf-hybrid in Alaska; however,

Noah and Army managed their way around that law. Utqiaġvik was not located within a reservation, but the North Slope held thousands of acres of tribal land. Perhaps Army could find a loophole for the bear.

Army shifted uncomfortably as he scanned sideways over at the sleeping cub in Noah's lap.

"Possession of wildlife in Alaska is illegal, Penny."

Okay, no loophole.

"Your mother could lose her veterinary license. Maybe even face fines." He continued. "A wolf-hybrid is a bit easier to conceal as it resembles a dog." His searching gaze traveled between Penny and Eelyn. "I could do a bit of research on the sly for animal procurement. Maybe rehabbing offers a path. It would be easier to pass him off once he is a few months old or by next summer. I won't even speculate. I would rather check and make sure. I do know that as fast as that cub will grow, if it lives…well, it will make it difficult to hide him by the end of summer. Even in Utqiaġvik."

Noah piped up. "I found a few different locations that would be far enough from town to raise a yearling cub. One place could be fixed up without anyone knowing. It's that old underground bunker and airstrip that John Reams has, thirty miles out east along the coast. He and his family live in Juneau." Noah saw the frown appear on his uncle's chiseled face. "Or we could ask him if we can use it. Oh, come on Army. You know he wouldn't mind. He checks up on it every summer, repairs things as needed. It would be a good place."

"Is no one worried that you would be raising a people killer?" Eelyn shrieked.

"Do you worry about me turning into a killer? Does any parent? Or do you do the best you can to instill morals and empathy into us so that we can make the best decisions?" Penny shot back.

"But you are human. Not a bear! I trust you to do the right, ethical *human* things in life. I trust Fjord to do what *bears* do, and with so much association with people that is implied by some of you, that places him in a different spectrum than your regular old, average one-thousand-pound, white-haired, hungry mammal that is known to stalk people. Now, I am all for waiting to see what we all can find for other options because I know Penny is against euthanizing him. But, at any time we determine that is what must be done, then that is what will happen. Understand?" Eelyn grew a bit wild and wide-eyed toward the end of her tirade

Give her a few feedings. She will fall for him, too, Lucy commented.

Uncertainty clouded Lucy's comment as she started to think their mother wouldn't cave. Adorable or not, she knew how much mischief young dogs could do. Case in point, Blue. She didn't own a shoe without chew marks no matter her attempted mental influences. A juvenile bear may do the same to their door or their couch. Penny sighed, conceding to her mother's wishes.

"Penny, you have any more visions?" Army asked.

Eelyn's head whipped around. "Visions?"

Penny rubbed the back of her neck and let out a slow breath. She peeked at Noah out of the corner of her eye and found he was staring at the mural behind Army. She followed his gaze, and her own landed on Edgar who sat ruffled on his perch.

"I did about this cub. Well, not actually about the cub. I dreamt about the death of the mother polar bear one night and then convinced Noah to go out looking for her the next day. I didn't tell him about it before so don't look at him like he did anything wrong. The scene we came upon was the same that I dreamt. And then further searching led me to him." She gestured to the cub.

Army nodded once. Eelyn looked unsettled.

Penny continued, "I haven't had any dreams lately about the scarred bear or the Shadowed Man."

The next day, Penny awoke early to pots and pans rattling and the delicious smells of bacon permeating her room.

Mom has returned, real breakfast, thought Lucy.

Penny's stomach rumbled in agreement. The morning staple of toast could not match her mother's cooking. Both girls giggled at the thought of "bread for toast."

You are very lucky with a friend like Noah, thought Lucy. *He is also so very, very easy on the eyes.*

Penny threw a shirt at her sister.

Luckily, she exited her room in her pajamas, t-shirt and sweatpants, but even those felt insufficient when she saw Noah sitting at the table.

Her mother looked her over. "Sleep well?"

"Yes. Making a lot of noise considering it is 6:00 a.m."

Noah grinned a Cheshire cat grin. "It's eight. Your mother wanted to let you sleep, so I stayed late to show her how we mix up Fjord's formula."

"Oh," she said as she sat across the table from him. "Well, thank you."

Eelyn placed the food on the table. Penny was so excited to be greeted with bacon, scrambled eggs, and cheesy hash browns with fried onions, she didn't think about speaking until she had her fill. In fact, no one spoke until every morsel was gone from their loaded plates.

Sheesh, save me some bacon, you bunch of pigs! Lucy mentally shouted to her sister. *So glad you all waited for me.*

Mother needs to get to work, Lu. Plus, you hardly ever eat with the family. Why would we expect a change?

"Very good, Eelyn," Noah said. "Don't tell my aunt, but you make a mean breakfast. She may try to hire you part-time."

Penny also complimented her mother.

Eelyn smiled. "Thanks guys. Just wanted a good meal before going back to work. Your aunt tried starving me with her current no-carb diet. I cannot emotionally survive without bread, cereal and potatoes. Seriously. Anyway, Penny, I made a few changes to your formula—vitamins mostly. I called a few colleagues who work at different zoos for some tips. And before you ask, no, I did not say we were currently housing a cub illegally."

Penny grimaced.

"I said it was for my own information as working with the research team spiked my curiosity on the cubs. They said they would send me more information. I hope to have it in

174

my email inbox this morning."

She rose from the table, checked her phone, and grabbed her coat. "Okay, kids. I am off to work. Sam is outside. He is giving me a ride so Penny can use the truck. Penny, I thank you in advance for cleaning up the kitchen. Noah, until next time. Be good." She gave Penny a hug and left.

Penny shooed Noah out the door, stating she was fully capable of cleaning up after her mother. She had loads of practice. She then placed a few strips of bacon and two slices of toast that survived on a plate and took them to her sister in their room.

Penny bowed upon entering the room. "Here you go, my lady," she said. "Breakfast is served."

Why, I do declare. You are such a sweet-hearted beauty, Lucy thought with a southern drawl. She coughed and continued in a more normal thinking projection, *please set it over on the dresser. I will get it when I get dressed.*

"Need any help, Lu?" Penny thought Lucy looked good today, if only a bit pale.

I'm good. You are dismissed. Lucy made a grand sweeping gesture with her arm, directing Penny back out into the house. Penny laughed as she retreated.

Later that afternoon, Army stopped by to be taught the secrets of cub feeding. Penny obliged. It was about time for Fjord to eat. He asked a few questions, clarifying what was proper and expected. She showed him how to hold the cub, propping him upright against the towel. Then he demanded she give him the bundle and get ready for practice.

"What?" she asked with surprise.

"Practice. You remember offering to help with wrestling? We can't have you just up and not show for the rest of the season. You have other responsibilities. And...people talk. Now go!" His raised voice startled the cub for an instant. Fjord whimpered, but he quickly rediscovered the nipple on his bottle.

Penny hurriedly changed and ran out the door, heart pumping in excitement. She could get out of the house! Noah greeted her with his crooked smirk as she took her place beside him on the mats during warm-up. The wrestlers and the coach all expressed their happiness at her return with exuberant competitiveness, performing their improved techniques more accurately than she could following a lengthy time off from exercise.

When Penny returned home, she found supper ready and waiting with Eelyn and Lucy spending time with Edgar. He had finally come out of his shell and was talking with their mother. Lucy reclined on the couch with Blue warming her legs. Penny was sore and happy. During their meal, Eelyn brought Penny up to speed on the state of Bianca. As usual, it was eventful. Two new boyfriends since her divorce. The most recent one was a biker.

"Oh, I saw Liam. Ran into him at the spa you two used to go to. Ivy something. Anyway, he was very talkative. Wants to come visit us. Misses you dearly. Apparently hasn't talked to you much lately?"

Penny shook her head. "It has been several…awhile. Boy, I need to call him."

"Yes, he seemed to not know much about what you have going on. Wrestling. Self-defense classes. Noah. I didn't tell him much about the women."

Dark thoughts bubbled up between them, their expressions troubled. The third deceased woman's autopsy revealed she had died prior to the bear mauling at her cabin. There were no additional clues to tie the three together, but officials thought it enough to announce the suspicions of a serial killer. Penny tried to shake off the bleak reflections.

"Well, then, he doesn't listen to me, because I am sure I told him about wrestling and Noah. About the whole crew. But that doesn't surprise me. He is a bit self-centered."

"Hmmm, I would say more distractible. His attention wanders. You know, like focus, focus, focus…squirrel! I felt like he didn't even hear the end of our conversation. He asked about coming up around Christmas. I don't have a problem with that. It would almost be like old times." A sad look crossed her mother's face.

After supper and the cub's feeding, during which Fjord

didn't eat his full amount, she tried reaching Liam via video conferencing. He answered on the first ring.

"Hey, lady! Long time no see! Your mom get back? She tell you we ran into each other? Chewed you out for not calling me more often, yeah right?" She realized she missed his big goofy grin.

"Hi! How goes it in the land of sunshine and glamour?"

What followed was a nice talk about his school, his current love interest, and his parents. Their conversation eventually steered toward Blue, who lay on the floor chewing on a new chew toy, the squeaking encouraging Edgar to mimic the noise.

Liam couldn't believe how large he had grown when Penny pointed the camera on the chewing canine. "He looks so much like a...wolf," he said over the din of squeaking. Penny walked into her bedroom where it was quieter with the door closed. She left it open a crack. The squeaking halted, and Blue nosed his way in through the crack, evidentially wanting to listen in on the conversation about him.

Penny smiled. "Except for his eyes, of course. Wolves do not have blue eyes. You should see the sire. Hey, you really planning on a trip up here?"

"If I can find tickets I can afford. I'm not a professional, yeah right? Not like you."

"Sure, that's why I fly all over vacationing. Due to my extremely high wages." She did not make much with an intern's salary. The cheap house rent and use of Army's vehicles was a blessing. That and monies invested from a settlement over the high school incident and her father's life insurance... Before her thoughts could tread down darker paths, she said, "Well, you are welcome to come anytime. Just give a heads up, you know."

During the next several feedings, Fjord continued to eat less and less. Penny thought that he didn't care for the new bottle her mother supplied.

He became listless, and Penny did a quick exam. His temperature was 105°F, and his lungs sounded different. She called her mother at the clinic, then Noah for moral support and a ride. After packing the cub in blankets, Penny and Noah set out to the veterinary clinic.

Eelyn examined the tiny bear, drew blood, and placed him in a neonatal incubator. She turned on oxygen and began gathering needed supplies. Penny ran the blood through the machine that would check for infection and organ function. Noah stepped in and assisted Eelyn when asked. Eelyn declared Fjord had pneumonia and that his prognosis wasn't good.

"I'll do what I can, honey. He's going to need to stay here, though. Both Vincent and Sam are away this week and next, so we can wheel the incubator into the office and keep him out of sight." Eelyn placed a hand on her daughter's shoulder. "We can hope."

Over the next few hours, Eelyn drained fluid from the cub's chest, started him on antibiotics and anti-inflammatories to fight the infection and bring his fever down. He lost his suckle reflex, a bad sign, so Penny watched over him, reaching in through the side to stroke his soft coat. Noah and Penny stayed the night watching over the bear, giving the medications and fluids that Eelyn prescribed. Noah easily dozed on one of the leather desk chairs, but Penny couldn't tear her eyes from the ailing cub. He seemed to wither with each passing hour.

In the morning, when Eelyn arrived with Lucy in tow, Noah rubbed Penny's back as they stood looking over the incubator.

"Come on, you need to get some rest. Your mother is here and will take care of him," Noah said soothingly.

"I just—" Penny palmed the tears that slid freely down her cheeks "—don't...he was doing so well. I don't want him to die."

Noah pulled her into him, wrapping his arms firmly around her. She curled into him, holding her face. In that moment, they bonded more firmly in their shared pain. When her tears subsided, her awareness of the warmth and hard planes of Noah's body holding her securely grew. She reluctantly pulled away. As she did, the memory of his heat clung to her.

"Sorry, Noah. I, ah, your shirt is all wet," Penny said, her ears warming, and her heartbeat escalated.

Noah eyed his shirt, smoothing the wrinkles. "That's alright. It will dry." He coughed. "Looking at him isn't going to help anything. Let's go." Noah put a hand on her lower back and steered her out of the room.

The next few days were touch and go for the little white bear cub. He perked up after the first ten hours and then relapsed into listlessness before her.

"It's because of the bottle I was using, isn't it?" Penny asked her mother. The guilt ate away at her, becoming unbearable.

"I can't say for sure. Aspiration pneumonia can occur with even the correct set-up. You did the best you could, honey." Eelyn smoothed Penny's long hair back from her face. "Don't give up yet. He's still breathing."

Not very well.

"Besides," Eelyn continued, "not long after you and your sister were born, you both were hospitalized with pneumonia. You each had an incubator, just like this. But you two fussed and fussed until the doctors finally placed you together in the same incubator. There were tubes coming out of your nose, mouth, stuck in your arms and legs, but you settled down. Your father and I never gave up hope. And neither should you. It's an unpleasant fact that what will be, will be. We just do the best we can and have faith."

Day four. I feel a change, Penny.

Penny rose for the morning, readied herself quickly and drove into town. She felt a change, too. Her connection with Fjord was stronger. Although her mother knew she was on her way, she did not meet her at the front door like normal. Linda waved her back to the office, indicating Army was there with Dr. Osborn.

Penny's heartbeat increased when she opened the door. The vacant incubator stood open. Army and Eelyn turned to face her; she did not see the bear cub in their hands. Disappointment surged as she took their startled expressions

179

to mean the worst. She couldn't understand it; the connection she sensed was stronger. Unwilling to digest what it could mean, she almost turned and fled. Then she saw her mother's face beaming.

"He's made a turn for the better! I just started to feed him. Do you want to take over?" Eelyn gestured with the bottle.

Taking the bottle her mother had been holding, Army reached behind Eelyn and withdrew a basket from the desktop. Inside wiggled Fjord, nosing around in the blanket folds.

"His fever broke last night, and he took some food from the bottle. I didn't want to wake you if it was a false alarm." Eelyn handed Penny the bottle, and she sat at the offered chair.

After Fjord's miraculous recovery, the days, or rather the lengthening nights, began to blend together with the reestablished routine. The endless nights would last until January 21, and Penny tried to make a mantra of, "it will only be sixty-five nights."

Army continued to fly home from teaching in Anchorage every weekend and sometimes during the week between lectures so that he could check up on his business in the north, which included now a growing polar bear cub. Between him and Eelyn, they offered their free time to allow Penny to continue her guitar lessons, assist Noah with maintenance at the airplane hangar, and just take a break. Noah took over care of the dogs, and Penny helped whenever she could. She found enough time between feedings to keep up with the incoming research data and work on composing the research paper with Army. Since feeding times occurred roughly every even hour and since she could easily sense when he was waking even across the few miles into town, Penny started slipping to the gym after the 6:00 a.m. feeding so that she could resume running.

Just before Thanksgiving and day twenty-four of life with Fjord, he opened his eyes to take in the vision of his momma bear and his world. His eyes shone a brilliant blue, a tad darker than Blue's eyes. As he became more active, Penny needed to be very careful about where she would set him when she required free hands. She filed down the tips of his claws to reduce the scratches on her hands. They didn't bother her, but she didn't want them to trigger any stares. Once he became larger, she was certain something more would need to be done.

Although he couldn't walk yet, he was scooting around well enough and weighed in at a whole three pounds. He made more noises, grunting and varied cries. The hair on the tip of his left ear did not develop; as his skin tone changed from pink to black, the tip shriveled. The black end curled in on itself. During a physical exam at home, Eelyn diagnosed frostbite. Fjord stayed inside the house, apart from when he was sick, as keeping a consistent ambient temperature was top priority during his early months.

Will be easy to identify him from other bears, Lucy echoed Penny's own thoughts.

Still going to chip him, though.

Yeah, like you will ever let him go out into the wild. Like he would be able to, being raised by humans.

Penny sighed at her sister's pessimistic but accurate sentiment.

As he began teething, Penny purchased human baby teething rings and froze them for him to chew on. Noah whittled a wooden ring for him, the skill shown with such a simple object both surprising and impressing to Penny. He also brought her a pair of fingerless, long sleeve arm warmers. His kindness never ceased to amaze Penny.

"So, my scratches aren't as hidden as I thought?" she asked him.

"Well, while his little paws do not contact me quite as often as they do you, they still are sharp. I saw these and thought they may come in handy for you."

The gloves were thick, tightly woven coverings with vibrant reds and greens breaking up the black color, like the aurora.

"See, lights out," he said.

"Thank you, Noah. For this and all the other gifts. And

your help with Fjord. You are amazing."

"Oh, I try."

Penny recognized her own craving for his nearness. Peering back at her, she saw a hunger reflected in his eyes. His expression deepened, and his lips parted as his gaze traveled her face. And abruptly panic tightened around her heart. Fear of rejection. Of mistaking his actions. And she stepped away where she could breathe easier.

New Girl

In the weeks leading up to the end of the year, Fjord continued to double in size each week. He was active and cuddly, and Penny could barely get enough of him.

Noah's self-defense classes began to focus on the varied techniques one would use to compete in the athletic challenges scheduled between Christmas and New Year's Day – the Inuit Eskimo Games. The games were challenges designed to imitate what one needed to survive the harsh climate. Several Native Alaskans who were participating in the World Eskimo Olympics in Fairbanks graciously stopped by the Wednesday night class to give demonstrations. Penny thought that Noah might be more focused on his own competition in the local games, but she withheld judgment, happy to share in the experience.

Other members of the class offered up stories, as was traditional. And although Penny had picked up a book on Native Alaskan folklore, after Noah had mentioned shamanism, none of the tales were ones she recognized from books. That Christmas was one of the happier in recent years, thanks to the warmth of the Volkovs. Noah finagled Penny into attending some of the week-long games. Between feedings, cleanings, and sanitation of bottles and food dishes (now that they had transitioned him to soft food), and more cleanings in addition to her exercise routine, guitar playing, and obviously work, less of her time was spent helping with the regularly scheduled activities like wrestling and self-defense class. Penny began to wonder if this was what a stay-at-home mother would feel like.

January snuck in quietly and by the months end, Fjord began walking, although it would be more accurate to say he stumbled and tumbled. His full coat now making him look like an overly large, fuzzy caterpillar most times. Penny attempted to help the little cub until Army saw what she was doing and told her to let the cub figure it out on his own. Penny submitted to his wisdom—at least while he was watching her. It was too difficult not to help.

His mental connection strengthened, and Penny now felt the constant feather-like brush against her consciousness. He had a growing curiosity, and she acclimated easily, unless his desires spiked. Then it was like a mosquito buzzing her head.

Fjord's feeding schedule was rigid due to the little bear's own internal clock. Penny was unable to alter it enough to free her time to attend wrestling and self-defense classes. Because she was able to fit in a fitness routine and still hang out with Noah, the lack of the other activities didn't bother her. She heard about the new teacher who had moved into town a few months earlier as Noah drove her to self-defense class for the first time in several weeks. Marie Felter. She filled a vacant position at the high school, and everyone in the class seemed to know her well enough. They were very friendly toward the outgoing female, especially the males. Even the six-year-old in the self-defense class clung to her instead of his usual place by Penny.

Of course, as soon as Penny saw her, she understood the infatuation. Marie was a fit young woman with long blond locks. Her eyes were a brilliant green, and her skin pale with a perfect rosy blush on her cheeks. Her smile was easy and frequent. Penny couldn't help but like her—until she saw how much Noah seemed to like her. Then Penny wondered if it was worth liking this girl.

*Really, Pen? I thought you and Noah were just, uh, you know...*friends? chided Lucy.

Penny sighed. *Fine, I'll go with my first impression.*

Oh, we both know you suck at female relationships, present company and mom excluded. If you made her shorter, added tattoos, changed her hair color to brown and eyes to blue, she could be like Rainy. Ms. Summers, I mean.

Ah, sure. That might work, Penny replied with more than a

hint of sarcasm. Lucy was referring to Penny's almost-enthrallment with her Family and Consumer Science teacher in high school. She was cool, everyone had a crush on her, even the women. She rode motocross and could decorate a five-tier wedding cake. Not skills that usually coexisted together.

Noah approached her and asked if she would mind pairing up with Marie. During a brief introduction, Penny learned Marie participated in multiple self-defense classes at her previous residence in Colorado, so Penny didn't need to dwell on too basic of moves. They practiced behind grabs, choke holds, and weapon deflection moves. After twenty minutes, Noah called for the pairs to switch. Noah asked Penny to spar with him for a demonstration.

He told the class that the key to deflection and escape is to repeatedly perform maneuvers so that they become instinctual. Practicing under stress will help with focus so that you are more apt to keep a level head if attacked. He offered a competition to members, seeing if they would like to spar on occasion with unknown attack moves. They all enthusiastically agreed.

"No situation will be the same—but you should learn some basic moves that can help. Being attacked by a person is less likely to happen here in Utqiaġvik than, say, being attacked by a walrus. But we live in a cold, dangerous world and walruses are moving close to our community. Being aware of surroundings is good on many different levels. So, enough talking. Penny and I will show you some techniques and moves that utilize objects in your surrounding environment."

Penny stood in the center of the mat. The others sat or stood around them in a circle. Towels, water bottles, and shoes scattered around them. Noah disappeared from her view. He approached her from behind and placed a choke hold on her, pointing his finger in her back like a weapon. Penny quickly extricated herself from his grip by lunging forward and down, throwing him to the ground. Before she could strike him, he rolled up and attacked again. Again and again he attacked, and she returned with a defensive move and sometimes counterattacks. She grabbed discarded towels to temporarily bind his wrists, a shoe she used to strike at his temple, a soft plastic water bottle opened and the contents sprayed in his face. They moved quickly around the mat, as if dancing a dangerous duel that could result in one's injury or perhaps death, if at a different place and time.

Although they both held back any injury-causing blows, Penny was certain she would suffer some bruises from the demonstration, as would Noah. He was dripping wet thanks to her water attack. His glossy curls hung heavily, weighed down by the moisture and fell into his eyes

Both were breathing heavily as they finished, and Noah threw an arm around Penny's shoulders.

He then announced with a smile, "Penny here, as I said before, is not as advanced in training as I, but she uses everything she can to defend and attack, like when she picked up Frank's shoe and flung it at me. That is an important thing to keep in mind. Anything can be used as a weapon. How many things in this room can we use? Please, start naming them."

As they did, Noah and Penny were given a chance to catch their breath. Noah squeezed her shoulder, unknowingly sending a warm wave of goosebumps down her back and arms. He winked at her and whispered, "Great job, Momma Bear." Then turned his attention back to the responding group.

Penny's heart skipped several beats and, as she gazed after Noah, she caught Marie staring at her. Penny smiled, and Marie returned with a smile of her own.

They went through another twenty minutes of technique work with different partners before the group began to cool down. As they stretched, Marie sidled up next to Penny and asked where she had learned to fight like that.

"I've been in training since fourth grade," Penny replied.

Marie and she chatted easily during cool-down, which had involved Marie asking Penny questions about why she moved to Alaska, what type of research she was involved in, how well she knew Noah.

As they readied themselves to leave, Marie asked Penny if she wanted to get together for lunch some weekend.

"There are a few single dads who think a single teacher would make a good step-mom, but I am not buying into that," she said conspiratorially.

"I think I would enjoy lunch some time." A thrill of joy at the possibility of a female friend coursed through Penny, who never really hung out with anyone other than Lucy and Liam. And now Noah. She kept in touch with a few girls from her class, but girl time was time at home with her mother or Lucy. Rita was fun to hang out with, but usually Bill was along, limiting any girl time.

I don't know, Pen. She seems like she may not be the right kind of friend. Lucy's pensive thought entered, tamping down Penny's happiness.

Best to not make a judgment just yet. We just met her.

They exchanged numbers and promises to call.

In all your free time, Lucy commented.

You're right. Probably won't work out. She and Noah will begin dating, and I will be down two friends.

Oh, come on, don't be so pessimistic.

Noah asked for a ride home with Penny following class since Army had dropped him off earlier.

"I was thinking about Marie," Noah said after some time in shared comfortable silence. "You two seemed to hit it off well tonight."

"She seemed nice. Outgoing." Penny said as she swerved to avoid a rut.

That brought a chuckle from Noah. "Quite the opposite of you. Not the nice part, Penny. The outgoing part. You're like me, quiet, unsocial. The intelligent, attractive, quiet ones are intimidating for most people. But fortunately, I am not most people. So, you do not intimidate me. Marie, though, has been struggling here in Utqiaġvik. She is more of a social thing and hasn't yet found her place in the community."

"Do you know her quite well?" Penny asked, a sour bubble blossoming in her gut.

"Not really. I listen to the gossip." He tapped his temple. "The quiet one who picks up useless info."

"You listen to gossip?" Penny said, feigning astonishment.

As he continued, Penny found her attention wandering back to a previous comment. Attractive. *He called me attractive!* Butterflies fluttered inside her, fanning the waves of jealousy away.

"I hate for you to only hang out with the research team. And I know Marie is new, but maybe the two of you will hit it off."

Although Penny didn't care to hang out with other people beside the few she knew in Utqiaġvik, she recognized the fact that Noah continued to look out for her.

The sun began to peek over the horizon toward the end of January, which marked Fjord's three-month rescue anniversary. His left ear, mostly a shriveled black tip, was more noticeable. Army complained to Penny that the cub had grown fat and needed exercise, just like Army. She found it hard to take offense. Fjord was plump, weighing in at nineteen pounds, and after her mother consulted with her colleagues, no changes were made to his feeding schedules since he measured in like cubs his age at zoos.

Penny considered options for taking Fjord outside for short romps in the snow now that he was walking. The yard would be fine for short outings, but the vacant research station a much better location, far away from prying eyes.

Romp and Roll

The door chimed when Penny entered the veterinary clinic. The familiar pet odors mixed with chemical disinfectants and the smell of ozone from her mother's favorite air purifier wafted over Penny, inciting nostalgia from years spent assisting her mother. Although she never desired becoming a veterinarian, there was something comforting and respectful about the profession.

"Penny, so good to see you! Haven't seen you, what, in a few months! You are just as lovely as ever," called out Linda, who sat at the front desk overseeing an empty waiting room.

Penny blushed. "Good to see you, too. You're sweet, but I think your eyes might need to be examined."

"Don't be so humble. Oh, do you have a puppy for your mom to check out? Is it one of Army's?" Linda perked up even more, if that was possible. She had an obvious weakness for Army, fawning over him whenever he visited.

Fjord yawned inside her jacket. Well, not her jacket. Noah's larger coat hugged the cub close to her, only the top of his white head visible. Fjord had just eaten and was ready to sleep.

"Um, no it isn't Army's. And he's very shy. I'll hold onto him, if you don't mind. Where's mother?" Penny refrained from correcting Linda's assumption. The cub was not something she was able to expose to those outside her circle.

"Oh, finishing up with a c-section. Here, do you want me to take him for you?" Linda rose and held her arms out.

Blue wound around Penny's legs. "No, that's fine. I can kennel him. Thanks, though."

Linda smiled and resumed her position on the swivel chair. The phone rang, and she quickly answered, "Hello!

189

Veterinary Clinic, Linda speaking. How can I help you?"

Penny took Fjord into the office Eelyn shared with Dr. Vincent and placed him in a small pet carrier stored beneath the long table that served as a desk for both veterinarians. It struck Penny that she and Dr. Vincent had never met. Then again, she only ever visited the clinic when her mother worked, and she worked when Dr. Vincent did not.

Fjord curled up in his blanket. Penny regarded Blue and mentally focused on him staying with the cub. Blue peered at the carrier and then at the door. He barked his displeasure. Penny imagined the great responsibility of looking over the cub. Blue cocked his head to the side and whined.

Just stay until I come back, she finally projected, leaving the puppy with her twenty-three-pound cub.

When Penny walked into the surgical room, Eelyn was closing the c-section. The copper tang of blood and surgical disinfectant scrub assaulted her. She held her anxiety in check and calmly entered.

"Hello, daughter of mine. How are you this afternoon? Did you enjoy the half-hour of sunshine today?" The sun rose above the horizon, but fog obscured the show that marked the end of the endless night and the promise of sunlight to come. Her attempt at humor aside, her mother looked unsettled, a long blood spatter on her left cheek. "Ah, would you mind helping Sam with the puppies?"

Sam was in the corner with a towel, massaging a pup. Penny grabbed a soft towel from a pile and one of the other puppies from the heating pad. Could have been Fjord's very tiny twin – solid white with a black left ear.

A total of twelve puppies were delivered in all, but three lay still off to the side. The largest was puffy looking. As Penny inspected it, Sam informed her it had been the one stuck in the birth canal. Penny gently massaged the puppy until it showed more vitality; then she changed to a different pup.

"This one looks like your pup," Sam said with a friendly smile. The creases around his eyes multiplied as he grinned at her.

"Umhmm," she agreed.

Sam chatted about the surgery and easily filled up the silence while her mother finished up and moved the mother dog into the next room. He was chatty and fortunately didn't seem to mind that Penny was not.

As they were transferring the lively puppies to their mother, Sam asked, "Eelyn, I'm going to grab some food. Want me to pick up your usual order at The FrostBite?"

Eelyn drug her hands through her hair. Penny could see her weariness from staying up late with Fjord last night only to be greeted with an early morning emergency.

"Sure, that would be great."

Penny raised her eyebrows at her mother after Sam left. Eelyn pulled her daughter into the office and shut the door.

"Nothing going on, he's being polite," she said. "Where's the bear?"

Penny pulled Fjord's comatose form from the cramped carrier and helped her mother draw blood for tests.

"He and Rose aren't dating anymore, right?"

"Penny, knock it off. It's not like that." Her mother answered in a clipped voice. "No one will ever replace your father."

Trying a little more gently, "You don't need a replacement. Or a fill-in. No one would judge you for dating."

Staring absently at the opposite wall, Eelyn's face fell suddenly. "No. I am not ready. Maybe someday."

Eelyn finished up, and Penny gathered her charge once again, stuffing him inside her jacket. Fjord was almost too much to fit when he was sleeping; when struggling, he made it difficult to stay concealed.

"Ouch, dude. Watch the claws," Penny shifted the cub around, trying to convey her desire for him to be still for just a few minutes longer. Once Noah picked her up and they set out for the research station, the cub would be freed to roam about.

A knock on the door startled them both, and Penny kept her back toward the door until she saw Noah standing there with a grin.

191

"Ready to go, Momma Bear?" Noah was a vision with his hands tucked in his jacket pockets and glossy curls framing his face. She stared at him; something was different, but she couldn't put a finger on what. She realized she was staring and looked away only to return her gaze.

What was different? Was it because he wasn't wearing a hat?

He shifted under her stare. "Um, is there something on my face?" He half-smirked and bent down to pet Blue, who was wagging his tail, vying for attention.

Penny closed her mouth. He didn't have anything on his face. *How could he be even better looking without the beard?*

"Oh, Noah. You shaved!" Eelyn stated the obvious. "You're just as handsome under all that hair! How long has it been since you were clean-shaven?"

Rubbing his jaw, he squinted. "Years. I feel nekked."

Penny ducked her face, heat rising on her neck; she stifled a giggle.

Blue sat in the back with Winter as they drove out, each dog looking out a window. Fjord sprawled on Penny's lap, dozing. Penny felt as if she rode next to a stranger, catching herself doing a double take more than once. Noah seemed to mostly ignore her, although when their gazes connected, he smiled and gave her a wink.

Noah started shoveling snow from the front door of the building while Penny went inside to start the generator and turn lights on. She put Fjord in the wooden box Noah had built for the cub, a play pen of sorts. It had a warmer inside and heated up quickly, quicker than the open room. She eyed it with the bear walking around the cramped quarters. It wouldn't work for too much longer. He chuffed and rose up on his hind legs, pawing at the sides. Winter jumped up against the outside and peered in at the bawling cub. He leaned down and licked Fjord's face.

Just wait, buddy. Just a little longer. Down, Winter. You can play later. Penny shut the cover and continued with an inspection of the interior, Blue trailing her like a shadow.

Noah stomped his boots off when he entered, placing the

shovel next to the door. "No issues outside. Everything look good in here?"

"Yep. I'm going to check on a few things while we are here, if that's okay?" Penny turned off the lights in the back and sat at a desk in the front, pulling her computer from her backpack.

Once she finished her work, she pulled the polar bear hide leggings from her bag. They had been a Christmas gift from the Volkovs, made from the hide Noah removed from Fjord's mother. They matched the pair Noah had donned, also a Christmas gift, but from another bear (one taken during an indigenous hunt).

Fjord's first major outing was one part exciting and one part poignant. The snow was fluffy and deep in places, unlike around home where the dogs and vehicles trampled down the powdery fluff.

He was thriving, her little bear cub. Penny took pictures of Winter, Blue, and Noah playing with the cub. At first, Fjord walked like a cat with tape on its feet, picking up his paws high to shake the cold snow from his toes. Once he became used to the new sensation, he stuck his face into a snow drift - a long bout of sneezing followed. Noah offered to photograph Momma Bear and her clan. With her mind, she called both dogs in to sit on either side.

"If that isn't spooky..." Noah huffed and took several. Then he turned around and leaned against Penny to capture a group picture. Of all the photos of Fjord, that picture would become the one she admired the most. Fjord's front paws were raised toward the sky and his tongue poked out of his mouth. Winter nosed Noah's flushed and smooth cheek, and Blue lifted his paw as if to high five the little cub.

It wasn't until mid-February when the sun provided more than six hours of sunlight. Marie and Penny met one Saturday for afternoon coffee. Eelyn was happy to cover baby duty during her brief absence, almost too happy over the potential girl pal Penny might gain. Lucy not so much.

Watch that one, Lucy thought as Penny left.

The get-together started out enjoyable. Until Marie opened

her mouth and bombarded Penny with questions. How can she stand the lack of sunlight? Isn't the foggy weather insane? Didn't Penny shop outside of town?

Penny surreptitiously glanced down at her clothes as Marie ogled the restaurant patrons. Her blue plaid shirt that Noah gave her (it was too small for him) was unbuttoned and the yellow and blue "Utqiaġvik Pride" peeked from beneath.

Did you just roll your eyes at her? Her sister remarked.

And here I roll my mental eyes at you, she retorted. *I like my clothes.*

"Ah, I wish there was some place to go out dancing here," Marie complained.

"There's dancing every Sunday night at the Lodge," Penny replied, knowing already that the lodge was not the kind of dancing Marie would like. Noah had asked her to play guitar with Army and him in a couple of weeks at the lodge, but she was still waffling about performing in front of a crowd. Small groups of friends were okay, but crowds...the thoughts churned her stomach.

Marie scoffed, and Penny responded with a smile.

"Noah and I go there occasionally. It's not that bad. Nice time to visit with people."

This comment sparked a string of questioning involving Noah. Penny was reluctant to give up much, not that she had really given many answers since the visit started. Marie either talked over her or seemed completely uninterested in her responses. That was until now. Marie seemed annoyed at her shrugs and one-word responses

"You two are very chummy. Well, do you *like* him or what?" Marie asked.

A long pause followed.

"I am beginning to think your silence is a definite yes." Marie smirked.

Penny wanted to tell her yes but no at the same time. She wanted the voluptuous blond girl to stay away from Noah, but then again, she held no claim on him. She held no claim on anyone. She recalled the innumerable times his fingers brushed her hand or touched her shoulder. She focused on wiping the condensation from her glass, secretly hoping Marie would let the topic go.

If Marie's intense stare was any indication, the added throat clearing struck her point home.

"Yes, of course I like him. Everyone does. We work together. We are neighbors. He is my closest friend." Penny pulled her right shoulder up in a half shrug.

He takes me on overnight survival trips, visits my house in the middle of the night to feed a polar bear cub, meets me in the bunker to goof off on the guitars, she added to herself.

He finds you attractive and flirts with you, added Lucy. Penny hid a small smile.

It's been months though. Wouldn't he have asked me out by now?

"Does he tell you about the girls who ask him out? Word around town is quite a few do, you know."

Penny didn't know what the word around town was. For a handsome, single man like Noah, how could she figure girls weren't trying for his attention? But she didn't want Marie to know.

"As far as I know, I am the only girl he hangs out with." Penny smiled with indulgence although she began to wonder to her sister. *How many girls ask him out?*

You could always ask him. Close friends and all that, Lucy chided.

"And you two are seriously not a couple?" Marie asked, as she eyed the pendant hanging around her neck. Penny fingered the claw unconsciously. "That is a strange necklace. Matches your wardrobe." Marie then smiled sweetly. "Well, maybe he hasn't been asked by the right girl yet."

Penny considered that. Was there a way she could find out if he wanted to date her without ruining their friendship? Did she even want to date him? She snorted at that. Marie gave her an odd look.

Fortunately there was no more talk of Noah.

The week passed quickly without a chance to ask Noah much of anything. Penny agreed to a second coffee excursion with Marie during which she gossiped about the town folk and their children. The only time she included Penny was to ask if she agreed with her. A noncommittal "hmm" was the only response Penny gave.

Penny refrained from commenting and was having a hard time not staring at the girl in shock. Marie's apparent fondness for criticizing people didn't sit well with Penny. After all, the girl was a teacher—someone children could look up to— a model for civil behavior and good manners.

The waitress, Gigi, stopped by to check on their orders. Marie complained her coffee was too cold. Penny barely kept from shaking her head in bewilderment as she had watched Marie add ice cubes to her coffee to cool it down. Instead, she gave her attention to the tall, dark-haired girl waiting on them.

Penny knew Gigi from self-defense classes, which the girl attended on an infrequent basis. Looking more closely at the tight smile Gigi was giving, Penny wondered if it was just Marie's complaints and shallow comments on the restaurant that weighed on her.

A shiver of foreboding fell down Penny's spine.

"Hey, how are things, Gigi? You haven't been at classes lately. Been busy?" Penny pushed down the rising sick. What was wrong with her?

"Are you still dating Robbie?" Marie probed in a soft, sugary-sweet voice, sticky upon Penny's ears.

Gigi glanced at Marie, her eyes troubled. She ran the back of her hand across her forehead before responding in a breaking voice, her eyes glistening.

"Things are alright. Thanks for asking, Penny. No, Robbie and I are taking a break, Marie. But you would know that, I think. Let me know if you need anything further." Gigi left their bills and spun around, her long black hair flying up, trailing her like ribbons on a kite.

Marie smirked. "He wasn't worth it, not if he grazed in other pastures."

Penny wondered in whose pasture Robbie grazed. Had it been Marie's? Even so, in a debauched way, Marie was right. Penny readied to bid Marie goodbye, feeling more than a little uncouth for associating with the young teacher. Before she worked up an excuse to leave, Marie caught her attention.

"Did you hear about the girl they discovered in Juneau? They think she was murdered. Possibly by the same one who killed the girls around here."

Stunned by the comment, Penny sorted through recent conversations with Army and Noah. Neither had mentioned any additional killings.

Marie showed Penny an article on her phone. The photo of the deceased girl looked familiar. But her name was unfamiliar. Troubled, Penny knew she would ask Army and Noah about it later.

"Wow, that is very scary," Penny said as she handed the phone back to the girl.

"Scary? I'm glad it was in Juneau. Must mean the killer moved away. Well," Marie drew her coat over her shoulders, "I best be going."

Anxious to get back to resume bear duty, she paid the bill and left wondering if she really wanted to hang out with the girl again. Penny also wondered about Marie's words. Would Noah go out if someone asked him? The thought troubled her.

Maybe girls around here just know he isn't interested and don't ask, Lucy offered.

It is not like that is a topic we discuss. I mean, I ask him about doing things, not date things.

Lucy snorted. *Yeah, okay. Cooking him dinner and watching a movie is not a date night kinda thing.*

Oh, come on. Friends do that, too. And he has asked me to do things. We go out to movies, go to the restaurant. If he started dating someone, I would lose all of that.

And you would be hurt. Come on, admit it. You like him. You should just tell him.

Penny blocked her sister for a few moments, a gift she had improved to hide her constant state of weariness from Lucy. What was the point? If Noah had any interest, wouldn't he have initiated something? Their brand of flirting was mild. No different than Army "flirting" with the waitress or her mother for that matter. Compliments are not equivalent to flirting, except in Lucy's mind. Harry's brand was overbearing. Noah's and her bantering was...warm. Friendly.

Life goes on, Lu. If something is meant to be. Penny returned to their connection.

I get it. You are too afraid to do something. To take a chance. To see if you could be happy having someone closer to you than a friend. Whatever. Why would you listen to me anyway? Like I know anything about real life. I am a watcher. Not a doer. How could I know anything, except for what I wish I would do in your place?

Lucy closed herself off after she finished her rant and Penny could not get her to open again. She mulled over what Lucy said and what Marie mentioned at lunch. She felt a connection with Noah, but was it all in her head?

Later that night, curled up in bed with a book, dog, and bear, Penny's phone alerted her to a text.

Noah: *Hey Momma Bear, lights out.*

She checked the clock: 9:42 p.m. Lucy and her mother were still out at the clinic to check on a patient.

Penny: *Meet you out front.*

She left the slumbering pair of animals in her bed, pulled on a pair of jeans, and headed outside.

A heavy fog had developed soon after her lunch with Marie. It matched her mood up until now. The fog clung nearer to the ground, not as heavy as earlier, and glowing orbs from the lights from town showed here and there. Even with the fog, intense ribbons of green and red wove through the heavens above her. Noah quietly approached as Winter nosed her hand in greeting.

She thanked Noah as he gazed transfixed at the sky. He glanced down and gave her a wink. Penny's happiness at Noah's calls or messages whenever the aurora displayed itself seemed to spike with each flare of the lights. Whether it was 3:00 a.m. or 5:00 a.m. didn't matter. Both were accustomed to sleepless nights, either due to dreams or night cub duty.

Thoughts about what Marie said earlier in the day and

Lucy's comments invaded her mind. But then the image of the red-haired girl, the one found in Juneau, flashed in her memory. The blood drained from her face as recollection set in. The reason the girl seemed so familiar to Penny was that Penny had seen her before. Not in person, but in a vision. The one she had already spoke to both men about.

"Hey, where did you go? You look haunted," Noah touched her cheek with a cool hand.

"Noah, remember before I found Fjord, I had a vision that showed a girl's face? The one that didn't seem familiar?" she croaked.

He squinted at her as he dropped his hand. Then he nodded once.

"I saw her earlier today," she began.

"Where? In town?" he asked, his brows drawn together.

"No, not in town. In a picture. She was found dead in a hunting shack in Juneau, and the authorities said she was missing for months. She disappeared after work one day. In September." She paused, swallowing back the bile. In a whisper, she continued, "I think that was about when I saw her and heard her scream in my head."

The silent lights, reflected in Noah's eyes, shifted and danced above them.

He grabbed her hand and pulled her in the direction of his house.

Army dozed on the couch, a newspaper draped across his chest. When Noah shook him gently, Army shot up, yelling a garbled word that sounded very much like a curse.

"Sorry. We need to talk," Noah said.

Penny relayed her story. While Army made a few calls for more information, she paced the living room floor.

"Well, kids. Penny ought to go home. Nothing more we can do. The authorities will look at every possible connection, but for now we should all get some sleep."

Penny glanced at the clock, surprised it read 11:13 p.m. Noah walked her back home beneath the lights that still danced overhead.

The next day, Lucy agreed to go to The FrostBite with

Penny for lunch to find Gigi was once again working.

She keeps looking over her shoulder, her sister commented.

Lucy left to use the restroom before Gigi delivered the drinks. It did not go unnoticed by Penny that the girl slammed the glasses down harder than necessary.

"Where's your friend?" Gigi asked.

"My sister…"

The other girl shook her head. Penny cocked her head to the side and began, "Noah?"

"No, the blond."

"Ahh, well, I have no idea. Causing problems for someone, I would imagine. We aren't close friends, Gigi. I am very sorry, for what it is worth."

Gigi responded by lifting her chin before turning to go.

"Hey, are you okay?" Penny called after her.

The girl turned back and smoothed down her apron. Dark blemishes stood out beneath her eyes. She sighed.

"I'm okay, Penny. Just tired." She huffed. "My roommate's been staying with her boyfriend more and coming home to an empty place is lonely. My phone has been ringing at odd hours, private number but no one answers. Stupid robocalls. Kinda freaking me out, I guess."

"Really? You don't know who's calling?"

"No, I thought maybe it was Robbie at the beginning, but he said it wasn't. And I believe him. It's just that…" She broke off, looking around the crowded room.

"What?" Penny motioned the girl to sit in the empty red bench seat across from her. Gigi fell into the cushioned seat.

"Well, I remember Katie told me she got calls like that. She would answer them at first. That was the week before she disappeared. Then she called in sick for work and never showed up."

The hairs rose on Penny's neck. Katie was the girl found dead a few days after Penny arrived.

"It's probably nothing. I get those robocalls, too. Let me know if you need anything," Penny put a hand on the girl's arm. Gigi nodded her thanks before returning to work.

A throbbing temple headache descended on Penny, and she apologized to her sister for her desire to leave early.

On her way out of the restaurant, the cold and vertigo hit Penny simultaneously, and she fell to her knees. Faintly, as if in the distance, Lucy called her name. Danger pulsed through Penny's veins as the Shadowed Man flashed in her mind.

Someone grabbed her arms and hauled her upright. Noah gazed down at her.

"Are you alright?" he asked.

She shook her head, clearing the cobwebs. "Sure, I'm fine."

"When a woman says she is fine, she most certainly isn't," he rebuked. Lucy stood off to the side, shadowing Penny, a protective hand resting on the small of her back.

"I saw the shadowy person again."

"No one else?"

"No, no one else." She fought off the disorientation. "But Gigi said she was getting phone calls from a silent caller. Just like Kate Kingston did before she disappeared. Has there been any more word on the deceased girls?"

He shook his head. "Nothing. No suspects either. And I overheard Army mention repeat calls from an untraceable phone the week prior to her disappearance."

"Do you still think I am having premonitions of the killer?" she asked, her voice close to a whisper.

"I have no doubt."

"Noah, I am worried about Gigi. I just have this feeling. I think she may be a target."

"Tell me as soon as you have a vision, okay Penny? Call me. Message me. Knock on my door. Anytime. Alright?"

She nodded.

"Do you need me to drive you home?" Goosebumps pricked her skin as she became aware of their nearness. She placed her hands on his chest, steadying herself. She turned away, guilty for wanting to ride with him when her sister was waiting for her.

"No, I am fine, Noah, really."

His skeptic gaze suggested he was aware of her lie. "In

that case, I think I might have a chat with Gigi. Make sure she lets me know if anything odd happens. Sound like a plan?"

Heart falling, Penny nodded. It was for the best, to advise the girl to be extra careful. What better way to be extra careful than to have Noah looking out for her? Penny hoped he still had time for her.

Jealous

Turned out Noah had plenty of time for Penny. Several weeks later, Valentine's day, he convinced her to play guitar with Army and him at the lodge. Eelyn kindly offered to watch the cub so Penny could have more than a couple of hours off. Her mother also planned to visit between feedings, so she could enjoy the evening, too. Lucy tagged along and sat at a table, mentally singing along with her sister while clapping like a fool after each song.

Penny had played guitar almost her entire life but never played in front of a crowd like this.

The bright lights shining in her face made it difficult to see the crowd, so all the people she saw as she entered the lodge could have up and left and she wouldn't have known, excepting for the applause after each song.

During a break for the performers, a server brought refreshments. As she grabbed a water, she was hit suddenly with vertigo. Once again, she saw the face of the polar bear, but without blood on his face. He was looking away from her, rather than at her. His profile dissolved, and a shadowy human form took its place, piercing eyes of ice staring into her soul. The hairs on the back of her neck stood up. She broke out in cold sweat, and her hands began to shake. She pulled the water bottle in tight to her chest and willed the image to disappear. It didn't.

She jumped as a hand touched her lower back.

"Hey, you okay?" came the quiet voice of Noah. He searched her face, his brow furrowed. "What's up? Are you sick?"

Nodding was all she could do as a surge of nausea rose within. He pulled her over into a corner, and as she sat, he mothered her, feeling her forehead and checking her pupils. Laughter bubbled up her throat only to come out as a gasp. It was fortunate her mother and sister left earlier so that they did not have to see her like this.

"Was the playing too much?" he asked, genuinely concerned.

She shook her head as she focused on Lucy's whisper in her mind that she was alright.

"Sorry, Noah. No, the playing is fine. I just...became dizzy and then saw the bear..." she said, not wanting to relive the vision.

"The bear or the Shadowed Man?"

"Both," she answered.

At that moment, Marie sidled up next to Noah and managed to stand in front of Penny. In prime form, Marie praised Noah's skill at the guitar in a sugar sweet voice. Penny heard that voice too often at the vet clinic and may or may not have used it once or twice herself when talking to baby animals. Shifting around Marie's curvaceous frame, Noah glanced at Penny. Concern was still etched on his handsome face, stubble darkening his jaw. As Marie rambled on, Penny mimed vomiting into the ash tray behind her back. Noah barked out a laugh and quickly attempted to cover it with a cough. "Marie, it is nice to see you, but could you please excuse us? I need time alone with Penny," Noah said. He missed the irritated look Marie flashed at Penny.

"Oh, Penny, are you sick?" she recovered, asking in a mock curious tone. "Do all these people watching bother you?"

"No, I just got, ah, got a cramp in my hand," she said as she dropped her gaze to her lap and rubbed her right hand. Noah took the hint, squatted in front of her and began to massage her hand.

"We will be a few minutes," he said in a tone that meant he was done talking to her. Marie spun around and retreated towards the bathrooms near the opposite side of the room.

"I am better, Noah, really," Penny said as she reluctantly tried reclaiming her hand. But his grip held firm. "Get up, you look silly."

"Did you see any faces?"

Resigned that the striking man was also stubborn, she spoke, her voice low so that it carried to his ears only.

"No. No other faces. Not the Shadowed Man's. No woman's face. Just doom and gloom, urgency and malevolence." She closed her eyes and willed darkness to blot out the images. It didn't work, so she opened her eyes, meeting Noah's gaze. "I don't think I'm a target. I think I would see his face. I hope I would..." Deep down she knew. At least not yet. The sapphire blue of Noah's eyes sparked a memory. "He has pale blue eyes."

"I'm not sure that helps narrow things down. People can wear colored contacts."

He continued rubbing her hand.

"Noah, you can stop with my hand." He didn't and smiled at her.

"Massaging is supposed to help with cramps. Besides it being Valentine's Day and all, holding someone's hand is completely acceptable, yeah?" His smile and upbeat tone did not erase the concern from his face. "I will make sure you get home tonight. If you want, you can sleep in the bunker."

Sighing, she stood, the weight of the menacing images dragging her down. He kept hold of her hand as they walked back to the small stage and said, "Come on, Momma Bear. You got this."

With that, she managed to pull herself together to complete the rest of the night's music.

The remainder of that night and the few weeks that followed sailed by without any missing person alert or discovery of a body. It was unsettling - not knowing why the vision had struck. How soon would something happen? Would something happen?

In addition to escorting her everywhere, which both annoyed and thrilled Penny, Noah was an almost constant presence at the Osborn household as he continued to help with the cub. She was annoyed because she was unable to behave how she normally did: drive herself, run through taekwondo patterns, do push-ups, walk around in comfortable clothes. But she was thrilled because they played more guitar (Edgar sat on Noah's shoulder now instead of Penny's), watched movies, cooked, and baked together. Noah often requested her French Toast cupcakes, and luckily, Penny was able to give more away than keep in the house. Those cupcakes called to her at all hours of the day and night, and since she was up most hours of day and night, the temptation to submit to the decadent blend of maple, cinnamon, and cream cheese in a tiny cake was too powerful to keep in the house for long.

Lucy spent much of her time out of the house away from the pair, insisting she would rather help at the vet clinic than be a third wheel. Penny swore there was no reason for her to leave. Noah and she, sadly, had nothing more than a strictly platonic relationship. Standing firm, Lucy hoped her absence would encourage the relationship status to change into a more romantic one.

Due to Noah's pestering, Penny continued to attempt the recommended meditation. Although it neither incited additional visions nor clarified them. There were benefits to meditation, chiefly a calm mindfulness.

It was during one of her meditative naps on the couch that her mother came home from work. Noah was also visiting, or rather snoozing on the opposite side of the couch, her leg pillowing his head. They roused at the sound of the door closing. Noah yawned and stretched before greeting her mother.

"Anything I should be aware of?" asked Eelyn after he had left.

"Nothing as exciting as a boyfriend, I assure you. He's just worried about my visions," Penny said, choking on her words.

Seeming to take it in stride, Eelyn asked, "Are they getting worse? Changing?"

Penny answered no to both. "But they are not getting better or less frequent."

Eelyn's sharp gaze met Penny's. "And you still think they

could be connected to the seri…ah, deceased women?"

Penny gazed down and chewed on the inside of her lower lip. "I think so. I don't ever get any clues that might reveal who he is or where he might strike next, you know? They happen before a body is discovered or before he strikes. Or when he strikes? I don't know. Noah is just supportive. Slightly overprotective. If he can't protect everyone in town, then he will at least try to protect me." She shrugged.

"Is the man ever attacking you?" her mother asked.

"No. Never a clear picture of his face. Army's meditation isn't helping."

Eelyn gave her daughter a hug. "Better to not take that level of companionship for granted. He is loyal." She leaned back and searched Penny's face. "But…not your boyfriend?"

Penny sighed, and Eelyn took that as her answer. She patted Penny's cheek.

"The best things come to those who wait," she whispered.

"There is no vaccination for impatience," retorted Penny, desperate to change the topic. "Have you seen that journal I bought for Lucy? The leather one from Christmas?"

Pursing her lips, Eelyn shook her head.

"Hmm, it's missing."

"I'll look for it with you later," Eelyn rubbed Penny's arm. "I have an emergency to see, and I need to get going. I'm sorry."

It was Penny's night to cook and take care of Fjord. For once, Noah was not spending a Saturday evening with her, helping to feed the cub and play guitar. Apparently, he needed a break on occasion.

Fjord was now eating more at one time and sleeping longer periods in between, so her chances of getting enough sleep were very good. The realization that there would not be garlic toast for her evening meal hit her midway through the preparation of the food. She cursed herself for forgetting. Her mother, in the shower, would not be of any help. Nor would Lucy, who was in bed with a headache. And so, Penny left a note and grabbed her coat to run up to the Dolores' restaurant. No visions plagued her that day, nor in several

207

previous days, so she felt comfortable going out on her own.

As it was every weekend night, The FrostBite was busy. Dolores was working at the till when Penny walked up to pick up her order that she had called in during her drive.

"Oh, I have it ready for you here, Penny. Do you need to rush off or can you stay to visit with Noah and the rest?" Dolores asked.

"No, working on supper." Penny smiled and refused the urge to look around the seating areas.

"That's too bad. I think he would prefer you visit," his aunt commented as she rang up the bill. Penny met her eyes then glanced in the direction Dolores indicated with her head. She felt her heartbeat speed up at the thought of seeing him.

The sight she focused on was not what she anticipated. Easily recognizable by his thick, curly black hair and the usual blue flannel shirt, he leaned against the far counter, facing away from her. Several other men and women that gathered near were familiar from self-defense classes or casual meetings with Noah. One of the women was Marie.

Her mouth formed an *oh* as she saw Marie lean forward into Noah. Her far hand traveled up his arm and around his neck as she pressed herself into him. Penny whipped her head back to the till, thoughts jumbled.

"No, Dolores, I think he is busy."

Dolores looked over quickly and slammed the till shut. She started to say, "Why that..." with the rest trailing off under her breath.

Penny quickly turned to leave and heard Dolores yell something incomprehensible. The door's loud chime reverberated in Penny's ears as the images burned into her mind.

Hey, you don't know what was happening. There are two sides to every story, thought a supportive Lucy.

Not when both sides had their arms around each other.

No, Penny, he did not have his arm around her. She sidled up to him. Like a snake. Lucy's thoughts trailed off into cursing.

Penny's thoughts grew dark and tormented. He did not

push her away, so what did it matter? What could she do? Nothing. Go home and finish supper. Realizing she had blocked her sister, she opened her mind again, and Lucy's comforting thoughts soothed her. Both remained quiet for the rest of the drive.

As Penny walked through the door, Eelyn, having finished her shower, called from her bedroom, "Noah called. You left your phone here, so I answered. Sorry. He wants you to call him back."

"Sure, thanks." Penny went back to the kitchen. She realized she was no longer hungry for her favorite dish. Her stomach roiled at the normally appetizing aroma of spaghetti sauce. The day Penny's appetite for spaghetti disappeared was a bad day indeed.

As Eelyn ate and Penny picked, she grew angry at Marie. Her mother tried starting several conversations, but with Penny aloof or short, Eelyn's attempts ceased. Penny longed to hide in a dark place, so she created one in her mind, closing herself off from her sister in the process.

While she was cleaning up the kitchen, an alert sounded on her phone. A message from Noah. She ignored it. His call came quickly after. She ignored it. Marie sent her a photo message in addition to several other messages. She ignored all.

Someone could be hurt, Lucy offered.

Then let him call Army.

Eelyn heard the incoming messages and calls but said nothing. Penny muted her phone and threw it on the couch after the seventh chime. *Just quit!* she shouted in her head.

You'll have to talk to him tomorrow when he comes over for night duty, Lucy reminded her calmly.

Penny's response was a polar opposite to her previous outburst - silence.

There followed no mental sigh, but Lucy began a melodic narrative of a recent science fiction novel that was by Penny's favorite author. Around 2:00 a.m., Penny couldn't help but check her phone. No further calls or messages since muting. She toyed with the idea of sending him a quick message of, "Sorry I missed you." But then she scoffed at the notion. She had seen him...and her.

She finally decided on: *"Headache tonight. Talk to you later."*

The next morning, she barely spoke to her mother or Lucy. Instead, she settled into a sullen silence. Fjord suckled on her hand, his high trill that normally made her smile failing. He rolled on the floor, tangling himself thoroughly in a blanket, attempted to rip an ear off his stuffed polar bear and growled at Blue. Blue only cocked his head at the less than ferocious ball of white blubber and fluff. Fjord bawled after her when she put him in his box.

Half an hour before Noah was due to show for an early start to his night duty, Penny left the house for a run at the gym.

As she approached the gym doors, she noticed Marie standing next to the treadmills with an older man and two young kids. She groaned inwardly and turned around, walking back to her vehicle. Not knowing where to escape to, she drove around the bland town a bit before heading home, taking great interest in any brightly colored (chipped and peeling) dumpster. She longed to walk along the beach, but the dark skies barred that idea. Just because she hadn't had any visions didn't mean she was going to look for trouble.

Instead of parking at home, she parked at Army's and jogged up to the house. It was only 10:00 p.m. and the lights glowed from the few small windows, so she figured Army was home and still awake. Army beckoned her in after the first knock.

"Well, what are you up to this late at night, girl?" asked Army.

Penny shrugged, unsure what to tell him.

"Been having more visions?"

"Not since the night we played at the lodge," she admitted.

"The meditation helping?"

She replied with a one shoulder shrug.

"I have been thinking on it, Penny. I still think this bear with the scars is your spirit animal or even guardian angel.

One that can jump into a living creature's body when necessary. Do you think that strange?" He watched her with a raised eyebrow.

She sniffed, her expression salty. "Strange? You mean strange like having premonitions?"

"I think extraordinary might be a better term for your visions, Penny. As for the guardianship idea, it would explain why you see him in your thoughts as well as in real life."

Thinking about the bear in that manner brought some manner of comfort. Provided the bear refrained from attacking her, either in the visions or in real life.

Tapping her temple, she said, "Unfortunately I haven't got a tap on his thoughts to confirm this theory."

"Well the more dangerous of the two in your visions is the unidentified man. You can monitor the bear," he broke off waiting for her confirmation, then continued, "so he won't be sneaking up on you at least. Either way, neither is a good reason to stop living life to the fullest. Embrace all challenges that you face and be thankful for what you have."

After wishing him a good night, she descended into the bunker to practice guitar, already deciding she would use Noah's Gibson.

Penny, come home. It is almost midnight. I am pretty sure Noah is dozing. You should be able to sneak in.

Penny checked the clock to see that Lucy was right. Having done nothing more than strum chords for the past hour and stare blankly at the ceiling, it was probably best to just call it a night and try to get some sleep. She could sneak up into her room through the back door of the bunker. On the other hand, she could just sleep in the room with the hammock and twinkling lights.

Whatever. You will need to talk to him some time.

Penny dreamt of running through the snow while fresh heavy flakes fell all around her. She stopped to spread her arms out, catching flakes in her hands, on her arm. She heard a voice calling to her. A voice she recognized. One that comforted and thrilled her at the same time. As she looked around for the source, the wind rushed up, blowing the snow

211

around her and blocking her view.

"Penny, hey Penny. Wake up, Momma Bear."

She opened her eyes to find the most intriguing eyes gazing down at her. She sucked in her breath and wiped at the drool on her cheek

"Hey, I saw you didn't come home and thought maybe you wound up here," Noah spoke, his low voice soft.

"You checked my room? That's a bit creepy, Noah." She struggled to sit up, the blanket effectively binding her attempts. Noah tried to help, but she pushed him away

"So, are you avoiding me?" he asked bluntly

"No," she replied. As she gazed up into his eyes, she felt the weight of her lie. "Yes."

He nodded. "It isn't what you think."

She sighed, trying to extricate herself from the protective blanket. "Look, it doesn't matter. If you like Marie and she likes you, then what does it matter what I think?

"I don't like Marie. Not like that. Not like anything. And it does matter what you think."

Penny peered up sharply. She noted the intensity of his face matched his statement.

"It sure seemed like you liked her more than a friend," she said quietly.

Noah was shaking his head slowly. "You didn't see the whole scene. A few friends invited me out to visit, and she just showed up. She wanted to take a picture with me to send you. To encourage you to come out and hang with us. I agreed because I thought you would enjoy the guys I was with, but I also knew Fjord would keep you busy. Then I thought maybe you could sneak away for an hour. And she was persuasive, so I went with it. She started hanging on one of the guys who seemed fine with it. When she did the same with me, well, that was when you saw us."

Penny hated that the vision continued to flash before her eyes. She looked away and squeezed her eyes shut, trying to imagine a different scene, the one Noah was describing.

"I heard Dolores yell and saw you walking out."

Penny saw that Noah did look bummed.

"She is a looney, and I don't mean a Canadian," Noah said. "She went nuts after I pushed her away and started crying and lashing out at the guys I was with. Dolores pried her away from us and sat her down in a booth. Tried talking to her. She was drunk or…something. Punched Dolores in the chin."

"She hit your aunt?!" Penny asked, amazed.

"Yes, but Dolores blocked the worst of it. I was worried you got the wrong impression. About me. I am…I am not like that. In fact, I consider myself unavailable."

"I was just shocked, I guess. I never pictured you with someone like her. I mean, she is super-hot, but just everything else about her didn't seem like…"

Penny's relief made her almost floppy. She leaned back, but then the realization he had used the word unavailable worked its way through Penny's brain. His nightmares must not have been improving.

Noah's intense eyes bore at Penny. "Who do you picture me with?"

Penny looked away before her blush hit her full on. It was so strong she felt her scalp burn. She couldn't look at him as she replied, "Oh, I don't know. Someone like…more. Just someone more." The temptation to ask was too strong. "Um, why are you unavailable?" She picked at the blanket.

He leaned closer to her and whispered, "Why do you think?"

Their eyes met, and Penny momentarily forgot how to breathe. "Ah, nightmares?"

A half-smile lifted his face, the twinkling lights reflected in his eyes making him look mischievous. "While there is that, I can't stop thinking about a certain brunette. But I'm not sure she likes me in a romantic way."

Her blush became so intense she was sure her head would light the room red. She cleared her throat before replying. "Well, might be a good idea to ask her."

"I've thought of that. But what if she doesn't like me more than a friend. Would that affect our relationship in the future? I would rather have her as a friend than nothing at all."

213

Penny's eyes leapt between each of his, as if trying to discover which eye held the key to what he implied. Finding no concrete answer in either, she stared back down at her hands. "I can see how that would be a difficult choice. But wouldn't it be better to know for sure? Especially if she feels the same way?" Deep in her heart she hoped he was referring to her, and yet uncertainty needled its way in, reminding her that there surely was someone else.

"There are no certainties in life," he said as he stood.

"Except time," she glanced at the clock that read 4:23 a.m. "I should get back home." Misery welled up within her. It was not her that he had secret feelings for.

"I'll walk you back," Noah offered her his hand. She accepted the strong, calloused grip and allowed herself to be pulled up out of the warmth and security of the hammock. The fact that he kept hold of her hand until they reached the ladder leading to her room caused the bubbles of hope flare to life.

"So, how long have you known about the back access to the bunker?" he asked as he turned to face her.

"Army said I could come down anytime, from any route, so…"

She felt awkward standing so close to him. *Crap, what should I do?*

How about keep breathing and get up the ladder? Her sister offered.

Penny started. *Really?*

Well, if I told you to sneak a quick kiss on his cheek, you would be mortified, so I went the safe route.

Penny grabbed the rung above her head and paused, thinking about her sister's comment. She turned and faced Noah, her hand still on the rung.

"I'm sorry she turned out to be so crazy," she said breathlessly as she rested her chin on her shoulder.

A soft smile lightened his face. "Don't be."

She turned back to head up the ladder when he called to her softly, encouraging her to turn back to face him. The soft, red glow of the corridor lights cast shadows across his face, and his eyes gleamed darkly as he stared down at her. His gaze traveled her face, over her lips before meeting her gaze once again.

Her heart beat so loudly in her ears she almost didn't discern his words.

"You probably shouldn't tell your mother about this ladder."

She nodded and cast her gaze downward ready to make her way up the ladder. Disappointment welled up until she felt the heat radiating from his skin, and she realized he had her caged against the metal rungs. She glanced up and saw such vulnerability on his face.

His voice was husky when he whispered, "Penny."

Then he leaned down and brushed his lips against hers. They were soft and warm, tentative before he broke contact and rested his forehead against hers.

In the scarlet shadows, his warm breath caressed her skin. An intense need hit her, and she reached for his face, trailing her fingers along his strong jaw as they moved to the back of his neck, the short stubble rough against her fingertips. The pulse in his neck thrummed as she pulled him closer.

The half-smile that made her heart flutter played on his lips as his face hoovered mere heartbeats from hers. His skin was fire, and his gaze the northern lights. He grasped her around her waist and pulled her tight against his body. He ran a hand up her spine and cupped her neck, tilting her head back. She met his lips and kissed him with a hungry abandon she didn't understand but that made her entire being sing. She pulled back after only a few moments, their breathing ragged. Her heart beating like she had just run five miles.

Invested

Marie did not appear at the next defense class nor any other class for several weeks, for which Penny was grateful.

"She probably moved on to something more fun, someone else whose life is more interesting to interfere in," Eelyn commented after hearing a short synopsis of the soap opera that had been Penny's social life for a few short weeks.

Penny and Noah continued with their friendship as if nothing happened—but something most certainly had. His lack of additional affection made her uncomfortable, questioning whether the kiss had happened. He maintained a continued presence, but Penny felt a strain.

Maybe he regretted it. Maybe he didn't really like her. Maybe he changed his mind.

Maybe you both are colossal chicken butts, commented her sister on more than one occasion. *Unfortunately for cupid,* as Lucy pointed out, *you both are too timid to do anything about it. He has feelings for you, you dummy. Throw him a bone, would you? Give him some sign that you are in love with him.*

I don't know if I should. I mean, I have another year and then will be heading back to Anchorage, right? Is it worth it if I end up ruining our friendship? Or what will happen when I must leave? Long distance relationships don't often work out.

Seriously, why worry about that? What will be will be, you know?

Right. So. I'll just give him more time. That sounded about right to Penny.

Take a chance already!

You know, you need to be putting more energy into

finishing your book than trying to figure out my life story.

March brought with it increased daylight hours—from nine hours to over half a day. The tagged polar bears were still out on the ice, far from shore according to the computer that Penny continued to monitor. Temperatures slowly rose and reached the mid-thirties by 8:30 p.m.

One night, Penny needed to get out even if it was dark, just for a break to clear her head. She didn't need a chaperone for a short walk with Blue, and the absence of any terrible visions led her to conclude that all would be fine. Like Army said, she must get out and live life.

Lucy continued with her suggestions and lecturing on how Penny should conduct herself around Noah.

Get out of my head! Let me enjoy this walk without you, without your thoughts. I have enough of my own to deal with! She mentally screamed, the force of it causing her to bend over. She grasped her head in her hands, her breath ragged. Blue sniffed her gloved hands and whimpered.

She heard nothing in response. Finally. Her sister had pulled away from her. Penny rubbed Blue's head before standing straight. "Sorry, buddy. Personal things to take care of."

He licked her cheek and turned to resume pulling on the leash.

After a few minutes of refreshing silence, she heard a vehicle approach. She reached for her cell phone just in case. A small SUV pulled up beside Penny. The window slowly rolled down as Penny's hair stood on end.

"Hi, Penny! Long time, no see!"

Penny's stomach curled at the sound of the all too familiar voice. She forced a polite smile as she turned.

"Hi, Marie."

"Oh, Blue has gotten so big! Penny, this is my boyfriend, Steven, and his two boys, Alex and Axel." Marie placed a lot of emphasis on the term boyfriend.

Penny nodded and smiled. "Hi." Blue pulled on his leash, away from the SUV.

"It's been ages since I have seen you," Marie gushed.

"How are things going?" Her eyes seemed to sparkle in the interior lights of the vehicle.

"Oh, great! Really great. Staying busy." Penny smiled widely and wanted to add something about Noah but failed to see the point. Blue continued to lunge away from the vehicle. He was not immune to Penny's feelings.

"And Noah. How is he?"

And she went there, Penny thought.

"Awesome."

"Good."

"Good."

Marie cleared her throat and spoke quietly to the driver. She turned to Penny. "Okay, well, we will leave you with Blue. Looks like he wants to keep going." She smiled. "See you later!"

Penny wondered at the exchange and why they were out driving, here. The road led to more than just Army's, she supposed.

As the vehicle sped away, Blue sat with his tongue lolling and his cheeks pulled back in a sort of grin. She smiled at him and gave his head a quick pat.

"Are you helping me?" She wondered aloud. He barked once.

Upon their return to the house, Penny found Noah had left more wooden teething rings that he had carved for Fjord. With Fjord's canine teeth erupting, his pains became Penny's. He stopped eating for several days while his chewing intensified. Eelyn once brought some freezable child teething rings for him to try. They worked for a bit, but once the swelling in his mouth subsided and the teeth poked through, he quickly destroyed the teething rings

"This inside stuff is nontoxic, right?" Penny asked her mother

"I think so."

Penny switched to frozen washcloths for him to chew on until Noah made the wood rings.

The weather was warming, and a good length of freezing rain struck the night before a needed trip to the research station. A thick layer of glass covered every outdoor surface the following morning.

As she stepped out onto the small landing outside the front door, she slipped on slick ice, landing roughly on her backside. Sharp pain shot up her tailbone, forcing the air from her lungs.

Are you hurt? her sister asked as Penny blinked back the rising tears.

Nothing to be concerned about. Just a crack. Penny began giggling. That giggle grew until a snort erupted, and her laughter bordered on hysteria. Thankfully, no one had observed her graceless fall.

"Careful, goofy. You'll slip again."

Surprise. So, Noah had witnessed her fall.

He offered his hand, but her feet struggled to find a grip on the icy wood. Noah let go before he too went down. Waves of laughter hit her again as she struggled to rise. Groaning, she blinked away the tears and rolled to her side so she could grab hold of the railing and pull herself to her feet.

"You okay?" Noah asked, barely able to conceal the grin.

The laughter rose once more as she said, "Just a crack." She slipped again in her fit of hysteria.

He shook his head, and his laughter joined hers. He asked where the spikes were that Army gave her yesterday.

"Um, inside on the counter."

"What are they doing there?"

"Being completely unhelpful."

"The spikes are supposed to help you."

"No shit."

She took deep breaths in an attempt to regain composure. "Probably need de-icer for the steps." She giggled.

"You think?" Noah brushed off the back of her jacket, and she held up her arms signaling him to wait.

"I'll dust off my pants, thank you. I'm fine, really."

They loaded up the truck and set out, Fjord chewing on the seat and awkwardly crawling between them in the front seat. Both dogs lounged in the back. The truck, in four-wheel drive, skidded several times on the trip through the quiet town and out to the station. When they reached the station, Penny grabbed the little bear and set him down outside the truck next to her feet. He sat for several seconds, squinting in the sunlight before he grabbed her polar bear-hide-covered leg and attempted to climb up.

She walked forward, brushing him off as she walked. He followed like a puppy on all fours, calling with his high-pitched squeal. Winter and Blue jumped out of the back and started sniffing around the interior of the research fence. Whenever she got too far away from him, Fjord would cry out.

"He kinda sounds like a goat."

"He does not. Goats sound like polar bear cubs," Penny shot back, sticking her tongue out at Noah.

As Fjord continued to venture further through the snow, Blue approached him and rolled him easily on his back with a paw before calmly walking away. Fjord struggled to right himself and clumsily jogged after Blue. Penny sat down on a snow-covered barrel, thankful for her caribou face mask and polar bear leggings. Noah sat next to her and called to the little cub. Fjord ambled over and rubbed up against Penny's legs, standing up and falling over in his attempt to climb. Penny reached down and lifted the cub into her lap.

"Oh man, buddy. You are heavy," she huffed.

"How much does he weigh now anyway?" Noah asked, the skin around his eyes crinkled against the glare of the sun reflecting off the snow.

"Fifty-two pounds."

"Fifty-two. He was only fifteen."

Noah stood up and walked away a few feet before sitting back down on the snow. He held out his arms. "Here, release the kraken!"

Penny lowered Fjord to the ground again only to find that he tried once again to climb her legs. So, she stood and walked over to Noah. Fjord followed slowly behind. As Penny looked down at Noah, he smiled and reached over to pet her furry leggings. Before she knew what happened, she was lying on the ground beside him. "You should be more careful. The ground is slick there."

She threw a handful of snow at his face, which he successfully ducked. By then, Fjord had reached them and was noisily climbing her legs. The dogs had also jogged over to join in the action. Noah played with Winter and Blue while Penny played energetically with the small bear, spending more time deflecting him from her face.

"Get off, you nose licker, ew!" she said as Fjord reached up to paw at her hand as she pushed his little black nose away from her face.

Blue finally dropped down beside Penny, his tongue lolling. Fjord half-crawled, half-fell off Penny's back and climbed Blue. Blue shook the cub off and pinned him with a front paw, judiciously licking the cub's wriggling body.

Penny and Noah laughed. Penny could sense the weight lift from her shoulders. Had she really been that tense? The wind was light today, and she imagined it carrying off her anxieties, her cares. Noah propped himself up on one elbow and watched the dog and the bear.

"So, I was thinking we should increase the amount of time we spend outside with him. I was also thinking about taking the sled out away from town so he can get different terrain. Take him down to the coast."

"You've been thinking a lot," she said wryly. A handful of snow hit her in the side of the face. "I was just worried you would hurt yourself, all that thinking," in her giggling, she inhaled snow and coughed.

"We could even go visit the Burnirk site." He was referring to the archaeological sites where prehistoric mounds had been discovered.

"Not sure we are allowed to go there, much less with a bear and two dogs in tow." She stared off at the horizon.

"Oh, you forget…I know people. We could go to the coast and dig for mammoth tusks. Need something to match your narwhal tusk, right?" He smiled mischievously.

She imagined the five of them digging feverishly in the exposed permafrost. Blue carting off a tusk much too large for him to carry. A smile tugged at her lips even as she cringed. Fjord screeched and bit and swatted at Winter's tail. Winter smacked the cub in the face with his tail, and Fjord growled and rolled over backwards. Noah laughed.

As her thoughts transformed, Penny nodded, absentmindedly chewing the inside of her bottom lip. She began to construct an image of her and Noah, decked out in polar bear fur, wandering the countryside with an ever-growing polar bear cub. Winter and Blue ever in the image. As her mind wandered, she paid less attention to Noah's rambling.

"...permit for a sanctuary." She turned her head quickly, flopped down and propped her head on her hand, mirroring Noah, and asked him to repeat what he just said.

Noah smiled. "Repeat from where I started or from where you started getting glassy-eyed on me?"

"Sorry, I just started thinking about what is yet to come in the saga of the growing polar bear and his peeps. What were you saying about a permit?" Penny smiled meekly.

"Army thinks he can get a permit to reopen a wildlife sanctuary. There was one not far from the research station that housed polar bears at one time. It was a way to rehab injured wildlife and once healthy enough, they returned the animals to where they had been found, equipped with tracking collars and the like. The place has been abandoned for at least four years now. He thinks there is a slight chance he can get it, and slight is better than none. I like the idea better than the place thirty miles away. Or a zoo. At least with the sanctuary we would be reasonably close to town."

The cold started seeping into her feet and fingers, but her heart warmed when Noah said "we." She mentally chided herself for her reaction, but with a smile responded with "let's hope so" before standing up and brushing herself off.

On their way back after several hours of playtime, Blue and Fjord fell asleep in the back seat on the ride home, Fjord curled up beneath Blue's lanky frame.

Army surprised her with a larger, more sturdy wood box for Fjord when they returned home. This update included a hinged cover that kept the holding area dark and warm. It also became his playpen as too often he ventured away from Penny, chewing on anything that was within reach. Like her boots. Eelyn's boots. The broom. The chairs and table. Penny obsessed about the chewing on the furniture and asked Army how best to prevent the chew marks. The bear was mostly unresponsive to her mental persuasion against chewing.

"Well, it isn't expensive furniture at any rate. More important to keep the electrical cords away from him. I don't care for fried bear cub. Maybe it would be best to put up a fence and restrict him to one area. Yes, that would be good but should protect the wood, too…" He trailed off in thought. "If we section off part of the living room near the back door…we could even throw together a rough shed to sit outside the back door."

"Oh, no need for that." Guilt pressed on Penny. Army did so much for her already.

He is invested in this cub's survival, too. He hired you to work on the problem of the changing climate and the impact on these bears, reminded Lucy.

"He is going to get bigger, Penny. We all know that. Knew that before agreeing to be involved. Won't be too long before he won't fit in your house anymore. Might as well do everything we can before kicking you out over the loss of my furniture." Army smiled and patted her shoulder before he stood up to refill his coffee cup.

Chaperone

As he grew, Fjord interacted with only a select few people except Army, who, due to teaching responsibilities in Anchorage, spent less time with him than the rest. Fjord's shyness turned into an aggressive playfulness around the man.

The pot came to a boil one day. Fjord stalked Army, but he pretended not to know the cub was behind him. Then all at once, Fjord pounced on the old man, grabbing his calf with his tiny jaws. Army clasped Fjord around the jaw and shook his head from side to side.

"Well, hello, pup. Need to establish our boundaries, eh?" Fjord quickly submitted to the human.

Fjord approached Army slowly with his head down, indicating he was no longer a threat. He displayed the behavior for several days until unleashing wild abandon and rushing up to Army whenever the man visited.

In early April, Army invited Penny and Fjord to accompany him on the hovercraft to assist in monitoring the seal population on an ice shelf rich with natchik, or seal, lairs. No nightmares or premonitions had occurred in recent days, so she agreed. They set up at a breathing hole to wait for a seal to emerge.

Penny found that despite the cool temperatures, she was surprisingly warm as they sat there and waited. And bored.

Fjord was now seventy-four pounds. Every pound became impatient, like Penny, after ten minutes of sitting quietly. He sat still at Penny's side for a surprisingly long time before attempting to wrestle with Army, chewing on Penny's boot and going off to pee. After being reprimanded, he settled down to wait at a different hole than the one Army was focused on, occasionally peering in.

Penny settled her gaze on Fjord, her eyesight traveling in and out of focus as time passed. At one point she saw that he had fallen asleep. A seal rose silently from the hole before Fjord, startling him awake. Penny nudged Army, and they watched as Fjord reared up on his hind legs and then slowly, comically, toppled over backwards. The seal didn't retreat beneath the ice for several seconds, as if it, too, enjoyed observing the young cub.

A mother bear would hunt with her cubs in tow, making them mind while teaching them the skills they would need to survive. Their hunting technique depended on the ice. On a healthy shelf, a bear could lie in wait around a breathing hole until a seal popped up for air. Or, being able to hold their breath for up to three minutes, they approached unsuspecting seals below the surface of the water and attacked a seal sunning itself on an ice shelf. Their sense of smell was incredible with over ten-thousand nerve endings in their nose and a generous olfactory section in their brain that allowed them to scent prey twenty to ninety miles away, given proper wind. Their eyesight embraced red-green color-blindness leading to high sensitivity to movement, especially in dim light conditions.

Upon a tentative surfacing at the human hole, Army attacked the seal and dragged it out onto the ice, much to Penny's shock. As he dressed it, Fjord started nosing in and getting in the way. Army cut off a few pieces to feed Fjord away from the carcass.

"Aren't you supposed to be monitoring population, not scoping out the best hunting areas?" Penny asked innocently after she shook off her astonishment.

"Best of both worlds, Penny. Need to get Fjord some hunting experience. Since Momma Bear," Army picked up on the nickname Noah gave her, "has never hunted natchik before, Uncle Bear will have to do. Cubs watch their mommas do everything. Fjord is lucky enough with plenty of parental figures around. Hopefully we can teach him to be more of a bear and less of a dog-person." Army roughed up

Fjords neck, Fjord growled in response. The two humans chuckled.

"Of course, another bear would be better. But not sure your mother would approve of that," Army said, referring to Eelyn. "We can take the fat from this seal and render it down into an oil to mix in with his formula or top dress his food. Or you can just mix in chunks. I guess that would be much easier."

"Do you think we could fix up a shower specifically for him? Or a bath? Or a small swimming pool to swim in and get clean. I thought taking him to the beach would be good, but he will probably get just as messy before I get him back to the house."

"Good idea. It might be some time before I can buy that wildlife sanctuary. In the meantime, maybe you should try to get him used to sleeping outside. Maybe with one of the dogs. I think Noah and I could rig up a bath for him. He is going to be a messy bear, Penny, no doubt. But how best to get him acclimated to hunting? My people, thousands of years ago, learned to hunt from the bears. Now, I am charged with teaching a bear how to hunt?" He grunted, rubbed the cub on the back. "So, Penny...how are the visions? Still having them?"

She admitted some time had passed since her last one, uncertain what it meant, if anything.

"And the meditation? Has that helped fine tune them?"

Admittedly, Penny found meditation helpful to relax her mind, but the visions stayed the same. Terrifying, vague, useless.

"No, sorry. It hasn't really helped."

Army leaned his elbows on his knees and clasped his hands, his look contemplative.

"I still am of the mind that this scarred bear is your spirit animal. I hesitate to call him a guide, as so far he has been unhelpful." He smiled ruefully. "Please keep sharing additional visions with Noah or me. If there is the tiniest of information that could help solve this, help find the killer or help prevent another victim...well, I'm sure you understand."

226

Penny understood. Understood so much that she considered her inability to find anything useful more of a fault than the visions themselves. And there was guilt, if she were honest. Her attempts at meditation had not been productive.

Fjord finished his snack and started playing with Rosie, Army's tag-a-long hound for the trip. He all but dwarfed her in size, but she held her own, not taking any of his nonsense. The two furred creatures tumbled around until Rosie let him know he had gone too far and nipped him. Play time over, he returned to Penny's side and lay down to nap.

The end of April brought more sunlight to the area, although not that much warmer weather. Penny was asked to be a chaperone for the high school's spring formal dance, which she accepted and then immediately regretted. She would be required to wear appropriate clothing, and she did not own a dress. Her mother and Lucy helped her find one that they all agreed on.

The night before the dance she attempted meditation, if only to get a good night's rest. Once the calming sensations of the meditative state allowed her to drift inside her own mind, she attempted to draw up a recent vision. The shadowed figure materialized, dark and foreboding. But Penny held herself inside the tranquil bubble and focused on the figure, drawing him closer for inspection. Detail remained out of reach as a halo of light brightened. A hand reached up and toward her, as if to stroke her cheek. Her grasp on the peaceful state slipped as the words, "why did you go and mark yourself up like that, I can do so much better" swirled around her.

Her eyes fluttered open, and she breathed heavily against the fear that had surged within. The voice had been flat and indistinct, and the face still concealed by shadow. Apprehension flared as she replayed the words. They sounded familiar. Had the women been marked with tattoos? She couldn't recall any such detail.

Blue nosed her blankets from where he stood on the floor at her bedside. She scratched his head and willed him to go back to sleep. Lucy remained undisturbed above.

Rising, she left her bedroom to get a glass of water. She checked on Fjord who was sound asleep in his box, a corner of blanket stuck in his mouth, wet from his sleepy time nursing behaviors.

Before getting back into bed, she considered messaging Noah to tell him of the voice. But she hesitated. It was late, and it was his night off. It could wait until tomorrow.

The rest of the night faded into a deep sleep, and when Penny rose early the next morning for a run, the voice had faded into the background noise of her thoughts, forgotten.

Her mother planned for a relaxing day, assuming bear cub responsibilities so Penny could get her work done and get ready for the dance without interruption. Alas, Penny was not one to sit idly by when her cub was playing. The dress prevented her playtime once donned.

They had decided on an iridescent pink and silver, floor-length dress. She was unaccustomed to wearing heels so opted for a new pair of comfortable, cork sandals. She wore little make-up, albeit more than normal. Her mother fixed her hair. And though Lucy and her mother insisted Penny looked wonderful, she felt extremely self-conscious in the unusual attire. Her hair, normally hanging straight down her back or in a simple braid or ponytail, was stacked upon her head, curls framing her face and tickling her neck. She almost didn't recognize her reflection in the mirror. She saw a woman, not a mere girl, staring back with dark, sultry eyes.

Before she left, her mother traced a fingertip along the feather tattoos exposed on her back between the two spaghetti straps. "Well, worst case, you could try flying away if it goes badly. Although, that might ruin the dress," she teased.

Noah had left before her, riding a newly modified motorized snow bike he had worked on all winter. Driving alone for the first time in a long time, she began to sweat during the truck ride and anxious electricity coursed through her veins as she stepped inside the school. She could face nighttime attacks, but not a gym full of sweaty high schoolers.

Because it was still early, the gym lights shone bright upon the few students milling about.

Must be the dance committee, Lucy thought.

The dance themed around the grandeur that was the aurora borealis. Long, colorful strips of crepe paper, varied in length, hung from above, and tiny twinkling light strands zigzagged stretching across the ceiling like so many stars. Hundreds of balloons littered the floor. Fallen stars, perhaps? It smelled a bit like sweaty socks, floor wax, and dusty crepe paper, and the rap music playing did not sound like the movement of the earth through the heavens.

Penny spied Noah off to the side smiling and laughing with a refined, petite blond woman. She walked in the opposite direction toward some students setting up a backdrop by the refreshment table.

"Penny, you look great! How have you been?"

She turned to find one of the teachers she was familiar with from the self-defense classes, Ms. Casey Kroh, the business teacher. A loud pop caused Penny to jump. The first balloon casualty of the evening. Penny fought back the spark of panic. *Everything is alright. Everything is fine.*

"Hi, Casey," said Penny. Casey nodded her greeting. "I'm good. You?"

"Every day is better than the last! Will you look at that! Aren't they cute together? Did you know that they used to date in high school? We all thought they would get married." Casey giggled at the scene across the gym.

Penny looked around and saw Noah and the girl still talking.

"Oh, cool," she responded.

Casey smiled and walked away. Penny's gaze followed her, her mind tumbling over the comments. She turned back to what she was doing.

Oh my, are you jealous? You know, you've been tight lipped since…

Shut up, Lu.

"Hey, hey! Who is this? Miss Penny? You sure clean up

229

nice!" said Pete, a senior she knew from wrestling. His southern drawl was smooth and in sync with his handsome looks.

Penny whirled around to face him. "So, what? I normally look terrible?" she said, a little too sharply.

Pete's grin melted off his face.

Lucy's thought flowed into Penny's. *Obviously not the response he was going for.*

His friends, flanking him, quietly took a step away from Pete. Noah appeared behind him and whispered loudly in his ear.

"Tread wisely, my friend. Only tactful honesty will save you from a woman's wrath." Noah looked directly at Penny while Pete and the others searched for elsewhere to observe.

Several moments of awkward silence followed.

"Well, you look hot normally, but this is just...hotter," said James, another senior, as he gestured to all of her.

"Oh, well, thank you." Penny was more uncomfortable now. Hoping to cover her embarrassment, she urged, "Have a fun night! Don't spike the punch."

As if on cue, the lights dimmed, and music began playing.

Noah moved to stand beside Penny.

"So, no spiked punch? This is a damp, not dry, community, you know. Spiked punch is a must at a school gathering," he joked.

They both smiled. "So, who was the lady you were talking to?"

"Mrs. Samson. Laura. Political Science teacher. She and I dated briefly in high school before we learned we were related. First cousins. Shhh..." He put a finger to his lips. "No one else besides us, her husband and now you know that tender morsel of information. Gotta love those family secrets. She went on to date my best friend, who she is not related to, and they just welcomed their second kid in February."

"Wow, she looks amazing for just having a kid," Penny said.

Exit stage left green-eyed monster? Lucy thought.

Sure, sure. Let it go.

"So, shall we chaperone?" Noah asked, holding up his elbow.

She placed her arm through his. "Yes, we shall." Penny smiled and they walked off to move among the students.

Throughout the night, several students and teachers asked Penny to dance, which she declined. She talked with the teachers, including Mrs. Samson, who was thoroughly entertaining and was undeniably in love with her husband.

Penny took the opportunity to photo bomb several students' pictures. She was vaguely aware that she might have been the subject of other photos but was enjoying herself too much to bother with it. Later when she checked her phone, she saw someone sent her a photo of her and Noah. He was smiling and whispering in her ear while she laughed.

The music ended and the announcement came that the dance was over. As the lights brightened, Penny said multiple goodnights as she started to help clean up. The dance council was to meet in the morning to put away tables and chairs, but Penny helped the other chaperones remove table covers and garbage.

She packed table toppers into a box and left the gym floor to stow them in the janitor's closet. When she returned to the auditorium, the main lights were turned off again, and the dance floor illuminated with a thousand twinkling white lights.

She looked around, startled to discover that she was the only one left in the gym. A voice caught her by surprise from behind.

No, not alone.

"Would you dance with me, Momma Bear?"

"I specifically recall reading that the chaperones are not to dance. And besides, bears don't dance!" Penny replied.

"Actually, bears dance in circuses."

Noah gazed expectantly at Penny. She looked down. "I don't know how to dance."

"What?! I hardly believe that. You ace anything you do… and fighting is sometimes considered to be a dance." He looked more closely at her expression. "Wait, seriously, you don't know how, or you have never danced?"

"This is my first dance. I mean, I danced in my home with my parents," Penny said, her nerves flaring with the foolish disclosure. And there was that one fathers-daughter dance she and her sister attended with their father. In fifth grade.

Noah ran his hand through his hair and smiled a brilliant smile. His hair, more curly than usual since a recent haircut, sprung back like the springs it resembled. The smile he wore warmed her to her core.

"Penny," he walked backwards to the center of the gym floor, beckoning her with his index finger. "Come hither."

She snorted and offered a shy grin. "Hither? Really?"

Noah reached for her hand and pulled her to the center of the gymnasium.

Her gaze traveled over his perfectly cut, black-vested suit that held his manly scent. Her eyes weren't sure where to focus until she found the toes peering from her sandals. It was a fascinating picture that she focused on. He took her hand in his, lifting her gaze to see something beautiful. Incomprehensible. Her heart expanded more than she thought possible.

"Um, Noah...there isn't any music playing."

He smiled, lifted his phone from his pocket and pressed the screen.

"Do you recall telling me what your favorite song was growing up?"

"My favorite?" She quietly thought about it and told him an old song her mother used to play. "Sinatra, 'Fly Me to the Moon.'"

The big band sound began blaring through the speakers.

He placed his right hand on her waist and grasped her right hand in his left. She looked up at him expectantly as they stood in place.

"Okay, you may not believe this, but I don't know how to dance very well myself. So, let's both fake it," he said.

A nervous giggle erupted from Penny.

Blind leading the blind, she thought.

Don't think, just dance, her sister thought back.

Penny closed her eyes as they began moving in time with the music. When she opened her eyes, she found Noah looking down, a lopsided grin on his face. Around the dance floor they went, gracefully, perhaps—off-time with the music, most definitely. When the music ended, their arms stayed wrapped around the other.

Noah's gaze intensified, flickering about her face.

"You've been avoiding me," he said. All those nights he stayed late, and she fell asleep (or pretended) while watching a movie began to catch her off guard. "Better option came along?" He smiled, but his eyes searched hers.

"No, no option could come close. I just—" She broke off as he closed the distance between their flushed faces.

"Just what?" he asked against her cheek, catching her earlobe in his lips. Her stomach tightened, and she lost herself in his touch.

The lights flicked on, and a voice called out that the building would be locked down in five minutes.

Penny sighed and pulled back slightly, meeting his intense gaze.

"Penny, would you want to go out on an official date sometime. With me?"

She chuckled, her unspoken yes endorsing his light kiss on her nose before leading her out of the gym.

While gathering their coats, Penny stumbled from the vertigo that slammed into her.

"Penny?" Noah began.

Dark images pulsed in her mind. She sucked in tight breath. "Noah, I saw Gigi!"

Without question and with urgency they left the gymnasium. Penny sent a message to Gigi as they jumped into Penny's truck. Noah drove—fast—and when they pulled up to Gigi's home, no light shone from the two small windows facing the street. Penny pounded on the door until the lights flickered on.

"Penny, what's going on? Noah?" Gigi asked sleepily.

Relief swept through Penny. "Um, I, we, ah-h, need to see

if you are okay?" Penny said weakly.

"I'm fine," she said.

"Look, I know this will sound odd. But you know me. You know I won't lie to you. Penny had this, sense tonight. That you might be in danger. Would you be willing to staying with a friend for a few nights? It's nothing, I'm sure, but we just want to make sure you are alright," Noah quickly explained. He could convince a snake to shed its skin by looking at it.

Gigi's eyes moistened, and she invited them in. Relief hit Penny, and she let out the breath she had held during Noah's speech. She didn't know the girl well, but something in their faces registered with the waitress from The FrostBite.

"The phone calls started again a few days ago. They bothered me before, but now that my roommate officially moved out and I am alone, well... Let me get changed," she said, then gathered up an overnight bag and left with Noah and Penny.

After dropping Gigi off at her aunt's, they drove back to the school to load up Noah's bike before heading home in a comfortable silence. Penny felt liberated, hopeful that they prevented Gigi from suffering the fate the others fell victim to.

To get her mind on other, less frightening images, Penny showed Noah the picture she received on her phone of her and Noah at the dance, unaware of who sent it.

"That would be from Laura. She sent it to me, too. Here, she sent me another." He tapped his phone, and Penny's hummed with the newly received message. The picture was of them posed for the camera in front of the photography backdrop.

"There, now you can say you went to a dance." He took hold of her hand, his thumb stroking circles along her knuckles resulting in a cascade of goose bumps up her arm. "You are beautiful, Momma Bear."

"You are not so bad, yourself, Mr. Volkov."

"Ok, don't spoil the moment by calling me Army's name," he said, grinning at her.

When they arrived home, she helped him unload his bike.

After a brief goodnight, she drove the several hundred feet to her own driveway alone.

Penny practically floated from her vehicle, but the doubt crept on slowly, like a migraine as she walked up to her house. By the time she opened her front door she was borderline miserable.

Her mother didn't appear to notice Penny's mood, worn out from cub duty as she was.

"Yeah, so that was more fun than my vet school emergency rotation with newborn twins." Her mother called out as Penny entered the living area.

"Did you enjoy yourself at least?" Eelyn mumbled.

"Yeah, I did, Mother."

"Well, are you two dating yet?"

"What?"

Did you tell her already? Lucy failed to respond, and Penny's dark mood deepened.

"He asked me out on a date. Does that count?"

"Good enough for me," Eelyn continued, oblivious to the conflict in her daughter. "I fed your little ball of fur, cleaned up his insane messes, and have been chewed on, peed on and pooped on. I didn't do that all for nothing. Not when there are future grandchildren on the line."

"You kinda just described a grandchild, didn't you? Isn't Fjord good enough for now?" Penny asked, trying to pull herself back toward lightheartedness.

"He looks nothing like me, although we are starting to smell alike." Eelyn groaned and lifted her weary body off the couch. "He last ate thirty minutes ago. Good night."

Penny stood for a moment and then went to her room. She removed her dress and put on her pajamas. She slowly removed her makeup, brushed her teeth and went to her bed.

Lucy?

What?

I wish you came tonight. It was a lot of fun.

I saw, Penny. I am glad you enjoyed it.

Don't you want to learn to dance, Lu?

Penny, someday I will be well enough, and you will take

me dancing all night. Penny could sense the sleepy smile, so she bid her sister good night.

In her dreams that night, shadows flickered around her. Headlights glared, and she faced a figure in the shadows. The Shadowed Man. She didn't feel the fear she had experienced before, just certainty that it was time. As she approached him, a large white-haired figure launched itself on the Shadowed Man. Penny watched as the bear with three black scars on his right cheek dragged the limp man away from her, the man's head in the bear's great jaws. She awoke to Blue standing above her, his nose in her neck. Blue curled up against Penny, and she was grateful for the warm dog to cuddle.

Flare

The day after the dance, a frazzled Penny tried, but failed miserably, to be upbeat.

While she rushed between her many errands, her mother sent her a "Good Morning - full day at clinic. Love you" message. Lucy had tagged along with their mother and was out of reach. Noah sent her numerous messages, but nothing indicating his undying love for her. No date requests. Well, what was she to expect? Besides, on the edge of her mind something important waited, something she needed to tell Noah. But she failed to recall what it could be.

After finishing up the reports that Army wanted her to run, she met Vale for guitar lessons, which ran late. Then, she discovered Fjord had shredded her favorite pair of running shoes. And apparently he liked studs, too, as she found the pair Lucy gave her in a pile of his poop. They were shitty, no way around it. And now, she needed to run back to the station for a zip drive that she was always supposed to keep with her.

And so, in the dark, with Blue riding shotgun, she found herself heading back to the station in the purpling twilight. Noah wanted her to wait so that they could go together, but an independent streak sparked within her and she wanted to get it done. He needed to focus on his aunt, whom Noah and Army had rushed into the hospital for her heart. They didn't need to oversee her every move.

The truck bounced along over the rough road and snow drifts that had re-established themselves since her trip earlier in the day (when she forgot the zip drive behind). Stupid wind. Noah called to update her on Dolores' condition. She was going to be fine. It had been nothing more than heart burn. Déjà vu flooded her mind when she spotted a lone vehicle on the empty road.

"There is someone stopped on the road," she told him through her phone connection via earpiece.

Noah's voice muffled as he spoke with someone on his end, then she heard, "What?"

She repeated what she had said then read off the unfamiliar license plate. "Dark color, maybe grey? No, it is a very dirty, white van. Hood is propped up."

"Doesn't sound familiar. It is a guy?" He meant *the* guy. The Shadowed Man. She didn't know, but an ominous weight seemed to have settled on her chest.

She lowered the passenger window once she was next to the driver's side of the van. A shadowed face sat within the van as the driver's side window rolled down half ways. Common sense warned her against helping whomever it was, but the road was only traveled on by those who worked at the research station, and the weather was brutal.

"Hey," she called. "Need any help?"

The face nodded and a hood was pulled up over his head as the window rolled shut. The man stepped out of the vehicle.

"Noah, I can't make out his face. His hood shadows it. He is about six feet tall," Penny began her description quietly as she placed her vehicle in park to idle.

"Penny, stay in the truck," Noah warned.

The man turned and smiled. "Good evening, darlin'."

The voice brought with it recognition. "Oh wait, it's Sam," she told Noah.

"Don't hang up. Keep this line connected," Noah demanded.

She exited her truck into the dark cold, tucking her phone in her pocket and wishing she had turned off her headlights so she could adjust to the dim light and see the situation better.

"Vehicle overheated. Trying to cool it off. Think I'm low on antifreeze," came Sam's voice. It sounded duller than his normally animated voice. But then again, Penny found it hard to hear him over the wind. She repeated what she thought he said more to calm herself than to repeat to Noah.

The hair stood on the back of her neck.

"I'll grab a flashlight. How about you open the hood, if it seems cool enough." She kept an eye on him as best she could as she walked around to the back of the truck to look inside the toolbox. Noah warned her to be careful. Blue jumped out, and she probed his thought, asking him to stick close to the truck. She didn't want Sam to see Blue.

As she returned and approached the front end of the van, he shook his head and gestured with his gloved hands. "Can you do it? Sorry, my hands are painful, too cold." There was Sam's normal, charming voice.

She sensed Lucy brush her thoughts to get a grasp of the situation. *How are his hands too cold if he has been sitting in a warm vehicle?*

"So, where are you headed?" she asked as he moved out of her peripheral view. "The research station is really the only building out here." She removed a glove and touched the hood while trying to keep him in view. It felt warm, but not abnormally so. As he slipped out of view again and she repositioned, she felt her hood yank back. She gasped in the cold air, dropping her glove.

His arm went around her neck, tugging her earpiece out of her ear. Something hard and sharp poked into her back. Her mitten-covered hands clawed at the arm around her neck.

She paused as he spoke. "If you don't struggle, it will be so much easier for you."

"Is that a gun, Sam?" she asked, hoping Noah could still hear over the wind what was going on although she could no longer hear him. She silently cursed the wind and its seemingly ever-desperate course at annihilation of life.

"Shut up!"

A glinting item shone in front of her, the hard poke in her back gone. A long knife, its grey metal gleamed in the headlights.

"Put your hands on the hood. Slowly." Below the arm wrapped around her neck, the knife edge contacted her skin. She didn't feel any pain, but warmth trickled down her neck.

The bastard had cut her.

"I sure hope you didn't cut through my new jacket," she said calmly. She pictured Blue attacking the man from behind. The guy gave a sharp, startled cry and slightly released his hold on her.

"What the—" he said.

She started raising her hands, ready to attack. Out of the corner of her eye, Blue darted away from Sam.

"I said hands on the hood!" He screamed as his attention returned to her.

She slammed her head back into his nose. With the same burst of speed, she grabbed the knife hand and jerked it down away from her neck. She spun around, punching him in the throat and kicking him in the stomach. He lunged for her, but she dodged, grabbed his closest arm and bent it around behind his back. As she did, she swiped her leg around behind his knee closest to her, knocking him to the ground. She slammed her cowboy boot down into his crotch and backed away. Somewhere during the struggle, she lost her mittens.

After readjusting her earpiece, she regained full connection with Noah. He sounded breathless as he shouted, "I am on my way. Under the seat. Check under the seat."

She looked over to see the man rolling back and forth on the ground. Blue padded up and set up point, his hackles high. She felt his growl in her chest more than heard it with the wind. She ran to the truck and checked under the driver's seat, finding a small handgun.

Handy but illegal, she thought.

And potentially lifesaving, her sister quipped back.

She put it back and instead pulled out the flare gun. As she returned, Sam started to roll up on all fours.

"Stop, or I'll shoot."

He mumbled, and she yelled at him to speak up.

He spit as he continued to try to stand. She fired a warning flare into the ground beside him. He shouted unintelligibly as the flare momentarily blinded him.

From behind the man, emerging from the black belly of

night was a very hefty, very red bear, illuminated by the flare's light. Blue retreated to Penny's side, whimpering. The bear towered above an unsuspecting Sam. It dropped his front legs down onto the man and grabbed him by the back of the neck. He shook his head once, snapping the neck, and Sam went limp. The bear dropped the man on the ground and grabbed him by the head. Penny stared after the bear as it slipped back into the night, Sam's feet trailing behind, departing the flare's circle of crimson light. She retreated to her truck and locked the doors, describing the events to Noah, who remained connected to Penny via their cell phone link.

Blue leaned into Penny on the seat of the truck as the music on the radio fell into static.

Noah and Army arrived moments later with a police vehicle, its lights and sirens blaring, not far in the distance. Penny exited the truck and handed the flare gun to Noah as he approached.

"I'm fine. Can you check the back of my coat? I need to know if the knife ripped through it," she asked in the bright lights of their vehicle.

"Let me check your neck first. It's bleeding," he said and tugged at her collar. As he poked and prodded gently, Penny winced. "It's alright, only superficial."

He checked her coat quickly and told her it was fine.

"Where is he?" Army called.

She described the bear attack once again. When she mentioned the three black scars on its cheek, Noah's look was intense.

The law enforcement spotlights managed to locate a body several hundred feet away from the vehicles. His head no longer attached. Bloody tracks led away from the scene. The bear was not to be seen.

"It was Sam? Are you sure?" Army asked.

"Yes, it was Sam."

She inhaled slowly, released the breath and repeated this several times, her eyes closed as she tried to find a calm space in the current chaos. She knew the arrival of the police would lengthen her time in the dark cold of night. She felt Lucy's warm presence and took another steadying breath. When she opened her eyes again, Noah was standing in front of her, anxiously searching her face with troubled eyes.

"I'm okay," she breathed.

His arms wrapped around her, pulling her close in the cold night air.

"Of course, you are," he said.

Army called to them to go meet the officers approaching. Penny was more than happy to oblige. The officers placed Penny and Noah into the back of one of the two police SUVs while they took stock of the situation.

The outside sounds were muffled inside the vehicle. The high heat thawing Penny and her emotions. It was Sam. How could it have been Sam? What were the warning signs she missed? They all missed?

"What the hell?" said Noah as he hit the back of the driver's seat with his fist. "It was him, wasn't it? The Shadowed Man in your visions." Fortunately, no one was in the driver's seat.

Penny moaned. "Where is Blue?" *He had been at my side since the bear...since Noah came...*she felt the world tip as the strong, solid ground beneath her crumbled.

The door opened, and the heat that leeched out was replaced by a large, furry body. As Blue wedged himself between Penny and Noah on the floor, he placed his head on Penny's lap. In that small movement, the world rebalanced. She sensed his discomfort, his tension and his confusion infuse her own similar thoughts, but now she calmed him with the strength that still flowed through her. Noah's reassuring embrace further aiding in settling her.

Knowing the killer had been discovered and stopped became the talk of the town. It even made national news as following his identification, additional murders outside of Utqiaġvik were being linked to Sam. Who knew how many the total would end up?

No matter how busy Penny made herself, flashes from that night cut through any peaceful moments, blinding her with violence. Thoughts of what the victims went through flooded her mind. She growled and bristled at her family and friends more than her polar bear before blinking back surges of tears, pulling it all inside and forcing an act of complete interest in whatever task was at hand. She shouldn't have survived. She had survived. The man was a monster. What had she done differently than the others? Had it mattered that she knew him? How had she not known he was the killer? She *knew* him!

Her mother fought with similar emotions having worked closely with him. Penny did not see Rose in the first few days following the incident, but she wondered how she was coping since she had dated Sam. When Penny had moments alone with Army, he suggested she was faring as well as expected. So, not well.

"And, how are you?" he had asked.

Penny shrugged.

"We owe you our thanks," he had said.

"We?" she was confused.

"The town."

"I didn't do anything, Army."

"You stopped Sa—the killer."

"No, the scarred bear did." She knew she had immobilized him before the bear attack came, but it still felt unreal.

"Do you still have visions?"

"No."

Army grunted. "That's good. If you have them again, like before...well, please let me know right away."

She had nodded absently knowing her visions were done with regards to the shadowed man. He held no further shadow while stored in the morgue or buried, whichever it was.

Whenever out or near other people, their eyes signaled pity...kindness...sympathy. She wanted none of it. She wanted all of it. But she would not allow herself to be the victim who survived.

Following the whirlwind of physician visits for the cut on her neck, counselor consultations for her anxiety along with subsequent prescriptions, an officer at the police station called Penny in four days later.

"So, the body we found," the officer began.

Penny nodded.

The officer, Felton Kim, confirmed the attacker's identification. Gregory Von Dixon, alias Samuel Little, corresponded to the description of a man suspected in multiple missing persons in Juneau, Fairbanks and Anchorage. His DNA matched several of the female murder victims, but since he wasn't booked for any crime, he had been unencumbered in his rampage. In addition, authorities were cross-checking a string of suspected serial murders dubbed the "Midwest Murderer" in the lower forty-eight.

Any other person, Pen... Lucy's thoughts trailed off, the potential ominously haunting their periphery. *He might have gotten away with another murder. You know, finding out who the guy is, is almost more terrifying than when he attacked you. At least for me. I still get the chills when I think about it.*

An involuntary shudder shook Penny as she agreed. Noah wrapped an arm around her shoulders as the officer continued to speak.

While I am relieved, I wish he chose a different road that night. Just one more demon to haunt my dreams.

There was a pause before Lucy thought, *What about Mother? How do you think she is holding up? Or Rose, for that matter?*

Penny considered her mother was holding up quite well. Then again, it would be in line for Eelyn to act with outward happiness to help others adjust, all the while shameful and grieving inside.

Rose dated Sam, but their mother...no. They had not been close; although the way their mother dealt with the situation indicated it had been a near miss.

And Gigi...well, let's just say that Gigi had accepted the news of the killer's death and had returned home, thanks to Noah and Penny.

Noah and Penny didn't speak after the meeting at the police office. In fact, they had already discussed everything that happened at length. They mulled over whether the outcome could have been different had she shared her prior premonition with Noah. In her defense, Penny argued that it had turned out for the best. Even if Sam's face had appeared, she doubted she would have realized the significance of it sooner.

Had I changed one thing in my past, taken up soccer instead of taekwondo, our paths might not have ever crossed. I am happy. No, not happy. Satisfied the evil stopped with me. Life graciously taught me that we don't always get what we want.

Noah's support, silent and physical and verbal, meant more to Penny than she could ever verbalize. He sat with her until she fell asleep every night afterwards. Nightmares troubled her: a lattice of the attack, her father's death, Fjord growing up to become a menace, Noah saying goodbye. Noah all the while stroked her hair, calmly telling her it was over and that he would protect her. She tried to allow his calm to infuse her, but she couldn't get past the fact that he had not protected her from Sam. She was the only one who could protect herself.

The sleeping aid the doctor had prescribed sat on the shelf in the bathroom next to the mirror, taunting her daily. After a few sleepless nights, she relented to their call. If not more because she observed Noah's sleep deprived state. Blissful, dreamless sleep enveloped her with each dose.

Penny insisted she return to help with defense classes the following Wednesday. She questioned her abilities, even since she had subdued Sam (because if the bear had not arrived, she couldn't say for sure she would have survived). Pushing herself on the treadmill and lifting weights would only do so much. She needed to be better able to defend herself. She needed the extra resistance training.

The twelve other people gathered were engaged in friendly chatter, hovering at their favorite spots on the bleachers. The few Penny knew waved and offered friendly smiles. She nodded in return, unwilling to engage in chatter.

A visiting instructor, Kyle, began by explaining to the

group that they would be starting by sparring under some extreme conditions. Noah stuck by Penny's side as the auditorium went dark. A strobe light started a slow pulse, making Kyle look like a stop motion film as he spoke. Penny felt her heart rate increase. She had wanted to try out such an exercise; still, her anxiety spiked well above the normal sparring. Perhaps she should have taken the anti-anxiety medication. One pill couldn't have hurt or made her a zombie.

"An attack never comes when you expect it or when you are ready. That is the key. To always be prepared. Will you be attacked at night while a strobe light flashes in time with metal music? Probably not. But if you are attacked in broad daylight while having coffee with your dog..." Kyle let the sentence hang as the lights came back on. He was good at theatrics.

He gave one last piece of advice before the lights went out again.

"Remember, if possible, always focus on the attacker's chest. Not the weapon or their face. Their chest will not lie, but they can feign moves with arms and legs. Listen. Listen to the sounds that are not typical. Feel the movement of the air around you."

Lights out.

Strobe.

"Fight."

Heavy metal music began blaring—more specifically, the song that had played from Sam's speakers.

Penny sparred for several moments, and then backed off to the side of the room away from the others as the song shook her core. Her heart rate increased as a vise began to squeeze on her head and her chest.

Pen? Penny? Are you alright? her sister asked.

"No," Penny croaked. She knelt; her hands covered her ears as she leaned forward. Her head tapped the ground as she began to whimper. While she blocked her sister from her head, someone else shouted.

The lights came back on, and the music cut out. Vaguely

she sensed someone approach.

No, no, no, no. Please, calm down. It's okay.

Penny wanted to stand. To pretend it was fine. She was fine. But it was not. Not now. She needed to reconnect with her center.

Distantly, she heard the group, a hundred miles away. Warm hands clasped her shoulders, and she released a shaking breath.

"Hey, Momma Bear. I need you here with me. Come back to me, okay?"

The tender voice broke through her fears.

I am okay. Okay. Okay. Just sparring, to prepare. To practice. With friends. Her thoughts skeletal. Her emotions raw. Her body reacted to the warm touch.

"Noah, I think I need a break."

The moments that followed were hazy. She knew that class was dismissed. She knew that many, maybe all, the students offered consoling words. She also knew that someone gave her something. Water. A pill. Don't chew. And sleep came.

When she next woke, Noah and her mother conversed quietly in the living room of her house. She approached them from her bedroom.

"Baby, how do you feel?" Eelyn asked as Penny walked out of her room and approached the couch.

She felt her shoulders rise as if strings pulled them from the ceiling, not of her own volition.

"Tired. How long did I sleep?"

She noted the look that passed between her mother and her friend.

"A while. Perhaps not long enough?" Noah said.

"Look, it was an anxiety attack. Had them before. More are likely to happen. Sleeping for the rest of my life does not equal recovery. Although, if you don't mind, perhaps a few more hours? I am sorry, Noah. I didn't mean to ruin practice."

"No worries, baby," Eelyn said.

"You didn't," Noah said simultaneously.

"Fjord will be taken care of. You get some rest." Penny's relief at their words was almost palpable. She returned to her room and sleep pulled her under and away from reality.

That night she dreamt of the scarred bear. Relief at seeing his large form filled her. He stood silent, his brawny frame still. Not a muscle twitched. He was a magnificent beast. A field of brightest purple fireweed surrounded him for as far as Penny could see.

She walked closer, knowing this was not a vision, and stood near him. He turned his large head toward her, his gaze piercing the depth of her soul. She felt lighter the longer she stared at him, like she could raise her arms and fly out across the ocean.

He chuffed, the sound reverberating deep in her gut. She stepped closer still and placed a hand in the thick hair on his neck. A deep peace settled inside her as she breathed in clean air and the musky scent of the bear.

Huge, white snowflakes began to fall, cool against her skin with each landing. A white blanket covered the land, dousing the showy purple and illuminating the land with a silvery radiance.

The bear blinked slowly, his piercing black eyes peering into her soul. Her world ended and began, ended and began once again.

Liam

Research resumed during the end of April, the research she initially signed on for and welcomed wholeheartedly. The small projects Penny had worked on over the winter months and her other duties, including the cub, were not what she had imagined when she signed on for the opportunity to work in northern Alaska.

Saving one bear, Fjord, was a definite positive.

She associated the data from the animals they tagged with the bio chips with data from NOAA. Evaluations of the information would start once the team was all together.

Now, though, the members slowly reconvened in the North, and the work returned to "snagging, tagging, and bagging" as Bill liked to call it.

Penny made sure to socialize Rita and Bill with Fjord, so that they didn't think she was shirking on her duties while she was absent. They reacted with excitement and without fear. Fjord crawled his ninety plus pounds up on Bill's lap and fell promptly asleep after suckling on Bill's hand.

Rita laughed, "Opposites attract is right! One white bear and one black bear!"

In that time, she had been dream-deficient, which was most likely due to sleep aids, for without them she relied on the anti-anxiety medications too much.

Aunt Bianca came up to visit in May and brought a rather large surprise for Penny—Liam. With Penny taking care of the now ninety-five-pound cub, working, giving guitar lessons and having daily workouts with Noah at the gym, she had maintained minimal contact with her old friend, Liam. Up until the move to Alaska three years ago, Liam had hung out with Penny on her birthday every year since fourth grade.

She hadn't realized how much she missed him until she saw him walking toward her at the small airport terminal alongside her aunt.

"Lee!" she exclaimed as she ran up to him. He pulled her into a bear hug, lifting her off the ground. "Wow, man! You look so different!" He had filled out. His strong, squared jaw line now held dark blond stubble. She remembered him always longing to shave, and now he needed to.

"Are you surprised? I told you my present for you this year was going to be big, didn't I," he said, smiling devilishly.

Yes, it was a huge present. Startling. Stunning. Surprising.

She smiled at them both, her aunt's arm draped across Eelyn's shoulders. The sisters were as different as Penny and Lucy were alike. Where Bianca was dressed in a designer pantsuit, with her hair coiffed and full-on makeup, Eelyn wore jeans and a sweatshirt, hair pulled back into a messy ponytail and no makeup. Of the two, Eelyn looked much younger than her younger sibling.

"Oh, well, you know me. Always so dramatic," Bianca said.

"I never pegged you for a cold climate girl," Liam said as they removed bags from the back of the truck at the house.

"I never pegged you for an Alaskan adventurer, either. But here you are," Penny said.

She smiled, but inside she bristled at his comment. *Does he not understand why I am here?*

This is Liam you are thinking about, right? thought Lucy. *He was always a bit self-centered.*

With Bianca and Liam visiting, hotel arrangements were a necessity. They would all spend a lot of time at the house, though, because of the bear. Bianca didn't want to mess with the cub, and Fjord didn't want to be near her anyway, so that worked out fine. Liam did want to play with the cub, but Fjord kept his distance. When Noah stopped by to meet Liam, Fjord cried out in greeting and attempted to crawl up Noah's leg. As Noah held the overly large cub in his arms, Fjord seemed to stare disapprovingly at Liam.

Liam said as much.

"He just doesn't know you yet," Penny said. "Give him time to warm up to you." She reached out to rub the cub's head. Fjord chuffed. Liam frowned at the exchange.

"Liam, this is Noah. Noah, Liam," she introduced.

"So, you guys just stay in and play house with the bear around here, or is there something else to do for fun?" Liam asked.

"There are other things to do," Penny said. "But honestly, Fjord does take a lot of my time. Depending on the weather, we could go out on the boat, go for a flight or take the dog sled out. What interests you?"

He shrugged. Clearly deciding on a sulk.

Bianca rushed in after a brief awkward silence.

"Well, I would like to go out on a dog sled ride. That sounds like a lot of fun!"

Noah nodded and began describing the dogs, how many they could take out at a time and where they could go. As they talked about it, Penny walked the cub to his play area in the living room and began making him some food. Eelyn helped her while Penny took a moment to work out just how the next few days could go.

"Is it me or did this house just get incredibly cramped?" Penny whispered conspiratorially. Eelyn gave her a questioning look. With raised eyebrows, Penny rolled her eyes and shook her head.

"Oh, what fun awaits us this week." Eelyn laughed.

They spent the rest of the day catching up. Liam told her of various things he was doing. He graduated earlier that month and was taking a break before starting his new job at a computer software company. The meaning of half the words he used when he described what his job entailed were lost on Penny. He spoke a technology language unbeknownst to her. When Army called Noah on his wrist communication device, Liam perked up and asked where he got it.

Noah looked at Penny before replying. Her smile came out more of like a grimace as she began to see the complications that could arise.

"Penny gave it to me for Christmas."

She had picked out a model that synched with his cell phone and came with an earpiece like his old version that had quit working right before the holidays. It certainly came in handy when out sledding.

Liam looked at Penny. "She did?"

"We go out on the sleds so much that this seemed a better way to communicate without freezing our hands," Penny offered weakly. She thought of the gift card she had gifted to Liam.

"Awesome! Been thinking about getting one myself. Can I see it?"

As Noah showed him how it worked, he said, "It is just like Penny's."

"So, are there other people your age you guys hang out with here?" Liam asked.

Noah just shrugged and leaned back into his seat. "Not really for me."

Penny explained how she spent her time with the research crew and the people she gave guitar lessons. "And once school starts, I help with self-defense classes and wrestling."

"I remember," Liam said.

"How about you? What is the lady in your life like?" Penny attempted to take the conversation back into his court.

"She is not quite who I thought she was," was all he said as he looked directly at her.

Noah stood up to leave. "Need to grab some things uptown before heading home. Good night, everyone." He winked at Penny as he walked by her and squeezed her shoulder. "Don't stay up too late."

"That boy is fine," Bianca commented once Noah left.

"And taken. At least, I think so," Eelyn said, glancing at Penny with a sly smile.

"Oh, sis. I'm not looking," Bianca asserted, winking at Liam, who looked irritated.

Penny sighed.

"Oh Liam, don't be jealous. You are gorgeous, too," Bianca added, blowing him a kiss.

Good ol' Auntie, trying to smooth things over after she rocked the boat.

Bianca sighed. "Well, we should get ourselves to the hotel. Get some sleep. I am tired!"

Liam asked so only Penny could hear, "It's okay that I came, isn't it? You seem irritated."

Penny smiled with what she hoped was a genuine smile.

"I'm just worried there will be a pissing contest on who is my better friend. Also, this bear takes up a lot of time, but he is mobile. So, I hope you can make concessions with that. I am happy to see you. It has been a long time. Too long." She reached over to squeeze his hand.

He squeezed back. "Don't go out of your way to make me comfortable or keep me entertained. Just having time with you will be enough."

Bianca called to Liam to leave. After they left, Eelyn sat down beside Penny on the couch and held up her hands to ward off questions from her daughter.

"No idea he was coming along. I got the impression from Bianca that there was something going on, but I never expected this. She could hardly talk about anything else besides him. He is almost twenty years younger than her."

The comment caught Penny off guard. She looked at her mother. "What?"

"Well, I thought perhaps you figured it out that they… well. I could be wrong." Eelyn gave her daughter a hug and set off for bed leaving Penny to wonder.

That would certainly make things easier, you know. Lucy thought.

Would it really?

As they sat in the living room the next morning following one of Fjord's feedings, Penny, Noah, and Liam discussed plans for the day. No one brought up Penny's recent attack, for which she was thankful. Having company and the chance to take her mind off her anxieties was a welcome prospect.

Bianca and Eelyn whipped up a birthday meal for the twins that included a fancily decorated cake, courtesy of Bianca. Naturally, the Volkovs and the research team were invited. Lucy gave her opinion from beneath the depths of her down comforter on what they should do for fun. Per usual, she would not be partaking in the extra festivities outside the birthday party. The family party would be enough for her.

Technically the birthday party was on Penny's birthday, not Lucy's—Penny being born several minutes before midnight and Lucy several minutes after, hence different birth dates. Lucy readily accepted celebrating her birthday early on her sister's date.

"Well, what do you want to do for your twenty-second birthday? Or, should I ask, what can we do in this town? Are there any clubs?" Liam asked.

Noah chuckled. "No. No clubs. And this is a dry town. No alcohol sold." It was damp, meaning alcohol could be brought into the town, just not sold.

Liam looked aghast. "What! How do you all let loose?"

Bianca tapped him on the head.

Liam shook his head glumly. "Oh, that explains the liquor Bee stashed in her suitcase."

"Well, up north to unwind, we indulge in decaf coffee, tea, soda, or hot chocolate," Penny joked.

That's what you usually drink when relaxing, thought her sister

Yah, true that, but better to make light of it before he has a meltdown, Penny thought back.

"We can go to the Underground," although Penny had not yet gone. Rita told her about it when she first arrived. "It's a bar, well, set up like a bar without alcohol that is inside an underground bunker. It's pretty cool, I heard."

"It is okay," said Noah. "Nothing special really." He winked at Penny and was rewarded one of her many blushes. Liam spoke on about the clubs he visited in California and how it was too bad she missed out on such opportunities.

"So, what kind of clubs do you visit?" Noah asked.

As Liam droned on about various ones, Penny rolled her eyes before excusing herself to grab a snack.

Great, he will never shut up. How come you get to hide

from this? Migraine still? Penny sensed a slight discomfort in her own head, an effect of Lucy's state.

Yeah, headache. I am going to try to rest. Your conversation isn't helping my pain.

Har har, Penny thought and wished her good night. As she returned her attention to the conversation in front of her, she realized that a tension had settled in her absence.

"What did I miss?" Penny asked.

"Liam asked about the outdoor survival practice. I was telling him about the northern lights we saw during our last camping trip. With the sun not setting during their time here, no chance to see them now."

Penny checked her phone. "Right. But we have clear skies forecasted, so we could take a team out," Penny hesitated when she saw Liam's grimace, "Do you think Bianca would want to go?"

Her mother and aunt left for town to pick up a cake at The FrostBite.

"Yeah, sure. Probably." Liam abruptly stood and walked to the window to peer out. The window faced away from town; the vast expanse lit up beneath the clear blue sky.

"Don't you get lonely here?" he asked. "It is so desolate."

Penny answered first, to his still turned form. "It is peaceful here. No traffic to deal with. No crowds. Everyone knows everyone and yet leaves you be. The pets are cool." Penny scratched Blue as he lay beside her. Edgar cawed, unwilling to be left out.

Noah smiled and reached down to do the same to Winter. Liam warily eyed the wolf-hybrid before turning back to face the small window.

"I feel trapped," he said.

"Let's get ready to take the team out. We have plenty of time before the feast tonight!" Penny said with a false happiness.

By the time her mother returned, Penny's mood had lifted in response to the dogs' excitement for a run. Noah took Bianca on his sled, and Penny settled Liam in hers. They rotated on the way back to allow the visitors to take control

255

of the teams.

The birthday celebration that they planned passed peacefully. Fjord paced around the table, searching for scraps. Penny chewed out anyone who handed offerings to the cub, but she still worried about his digestion. Blue, knowing better than to try, sat patiently next to Penny.

The next day greeted them with more sun and clear skies. They drove out to the point and then back south through town and along the coast, the area's attractions on full display. Bone pile, archeological dig, marina, research station, and eventually arriving at a dilapidated old building that marked the site of an abandoned wildlife refuge.

After returning to Penny's house, Aunt Bee and Eelyn were out. Since Fjord required near constant supervision, Noah offered to take Liam out, meet up with some guys. Liam looked to Penny as if seeking approval.

"Sounds like a plan to me. Go. Get out, both of you. I must take care of this thing. Yes, leave Winter here, too. Have fun!" She called out as they departed. She felt the proverbial weight lift from her shoulders.

She was awake when she received a message from Noah that Liam was coming in.

She noted the time–2:00 a.m.–and replied with a question mark.

Liam stumbled in through the doorway, clearly not in the best state.

"Have you been drinking?" she asked. A whiff of his breath was a good enough response.

"Noah and I hung out. He told me all the things you two do together. Is that why you are too busy to call me?" he asked.

"I don't know. I am sorry, Liam. But I am busy up here." Plus, he was not implying what she thought he was. He was her sister's ex, for crying out loud.

He walked up to her and grasped her head in his hands. As he leaned down to kiss her, Penny stepped away, swiftly breaking his grip. If he continued, she might break more than that.

"What is wrong with you?" she asked.

"I miss you, Pen. You used to be mine," he said, stepping toward her again.

"We used to be friends. We are friends, Liam. Nothing more," she said as she pushed him back. He stumbled and lunged at her again.

"I always wanted more," he whined.

"That is all I see when I look at you, always. You know that. You will always only ever be my friend. Why are you trying to ruin that now? Noah is my friend as well. The cub is taking up all my time. I have lived in Alaska for over three years. This is the first time we have seen each other. Why would you think there was anything more between us, Liam? You were in love with my sister, not me. Just because she rejected you doesn't mean that I will fall into your arms."

Her words fell flat.

"Noah says you two are more than friends," he said.

She blinked.

"Penny, I miss you. I love you." He tried to kiss her again.

I hope you get sick and pass out, she thought as she pushed him away again.

She felt a slight pressure behind her temples as a headache started. *Why did he have to ruin this?*

"I think I'm going to throw up," he said as his face changed from pale to green. She grabbed the garbage can and placed it in front of him just as he threw up. She gave him a towel to wipe his mouth and then directed him to the couch.

Nah, she thought. *Just a coincidence.*

She heard him mumble, "I'm sorry, Penny." Then, he was out.

She changed out the garbage bags and placed the garbage can by his head. She also placed a roll of paper towels, a bottle of water and two ibuprofens on the table, hoping that he would see them should he wake up.

What a nightmare. He has never acted like there should be more to our friendship.

Penny's thoughts whirled in her attempt to recall where she gave the wrong impression. She could only think of all

257

the times he talked about the girls in his life.

I think he is just jealous that Noah has basically taken over the role he used to play in your life, Lu yawned. *And maybe he has always wanted to be more than friends with you, Pen. It is not worth worrying about. It will work itself out. He probably won't remember anything in the morning.*

Yeah, okay. I am a bit riled, though, so I think I will go play guitar for a bit to clear my mind. Fjord should be good for the night. Rosie slept in Fjord's box in the dog shed, which fortunately resulted in full nights of sleep for everyone.

She locked her bedroom door to keep Blue away from Liam who would stay the night on the couch. Her mom was spending the night with Bianca so that Liam could hang out with his friends.

Throwing her rug to the side, she pulled on the latch to the hidden door.

Don't wait up for me, she thought to Lucy.

Never do!

Penny turned on her flashlight after she stepped off the last rung, then made her way down the long tunnel to the playroom and found the light switch. The loud buzz faded as the lights warmed up.

"What are you doing here?" called a disembodied voice, startling her.

"Noah?" she called out. "Where are you?"

His head appeared over the back of the couch, which was facing away from her. He waved and sat up.

"I ask again. Why are you down here and not up there with your friend?" Noah said, bitterness escaping on the last word.

Penny took in a deep breath and let it out. "That guy up there is an exaggerated version of my old friend. I am not sure what is up with him." She approached Noah, who patted the spot next to him. She sat down beside him and laid her head back against the couch.

"He was drunk," she said.

"Um-hmm."

"But you are not?" she asks.

Noah grunted and shook his head. "I know better than to drink the juice Old Bob peddles." Noah shook his head. "You are asking for trouble with that stuff." He took a sip of his drink and offered some to Penny who shook her head.

"This is just cola, diet." Noah said as he offered her an unopened can.

Penny accepted it with a sheepish grin.

"How was ol' Lee when he came back tonight?" he asked with more than a hint of sarcasm on Liam's name.

"He was an ass. But that quickly morphed into a vomiting event, and then he passed out."

"What could I say, he was in a mood and nothing I could say or would not say mattered. I thought you said he was an alright guy."

Penny chuckled at this. "Yeah, he used to be. We have been friends since the fourth grade. I just don't get it. He usually isn't like this. I mean, the attitude, yes. He is a bit full of himself."

"Maybe he came to realize the best thing in his life was you. And he doesn't know how to deal with not having you."

A loud snort exited Penny. She began giggling uncontrollably and could not speak for several moments. When she regained her composure, she said, "Like anyone could ever 'have' me. Anyway, Liam never showed any interest in me. He was always going on about his latest girlfriend, after Lucy dumped him. We didn't spend as much time together after that. We didn't grow apart either, just saw each other less."

"There aren't many of my old friends around here anymore. They left or are married or have kids. Our lives all move on, whether we want it or not," Noah said.

They reflected within their own thoughts for a time.

"Speaking of change, it's been awhile since we played guitar together," Noah said.

Penny realized the truth of the statement. "Do you want to now?"

"Nah. I'm too comfortable."

"I'm considering writing a book. Or more of a story,"

Penny said.

"Really? About Fjord?" Noah looked at her curiously.

"Yes. And what happened before. I don't know." They sat so long in silence that Penny began to doze. Then Noah asked where she learned to ride motorcycles.

"The exact opposite of you. In the desert on a dry lakebed. My family spent a weekend there once. Big campers, tents. It was like a festival. They hired in a food truck, a magician for the kids at night. Shot off fireworks, illegally. Shot at explosive targets with 22s. I think I was like eight. Someone brought a little 50cc dirt bike that they let me try out. My mother said she was glad it couldn't go very fast, otherwise I might have driven off and left them behind."

"Penny, how is it you are not even aware how cool you are?"

Penny gazed at him in disbelief.

"Seriously, people talk. A lot. About you and how wonderful you are. How you help Mrs. Ferguson with her groceries and how you changed Mr. Anitpauk's tire when it blew on sixth street. They talk about how poised you are and health conscious. How beautiful you are and how lucky you will make some man." Noah seemed to choke on the last words.

"You know, choking on the part where you say I am pretty is lessening the effect," she commented, trying to sound funny.

"Honestly…" he said as he leaned forward to set his drink on the table, "…I choked on the part where you will make some man, other man that is, very lucky." He leaned back and looked at her intently.

"Other man?"

"Yeah, I mean…"

Nervous at what he might say, she cut him off. "Um, it is late. Early. It is close to 4:00 a.m. I should probably try to get a few hours of sleep. Goodnight, Noah," she said as she rose to leave.

He closed his eyes and leaned his head back on the couch. A pained expression momentarily crossed his face.

"Penny…"

She spoke softly, "I don't know what I am supposed to do, Noah. I've never dated. I don't want to mess this up." An uncomfortable silence settled after she motioned between them. What was she supposed to do? Throw herself on this man beside her? She would be leaving, and… "I'm scared of what I might lose," she whispered.

"I'm scared, too. But maybe we don't have to be." He stared at her as he leaned forward invading her personal space. Her nerves tingled and emotions sparked as he grabbed her hand and pulled her down onto his lap. As he nuzzled her neck, she melted beneath his touch. His tender words and her own responded desires were for their memories only.

By the next morning, a fully recuperated Liam behaved like a complete gentleman. He and Bianca did seem rather close and neither of them stayed either late or alone at Penny's for the rest of the trip. While Penny was happy to hang out with Liam and her aunt, she secretly was happier when they left, and she was able to get back into her normal routine.

Sanctuary

By summer, Fjord weighed in at one-hundred-and-forty pounds and was ganglier than before, if that was possible. He was also taller and broader than both Blue and Winter. He could still easily fit on the couch with Penny to take naps but sitting on her lap while on the chair became more of a challenge. She had not thought of moving back to Anchorage to finish college in some time. With the growing bear demanding so much of her attention and the unfurling relationship with Noah, she couldn't picture her life without either in it.

As Fjord swatted at Penny with a gentleness that would someday come packed with much more force, she considered how his molting had become downright embarrassing. They went through hair tape and other hair removal devices regularly. The day she first realized he started dropping his hair coat, she wore her black yoga pants. Noah stopped her as she walked by him and tried brushing her leg off. She laughed and pulled away, asking him what the hell he thought he was doing.

"Trying to help you not look like a crazy cat lady," he commented, his smile stealing her breath.

When she looked down at her pants she gasped.

"Oh my. That is a lot of white hair." She looked around and realized Fjord's hair was all over. She began brushing him daily with a special comb to remove the shedding hair more quickly.

He reached a size that made it difficult to stay in the house. Even with the small shed Army and Noah hastily added to provide a cooler area for the bear.

Army showed up unexpectedly one Saturday waving papers in his hand, a broad smile lighting up his face with

Noah hot on his heels. Blue greeted them at the door.

"What's up, gentlemen?" asked Eelyn, drying her hands on the kitchen towel.

"Found a place for Fjord to go," Army said.

Penny's heart sank. Although she knew Army was working on that, she never really considered that the bear would be placed in a different home, one that did not include her. It took great effort for her to fake a smile but fake one she did as she rose to join the three gathered around the kitchen table. Fjord, who woke from his nap beside her chair, pawed at the fencing that prevented him from entering the kitchen. It rattled noisily, his outcries ripping at Penny. She returned to release him since her thoughts were not enough to soothe the cub. He calmed and padded quietly beside her, sitting near her legs at the table.

Eelyn asked the big questions...where, who, when. But Army waited until all their attention focused upon him. Penny glanced over to see Noah leaning expectantly forward, curiosity etched into his dark, handsome features.

So, he doesn't know either, she thought.

He would tell you if he knew, sis. Lucy's statement did nothing to quell her anxiety.

Army cleared his throat, drawing them in further with several seconds of silence. The ticking of the wall clock was audible in the room. Penny forgot to breathe.

"As you all know, I'm working on a contingency plan that will enable Fjord to continue to be a bear. We discussed several possible options at the start of his life with Penny, and as he has thrived and captivated our hearts, other possibilities arose. I believe I hold in my hands the best possible outcome for everyone." He laid the papers down in front of them. Tapping them with his finger, he continued. "Within this document lies an agreement re-establishing the North Slope - Utqiaġvik Wildlife Sanctuary." Noah sat upright in his chair. "And I, one Armstrong G. Volkov, am sole proprietor of said sanctuary."

"What does that mean, Army?" Eelyn asked gently.

His eyes twinkled. "It means that with my newly acquired

license and land parcel, if Penny agrees to become head caretaker and Eelyn concedes to veterinary services..." his pause stretched out for a year or more before continuing, "... then Penny and Fjord can move in without further disrupting your home and the town."

"Where is this sanctuary?" Penny asked, her anxiety over the possibility of losing the bear transforming quickly to cautious optimism that he wouldn't be too far away.

"Well, it is the one and only wildlife sanctuary, sitting five miles from the research station."

"You bought this place?" Noah asked, his eyebrows raised as he pulled the document closer to page through.

"Yes. Got it quite cheap from the tribal council. With the polar bear population in such a steep decline, as well as other polar species, a place for rehabilitation was given careful consideration. I put Bill down as a consultant, what with his background in polar species. And Eelyn's recent education in arctic species biology, plus her Doctorate of Veterinary Medicine, helped with the application."

Penny looked sharply at her mother. With Fjord and Noah taking up so much of her attention, Penny forgot her mother took online college courses.

Penny wondered what else she had missed.

"How soon can we move in, you think?" Penny asked.

"Well, the place needs some work," Army said.

Noah snorted.

"Okay, it needs a lot of work, but I checked on it before signing anything. The electrician and plumber from town looked it over. Minimal work is needed to make any of those repairs. The living quarters are, well, another story. Much more cleaning and fixing. It looks like a bear broke in and lived in the place for a summer. Maybe even a gaggle of geese. Lots of goose feathers. Anyway. I think it will work."

He looked expectantly at Penny who turned her gaze on Fjord. Thoughts whirled in her head, none of them allowing her much time to dwell. She nodded absently. "I think I will be glad to live out there with a bear for a roommate. Will help the transition to living alone, I guess." She glanced at her mother.

Funny. Like I won't move with you, her sister commented.

"Well, it is big enough. We can all come stay with you at some time or another." Army cast a meaningful glance at his nephew.

Once the realization hit her that her little bear would be staying with her, Penny felt an easing leach into her bones. She rose slightly to hug Army across the table, trying not to disturb the sleeping cub on the floor beside her. Eelyn squeezed her hand, and Noah threw his arm across her shoulders pulling her into his warm embrace.

She held her fists up next to her head and gave a weak "yeah!" as tears escaped her eyes.

Penny spent the remainder of the summer working on repairs to the buildings that made up the refuge. Army envisioned and placed orders for a high, chain link fence around the perimeter with other varying sizes of fenced-in areas to separate the sick, young or old. There was more than enough land for Fjord to exercise. Donations from town included empty plastic barrels, metal barrels, and scrap tires from one of the big pieces of machinery.

With encouragement from Army, Penny returned to blogging, something she had briefly tried in the fall before Fjord's appearance and even set up a donation website for the upcoming refuge. Eventually, there would be cameras to live stream the animals' activities, perhaps even veterinary exams or treatments, once there was no longer fear of losing Fjord over some technicality. She delayed her work on a master's degree since the refuge and her continued work on the research team was all that mattered in the short term.

Army took care of the legalities and specifics while Penny and Noah began fixing up the buildings and the enclosure. Whenever Bill and Rita were able they added their muscle and insight. Very few bears remained in the area to be tagged.

Penny began to realize something. She shared her thoughts with Lucy one night after a long day of scrubbing and painting.

When Army took on my research proposal and asked me

and Mother to take part in it, he really didn't need our help, did he?

Lucy's mental shrug was the only response.

Fjord had entered another demanding stage and become a hindrance, sprawling down in her path and tripping her up on numerous occasions every day. His favorite thing to do for several weeks was roll onto his back for Penny to rub his belly. His chuffing and attention-seeking cries made it difficult to not give in to the man-sized bear.

Modifications to the main building, which housed Penny's living quarters, were underway in earnest. She requested a bear-sized doggie door to be installed so that Fjord could access part of the house and still feel close to Penny. Army requested it be constructed such that it could be concealed quickly and easily in the event of an inspection by state or federal agencies, since the animals needed to be separated from living areas for safety reasons.

The shed that sat next to the main building provided an area to thoroughly clean up Fjord. There was a solar-heated water tank housed outside, filled through an underground well. A tub, perfect for up to a five-hundred-pound bear, made for the ideal place to wash Fjord. He liked it so much he easily climbed in each time it was time for a bath. A crew put in a geothermal system to heat the main building and serve as a backup heater for the water.

The heated shed was kept just above freezing with a giant doggie-style door flap that allowed Fjord access from the ten-thousand square-foot play area. Army's twelve-foot-tall chain link fence with solar-powered electric fencing surrounded the outside perimeter. Penny knew it was not only to keep Fjord in but also to keep unwanted guests out. Scattered around the enclosed area were large boulders and a tree made from tractor tires for Fjord to play on. He loved that tree and tumbled off it repeatedly.

She knew that a lot was done to bring in the materials to build such an elaborate enclosure for her baby bear. Sure, a wildlife sanctuary had sat there prior in years past, but neglected, it had fallen into great disrepair. New electrical, new water and heating…it could not be a cheap venture. Penny wondered how she would ever repay Army for his kindness.

By late summer, the facility was deemed worthy of living in for the humans and animals. Lucy offered to stay with Penny for as long as she needed to, or forever, whichever worked best for all. But she helped their mother at the clinic and didn't care for driving herself around, so it was decided that she would stay on weekends or when Penny needed help.

Fjord took to the living quarters at the wildlife sanctuary with an enthusiasm only a bear could give. Penny moved in, living on her own for the first time; although, enough people visited making it seem like she was hardly ever alone. Lucy was always in her head, keeping her company when the nights grew a little too unbearable.

She would often run out to the ocean with Fjord to let him play in the waves with his tire-sized green ball. He was still on some formula but was consuming geese, fish and seals that Noah or Army would bring. He learned to lie down in the geese fields long enough for them to settle down around him. He would then jump up and grab one or two with his jaws and paws working together.

There was still quite a bit of whale left over from the community's June hunt. Army gathered his fair share, saying it tasted just like fried eggs, and the captain donated unwanted blubber destined to be discarded in the trash for Army's dog horde. Penny had tasted it once. It tasted like soy sauce because that was what she drowned it in.

One day at the end of August, Penny received a message: "Beached whale."

She hurriedly grabbed her coat and drove off with the cub in the truck two miles along the coast to meet up with Army and Noah. The scene that greeted her was not what she expected. No one else was present besides her and another truck. Army, Bill, and Noah.

As she approached, she noted that the whale was not her imaginary blue whale corpse. It was still enormous but smaller than a bowhead. The carcass was white in color with a slight hump where a dorsal fin would be. As Fjord approached, all three fell silent and backed up to Penny.

Bill said, "So, we think the whale washed up within the last twenty-four hours. There are already scavenge marks on it, indicating bears already found and tasted the creature."

Penny worried about allowing Fjord to be out on his own, but Noah convinced her it was safer to stay away from the whale in case other bears showed up.

She sat with Noah on a ridge carved out by years of tides and ice overlooking the sea. Bill and Army retreated to one of the vehicles. The sea sent up mist, obscuring the sky. The moisture clung heavily to their clothes, but Penny reveled in the outdoors.

The ridge gave them a good vantage point of the area behind them as well, so they took turns scouting the area for additional people or predators. After a few hours, Fjord wandered away from his feast to play in the waves. As he was essentially cleaning up, two larger bears approached from further south. Penny and Noah watched. The new bears appeared but did not notice Fjord out in the waves and began to feast on the whale. As Fjord lumbered back onto the shore and shook off, one of the new bears spied him and stood up on their back legs. The second bear followed suit.

Fjord stood quietly as they inspected him. At two-hundred pounds, he was easily the smallest bear. The first bear lowered himself to all fours and sounded off with a loud growl. Penny and Noah heard the noise thanks to the wind carrying it to them. Fjord began to approach the bears, walking slowly with his head down. The first bear, who seemed to be making the most noise, suddenly ran at Fjord. Fjord turned sideways and began scooting away quickly. The first bear stopped and watched. Fjord continued to move away while keeping an eye on the aggressor.

As he was already on their side of the whale, Fjord's movements brought him closer to Penny and Noah observing the scene. Penny let out a shaky breath. Noah patted her back and climbed down the ridge, opposite of the bear to keep out of sight.

"I doubt there's much interest in anything besides eating right now. But I don't want to stick around long enough to find out, right?" Noah whispered to her.

Fjord caught up with them several minutes later. They walked slowly back to the truck, Fjord scrambling into the back. Army and Bill followed on the way back to the station. Penny was pleasantly surprised how well Fjord cleaned himself.

"A bit fishy smelling, but that's normal, hey big guy?" He pushed into her as she rubbed his neck.

During her second year in early September, Noah and Penny decided to take Fjord and half the sled team out for a couple of nights. On the second night, a freak snowstorm set in, grounding them for three days. Noah and Penny tethered themselves to the tent with ropes to safely feed the dogs.

Penny wondered where her visions were when she needed them, but then the visions never cooperated, not really. Being fully rested and not anxiety-ridden without the deadened emotions had been a plus. Well, perhaps the emotions were a bit leveled. Then again, that was the point. And, the lack of visions also comforted her. The threat of the shadowed man was no more, and the scarred bear moved off away from town, almost like he no longer needed to hang around, having finished his job.

Winter and Blue stayed inside the tent, used to being inside the house. Fjord stayed close to Penny outside, the thin fabric of the tent separating them.

Noah worried the bear would rip the tent down, but Penny convinced Fjord through a series of mental pictures that his spot was outside the tent. Fortunately, he responded better to her verbal and mental commands. He willingly complied, surprising Noah. Although Army suspected, and possibly Noah, that Penny held some strange control over the animals, she had yet to elaborate on her effect in the bear's decision to behave. One secret that she held from the world.

To occupy their time in the tent, the two of them played card games, tried to stay warm, ate protein bars and melted snow with a small butane torch. Everything seemed like they were dancing close to a raging fire but stayed just out of harm's way.

Noah spoke more of his travels during his time in the military, especially when he was in Australia. "I would like to go back one day. Travel more of the countryside."

"Don't they call that a 'walk-about' or something?"

She heard the smile in his voice. "Yeah. You wanna go on a walk-about with me?"

"I think that would be wonderful," she said, snuggling in closer to him.

"I think it would be wonderful if you stayed here," he answered quietly.

"Well, who else could take care of the beast if I left? I mean, you're pretty and all, but you are not momma bear material." Her attempt to lighten the mood struck a hollow note. She cleared her throat. "I want to extend my stay. I mean, running the refuge sounds more appealing than heading back to finish my graduate degree. Army suggested I work at it online if I decide to continue with it. You, ah, think you could handle me around for longer?"

"I could handle having you around forever." A warming thrill coursed through her as he continued. "It takes a long time to piece yourself back together, doesn't it?" Noah shifted. "When you showed up last year, I was pretty messed up yet. Still am, I guess. I still feel terrible about attacking you. Good thing you can kick my ass." He smiled before continuing. "Your spark and fire helped me more than you could ever imagine. Sometimes letting someone else in is the hardest but most rewarding thing. Makes it easier to find light in all the darkness."

In the silence, Penny wanted to say more but unsure what exactly could be said. Soon, exhaustion won out, and she fell asleep.

Penny woke up to silence just after 1:00 a.m. No, not quite silence. There was the quiet breathing of Noah and the dogs next to her. She thought she could even hear Fjord snoring softly across the tent panel outside. The wind subsided, leaving behind an eerie stillness that unmasked the other noises.

She unzipped the tent flap and a brilliant display of the aurora danced across the moonless sky; the Milky Way barely visible beyond.

She kicked out her foot in a blind attempt to wake Noah. Except she misjudged and nudged Winter, who silently jumped to his feet.

He glanced at her with his intimidating amber eyes before slipping past her into the night. Blue slipped past immediately after him. She watched them as they paced out beneath the dazzling spectacle. Fjord's body blended into the white ground, difficult to see until he rose. He shook his hulking two-hundred-and-fifty-pound mass and ambled toward the free dogs, Blue and Winter, nosing the other four-legged companions sheltered beneath snow mounds.

She crawled back to Noah and shook him gently. He groaned, and she started to say his name when howling cut her off. She held her breath as the voices swirled around her, shaking her to her core. She crawled back to the tent flap to glimpse the silhouette of the team and watch the bear and the dogs as they played beneath the dancing sky. The dogs were positioned in various stances: some standing, some sitting or lying down. The eerie chorus of canine voices raised a tribute to the end of the storm and the beautiful display above them, their fur shimmering in the flickering light.

She felt Noah stir before his head appeared beside hers—sleep still clouding his eyes.

She crawled out into the white wonderland and stood, stretching out her limbs and twisting away stiffness. He followed suit and then leaned into her, draping his arm over her shoulders. She reveled in the closeness of the aurora. The closeness of him. Blue trotted up and sat beside her and nuzzled her mittened hand. She thought about trying to capture the moment in a photo or video but then decided she didn't want to move.

Noah nudged Penny with his shoulder and tilted his head in the direction of the two youngest team dogs rolling around.

"After the storm and such a heavenly display, kinda makes you want to roll around in the snow, too, right?"

She looked up at him, catching just a bright flash of white as he smiled. She reacted and pushed him to the ground. The new snow provided a soft place to land.

He laughed and said, "Oh, really?!" as he collected snow into his mittened hands.

She took the handful of snow in the face.

Squealing, she dumped an armful on top of his head. Winter and Blue jumped into the melee, sticking cold, wet noses into the human's hoods, play-biting at their coats and pant legs. The dogs then launched themselves on Fjord. Noah finally gained the upper hand and straddled Penny, holding her hands above her head. Thoroughly pinned, he released her hands and sat back on his heels.

She propped herself up on her elbows, her gaze flickering to the aurora above. A radiant aura draped behind Noah. She was mesmerized by the glow and shadows that played on Noah's face. How heavenly he looked. Her eyes adjusted, and she found him looking back at her.

Breathless, she smiled. "Amazing, isn't it?"

Her laughter inside subsided as she wondered on his expression. She ached to touch his face, but her fingers were tucked warmly inside her mittens.

He cocked his head to the side. "No comparison to you." His raspy voice sent shivers of electricity dancing out from her chest.

"Don't be silly," she breathed.

He leaned down toward her. She pushed herself up, meeting him halfway. The kiss was gentle, tentative. Noah pulled back slightly and looked into her eyes, smiling.

She threw an arm around his neck and pulled him closer as she lay back on the ground. He trailed kisses along her cheeks, her jaw and back to her mouth. In the cold she felt feverish.

"Maybe we should take this inside where it is warmer," Noah laughed and then groaned slightly. "I hope I didn't sound like my brother saying that."

Penny nuzzled her cold nose against his.

The dogs broke out into another chorus of howling, sending more chills than she thought possible down her spine. Noah helped Penny to her feet, and they looked around. The colors sharpened considerably, if that was even possible.

"The tent needs a see-through top," Penny mused as the shivers began.

Noah told her to brush as much snow off herself as she could while he led her to the sled. She slipped her face mask up over her cheeks.

It must be around 20°F. It's not that cold.

He rummaged around and found two additional blankets that he wrapped around them. They lay down on the sled side by side. It was terribly uncomfortable until Penny turned to her side and nestled her head on his shoulder. The display continued for minutes or hours. Time didn't matter.

Fjord lumbered over and tried to get in the sled with them until he realized the effort was futile. He instead lay down next to Penny and started chewing on something.

When the aurora ebbed, Noah pointed out various constellations, telling her the Inuit names, and she followed up with the names with which she was familiar. Taurus was Nanuk, the spirit of the polar bear. Cassiopeia was the Lamp Stand. Ursa Major was Caribou. Ursa Minor was the More Red Man. The Milky Way was called the Divider. The belt of Orion was the Three Hunters following the Polar Bear. The aurora was their ancestors calling out to them, watching over them from the spirit world. If you got too close to the aurora, your head could be cut off and used to play ball.

"No," Penny laughed. "That is terrible! Did you consider your ancestors to be angry or jealous of you or something?"

Noah laughed as well. He went on to explain that when he grew up, falling stars were known as "star poop," earning another laugh from both.

"Usually we aren't able to see the stars. The fog, blowing snow, clouds and the aurora block our view."

A comfortable silence settled between them as the aurora

flared. She strained to head the inaudible music that played before her.

I am so glad you got to see this, Lucy's words echoed in Penny's mind.

Finally, Penny drug herself away from Noah's embrace. The cold was heavy into her muscles. They returned the blankets and themselves to the tent. She rubbed Fjord before she climbed in. He rolled about in the fresh snow, happy for the cold. Blue and Winter weaseled back inside the tent. Fjord chuffed and nosed around the zipper until Penny told him "no." They crawled back into their sleeping bags and slept for the few remaining hours of night.

Cracks

Lucy excitedly but carefully handed Penny the leather journal that Penny had given her last Christmas. Neatly scrawled across multiple pages was the short tale of a lonely queen. Penny hungrily delved into the story.

What did you think? Lucy asked her twin hesitantly about her thoughts on the short tale.

"This is one you started ages ago, isn't it?" Penny asked.

Lucy nodded.

When they discovered Lucy's debilitating illness, the twins spent many late nights discussing what it might be like to lose each other. Lucy assured Penny that she would wait for her just past death's door. Whether it would be months, years, decades, she would wait. The story was an idea that stemmed from her fear of dying young.

Seriously? It isn't obvious? Penny thought as she wiped her eyes, unable to choke out words.

No, your emotions are muddling our connection a bit...

Penny closed the book and walked over to where Lucy sat in the room. She insisted on being out of sight while Penny read, but eventually curiosity led her back into the room. In a way this was humorous, as Lucy may be out of sight, but she was never out of mind. Penny smiled at the thought.

Lucy, it was amazing. I really liked it.

But... she paused dramatically.

No buts. It was good. Penny lay the book on top of their shared dresser.

She showed a rare, sweet smile. *I'm glad you like it.*

What about a title? I don't recall seeing one.

Oh, forgot to write it. Yes, I thought I would call it "The Queen." Lucy twisted her hands as if in worry.

I like it. When are you going to show Mother?

As soon as she gets home. I wanted you to be the first to read it.

Before Fjord's first birthday in mid-October, Army purchased a new white utility van to transport the critter around. Fjord approved of his new ride, as evidenced by his immediate slumber upon entering the padded back of the white utility van. Their first trip was to the shipping docks to use the scale.

"Caught me a whopper," said Army when he read the weight and whistled.

The scale read three-hundred-and-eighty-eight pounds.

Penny stood in awe as Fjord stepped off and pawed at her leg. She pushed his paw away and rubbed his head. He wiped his head across her thigh, pushing her off balance. As usual, she ended up sprawled on the ground, Fjord taking advantage of the situation. With a paw on her chest, he licked her face.

They celebrated Fjord's first birthday with a fish and muktuk cake out at the wildlife station. Army acquired several more tractor tires, Penny presumed from the fishermen, several tree trunks, mostly driftwood, and more large inflatable balls. Noah presented the bear with a stash of reindeer antlers that incited several tug of war games between Fjord and Blue. The larger he grew, the more Penny wondered what was in store for her.

She tried weaning herself from the sleep aids and anti-anxiety medications, wanting more normal-feeling days, but every time she tried, nightmares from her past plagued her nights. Living on her own was a big change even though she saw her family, Army, and Noah every day.

Although Bill and Rita had left months ago, the team still had some work to do. The week following Halloween, Penny joined Noah on a three-day trip out with the dogs and Fjord to gather information on the ice freeze and to discern the status of oil contamination in the area. There was growing concern over oil levels in the seawater following multiple oil leaks from the drilling rigs during the summer.

"There are reports of dead seals and polar bears scattered

along the ice. Normally, the water drags a carcass down, which is why we have limited knowledge of bear pathology. So, this sudden increase is disturbing. We should gather core samples at multiple sites so we can share and compare with other research groups," Army said. His new motto morphed into "share and compare."

The extent of the effects surprised her.

They could get there more quickly with snow machines, but Army currently had zero out of the two that actually ran.

The site Noah and Penny headed to was west along the coast. With just over five hours of daylight, they would travel out on day one, collect samples on day two and head back on day three.

With help, Penny slept well the week before they set out. Her energy and excitement invigorating. No visions plagued her dreams before the trip.

Lucy, who decided not to make the move with her sister, stayed relatively busy, rarely around when Penny dropped in to visit, often staying in her room if she was home. Penny stayed extremely busy; so busy in fact, her guitar sat untouched for weeks.

Okay, Lu, I'm off to save the world! No just kidding. Just headed out to take ice samples. Pretty excited—I've never done that before.

There was no response from Lucy. Her mother hugged her tightly and told her not to worry. Or she told her mother not to worry? Penny couldn't shake the sense of foreboding that crept up on her as Noah and she set out, Fjord running along behind.

They traveled mostly along the fast ice—ice attached to the shore and seabed—as it provided a relatively flat run. When they arrived at the coordinates on the next day, Noah suggested Fjord go off on his own to hunt. Since there was a recorded healthy population of seals in the area, Noah thought Fjord might find some success. The bear's natural instincts kicked in as he sniffed the air, catching a scent that ensnared his attention. Not long after their camp was set on the shore, Fjord lumbered off. Penny and Noah decided to drill the ice at different sites to speed up the process. They took the sled out on the ice to gather the samples.

Penny checked one last time to make sure the dogs' tethers held before walking away from Noah. He quickly pulled up a core sample before she arrived at her site. She knew this because he already started his count, his voice coming through in her earpiece.

"Penny, this sample is pretty thin."

"How thin?" she asked.

He read the measurement, and her insides tensed. Much thinner than expected. A 'we shouldn't be here' kind of thin.

"Probably an error. A fluke. Let me move and take another," he said.

"Be careful, Noah," Penny cautioned. They both knew the dangers, and she tried to force down the rising tension, reminding herself about the lack of premonition prior to the trip. The hairs stood up on the back of her neck.

While only separated by two-hundred yards, an ice pressure ridge and snow formation that looked like an angel with its wings partially extended blocked her view. Penny stopped drilling and adjusted her stance so her video recording device on her headband captured the scene with the angel.

What an awesome picture.

Returning her attention to the job at hand, she collected her first sample. Read the measurement. It validated Noah's reading as not being a fluke. His voice in her ear startled her.

"My second one is thin, too. We need to move."

She began to respond, but a loud sound and vibration beneath her feet caught her attention. A loud crack. Startled, the drill slipped and fell to the ice.

As she glanced at the drill and began to reach down for it, she felt more than heard the low moan. A spider web of tiny cracks shot out across the ice below her feet

Jump. Now!

Penny launched herself as hard as she could away from the spot and landed hard on her stomach on the ice. Her boots provided little support as they slid against the now loose ice.

Frantically, she struggled to grab onto something and pull herself away from the hole. She felt the icy water find its way into her boots as her legs sank into the hostile water. She was shouting for Noah against the wind that had picked up. As she turned her head, she saw the microphone that she had clipped to her hood lay on the ice, smashed beneath her mitten. She screamed.

"Help!" The wind carried her plea away from her would-be savior. "Noah! Noah! Help me!"

She slipped further down; the glacial water pulled at her legs and then her belly. Cold shock set in, and she started to hyperventilate. Slipping, she scrambled at the lip of the hole, hoping to hold onto the edge, but the ice rim broke. Her head stayed above water for mere seconds before the current pulled her under. She found the strength to pull herself back up, breathing in the cold air.

Lucy! Lucy! Fjord! Noah! Noahnoahnoahnoah! A strong buzzing filled her head. She opened her mouth to scream but saltwater invaded, and she choked.

Submerged a second time, Penny heard Lucy screaming for her to hold her breath. Penny's body was pushed and pulled against the underside of the ice by the water that steadily gurgled its displeasure at the intrusion. It wrenched the warmth from her bones. Her eyes burned as she searched for the light. Her lungs spasmed. Weak light filtered down through the hole, so very far away. Penny felt a bump with her foot and pushed off on it, clawing her way back to the hole. She was awarded with a taste of the blessed air once again.

Noah, Fjord, Blue, Lucy, she chanted over and over. *Help me!*

She was cold. So very cold. Her arms became lead without feeling. As she began to dip beneath the surface again, her body stopped responding. No amount of will could make her legs move. She held her breath, thinking that the burning in her lungs would warm her. It seemed to work. Warmth spread through her body. She no longer felt the pain of the cold. No more shivering. It will be okay. She opened her eyes to watch her thoughts ride the bubbles tumbling lazily away from her. The dark water roughly embraced her, pulling her down with its temptation of eternal relief.

Fjord, where are you?

Noah, Noah!

Mother, Mommy…

Ohnohnononononononononono

She heard Lucy one last time before the darkness consumed all.

Fjord is coming.

Blinded by white light, she felt no pain although she sensed movement. There was a sense of being pulled. Something scraped against her legs. And then, the cloak of darkness descended.

Light. Pain rocked her body. She shivered. Something harsh ripped the skin from her face. She coughed, choking on the putrid saltwater escaping her lungs. The water sought its home back beneath the ice. Darkness descended once again.

THE PRESENT

Lucy

Ironic. No nightmares warned me of danger. Just a vague foreboding.

I am adrift beneath the water. In and out of consciousness, I ride the swells, a raft on the open sea. Up and down. There is an absence. The absence grows and nags at me. I do not know why.

There are voices. Some familiar and some not. I try to speak, but the water presses in on me and I am unable to open my mouth.

"...thank God you were there..."

"...don't know if I have the strength..."

"...love..."

"...there is a good chance she may never recover fully..."

"...without that video, we would have thought..."

"...please come back to me..."

"...Lucy...Ben..."

I wake, knowing I am waking but unable to take control of the speed. Too slow. I take a long breath in, release it slowly. My eyes open, but I cannot see. They feel dry, sandy, and I blink rapidly to clear them.

Focus.

My eyes adjust to the darkness, a strange blue light haloing the shadows. I turn my head to find Mother sleeping. Lost in dreams. Or nightmares. In the dim lights, I can make out the dark circles beneath her closed eyelids.

"Mother," I whisper. The sound is raspy, harsh. My mouth as dry as my eyes. I clear my throat and try again, louder this time. "Mother."

She sits up quickly, startled. Her eyes, the shadows clinging beneath them, find mine. Disbelief washes across

283

her face. Then relief. She cries and reaches toward me, the scent of laundry soap and my favorite hair conditioner coming to her as tightly as she to me. She smells like home. I can only weakly return the hug.

"It's okay," she coos. "I'm here."

A nurse peeks her head in the room. Disappears. Reappears and approaches. She has a warm, broad smile. She checks the monitor by my bed, checks my pulse. Pats my shoulder. Then quietly closes the door when she leaves.

"Oh, baby girl, I love you so much. I missed you." My mother is sobbing and smiling. A difficult thing, that. I smile through my own tears that now moisten my eyes.

"What happened?" I ask.

"You fell through the ice. Do you remember that?"

The memory of an icy embrace tightens around my limbs. The shivering begins even though I am floating in the heavy quilt from my grandmother. I'm too warm and so very cold at once.

A large, bearded man enters the room wearing a white coat with a stethoscope around his neck. Introduces himself as Dr. Tea.

He examines me, listens to my chest. Asks me questions that jumble together. What is your full name? What is your birthday? How old are you? Redundant, since I just gave him my birth date. Look directly at this light. Follow the light. How many fingers am I holding up? How do you feel? Can you tell us what you remember?

As I answer his questions, the memories slurry in my mind. The ice cracking beneath me. I remember jumping and then sliding into the water.

Lucy? Where are you? My thoughts are still sluggish, and the shivering has become more of a vibration deep in my bones.

"Lucy?!" I say out loud. "Where's Lucy? She's not here." My fingers glide against my smooth hair that someone has braided. Ugh, I need the pain to focus.

My mother doesn't respond. As she stares at me, her face pales and her mouth opens and closes slowly as she struggles for the right words.

A twinge had taken residence in my belly. "Did something happen to her? Did she go stay with Bianca?"

My mother still says nothing.

Lucy! Lucy! I scream in my head as I look around the hospital room for some sign. Something inside splinters, fracturing into a million sharp pieces. *I can't hear you! Where are you?*

"Mother, what happened while I was asleep?" I blink against the tears that fall, look at my mother who is shaking her head. Her hands are clenched tight at her sides.

"Penny, what do you mean you can't hear her?" she asks.

"In my head. Our twin-tuition. And she, me. You know about our telepathy. You said we could read each other's thoughts." My insides begin to shake. The heart rate monitor beeping escalates, and a warning alarm goes off. My words begin to slur together.

"Ican'thearhershesnotthinking..." My hands clutch my head as I begin to shake.

The doctor barks orders as nurses enter my room. He tells my mother that she needs to stand back.

Lucy! Lucy. Lucy...where are you...

I awake for the second time in the hospital room to the sound of a metronome and the hospital smell. The ticking waxes and wanes. Why is there a metronome in my room? Some sick joke? No, the clock on the wall. Just the clock on the wall.

My mother is staring out the window. Her face shadowed by the dim light outside. When she hears me sit up, she speaks without looking at me. As I come fully awake, she tells me a story. The story of my rescue.

Fjord pulled me out of the water. He, Noah and the dogs did their best to warm me up until an emergency crew flew in. Noah stayed back to bring the animals home. I have spent fourteen days in a coma that the doctors held me in to allow my body to heal.

"Noah can tell you details about your rescue later. The important thing," she says softly as she sits beside me in the bed, "is that you are alive."

"Lucy? Is Lucy…" I know. Deep down I know. Though I keep my eyes closed, I cannot dam the flow of tears. The steady ticking counting down my remaining time.

She strokes my hair. A soft kiss against my forehead.

I lost her again, I think.

I am not left alone for very long while at the hospital. The time I'm alone, I try to remove the clock batteries. Apparently, I haven't been the first to loathe the loud clock, or the cage securing it to the wall is standard protocol.

On the second day that I am awake, a new doctor with a wizardly beard and a kind smile spends time with me.

"Based on your preparedness for such an occurrence and your mother's stories of how thorough you are, I am frankly surprised that you are alive and well today. You undoubtedly will get more details from your mother and friends, but let me give you the basic story." This doctor prefers I call him George and continues with his speech, "After you fell into the water, your emergency beacon notified the EMS team here in Utqiaġvik. They immediately contacted your numbers, getting through to your mother to notify her of your distress call and to your friend Noah, who was able to answer your satellite phone." I nod. It was in my pack on the sled. "He was able to tell them what happened, and he stayed on the line with the dispatcher the entire time. The flight team locked into your signal and flew out to your position."

George pauses here, shifts his feet. "I mentioned your thoroughness before, and here again is where it comes to play. The video footage from the camera attached to your headlamp. Without it, we would seriously have questioned your friend's mental health or motives." He laughs, as if mental health was something that could be funny. "Anyway, the video matched his description of how you escaped from the water."

"I remember holding onto the ice, the current pulling me away from where I went in."

"Yes, your friend lost visual of you and was unsure how to get you back on the ice. He was speculating with the

286

dispatcher about going in after you himself. Luckily, he did not or neither of you would be here. A...ah...polar bear jumped in and pulled you out. Truly, quite amazing. And after your friend administered CPR and attempted to warm you, your dog sled team and the bear, too...yes...amazing...well, dog-piled on you and him to provide added warmth and protection until the helicopter arrived. Many cold-water immersion victims survive unspeakable odds, but it seems as if you are blessed with a huge and very hairy guardian angel watching out for you."

He tells me that I will stay a few more days for further assessment and to start physical therapy. An officer will most likely wish to speak to me to conclude the official report. And they would like me to speak with a counselor.

Mother has not let go of my hand for hours. It is cramped and sweaty, but I softly squeeze it.

"Are you okay?" I ask.

She huffs. Smiles. "Yes," she says.

"How's Noah?"

"He is fine. He is keeping track of Fjord. I know that was going to be your next question."

Fjord. "So, Fjord is okay? He didn't run off?"

"No, honey. Well, he did run away when the chopper showed up. But that was because Noah told him to go. He didn't want anyone mistaking Fjord for some hungry bear taking advantage of the situation, even though Rose was on the emergency chopper. Noah told her Fjord would be there. Anyway, after the chopper took off, Noah took the team out and found Fjord not too far away. Then he brought everyone home."

I leaned back after I realized I had shifted forward to listen to her words.

"Fjord really went in to get me?"

"Yes, the way Noah tells it, it was like Fjord knew you went under. Noah said he thought he heard you scream but couldn't see you. He found the hole right before Fjord came charging up and dove into it. I will let Noah tell you the rest, but without Fjord, I don't think you would be here right now."

The silence that falls is comfortable at first, but as it lengthens, my chest tightens.

"Mother," I whisper. "Where's Lucy? She's no longer in my head."

My mother rises, walks away from me and stands for several heartbeats. The air flows around her as she returns. She grabs my shoulders, as if to brace me. Or herself.

"Penny, can you please explain what you mean by no longer in your head?"

"Lucy has been in my head for as long as I can remember. And I could see her. I gave her presents every Christmas, birthday. She's always here." I rub my temples, an ache beginning. "Showing me pictures, listening to my thoughts. Our telepathy. You said you knew. You knew, right?"

"Shhh, Penny. Shhh, it's alright. Yes, I knew you two could read each other's thoughts. Shhh." She pulls me close and gently rocks me, while I compose myself.

"Can you think back to when you last saw Lucy?" she asks.

"I saw her the morning Noah and I went out on the ice. The morning I fell into the water."

Mother stopped rocking.

"Penny, honey, can you remember the last time you saw Lucy and me together?"

"Many times," I say, but I falter.

"When was the last time you saw me or anyone else talk directly to Lucy?" she continues.

Several moments pass before I go limp in my mother's arms. Quiet sobs hit me, my tears moistening Mother's blouse.

"Penny, Lucy died the summer before your senior year. Two years after she was diagnosed with terminal brain cancer. You held her hand when she passed away. Do you remember?"

I nod and find that the memories are there. I hate as well as cherish every second of them.

"I could hear her. Every day I talked to her, saw her in my

room," I say through a moan.

"Baby, I told you after she died that she would always be in your heart. And that you could always talk to her, even if she didn't talk back. Perhaps your mind chose to continue hearing her to protect you."

We take our time in the silence, my heart monitor beeping its quiet chorus.

"After your father died…" She faltered, then took a deep breath. "After your father died, I believe I said the same thing. That he would always be close to us, that we can always talk to him, even if it was a one-sided conversation. Do you hear him inside your head?"

Thinking about it, I shake my head. "I mean, I remember things he said to me, memories. But he doesn't respond to my thoughts. Not his voice. It has always been Lucy."

"Your father was taken from us so suddenly leaving behind this gaping hole that still hurts." My mother holds a fist over her breast. "With Lucy, we were granted time. We said our goodbyes. I didn't get a chance to talk to your father that morning." She shakes her head, blows out a quick breath. "You and your sister had a very special bond. One many of us probably wish we had and one that is difficult to prove at this point. I think it best though if we keep that part to ourselves. There is nothing that can be done about the past. And I doubt it will make your mental health look any better than it does." She leans back, peering into my face. Her fingertips slide across my cheek. "I think it may unnecessarily delay you being in this hospital. You will do better home with your friends and family."

I nod.

"All these years, those gifts to Lucy. I thought that was the way you chose to honor your sister's memory. They would show up in your room later. I never thought to ask you about them. Never thought to ask why you kept to yourself so much. You really didn't ever feel alone, did you?"

I shake my head.

"I am truly sorry, baby. Do you, I mean, do you feel alone now? Because you aren't."

I look at my mother wondering if my words would hurt her. "I know I am not alone, but my head feels…empty."

The thoughts and emotions swirl around, but are sluggish, weighted as if struggling though a vast, barren wasteland. The bright light that was my sister's voice is gone.

A new, young doctor sits down beside the hospital bed. I am surprised at how many doctors are in this small town. I hope none of them flew in on my account. Falling into the ice isn't an unprecedented ordeal here on the North Slope. Perhaps getting rescued by a man-eating bear is.

He takes his time arranging his larger backside on the small, uncomfortable looking metal stool. He then promptly rises and leaves the room, only to roll back a few short moments later with a larger padded chair. He plops down with a huff, taking several more moments to arrange his recording device on the table near my bed. I knew he introduced himself the day before, but I completely forgot his name.

"Please, tell me your full name."

Apparently, he has forgotten mine. My resentment wells up. Then, I sigh. No, not his fault. One more test. Here we go again.

After visiting with multiple doctors over the past few days, the repetitive questions reached tedious status. I bite back my bitterness and strike as even a tone as I can muster while trying not to let the crumbs littering his tie distract me.

"Penelope Diana Osborn."

"Where were you born?"

"In a hospital."

The doctor didn't even look up from his lap. "In what city and state?"

"Madison, WI."

"What is your age?"

"Twenty-two."

"Are you aware of where you are and why?"

"Yes. I am in the hospital in Utqiaġvik after waking up from a two-week coma."

"What is your first memory?"

290

"Of the accident? Or ever?" I look at the doctor, unsure of his direction. Not the usual line of questioning.

"Yes, the first memory of your life." He glances up quickly.

I focus inside my head for a few moments before responding, "Digging for bears."

After the doctor leaves, my mother enters the room. Warm cinnamon and vanilla trail her.

"So, honey, how are you doing?" she asks.

"The doctor says I suffer from psychological repression. My brain unconsciously blocked memories of Lucy when she died. He was more than happy to coax them out of hiding." I wipe my nose, hating the raw pain I hold inside.

Noah did not come to visit while I was awake in the hospital those days, though I did speak with him every night on the phone. His updates on Fjord dishearten me as the bear refused to eat during my absence. And Noah was concerned about another bear in the area that stayed close. The proximity seemed to agitate Fjord. Noah assures me it isn't the scarred bear. After the incident with Sam, the bear wandered off and away from town. It was like he was no longer needed. There are so many things to try to wrap my head around, this is one that I let go. He hasn't visited me via a vision while confined to the hospital. Perhaps he has gone off, leaving me in peace.

Army and Mother take me home.

I think back to what Army told me.

"There are voices in my head, too. Sometimes they are mine. Sometimes my parents'. I even heard you a time or two," he said as he gave me a hug.

The emerald leather-bound journal sits on top of my dresser where I last laid it. I sit down on the chair in the room to open the cover. The title page stares back. "The Queen."

How could I have imagined her for so long?

I take a deep breath and turn the page.

I bite into my fist to fight back the emotional pain. It is my handwriting that crawls across the pages.

A shadow falls onto the book. I close it. What could I say?

291

Hey look, here is a book that I thought my sister wrote but it turns out I wrote it. Crazy, right?

Mother broke the silence. "That's a lovely book. The one you set out for your sister at Christmas?"

I nod. I should be embarrassed, but I feel drained. Like my only emotions are worn-out.

"It holds a story I thought she was writing. How could I think that if I was the one writing it?" I place the journal back on the dresser and put my head in my hands. "Oh, Mother. I am so messed up. I feel so lost."

"Well, you are in your bedroom in Utqiaġvik. Not lost." She attempts a small smile as she walks closer. "We will find a way to get through this. You are stronger than you think." She reaches for the book. "May I?"

I offer up the book and shake my head to clear the fog settling in. Stupid medication.

"Don't try to overthink it. You are not crazy, no more than the rest of us anyway."

I want to return to the station as soon as possible, but I need to shower first.

Noah arrived as I finish, a cup of hot chocolate warming my hands. The warm cocoa soothes my worries for the moment. His strong hug soothes me more yet. He kisses me gently.

"Hey, Momma Bear. Need a ride anywhere?"

I smile. I missed him so much and cannot wait to leave with him. Have time alone with him. I grab my things and give my mother a hug. Before I leave, she asks if I will be okay.

Of course.

She hugs Noah and picks up the discarded notebook.

After we get in the toasty warm vehicle, he asks me what my mother is doing.

"She is reading stories that I wrote." Did I reveal the craziness?

He looks at me skeptically. "You wrote?" He begins driving. "Huh. I didn't know you wrote stories. I mean, you said you wanted to write, but I guess I shouldn't be surprised.

292

You did talk about journaling and showed me a notebook packed with your doodles. Just another form of release, right?"

The truck bounces along the frozen ground. Very little snow covers the area, instead it blows around in front of the headlights.

"So, you didn't come to visit me in the hospital..." I begin, trying not to let any disappointment shine through my words. Before he can comment, I continue. "It's okay, by the way. You did me a great favor, taking care of my baby."

"I did visit you. Every morning I took your mom's place, so she could do what she needed to do." A blush creeps up his neck. "I just...Fjord started acting out. He destroyed parts of his housing. And once you woke, your mom...well, I didn't keep you safe like I promised."

An ache forms in my chest.

"No one blames you. I certainly don't blame you, Noah. You rescued me," I say, hunching beneath the weight of all that has happened.

"No, Fjord rescued you. Your emergency beacon rescued you. I just warmed you up." He reaches over and grabs my hand.

"You always warm me up. Getting me back out was one thing. Someone took very good care of me between almost drowning and the chopper ride."

Pulling over, he parked alongside the road through town. His hair falls back as he tilts his head against the headrest and his knuckles whiten on the wheel.

"I would like to hear about how I was rescued," I say softly.

He nods and begins. I know the general story, thanks to my mother.

As I absorb the details, my insides bubble, and I feel slightly nauseous. Even though I was taking some medications to help me sleep before the trip, I still don't understand why I didn't dream about drowning before we left. Then again, I didn't drown.

"Wait, did you say you and I lay naked together? While I

was unconscious?" I say, trying to find humor through my shock.

He grins his one-sided grin, almost rueful, and sighs. "Yes. You know that is the quickest way to warm a hypothermic person. I was on my best behavior, almost losing appendages to the cold. Fjord and the dogs warmed us up efficiently. It was one hell of a dog pile."

"Thank you, Noah. For everything." I choke on my words as the grief tears out of me. He pulls me close, trying to comfort me in an uncomfortable position across the truck seats.

I change the subject to an even more painful one.

"My sister was Lucy. Lucille. She was born four minutes after me, after midnight on the next day. Identical twins with different birthdays. We could hear each other's thoughts. Telepathy, twin-tuition, whatever. She was diagnosed with brain cancer days before our fifteenth birthdays and died two years later. The summer before our senior year. We were identical twins, but I didn't get brain cancer. Why didn't I get the same thing?"

He is quiet and strokes my hair and my neck as I cry. His body shifts and the contents on the center cubby rattle as he fumbles for some tissues hidden in its depths. It's truly unbelievable how frequent my tears have become. My breath shudders as I take a deep breath, wipe my face and continue.

"We could hear each other's thoughts. When we were young, Lucy hardly ever talked. I did it all for her. A friend of my dad's did some testing on us when we were five. Nothing official or recorded, but his conclusion mirrored what my parents knew was happening. Since we could only communicate with each other and no one else, my parents accepted it and moved on. I don't remember hearing her after she died. I mean, I continued to think to her. But then when I lost my father, I think that was when I started to sense her again. The shock of losing him, of the school massacre... maybe I just couldn't deal with it all and so I let myself hear her. That's what the shrink said. My mind was full of my thoughts and her thoughts these past few years. She was just there, mentally talking to me. She was there in the water, encouraging me not to give up—that help was coming. But when I woke from the accident, she...she was gone. I went through losing her again." I find it hard to continue but push on. "You asked what my mother was reading. Those notebooks were filled with stories that I thought Lucy wrote. But I wrote them." I pause and catch my breath. "I worry that I am too crazy. I worry about what you will think. Of how to move forward."

"You are not crazy. You are doing the best you can in this life. The voice in your head...I have one too...I believe some people call it a conscience. Or, maybe she was there all this time. Your guardian angel. What matters most is that You. Are. Here."

My tears wash away the weight the world threw upon me.

Many quite moments pass, measured only by the slow, steady rise and fall of Noah's chest. When I'm ready, he starts driving.

"We missed you very much," Noah says as he shifts the truck into park. He blushes as he brushes my hair from my face. "Yeah, we. I don't think we should hold a contest on who missed you the most, though. Fjord might just sit on the rest of us so that he would win."

The headlights illuminate the small stretch of fence in front of us where Fjord paces behind. As soon as I step out of the vehicle and call to him, he stands on his hind legs and looks at me. Silent and still as a leafless white tree trunk. I can sense his scrutiny, his thoughts reach out to mine, and I respond, *Hello, baby.*

Fjord calls out to me with his voice and his mind, hopping his large body several times on his front legs before disappearing inside the facility. Heart racing, I run inside to find him waiting in his sleeping area. His head hangs over the railing. I run up to him and throw my arms around his neck. He sucks on my collar and emits a low, bone-rattling purr.

"That rubber band motor has developed into a chainsaw," Noah says as he approaches.

Fjord reaches a front paw up to bat at Noah. Noah catches

his paw and holds it to his chest.

"Steady, big guy."

Fjord noses my cheek, licks my nose.

"Ahh, you smell like fish, Fjord!" I laugh and rub his ears, his left scarred ear rough beneath my fingertips. "I missed my stinky bear."

Meanwhile, two smaller beasts assault my legs with their noses. Blue and Winter. Blue gets in a quick rear sniff, making me jump. Their minds are excited, and they weave between Noah, me, and Fjord's barrier.

I open the gate and wave the dogs through beside me. They both jog through and greet the bear, Fjord only giving them a passing sniff before returning his attention to me. I sit down on his heavy blanket, and the big baby lays down on his side and rolls onto his back with his head in my lap. He purrs while I rub his chin and throat. I can sense his happiness in my head; his thoughts are bright and airy. The dogs' excitement does not overwhelm me. Noah stands near the gate allowing me my reunion beneath his watchful gaze. As the animals' attention steers away from me, Noah pulls me up, his arms wrap around me, holding me to his chest.

"So, what was it like, hearing your sister?" he asks as we sway gently from side to side.

I think back to when Lucy was alive. "It felt just like it did several weeks ago. She was just there...in my head. Her voice. I could sense her emotions; see things she was looking at or thinking of."

"Have you ever heard anyone else? Or tried...thinking, I guess, to anyone else? Do you think you could? I mean, you have premonitions. And, well your connection to the animals..."

I wonder at his question. The dreams or premonitions. I shake my head with a slight one-sided frown. I tell him Lucy and I tried with our parents. But no one else shared the same connection with us.

I break away from his embrace as the animals go outdoors. I close the gate and walk into the living area. Noah snuggles in next to me on the couch.

"I have a similar connection to the animals." I hold onto his hand like it is my lifeline.

"That doesn't surprise me. Did your sister?"

I shake my head and lean into his embrace.

"What about the visions. Could she foresee the future, too?"

"No. It irritated her at first. Not having either ability on her own. But she experienced them through our bond. The visions were hardest for us. For me. They were rarely of anything good."

"No lottery numbers, huh?" he said, rubbing his cheek stubble against mine.

I sniff and smile. "Not yet anyway."

He cleared his throat, and I turn to him. "I can be very animal-like. Are you sure you can't hear my thoughts?"

I pull out of his embrace and gaze into his eyes. The inner vibrant green encircled by the dark blue of the deep ocean regard me with an intensity that brings a flush to my skin. My eyes flicker down to his lips.

"Not sure you are trying, but I believe you want me to do this." He leans in and kisses me gently on the lips.

He tucks my hair behind my ear and whispers, "I didn't know what I would do if I lost you. I still don't. I cannot picture my life without you in it. I love you, Momma Bear."

I sit outside on a lawn chair, enjoying the sun behind sunglasses. It is a rare, calm spring day. Temperatures are in the thirties. Not a cloud in sight. It's almost too hot. The mosquitos haven't taken flight yet. Soon, though, with the melt.

My sister's voice has been silent in the long winter months since my accident. I still try to talk to her in case she stepped away from her guardian duties. I know I only imagine the echo in the void. Perhaps she will return. Maybe the aurora grabbed her spirit from me and is playing with her. With the swiftly shrinking nights, they brazenly play now on the other side of the world within the darkness, their illuminating dance to the harmony of time and the world turning.

Although gone, she, like my father, will always be in my

heart.

Noah cannot sense me in his mind nor I him, and I am okay with that. Some of my thoughts are too deep. Intimate. Too embarrassing. There is still too much grief. Guilt, shame. To hear them all at once would be like pouring out a whole pot of boiling water when the other just wanted a cup for tea. I'm sure he would take it with open arms minus the teacup.

No troubling visions of shadowed figures have afflicted me in the many months since I awoke in the hospital last fall. The scarred bear has moved out of the area, and I still wonder what role he played. Was he my guardian for a short time? My spirit animal? I try not to overthink it. He saved my life, as did Fjord. I owe the bears more than I can ever repay. The refuge can do more immediate good while the benefits of our research work in other ways. I've decided to stay, postpone my graduate degree for now or at least any additional college. My learning will continue in the field, or rather, tundra.

I had a dream of Fjord standing guard over another bear, a sick bear. Behind them I recognized the outcropping of rocks within an eroded section of beach near the refuge. So of course, Noah, Fjord, the dogs and I went down to the beach early the next morning for a walk. With a sled. Just in case.

On our way to that area, Fjord ran ahead on the pebbled beach trailing the dogs. There is something marvelous in the great lumbering stride of a bear in pursuit. Noah and I hurried after and found Fjord standing guard over a very thin polar bear. Although conscious, she didn't put up any resistance as Noah and I rolled her onto a sled and took her back. Fjord fussed and was a pain until I reminded him, we were trying to help the bear. Big oaf.

Snow (Noah named her) stayed in one of the small indoor cages while mother treated her. Dr. Osborn consulted with wildlife and zoo veterinarians all over the world for Snow. A surgeon flew in to consult and then remove part of a front leg, courtesy of a long wound that became gangrenous. She developed pneumonia, and her prognosis was very poor following surgery. But she pulled through.

Once we knew she was responding to treatment, we began building another outdoor enclosure for her. Snow is young; we estimate around Fjord's age or a year older, although she has a much smaller frame than he does.

A month after Snow started to gain some weight, we began introducing the two bears across the chain link fence for short periods of time. This was to help acclimate her to the outdoors and socialize with Fjord. She adapted remarkably well on three legs and maintained a steady pace beside Fjord as they walked the length of fence between them.

After only a few days of socializing, Fjord put up such a conniption when we attempted to return her to her indoor enclosure. He had started to lose weight. If it weren't for the cameras, I don't think anyone would have noticed Fjord slipping the other bear his food.

When she started to resist parting with Fjord, we caved and allowed them to share Fjord's enclosure. I didn't, and still don't, have a strong connection to her mind and could only influence so much calm in those early days...but without any influence, the two beasts got on as well as any siblings. She's scrappy where Fjord is gentle. What a combination.

Late in the summer, a Berlin zoo veterinarian flew in to see the bears. Dr. Barry Kane. He was one of the veterinarians whom mother had consulted with extensively during Snow's initial treatments and who was now very interested in procuring a male for the zoo.

"He just wants to visit, meet everyone," her mother said.

Yeah, right.

Dr. Kane was around my mother's age. He played off his good looks—dark features, wide toothy smile—and accent to try to charm us into giving him Fjord.

He asked to have closer contact with Fjord and Snow. I relented with Fjord and even managed to not encourage Fjord to be (too) rough with the kind doctor. Fjord was such a ham, his attention seeking and rub-me-behind-the-ear-and-I'll-love-you-forever side on full display. I don't think I've seen a kid happier with a full bag of chocolates than that guy was covered in polar bear paw prints, his neatly combed hair askew with slobber and reeking of muktuk.

"You could come visit the zoo, see where he would be living," he offered.

Dr. Osborn seemed a little too eager at this suggestion. She did need a vacation, just not a European one.

Perhaps his youthful good looks won him much procurement for other creatures. His tactics were not successful as the decision was left to me.

"Sorry, doc. This is Fjord's home. He is not for sale or lease," I said.

Bill, with his lack of decorum and filter, grumbled insults within and outside of earshot. Something about candy canes.

"He's not European. He's from New Zealand. A kiwi," seemed to be his favorite gripe.

Barry asked me how we found Fjord as a cub. I told him I dreamt about it. And the female? I told him I dreamt about her, too. In defense, my mind was still amused and distracted by candy canes.

"The next time you dream of a bear cub, please contact me immediately. I will fly back here without question."

"Are you sure you don't want me to wait until we find a cub, have it in hand," I asked him.

He flashed a handsome, dimpled smile. "No. I do not wish you to become too attached."

"Well, I will leave it to Army to decide on what to do with future polar bears in need of care," Penny replied, not wanting to commit to something illegal.

Fjord is now approaching his second birthday. The lights are out, undulating and flaring overhead. They seem so close, that if I breathed in deep enough I might be able to smell their spectral aroma.

Fjord and Snow grapple nearby. Even if the lights danced to a specific melody, I wouldn't hear it over the growls and bawling of the bears.

They eventually move farther away, losing interest in playing, and roll instead in the new snow. The pink and green from above reflects off their coats and the snow. Such overwhelming beauty.

As it looks, some of the work I was involved in has come in handy. My goals, my life quest of becoming a marine biologist, are slowly coming to fruition although the direction has changed. Running a rehab station might not have been what I imagined, but it turns out to be what I need.

I am happy to be alive. Every day is precious. Life is not easy nor is it fair. But I choose to live it the best way I can.

The nightmares and darkness are hovering, always in the periphery, but I don't lose focus of what is in front of me. What the future holds. I have lost so much but have gained so much more.

I do not turn as he approaches. He stands quietly behind me, resting his chin on my shoulder. A bit of fur from my hood nestles between our cheeks, but he nuzzles my neck anyway. His hands find mine in my pockets. Time is nonexistent as we stand together, my fingers curled around my polar bear figurine.

This is home.

Epilogue

Penny, can you hear me?

The Queen

In a different time and a different place there lived a beautiful queen who ruled her kingdom from atop a high tower. Where once known for her exceptionally friendly nature with the people of the kingdom, for years she withdrew from them to watch over them from above. She was a sad and lonely queen.

It had not always been so. Once she had a king with whom she ruled. He was a kind and gentle king adored by all.

One day the royal family rode out to visit the countryside. The perfect morning greeted them with sunshine and light breezes, perfect for a ride into the country and a family picnic. Before leaving the castle gate, the wizened guard warned the king of a powerful storm he felt brewing within his bones. The king laughed and thanked him, assuring him the royal family would be back well before the storm hit.

The overly warm summer and limited rain was starting to take its toll on the crops. The king wished to meet face to face with the farmers to hear firsthand how things were progressing and offer kind words and support.

On their last stop before the planned picnic, they met a hunched man. His few wispy grey hairs danced airily around his head as he held his cap in his hands. He reverently greeted the royal family and bid them a speedy return to the castle as a storm was rounding the mountain pass. The king and queen looked and saw it to be true. Although the sky was clear and bright where they stood, great flashes of lightning began to appear between and below colossal billowing clouds assembling in the pass that led into the valley.

The king and queen thanked the man for his keen observation, blessing him and his family. The king's youngest granddaughter, astride a snow-white pony, rode up to the man and handed him the picnic basket. She asked him to make good use of the food within, since she and her family would not have need of it. The storm had put an end to their picnic. The man bowed and graciously thanked the young girl who returned thanks with a dazzling smile.

As the royal family hastened back to the castle, the storm continued to rally behind them. Clouds rushed in, blocking the midday sun, darkening the countryside. Loud, bone-shaking claps of thunder shook the air and grew closer, each strike of sky fire signaling its advance. The guards urged the family to move faster.

When they reached the castle, the flashes of lightning were blinding them. Stable hands and guards rushed to assist the royal family in dismounting, taking their horses as the storm panicked the steeds. The king led his stallion into the stable as no one, but he could handle the old horse. The youngest granddaughter managed to sneak into the stable and perched on the gate of her pony's stall to give him one last face rub.

A bolt of white ripped into the roof of the stable, setting it alight. Screams of humans and horses pierced the air. Stall doors were opened. Those leaving the stable tangled with those entering with buckets of water. The captain of the royal guard ordered the queen and her remaining family to find shelter within the castle walls while he and his men gathered the people stranded within the stable. The queen asked him to find the king.

The king and his stallion had become trapped when the bolt of lightning ripped through the roof and dropped a huge chunk of a beam on top of them both, leaving no chance of escape.

Fortunately, few lives were lost in the great fire. Many were injured, including the queen, who had rushed in to find her husband.

The queen felt guilty she had survived and was deeply afraid she couldn't rule as well as the king. Many years passed, and she grew lonelier and more anguished. She only held court with her council of advisors once a day to discuss the kingdom's affairs, with her sitting apart from them and speaking through a barred window.

Her family spent time visiting her, hoping to coax her out of the tower, to get her to understand the fire was not her fault. It was all in vain...she would see none of them. They eventually stopped trying and visited just once a year, during the kingdom's celebration of life.

There was one exception to her refusal not to see her family. The youngest of the queen's grandchildren, too young for formal schooling, came up every day after lunch to sit with her grandmother. She entered through a secret passageway. If there was any joy in the queen's heart, it was because of their visits. The girl's attentiveness and youthful exuberance helped to ease some of the ache in the queen's heart.

Each day the girl visited, she would begin by begging her grandmother to go outside with her and play. And each day the queen would refuse. So the girl would make up silly stories and talk about adventures they could have together if they left the tower. The queen would then weave her own tales of unicorns and fair maidens, dragons and valiant princes that would delight the young girl. They would giggle and smile, something no one else in the land would ever witness.

One day, the granddaughter did not visit. The queen did not fret as the child sometimes busied herself with other activities. After several days in a row of no visits, the queen became fearful something had happened to her granddaughter. She called on her advisors to find her, but they could not. She called on them to give her answers, but they had none. There was no knowledge of anyone visiting the queen, and they were unaware of the secret passageway.

The queen's doctor was called in as the queen became so distraught, she stopped eating and took to her bed. As the doctor could only speak to her through the barred door, she could not make much sense of what the queen was saying. As advisors became desperate and fearful for her life, they brought in the castle's metal worker who removed the hinges on the door so the doctor could enter and examine the queen.

During the exam, the queen constantly mumbled about her youngest granddaughter. The doctor ordered fluids and medications to be brought so she could treat the queen quickly. When the queen became lucid enough to understand what was happening, she asked her doctor if she knew why her granddaughter had disappeared. The doctor slowly realized what disease afflicted the queen and was saddened tremendously.

The doctor gently clasped the queen's hand. The queen gasped in disbelief as she heard the doctor's reply. Her granddaughter had perished in the fire along with the king. The queen remembered the visits with the darling girl so vividly and denied the claim. The doctor continued, gently explaining that her granddaughter was buried in the royal cemetery near the king's grave. The doctor gave her time to accept the reality.

The doctor then asked if the queen would like to visit her granddaughter and the king. At first, she declined, fearful of the pain such a visit would surely bring.

The queen continued to want to disbelieve.

But gradually her memories of all the visits and the absence of physical contact with her granddaughter began to feel surreal. She slowly allowed herself to remember the horrible day and the days that followed…the funerals of the king and her granddaughter, as well as a stable boy, who had tried to save her granddaughter. She gazed upon and rubbed at the scars on her hands and arms, the legacy of her attempt to enter the inferno that consumed the king.

At last, the queen requested that the doctor take her to the cemetery. They stood in silence in front of the graves for many hours. The queen asked why her dreams had felt so real. The doctor explained the mind, in all its power, can distort reality to protect the body from physical and emotional pain.

It took the queen many months to fully accept the truth of things, but she did slowly begin to go out from her tower. Her remaining family was delighted their queen and family member returned to them. Their love and support, finally accepted, began to help fix the broken parts the queen held hidden within her heart.

Although she never saw her granddaughter again, the queen knew that her granddaughter was always close to her heart, waiting for her, and she was glad.

Fantastic Books
Great Authors

darkstroke is
an imprint of
Crooked Cat Books

- Gripping Thrillers
- Cosy Mysteries
- Amazing Horrors
- Fascinating Historicals
- Exciting Fantasy
- Young Adult and Children's
  Adventures
- Non-Fiction

Discover us online
www.darkstroke.com

Find us on instagram:
www.instagram.com/darkstrokebooks

Made in the USA
Coppell, TX
07 July 2020

30443076R00187